In Duane Johnson's garage, the smell of gasoline in her nostrils, her partner put his gloved hand on her shoulder. He breathed into her ear. "You're excited."

He bit her lobe, a hot thrill shivered through her nerves. He grinned against her neck, probably thinking the kill made her horny. He had no idea.

"It's almost time," she whispered. "Get in place."

He crossed the concrete like a cat, tall and too skinny, blending into the blackness, an enigma. She knew him . . . but didn't really know him. Tonight he was fully engaged, but how long would it last? She couldn't hear him move or breathe over her own pounding heart. 11:10. Almost time for Duane Johnson to come home. Almost time for Duane Johnson to die.

Also by Allison Brennan

THE PREY
THE HUNT
THE KILL

SPEAK NO EVIL
SEE NO EVIL
FEAR NO EVIL

KILLING FEAR
TEMPTING EVIL
PLAYING DEAD

SUDDEN DEATH

A NOVEL OF SUSPENSE

ALLISON BRENNAN

BALLANTINE BOOKS • NEW YORK

For advice, guidance, and faith:
This book is for Kim Whalen.

ACKNOWLEDGMENTS

When I started researching this book, I knew only the basics about our armed forces. I read several books to put myself in the mind-set of the men and women who serve and defend America and our freedom. One book in particular helped me better understand the history and challenges facing U.S. special operations forces: *Leave No Man Behind* by David C. Isby. His dedication included the following quote:

"Let me not mourn for the men who have died fighting, but rather let me be glad that such heroes have lived."
—GEN GEORGE S. PATTON, June 7, 1945

A special thanks to several authors who were willing to share their knowledge, even when facing their own deadlines: Cindy Gerard, C. J. Lyons, and Karin Tabke. As always, the experts at Crime Scene Writers shared their time and extensive experience in all matters related to forensics. My friends and former colleagues, Trisha Richins and Ken Blodgett (who also designed my website), went out of their way to help with on-site research. And finally, Special Agent Steven Dupre, SSA Mike Rayfield (the real-life leader of Squad 8), SA Brian Jones (who let me set off an explosion even though my characters shoot better than I do), and all the Sacramento FBI Agents who have all been so generous with their limited free time to help me get it right. I may have taken a few liberties with rules and regulations, forgive me. And if I got anything wrong . . . I'm pleading no contest.

Behind the scenes, thanks to "special" agent Kim Whalen, my sounding board; my editor Charlotte Herscher who keeps my muse in line; senior editor Dana Isaacson who wields his pencil like a scalpel; Scott Shannon, the keeper of information and good will; and the rest of the incredible Ballantine team. I'd also like to thank the publishing team at Piatkus, who publish my books in the United Kingdom, for their enthusiasm and support.

Finally, my family deserves extra special thanks for not having me committed when I talk about my characters as if they're real people.

"Revenge is an act of passion; vengeance of justice.
Injuries are revenged; crimes are avenged."
—SAMUEL JOHNSON (1709–1784)

"If an injury has to be done to a man
it should be so severe
that his vengeance need not be feared."
—NICCOLÒ MACHIAVELLI (1469–1527)

PROLOGUE

They had debated killing Duane Johnson when he closed his restaurant, or outside the VFW Hall where he drank and played cards every week, but ultimately they decided that his house was the ideal place.

This late at night they would be guaranteed privacy. Neighbors were too far to hear Johnson's screams. She'd planned it down to the last detail. That was her strength. Planning the kill, executing the betrayer.

Karin's ultimate plan was brilliant. Not that she had shared the end game with her partner. Ethan was a linear thinker, focused only on revenge. He wouldn't understand that his pathetic vendetta was simply a means to end the life of her nemesis.

Her blood surged, the excitement rose, as she thought about destroying the one person who'd stolen everything from her. Giddy with anticipation, her face flushed. Murder was easy; vengeance was far more complicated and certainly more satisfying.

In Duane Johnson's garage, the smell of gasoline in her nostrils, her partner put his gloved hand on her shoulder. He breathed into her ear. "You're excited."

He bit her lobe, a hot thrill shivered through her nerves. He grinned against her neck, probably thinking the kill made her horny. He had no idea.

"It's almost time," she whispered. "Get in place."

He crossed the concrete like a cat, tall and too skinny, blending into the blackness, an enigma. She knew him . . . but didn't really know him. Tonight he was fully engaged, but how long would it last? She couldn't hear him move or breathe over her own pounding heart. 11:10. Almost time for Duane Johnson to come home. Almost time for Duane Johnson to die.

Almost time to start the ball rolling after thousands of days of planning and waiting and reflecting on the rightness of her kills . . .

If someone had told Karin that she was a serial killer, she would have laughed until tears ran down her face. She didn't even think of herself as a "killer," though she would acknowledge that she'd ended the life of those who deserved it. Those who had slipped through wide crevices of a pathetic, hypocritical justice system that cared more for the criminals than the victims. In fact, she'd often wondered if she was the reincarnation of the San Francisco vigilantes—the city would never have survived without that group of men dispensing law and order in their own way. Or better—Judge Roy Bean. Bean did it right, and when the law didn't fit, he forced it.

Justice in the purest sense of the word.

She was a woman out of her time. The Wild West was much more her element than twenty-first-century America, the land of the weak and pathetic.

Frontier justice pumped her heart. Vigilante. Had she not made one stupid mistake, she would have been praised from the top of the Sears Tower, proclaimed a goddess from the Golden Gate Bridge to the Brooklyn Bridge. A national holiday would have been named in her honor, and students of American history would study her life and philosophies and how she changed the system single-handedly for generations to come. Their teachers could only *wish* they had the guts to stand up against the failed system, to fight the predators.

They wanted to be her. Everyone wanted to be her, they just didn't have the stomach for it. She did. She'd *always* been able to punish the wicked. Especially those who wanted to hurt *her*.

When Ethan practically landed on her doorstep two years ago, Karin recognized she'd been handed the tools to finally destroy those who had deemed her a nonentity. A nothing. A mental case. In her forty-four years, she'd avenged every wrong committed against her . . . except one.

Her hands and jaw were clenched so tight that she almost didn't hear the truck. She froze. Johnson had arrived.

Heart racing, she willed herself to control her excitement. She wasn't supposed to have fun, this was business. An eye for an eye. But her mouth went dry and her vision sharpened. The trap had been laid, the hunt was nearly over.

You love to kill. Watching their eyes as they die.

The power, *her* power, flowed as the garage door noisily lumbered up on its tracks. She was in charge. She was in control. Duane Johnson had been sentenced to death and she was his executioner.

Earlier, they'd disabled the lights in the garage, but the streetlamps still faintly illuminated its depths, casting dark shadows and narrow beams of gray light.

Karin didn't personally know their victim. She knew his name, she knew why he deserved to die, she'd planned his death, but she didn't know *him*.

Somehow that made the entire affair all the more exciting.

The truck turned into the driveway, the headlights turning everything an odd, sterile white. Country music twanged from the radio. She stood flat against the wall, in a blind spot they'd scouted earlier. Ethan was on the opposite side of the garage, waiting.

Dressed in black, her hair colored to match, with her gun in hand, Karin was ready to fire if the plan didn't work.

The ignition cut out, and with it the music, but there wasn't silence. The *tick-tick-tick* of the engine cooling. The *click* of the headlights turning off. The door opening, the dome light on, and Duane Johnson singing in a surprisingly strong baritone the end of the song:

Oh, but love
Love is thicker than blood

Her eyes burned, her throat constricted, but her hands were steady as Johnson slammed the door shut. The car's interior light stayed on for a beat as he walked to the door that led directly into the kitchen. They had already been inside; he didn't keep that door locked.

Five years out of the military and he didn't have decent security.

He pressed the garage door closed, put his hand on the doorknob, then paused. Instant tension, as if his sixth sense clicked in.

Too late. The truck's cab light turned off and Johnson pivoted. She didn't see the glint of Ethan's blade, but Johnson's primal scream vibrated between her ears as her partner sliced the back of his knees, severing the hamstrings. The large black man immediately collapsed to the concrete floor as she maneuvered between the front of the Ford F-150 and Johnson's tidy workbench.

She had to give Johnson credit. Through excruciating pain and the inability to stand, he reached for his attacker's legs, trying to bring Ethan down to the ground. She holstered her gun and pulled out the syringe, plunging it into Johnson's upper arm. He stopped violently resisting, but the tranquilizer was mild. They didn't want him to be unconscious during his stint in purgatory—before they sent him to Hell.

"Wh—?" Johnson asked, his tongue thick, as she and Ethan grabbed him under the arms and carried him through his house to the family room. They'd already prepared the large room while waiting for Johnson to come home. The blinds were closed, their equipment ready—and the room itself backed to a wooded area. Private.

She prided herself on her physical strength, but Johnson weighed at least 240, and with the tranq, he sagged heavily. Blood from being hamstrung dripped on the kitchen linoleum and smeared as they dragged him. If they let him live—which they wouldn't—he'd be crippled for the rest of his life.

They sat Johnson on a kitchen chair they'd earlier brought to the family room, and he immediately rolled off, trying to escape. His pathetic crawl toward freedom was futile, his attempts to scream hampered by the sedative. It took only a few minutes before they had him restrained—ankles duct-taped to the chair legs, wrists secured to the armrests.

Ethan spoke, his voice calm, reasoned. He didn't

sound crazy; today was one of his good days. The lights were on and they made no attempt to hide their identity.

"Do you remember me?" Ethan asked Johnson.

Karin's stomach fluttered at what was to come. The seductive nature of death was a natural high superior to anything drug addicts injected into their veins.

"Fuh. Bahs." Johnson's eyes moved lazily. Panicked, but unable to focus.

"*You're* the fucking bastard!" Ethan turned to his special black box, with his special tools. She watched with wide eyes as he removed a long, thin, shiny steel needle.

"Darling," he said to Karin, "please hold Corporal Johnson's right hand."

She complied. Here, for the next hour or two, she was the subservient one. Within these walls, Ethan took charge. For this, she didn't mind relinquishing control. The anticipation of Johnson's reaction, his punishment, was exciting enough for her, and Ethan knew exactly how to elicit pain. She only knew how to kill.

But she was learning from Ethan, and she enjoyed her lessons.

Johnson strained against her grip, but Karin was strong. She bent back his pinky until he cried out.

Ethan snapped at her. "No games."

She didn't apologize, but released the finger. Watched the needle as her partner pushed it into just the right spot between the forefinger and the thumb. On just the right nerve to make Johnson . . .

Scream.

The scream was short-lived as another needle went in at the base of his skull. And another. And another.

"You left me to die!" Ethan sneered.

In went another needle.

She listened to the story again, though it was different now. Ethan had become a bit of a whiner. She didn't like that. She wanted to tell him to suck it up and be a man, no matter how much he had suffered. His plan—well, *her* plan that she gave to Ethan—was to make Johnson and the others suffer just as much.

Of course a well-placed bullet would have been just as effective, but this exercise wasn't solely about dying.

Tears ran in salty streams down Johnson's dark face, glistening in the harsh overhead light.

"Why?" His plaintive plea came out a whisper.

"Shoes," her partner commanded.

She removed Johnson's shoes and socks. Their captive's mild tranq would have worn off by now, but with his nerves in agony and his limbs restrained, Johnson couldn't fight back. He could barely cry out, though a shrill, high-pitched hiss came from deep in his throat as soon as the needle hit the right nerve between his toes.

She didn't think a man could hit that note.

CHAPTER
ONE

The homeless man's murder had been ritualistic, brutal, and efficient.

Megan Elliott swatted flies that swarmed near the body next to the Dumpster as she squatted beside the victim. It was midmorning and the temperature was already eighty degrees. The bullet had gone in clean, execution style, behind the ear. All signs suggested that he'd been killed right here, in a narrow alley separating a parking garage from the historic Cathedral of the Blessed Sacrament.

There didn't appear to be signs of struggle, but here in the decrepit underside of Sacramento, that was difficult to determine. While the city did a fairly good job at keeping most of the streets clean, on the north side of downtown, away from the Capitol building and closer to the soup kitchen, the grime and unwanted bred. Here, homeless weeded through the garbage off K Street for something edible when the city rolled up the sidewalks; or they slept against brick walls, clutching their meager possessions in a desperate grip.

No sign of struggle, and based on the lack of blood spatter, the victim had been prone when shot at close range. But he had the same outward injuries as the other two known victims. His hamstrings had been cut clean through, incapacitating him. His wrists had been duct-taped to something, as evidenced from the chafing and band of missing arm hair. And he was barefoot.

"What are you thinking?"

Megan stood and, though she was five foot eight, she had to look up at Detective John Black, who had to be close to six and a half feet tall.

"All the appearances of an execution, but you're absolutely right. The M.O. matches the murders on the recent FBI hot sheet." And to maintain good relations with local law enforcement, she added, "You were right on the money there. Thanks."

"His hamstrings weren't cut here. Not enough blood. No spray or cast-off."

Megan glanced around, but there was no blood on the brick wall or in the alleyway. Where had he been attacked?

Without touching the filthily clad victim, she inspected the deep gash in the back of his legs. She mimicked a slicing motion with her hand and then said, "I'll need the coroner's report, but it appears that the killer sliced right to left, cutting both legs with an even, fluid motion." She stood and said, "Turn around."

Black did, looking over his shoulder. She said, "You're much taller than the victim. If the victim was walking, the killer would have had to have walked up behind him and—*slice*—cut the hamstrings." She mimicked the motion against the back of Black's knees. "It's the only thing that makes sense. If the vic was lying down, why would the killer slice his legs across?"

"It would help if we could locate where he was attacked."

Megan agreed. "If the vic went down on his knees,

that should be obvious at the autopsy with bruising or evidence on his pants. But why shoot him here? Why did the killer move him at all after the inital attack?"

Wearing latex gloves and plastic booties over her shoes, an attractive, well-dressed woman who may have been thirty on her last birthday approached. "Nice theory, but maybe you should wait for crime scene analysis."

Black's lips twitched. "Simone, FBI Supervisory Agent Megan Elliott. Agent Elliott, Simone Charles, CSU Supervisor."

Megan nodded. She'd worked with the prickly perfectionist before. "We've met. So, what does the evidence show, Simone?"

"My team just came off a triple murder in the Pocket. Sorry for being late." She didn't sound sorry, but Megan noticed the red eyes and tight expression. She'd heard about the murder-suicide before she'd left FBI headquarters. A man came home early in the morning, drunk, and shot his wife and two kids while they slept, then blew his own brains out.

"You're not late," Megan said.

Simone motioned for one of her team to photograph the scene and the body. "I'll walk the area and be right back. You have a wide perimeter," she noted to Detective Black. "Any reason?"

"To keep the vultures at bay." He nodded toward the KCRA-3 van parked at the edge of the crime scene tape.

She grinned and walked away, dropping markers at specific spots.

Black said, "So was he killed here or not?"

Megan clarified. "He was definitely shot right here,

small-caliber handgun is my guess, twenty-two caliber, behind the left ear. A twenty-two is very effective at close range."

Megan had seen far too many execution-style murder victims when she was part of the national Evidence Response Team that went to Kosovo ten years ago. Which led to the question of why disable the victim first if only to shoot him?

If the evidence held true compared with the first two known victims, Megan already had the answer: between the time the victim's hamstrings were cut and when he was shot, someone had received sick pleasure from torturing him. Handicapping the victim was to keep him from escaping.

"We need to find out where he was attacked and tortured," Megan said.

The two previous victims had no visible marks until their clothing was removed. Then dozens of tiny pinpricks were obvious. "He plays before he kills."

"Excuse me?"

Megan had forgotten that she wasn't alone. The members of Squad Eight—the Violent Crimes/Major Offender Squad that she headed—were used to her talking to herself; she had to remember she was out of her element here, assisting SPD.

"Just thinking out loud."

Megan itched to inspect the victim's feet, but she didn't want to touch the body until the coroner's unit arrived.

First Austin, Texas, then Las Vegas, Nevada. Now Sacramento, California. The only thing those three places had in common, on the surface, was that they were large cities. The victims were single, male, between the ages of thirty-five and forty-five, tortured and murdered in their homes. While most serial predators stayed within one race, the first victim was black and the second and third were white. The first vic owned his own business and, though divorced, was by all accounts a devoted father. The second vic had never married, had a rap sheet for minor drug charges, and worked as a mechanic. There was some indication that he had a gambling problem, which delayed the local police from reporting the crime to the national database, mistakenly believing it was payback for an uncollected debt. The hot sheet possibly linking the two had only been sent out late last week.

As if reading her mind, or simply breathing too deeply, Black got on the radio and said to someone, "This body is cooking and it's only going to get hotter. ETA of the coroner?"

A gender-neutral voice replied, "On scene."

"Great." Black looked around, frowned, and said to Megan, "I'll find him." He stalked off.

It wasn't standard procedure for an FBI agent to go out to crime scenes alone, even aiding the local P.D., but there had been no initial certainty that this homicide was connected to the two other murders. Because her squad was already spread extremely thin, Megan had opted to check the scene herself.

But there was no doubt in her mind after viewing the body that the murder of this homeless man was connected somehow to the murders in Texas and Nevada. Why and how were the two big questions other than, of course, *who*.

She would wait to call it in until she had more information.

Megan frowned as she visually inspected the body again. Something else struck her as odd. Because the victim was homeless and had been living on the streets long enough to disappear into the backdrop of Sacramento, his age was indeterminate. At first glance, he could be as young as thirty, but the ravages of drugs and alcohol or simply the hard years living on the streets aged him. His clothes hadn't been washed in weeks or longer, so his hands stood out.

They were clean.

She looked around for someone from the CSU or SPD, but all she saw were uniforms, and they eyed her apprehensively. Her boss, Bob Richardson, had made great inroads working with local law enforcement, but there were always a few who blamed the "Fibbies" for everything bad that happened on a call.

She took out her BlackBerry and snapped a couple photographs. Not SOP, but she didn't plan to use the photos as evidence. She wanted to remember to ask the CSU about the hands, and this was Megan's reminder.

Were clean hands part of the killer's ritual? Or was this something new? Or special for this victim? Did this homeless man have some sort of hand-washing compulsion?

Or maybe there had been evidence on his hands and the killer had cleaned them. Very little could destroy evidence if the lab and technicians were good enough. But bleach or another caustic cleanser could be a sign that the victim had fought back and the killer had tried to conceal the evidence.

She knelt down and sniffed close to the hands.

From behind, a man cleared his throat. Megan looked over her shoulder. The tall Detective Black stood next to a short, light-skinned black man with a medical kit in hand.

She stood. "No bleach."

Black raised an eyebrow.

"His hands are clean." She was met with skepticism, so added, "He appears homeless. His face, his clothes, his hair—but his hands are clean."

Black said with a tone of self-recrimination, "I didn't notice."

The deputy coroner mumbled an introduction— Roland Stieger—before squatting next to the corpse.

They watched in silence as Stieger inspected the body. He made notes on a preprinted form.

"Help me turn him," he commanded.

As Black helped Stieger flip the body, Megan heard a slight rattle of metal, but when Black and Stieger started talking, it was clear they hadn't heard it.

She stared at the body and saw a distinct chain pattern around the victim's neck.

A veteran.

The prongs were so familiar she knew they were attached to dog tags even before she saw the tags themselves. She'd been raised in a military family, had buried her father with his dog tags, and she would never forget the sight of the chain or the sound the tags made as they slid up and down the metal chain.

Megan had always prided herself on her even temper and logical approach to problems, but suddenly her vision blurred and she wanted blood—the blood of the killer, the blood of a society that didn't value those who fought for them. Men like her dad . . .

She pushed him from her mind and focused on the homeless veteran. "John," she said, wanting an I.D. as quickly as possible. Wanting to know how this soldier had ended up homeless and dead.

Black looked at her quizzically. "Something wrong?"

"He's a veteran. The dog tags." She gestured. "We might be able to get a quick I.D."

"That'd be nice," Stieger said. "We have a few dozen unidentified homeless filling the deep freeze right now."

While Stieger pulled the chain out, Black asked, "So how do you want to handle the investigation?"

"It's your case, but I'd like to be involved. I'm fairly confident this is connected to the hot sheet cases."

Black agreed. "We'll need to have your boss and my boss talk, but I'm game. Joint task force?"

They both cracked a wry grin. There were so many "joint task forces" between local and federal law enforcement agencies that it was impossible to keep all of them straight. As a supervisory special agent, Megan herself sat on more than a dozen.

Stieger pulled out the chain. "Price, George L.," he read. "This looks like U.S. Army. No medical restrictions, blood type A negative. Christian. Have the Social as well."

Both Megan and Black wrote down the information. One of Simone Charles's crime techs snapped pictures. Stieger put the chain down and Megan didn't hear anything. "Wait," she said.

"Excuse me?"

"There's only one tag."

Stieger held up the chain again and felt along the chain. "Right. One."

Megan said, "There should be two tags. Either attached and separable, or the second tag on its own small loop."

"There's only one tag," Stieger repeated. "Maybe he lost it."

"Not likely," Black said. Megan glanced at him, and he added, "My girlfriend is a veteran. She still sleeps with hers."

He got it, and Megan didn't have to explain.

"Maybe the killer took it for a souvenir," she said.

Or maybe the victim *did* lose it. Or maybe he'd been injured or there was some other reason the second tag had been removed while he was a soldier. The missing tag felt odd to Megan, but she didn't have any facts to back up her instincts, so she kept her mouth shut.

"How long has he been dead?" Black asked Stieger.

"Decomp is telling me about twenty-four hours, but with this heat, could be as few as five or six."

It was eleven in the morning; Megan had been on scene for over an hour. The body had been discovered just after seven a.m.

"I'll have to do some calculations," Stieger added. "Factor in his clothing, the position of the body—fortunately, he's not in direct sunlight. I'll take a wild stab—and I mean a *not to put in your report* guess—at six to ten hours. I know, he looks and smells like twenty-four plus, but he's not. He's still in rigor, and heat speeds up that process instead of slowing it down."

Simone Charles, the CSU supervisor, approached and said to Black, "I found something you need to see."

Megan tagged along, though she felt as if Simone was antagonistic. Megan was used to it. It surprised her that in law enforcement, some of her biggest hurdles were fellow female cops and staff.

Black said, "So what did you find?"

"Follow me."

Megan and John Black followed Simone down the alley to 12th Street between J and K Streets. Instead of crossing the crime scene tape, Simone turned into the stairwell of the parking garage.

She pointed toward the cement outer stairwell at the same time as Megan saw what had to be blood.

"Cast-off," they said simultaneously. They were a half block from where the body was found.

Along the ground were bright yellow numbered cards and they told the story as Simone spoke. "We tested the wall, it came back positive for blood, but we'll have to retest it in the lab. The victim was walking west toward Eleventh Street, and the killer sliced his hamstrings, from right to left, and the blood spattered on the wall. But he had complete control of the knife because there are no drops consistent with him holding the knife after the attack."

"Which means?" Black asked.

"He sheathed it." Simone demonstrated. "*Slice*—he can't avoid the spatter because of the momentum and the suddenness of the attack—but he sliced, then stuck the knife right back in its case. Probably on his belt loop for ease of use."

She pointed to the numbered cards. "Those are from the victim. He fell here"—she pointed to an area just inside the stairwell that had a smeared, small dried pool of blood with two clean sections in between, most likely where the victim had fallen to his knees—"then he was picked up and carried up the stairs."

She moved up the stairwell and Megan followed.

Simone exited on the third floor. There were several crime scene technicians working the area.

"Wait," Megan said. "Did you say he was carried?"

Simone grinned like the cat who ate the canary, knowing she'd scored. Megan had to give her credit, Simone held that card nicely. "Oh, yeah. Carried."

Megan looked at the ground, the stairs, and the numbered markers, then saw what Simone saw. "No drag marks."

"Exactly." The criminalist beamed. "The guy couldn't have walked anywhere, so the killer would have to drag or carry him. The vic was pretty big, but I suppose a larger, strong male could have hoisted him over his shoulder." She frowned, looking down the stairwell.

"But then," Megan said, "the killer would have had his arms around the victim's legs." She demonstrated by pretending to haul something large onto her shoulder. "There wouldn't be this kind of blood trail. Maybe a few spots, but nothing this extensive." If the victim had been dragged up the stairs, the blood would have been smeared—not in this drop pattern.

"Exactly," Simone said in an admiring tone, as if she'd just realized that not all FBI agents were morons.

"There were two people?" Black asked.

Megan nodded. "Carrying him by the armpits, lifting him up." She followed the blood spatters. "You can see some small, narrow drag marks in places—nothing deep, probably from his shoes." She frowned. "He was barefoot. Where are his shoes?"

"He was homeless," Simone said. "Right?"

"He'd have shoes," Megan said. She'd seen many homeless dead, too many. Their shoes might have been too small or too big, but they wore shoes. "His feet weren't that dirty—he couldn't have been barefoot on the streets for long."

"Weren't the other victims barefoot?" Black asked.

"Yes," Megan replied.

Nowhere in the reports from the previous crime scenes had the investigators indicated any suspicions of the two perps. Megan's heart beat rapidly with the new and potentially valuable information. She couldn't imagine the police holding back from federal law enforcement such important information as a killing pair.

The three of them followed the yellow markers across the parking garage. "I've already called for all security tapes, but there're many blind spots. The main entrance, exit, and all pedestrian entrances are covered, but not every inch of each parking floor. Still, we should be able to view any vehicle entering or exiting. The garage opens at five a.m. six days a week, but it's closed on Sundays—only those with card keys can get in."

"So the killer had a card key?"

Simone shrugged. "I don't know. He could have tricked the system, or walked in and stolen a pass from someone else's vehicle to get his own in. We'll figure that out when we get the tapes from security. Or he could have come in before the garage closed at eight p.m. Saturday night."

"Do you need a card key to get out?" Megan asked.

John and Simone said in unison, "No."

"And they have tapes on all exit points?"

"Yes."

Megan was cautiously optimistic. If they had tapes of the vehicle, they may have a view of the driver. Or passenger, if there were in fact two killers as the blood evidence indicated. Make and model would be obvious, and very likely a plate number or partial plate.

In the center aisle of the garage, Simone stopped.

Three parking spaces had been cleared and yellow crime scene tape was posted. "People aren't going to like me. I closed the garage as soon as we found the trail, but there were already some people parked inside. They're not going anywhere until I finish collecting evidence." She pointed to what first appeared like nothing.

Then Megan saw the blood. She glanced behind her and saw the trail of numbered yellow cards, and they stopped here at the rear of the parking slot.

"My guess is a van," Simone said. "If they had a card key they could have gone anywhere."

"Then why dump the body in this alley?" Black asked.

Megan asked, "Wouldn't security have towed it?"

Black shook his head. "A lot of people leave their cars overnight. Drinking at a bar, going home with a girlfriend, working late."

"We have the list—security does note the tag numbers, but not the location. There were only three vehicles in the garage at midnight last night when the parking supervisor made his final rounds."

"Three?" Megan's heart raced. "One of them had to have belonged to the killer."

"Already ahead of you," Simone grinned. "I called in the plates and my office is running them."

It seemed too easy.

"What's wrong?" Simone asked. "I've practically closed your case for you."

"These killers have three victims under their belt and in the first two murders, no evidence pointing to a suspect. No witnesses. I don't see them being so dumb as to park in a public garage and let their license plate be recorded."

"Most criminals are stupid," Simone said. "Our prisons are bursting with them."

That may be the case, but Megan wasn't going to pop the champagne until an arrest was made.

"How did the killers return unnoticed?" Black asked.

"You can walk in from the street, just like we did," Simone said. "There's that half wall on the ground floor, plus walkways for pedestrians. They brought him in, up the stairs, did whatever to him, and left him dead in the alley a half block away."

Black frowned.

"What?" Megan asked.

"The exit is on J Street."

"And so?" Simone said.

Megan nodded. "The killers would have had to go around the building to dump the body."

"And J Street is one way. They'd have to exit J Street, turn on Twelfth, down L Street, up Tenth, then turn on Eleventh to get back to this exact spot. A wide circle."

Megan disagreed. "You're assuming they'd obey traffic laws."

Simone agreed. "At five in the morning, they could drive the half block down J the wrong way and no one would notice. Pull into the alley and pop the guy. I'm surprised at you, John. Making such a blanket assumption."

Black rolled his eyes. "I guess I assumed people obey traffic laws."

"Why didn't they just execute him in the garage?" Megan asked. "Why dump him in the alley? Even if they didn't follow the flow of traffic, they had to drive around to get back to the alley."

"Downtown is dead most nights, especially on Sundays," Simone said. "I could run around here naked and no one would notice."

Black raised an eyebrow, but didn't say anything.

"I'd like a copy of the tapes," Megan said. "And your forensics report. With security cameras on the pedestrian entrance we should get a face, possibly a good shot, and I.D."

"That's what I'm thinking. No problem."

Megan asked, "Is there any evidence that they took him out the same way? Not used the van, but brought him down the stairs?"

"Nooo," Simone said cautiously. "But after a little time, the injury would have clotted and there might not be blood evidence. We're still combing the crime scene—"

So that was a possibility. That was all Megan needed to know to confirm that these killers had a plan. Whether they drove out and dumped the body or carried him down the stairs and executed him next to the Dumpster, they had carefully determined that their way was the best way. Organized. It was risky to use such a public place for the murder, but clearly the location was important to them for some unknown reason.

As Megan walked back to the alley with Detective Black, she couldn't grasp the motive. Why go through such elaborate measures to kill a homeless veteran? Why kill him nearly a block from where he was kidnapped in a risky, public location?

It seemed both foolish and deliberate.

What did George Price have in common with Austin's small-business owner Duane Johnson and Las Vegas's Dennis Perry?

Why were they tortured?

Why were they executed?

And if the M.O. held, Megan would probably not learn anything else about the killers until they were caught, Simone's glee in having the three license plates to run notwithstanding. They'd moved around the country with ease, and if they'd killed Price at dawn, they could be three hundred miles away by now.

Fortunately, they had a lot more information than at the previous two crime scenes. Security tapes; a larger, public crime scene; greater chance of witnesses. With a little time and a lot of hard work, Megan was confident they'd I.D. the killers. She was good at working each piece of the puzzle until an identity was confirmed, a suspect arrested, and a killer prosecuted.

Megan didn't know that in twenty-four hours, they'd have nothing. No tapes. No evidence. No body. And no jurisdiction.

CHAPTER
TWO

Jack Kincaid leaned against the wall of El Gato during happy hour, a bottle of Tecate in his hand—his first and only drink of the evening. Scout, Lucky, and his other team members were celebrating their most recent success. They had rescued four medical missionaries in Guatemala who'd been kidnapped by rebels wanting their supplies. The rebels had thought ransoming the missionaries would yield more cash. After safely escorting the hostages to the U.S. embassy, Jack and his team returned to the jungle, retrieved the stolen supplies without incident, and in seventy-two hours were back at their base of operations in the border town of Hidalgo, Texas.

While Jack should have been more involved in the celebration, he was preoccupied. When he'd returned to the States earlier in the day, there was a message from Dillon that their younger brother, Patrick, had awakened from his coma. Jack weighed whether to visit Patrick. He wanted to see him, but he didn't want to see the rest of the Kincaids.

That wasn't fair. He didn't have a problem with his brothers and sisters. And certainly not his mother.

But his father had made it very clear two decades ago, reiterated more recently, that Jack was not welcome. And frankly, Jack didn't want to see Colonel Pat Kincaid either. Long ago, Jack had put the fuck-up in Panama behind him, but his father couldn't do it. Couldn't see that sometimes the rigid military rules were bullshit. That sometimes it was more important to stand for something than to take wrong-headed orders.

That Jack had moved so far up the ranks after Panama was a shock to Pat Kincaid, and in many ways to Jack as well. He'd almost walked away, but instead he'd remained steadfastly loyal. He had owed it to his unit and himself to see it through, stand up during the fallout, defend his decision, and take his punishment. In the end, however, Pat Kincaid had decided to bury the situation and "protect" Jack's future—something Jack had neither asked for nor wanted.

Then the Colonel had the audacity to demand an apology and a thank-you, or Jack need not come home for Christmas.

Except for weddings and funerals, Jack hadn't been home since.

But he wanted to see his brother. He simply couldn't plan a scenario that would guarantee he could go to San Diego, visit Patrick, and leave without running into Colonel Kincaid.

Life has no guarantees.

He'd considered watching the hospital and going in after the Colonel left. According to Dillon's message, Patrick would be released within the week. It would be easier to control the situation if Jack went to the hospital then to postpone a visit until his brother was home.

Scout walked over to Jack with Padre—Father Francis—at his side. The priest was drinking bottled water; Scout was on his third draft. Sitting at the table next to where Jack stood like a stone sentry, they all faced the door.

"Go," Scout said.

Jack didn't have to ask what his longtime friend meant. He didn't say anything, but glanced at Padre. *Padre* had been Frank's nickname since he and Jack met that first day of basic training when they both signed into the Army Rangers. Frank was a couple years older, and when it got out that he was a Catholic seminary dropout, the name stuck. Jack thought it ironic that when Padre left the army five years ago, he'd gone back to the seminary.

Padre had told Jack that the nickname saved him. Jack told him he'd saved himself.

Scout said, "We just got off a successful op, we have no pending assignments, now's the time."

"Something may come up."

Scout shook his head. "You're the last person I expect to make excuses."

Jack tensed. "The Guatemala situation came down fast. If we hadn't responded immediately, the outcome could have been worse."

"We're not the only guns for hire."

Jack frowned—he didn't like the expression, though it was accurate.

Padre interjected, "Is Dillon in San Diego, too?"

"Yes." Jack glanced at Padre. His friend knew what was important to him, and the irony that Padre—a man Jack had fought beside, a man he had saved, a man he had almost died with—had become his confessor wasn't lost on him. In many ways, Padre was a closer brother to him than his twin, Dillon; in fact, half-Cuban Jack looked more like the full-blooded Cuban priest than he did his fair-skinned twin. In other ways, they were worlds apart.

Scout drained his beer and centered it on the worn wood table and continued. "Do you think I couldn't handle the team on my own? Or was putting me second in command lip service?"

"You know it wasn't."

Scout shook his head. "You're fucking scared." He tipped his beer to Padre. "Sorry."

Padre smiled. The scene always played out the same.

Jack didn't respond. Fear didn't come into it. Rage did. He didn't know if he could stop himself from punching the Colonel in the jaw. All the wasted years when Jack could have been a brother to his six siblings, a son to his mother. All lost because Colonel Pat Kincaid couldn't accept Jack's decision in Panama.

What was he supposed to do? Let innocent civilians die because the intelligence had been wrong? He had been forced to act, even though by disobeying direct orders he could have jeopardized the mission. Jack had been willing to be reprimanded for that decision, even if it had resulted in a court-martial.

Pat Kincaid hadn't even allowed his son to take the heat.

"Take my plane," Scout offered.

Jack cracked a half-smile. Scout babied his Cessna. He didn't like anyone flying it, even Jack.

"You must want to get rid of me."

"I want you to see your family." Scout's fingers danced on the scarred table. "I have no family. I'm married to this job. But I'm older than you, I don't know how many more years I'm going to be able to do this. And then what? My parents are long dead, I have no wife, not even an ex-wife I can bitch about. No kids that I know of—a couple cousins I haven't seen in half a lifetime. You have something damn rare, and though you don't talk about it, I know you've enjoyed your visits with your brothers and sisters. Right, Padre?"

He nodded. "I'd say so."

Jack shuffled, under fire. "Dillon and I have come to terms." It was good to have his brother back, even though it wasn't the same as when they were kids. And he was getting used to Dillon's girlfriend, though he was still wary about the fed. Maybe because she seemed to know too much about him without trying. Jack demanded privacy.

"I've known you for how long?" Scout asked.

It was a rhetorical question, but Jack answered. "Nineteen years."

"Nineteen years," Scout said before Jack finished. "I buried your puke when you got malaria in fucking Belize, so I think I got some say in your life. Go to San Diego. See your family. It's not like the team and I are going to up and disappear on you."

Jack stared at his beer.

"You want to," Scout said.

"Jack." Padre spoke quietly and Jack looked at him. "Don't let your father stop you from doing what you need to do."

"I don't want a confrontation."

"I'm not going to tell you what you should do."

"You want me to forget."

"You can't forget."

Padre was the only person who knew exactly what had happened in Panama that caused Colonel Kincaid to disown his oldest son.

"You want me to forgive." Jack could barely say the word while thinking of his father.

"I don't *want* you to do anything. But I know how important reconnecting with your brother has been, how invested you are in your family's well-being, and how guilty you've felt over what happened to Patrick. Sometimes, face-to-face is better than a cell phone. You need a truce."

Padre was right. Jack wanted to be in San Diego for his family, but he also needed to be there for himself.

Jack turned to Scout. "You'll loan me your plane?"

"Hell, if I'd known it'd be this easy to convince you, I'd have said you could fly commercial." Scout laughed. "Yeah, you can borrow her. Just be careful, okay? She's a bit temperamental, prefers a light touch, and sometimes you're a might heavy-handed, know what I mean?"

"I'll treat her as if she were my own."

"God, no. Treat her like she's *my* plane."

Jack laughed and sat down next to Scout and Padre, feeling the tension dissipate. "I'll leave at oh six hundred, be back in twenty-four hours."

"Take all the time you want," Scout said.

"I can't take too much time off. Bills to pay," Jack said. "Twenty-four is about all I can spare." And all he could take, knowing everything could blow up if his father pushed.

The door opened and Chief of Police Art Perez and two of his deputy cronies sauntered in. "Great," Scout mumbled.

"Leave it alone," Jack said, not taking his dark eyes off the head cop. Perez didn't want Jack in Hidalgo anymore than Jack wanted Perez as the chief of police. Neither of them could do anything about the other, and Jack lived outside the city limits, so Perez couldn't even harass him effectively.

Except here.

Six foot two—a half inch taller than Jack, but with a paunch that suggested fifty pounds heavier and a disdain for regular exercise—Perez strode over to the table, hands in his belt. He had the demeanor of a man who had to prove his manhood each and every day.

"Father," Perez acknowledged Padre. His mother worked at the rectory part-time and liked Father Francis. Hispanic men almost always deferred to their mothers, especially in matters of faith.

But Jack wasn't a priest, and hadn't even made a very good altar boy thirty years ago. He hadn't won Mrs. Perez over.

"How are you, Art?" Padre said. "Would you like to join us?"

"Another time." Perez stared at Jack. Jack stared back. Perez turned to Scout. "I heard you had some excitement down in Guatemala."

"Not much," Scout said. "Maybe we can find some here."

"We have an early morning." Jack stood. The last thing he needed was Scout sitting in jail indefinitely for assaulting the chief of police. It had happened once before, when Scout and Deputy Leon started a bar fight.

Padre picked up on the cue, though Scout was slower on the uptake. It was earlier than his usual close-down-the-bar night.

"Yes," Padre took Scout's arm. "You need to fuel the plane."

"Going somewhere?" Perez asked.

"Personal," Jack said.

The silence was thick. Scout mumbled something about men with big guns and small dicks and Perez reddened.

Jack extracted them from the tense situation and they went outside. Nearly midnight and still warm, but the humid breeze off the Rio Grande felt good.

"Want to fly me out to San Diego?" he asked Scout.

"Naw, I have a date with Rina and the boys Wednesday morning."

"I'll be back by then."

"Maybe, maybe not, but I don't want to miss taking the boys to their first Major League ball game. Just take care of Carrie, okay?"

Jack had never named any of the planes he flew, though Carrie the Caravan was Scout's pride and joy. To Jack, planes were simply transpo.

"Of course. Let me give you a ride home."

Ethan—he'd dumped his first name in favor of his middle when he returned to the United States—didn't think it had been a good idea to snatch Price's dog tag, and he definitely didn't think it had been smart to mail it to the FBI, but he kept his mouth shut. He didn't want to upset Karin. He didn't want her to leave him. She'd saved his life and he needed her.

Far back in his mind, Ethan knew she needed him as well—she wanted him to teach her all the tricks of his trade, his unusual aptitude for acupuncture. But that was certainly a modest exchange. He couldn't have done any of this without her, and he'd be grateful for the rest of his life. The life he owed her.

"You okay?" she asked as he drove south.

"Fine, love." He glanced in the rearview mirror. Clear. "What are you thinking?"

"I don't want you to get in trouble," he said. "What if they trace the dog tags back to you? I can't lose you." His bottom lip trembled and he bit it hard enough to draw blood. He barely felt the puncture.

She leaned over and wiped the blood from his lip with her index finger. Out of the corner of his eye he watched her put her finger with his bright red blood into her mouth, then sucked her finger with her eyes closed, a half-smile on her lips.

He swallowed thickly and squirmed in his seat.

"They won't trace it to me, or you, or anyone. It's a game, Ethan. They'll be chasing their tails. I wish I could watch." She laughed, as if she were amused.

They'd gone out of their way to mail the package from Reno—not only far from their next destination, but it would point the police in the wrong direction. Because so far her plans had worked exactly as she'd promised, Ethan believed her. And he loved her.

They'd left Sacramento at three that morning, dumped the van, picked up another vehicle, hit Reno, then turned down Highway 395 and drove through the Owens Valley. The bleakness of the desert made him want to drive the truck off the edge of the next cliff. A few cars, a few trucks, and nothing. Highway 58 wasn't much better, and now I-40 cutting through the Mojave Desert as the sun set low behind them made him want to scream and jab a needle in the eye of the bitch riding next to him.

Ethan hated sitting in the car for hours doing nothing. At least she let him drive. He'd have blown his brains out if he had to sit in the passenger seat for fifteen hours.

He'd almost killed himself many times. Karin had stopped him. He hated her for it. Loved her for it. It depended on what memory came back and where it hurt.

"You're brooding," she said.

"It wasn't the same this time."

"Price was a worthless bum."

"I'm sorry I got carried away. I just wanted to try something different."

"It worked beautifully," she cooed.

"But he *died*. It didn't even take that long. I don't understand how it happened." And that's what bothered Ethan most of all. He'd studied and practiced and perfected his discipline. Price shouldn't have had a heart attack. It took the fun out of making him pay for the months of pain Ethan had endured.

She put her hand between his legs—close, but not quite touching him where he wanted.

"You didn't make a mistake. You tried something new and he had a heart attack. Maybe he had a weak heart, maybe he was a drug addict, we don't know. But think of what you discovered! When we're done with everyone on the list, we should explore the possibilities of serious damage."

"Nothing's permanent." Except memories.

"You don't know that. Look at what happened to Price."

"Like you said, he could have been a druggie or had high blood pressure or something."

Ethan had been a guinea pig. Punctured and pained to perfect the techniques of his captors. He would be better than them. They hadn't killed him—maybe they couldn't with the tools they'd chosen—but they had made him want to die. Wouldn't it be something if Ethan could slide in a couple of well-placed needles and cause a heart to stop? Had he done that with Price? Had he come up with something new? Better?

"I need to practice," he said.

"You'll have time. But first, we finish with the plan."

She touched him there now; he was hard. "Just a couple hours and we can take care of this."

He squirmed. He wanted her to suck him so hard it hurt. But he would wait.

They drove mostly in silence, though she was tormenting him with touches and kisses and whispers that kept him in a constant state of agitation. They arrived in Flagstaff as the sun disappeared. Here they would change cars again, rest, and tomorrow night take out another of the men who had destroyed Ethan: Frank Cardenas.

He shivered with anticipation. She thought it was about sex. Sure, sex had something to do with it. But more, he wanted to please her. To show her what he'd learned. He knew she enjoyed watching him poke the restrained men. He always asked if she wanted him to continue, and she always said yes. Keep it going as long as possible, until they pushed their victim to the breaking point.

The cabin they'd shared for the last six months was in the mountains above Flagstaff. He parked and got out, stretched, feeling free. The cabin was a large, spacious three-room A-frame with a loft. While he didn't like being confined, it was okay as long as he could see out the windows.

Ethan turned to her, putting their bags inside cabin. "Do you want—" he began, but her face had changed somehow . . .

"What?" he asked her.

"I'm excited about tomorrow." She took his hands and put them on her breasts.

"You like watching me work." It pleased him. He didn't smile much, but now his lips turned up with a rare grin.

She nodded and licked her lips. He cleared his throat and squeezed her breasts again, rubbing her nipples hard with his thumbs. Karin was pretty, older than him, but that was okay. She dyed her hair so often he didn't remember her natural color—maybe blond—but he liked it now, a reddish brown, long, making her look younger and sweet.

"It was fun, wasn't it?"

She nodded again as he pushed her against the wall.

"I'm glad I figured out how to stop him from screaming," he whispered.

"It was a neat trick. I didn't know you could hit a point and stop the vocal cords from working."

"It doesn't work like that. But to scream, you need air." He touched her neck, his finger trailing down her chest, across her nipples.

"But," he continued, "if the pain is so unbearable you can't draw in a deep breath, you can scarcely breathe, you can't scream."

"It helped," she whispered. "We were practically in the open."

That had excited her, too, that they'd been bold and almost reckless. *Almost* because she hadn't left anything to chance. They'd taken care of security, cameras, and had disguised themselves just in case anyone saw anything.

He leaned over and bit her ear, then sucked her lobe. He slid his scarred palm underneath her shirt, down the backside of her jeans and squeezed. She moaned and he lost himself in her.

"Watching men die turns you on." He rubbed her.

"No."

"You're lying."

"Am not."

She was lying. He felt her excitement, the forbidden thrills that pain and control and being gods gave them. He felt the power, the power that had been denied him for months. He'd been nothing, he'd been an experiment, poked and prodded and subjected to pain so intense, so vivid, it made him beg to die.

"Kill me. Kill me. Please. God no. No more. Kill me now. Now, God. Don't!" His plea came on jagged breaths as the man wearing black gloves slowly pushed the ultra-thin needle behind his testicles and made him scream so violently that his vocal cords became raw.

Months of screaming had damaged his larnyx to the point where Ethan could no longer speak without a rasp.

Now *he* had the power. The control. *He* would make them all pay. Those who'd left him to suffer. They should have killed him. *Why didn't they just shoot him?*

"Ethan." Her voice was low and he opened his eyes. He hadn't realized he'd had her pinned so hard against the wall she couldn't breathe. But she didn't look scared, never her. Karin wasn't scared of him.

She should be. Everyone should be.

"Admit it. You watched every needle go into his flesh. The poke. The slow pressure, his muscles tensing. The convulsions. The screams and panic and fear in his eyes."

"Fear," she breathed.

"Why aren't you scared of me?" he asked.

Her blue eyes, only inches from his, stared at him. "Why aren't you scared of *me*?"

"You don't even know yourself."

"You turn me on."

"Maybe I do." He shoved two fingers into her and she shuddered. His thumb pressed on her sensitive pressure point and she couldn't control her reaction; her arms tightened around his neck as a flood poured through her onto his hand.

"Oh, God, that was too fast."

"We're not done, are we?"

She grinned and pushed him away from her. She stripped. He watched, oddly disconnected. His penis had a life of its own, as if it watched and enjoyed the show, but Ethan himself was above it all. Watching his body, her body, reacting to the sight and smell of sex, but without fully participating.

She removed his clothes and took his hard dick in her mouth.

Ten minutes later he was still rock hard and she was frustrated. "Ethan."

"You know what to do."

She frowned, but her eyes lit with excitement. "I don't want to hurt you."

Lying bitch.

"If you want to help me, you need to do it. It's the only way." He was sweating and shaking. Was this like wanting heroin? Meth? The physical reaction was real. Too real. He needed her to do it. "Now, dammit. I need it." He grabbed her by the neck, pushed her back up against the wall. "You want it."

"I don't."

He slapped her. "You do. You need it as much as I do. You just won't admit it. But I know you better than you know yourself. Your eyes betray you." His lips touched her ear as he whispered, "Your body betrays you. You're shaking as much as I am. I'm in withdrawal. You're in ecstasy. Do it now, or I swear I'll kill you."

She pushed him away. "Don't threaten me." She opened his special black box. She was naked, had a curvy body, shapely legs, tight ass. Things he would have appreciated before. Things he would have enjoyed before.

Now he only craved one thing.

She turned toward him, the leather pouch in her hand. "Lie down."

He obeyed and lay on the hard floor. She took two needles from his kit. He quivered. She straddled him and sank his dick deep inside her. She shuddered. "I hate this."

She was a liar.

He could barely speak, but the words had to be said. "You hate that you enjoy it."

She held the two needles in front of him. Taunted him. He moaned. "Please. Please please please."

She moved and gyrated on top of him, sending him into agony not from sex, but from the inability to release. But it was always about her. Her, her, her, her . . .

. . . she found the nerve on the side of his neck and put in one needle. The pain surged through his body as his nerves reacted to the invasion. He'd taught her well.

"Kill me," he moaned. "God, kill me."

She then inserted the second needle high on his inner thigh and he screamed, tears streaming from his eyes, sweat pouring off his body as his hips moved violently.

The first time they'd done this, he'd bucked her off him, but he didn't care. It wasn't about her pleasure, it was about his pain. Now she anticipated it. Enjoyed it. Craved his agony so she could get off.

He exploded within her, the pain giving him the release he needed. He whimpered with humiliation and pulled out the needles himself. The pain subsided. A lesser man would be disabled for several minutes, but he'd had practice.

He flipped her over, holding her down by her neck.

"Don't make me wait again."

"I'm s-s—" she began.

He glared at her and for the first time saw that small glimmer of fear in the back of her eyes. He smiled, giddy, excited. She did fear him. She damn well should. He could kill her.

No no no! Ethan couldn't kill Karin. He needed her. What would he do without her? He couldn't survive. He wouldn't be able to finish their plans. He kissed her lips. Her neck.

"I need you." He started crying and hated himself for it.

"Don't, baby. Don't cry. I'll take care of you."

"Are you mocking me?" he asked.

"No, of course not!"

He didn't believe her. "Don't move."

"What are you going to do?"

He took one of the needles that had been in his body, and without hesitation, inserted it just under her nipple. The pain that crossed her face delighted him. He could see why she became so excited watching the others suffer.

She couldn't scream, she couldn't think. He counted off the seconds. *One. Two. Three.*

Ten seconds would feel like hours. He knew. He'd been there. He'd been through far worse. If only she knew. If only she'd been there. To watch. Would she have gotten all hot and horny watching him suffer? Hearing him scream? Would she fuck the man with the black gloves as Ethan froze in pain?

Twenty-one. Twenty-two. Whoops. Too long.

He pulled out the needle. She rolled over and threw up on the wood floor.

"Bas-bastard."

He stood, happy. Odd feeling, but there it was. Birds singing and a zip-a-dee-do-dah day. He laughed and dressed. "I'm hungry," he said. "I'll make dinner, okay? Your favorite."

Karin watched Ethan as he walked to the kitchen, whistling. Jekyll and Hyde. Bastard. She'd shoot him in the back for what he'd done to her if she didn't need him to finish teaching her the tools of his trade. She had watched him and had learned, but there was nothing like doing it herself. And he didn't let her do it often. When she pushed too hard, he clammed up and it was almost impossible to get him to open up again.

He was a fucking lunatic. But she'd forgotten that Ethan, though probably certifiably insane, was also dangerous.

She wouldn't make that mistake again.

CHAPTER
THREE

Megan went home late Monday night, the murder of George L. Price weighing heavily on her mind. She didn't know why it bothered her so much—murder was part of the job.

She poured herself a glass of red wine, kicked off her shoes, and sat heavily in her armchair. A white ball of fur jumped into her lap and meowed loudly.

She frowned at Mouse, as she called the cat, and said, "I already fed you." She'd never been an animal person. Her job wasn't nine-to-five, and she didn't want to be responsible for anyone else. Megan liked to come and go as she pleased. But her ex-husband had recently presented her with the furry creature, rescued by his new fiancée when someone threw the animal into a local lake.

Unconsciously, she stroked her pet, who immediately started to purr. The purr was surprisingly soothing, and Mouse kneaded his paws on her lap.

Megan sipped her wine and closed her eyes. It was close to midnight after a long, long day. Her squad was the only Violent Crimes Squad in the Sacramento Regional FBI Office, and she'd spent hours on the Price homicide, following up with Detective Black and Simone Charles several times throughout the day, reviewing the little evidence they'd thus far collected.

Their one lead—the license plates noted by the security patrol Sunday night—was still viable, though Megan wasn't holding out hope. Two of the vehicles cleared quickly—the owners had valid reasons for leaving their cars in the garage, and they had verified alibis as well.

The third plate was a possible. The plate was registered to an eighty-two-year-old great-grandmother. When Black went to her house, he discovered that the plates on her sedan did not match the numbers logged by garage security—someone had switched them with those off a black Econovan registered to a neighbor who had reported his vehicle stolen Monday morning. When Black followed up with him, the owner said the last time he'd driven his van was on Saturday morning, and he didn't know it was gone until he left for work on Monday. So far, the van hadn't turned up. Black was checking into neighbors and relatives. He was thorough and methodical.

In addition to this priority serial murder, Megan had to clear the paperwork piling up on her desk. She preferred taking care of her supervisory duties as they arose, not putting anything off too long, knowing how quickly the stacks of paper grew. But in the course of dealing with paperwork, she had to delegate new assignments, review reports, and attend a joint task force meeting on child prostitution while the assigned agent prepared to testify in a high-profile case.

She hadn't submitted her own written report on the Price homicide until after ten that night. But she left the office with a clean desk and a plan for tomorrow.

Now that she was home, she could think about why this morning's crime scene bothered her so much. Price was a veteran. He should have been taken care of by the country he had fought to protect, but instead he'd been marginalized and homeless. How had he gotten to that point? What had happened to put him on the streets? Drugs? Alcohol?

Megan's father had been a career soldier and had died on the field during the first Desert War. He'd been her hero, and while he hadn't turned to drugs or alcohol, many of his peers had. It wasn't just from what they'd seen or done as soldiers; it was also how they were treated when they came home. Megan had known too many veterans over the years who had serious medical problems, physical or emotional, and often did nothing about it. Partly because they were men—they felt they should be able to handle it on their own—and partly because the system was a bureaucratic mess.

What if her father had been discharged instead of killed? Her father had been a soldier. He couldn't have been anything else. But if he couldn't be a soldier, would he have walked the streets? Lost? Confused? Angry with his fate? What about Price's family? Did he have kids wondering where their dad was?

Men like Price often slipped through the cracks.

She was still waiting on the dead veteran's files. All they had was one of his dog tags—if they were even his. He could have picked them up off the street or found them in a garbage can. They'd take prints at the autopsy, and the coroner's investigators would track down family. Hopefully, they'd soon have his identification confirmed.

But Megan knew soldiers after being raised by one.

She couldn't imagine any of them tossing their tags in the trash. Not the men and women she knew.

Of course, maybe Price's wife or ex-wife had tossed them out of spite.

Nonsequitur, Megan. You are tired.

And thinking about her mother. If Caroline had still been married to William Elliott, she would have tossed all his medals, commendations, and the numerous newspaper articles Megan had carefully preserved over the years, intending to give him a scrapbook on his retirement.

The last page in the scrapbook was her father's obituary and a photograph she took of his headstone at Arlington National Cemetery.

Her cell phone's symphony ring tone startled her. She grabbed the phone from the table, looked at the caller I.D., and didn't immediately recognize the number. But it was after four in the morning—she'd fallen asleep in her chair.

"This is Megan Elliott," she answered, clearing her throat.

"You have to get to the morgue *right now*!"

Morgue. "Who's this?"

"Simone! Simone Charles, from Sac P.D. CSU. The army is snatching our victim. Says he's AWOL and wanted for attempted murder."

Megan sat up and Mouse jumped off her lap with an irritated *meow*. She couldn't believe the army CID was pushing for jurisdiction—and at four a.m.?

"I'll be right there."

"I called the district attorney and asked him to file some motion or something to stop them. But he thinks the U.S. attorney needs to do it. He's going to try to slow them down."

"Matt Elliott?"

"Is there another D.A.?"

"Sorry. You woke me." Of course the Sacramento P.D. would know the Sacramento district attorney, who happened to be Megan's brother.

"I'll call my boss," she said. "Hold them there."

"They'll have to arrest me before they take my body." Simone hung up.

Megan jumped in and out of the shower before the water warmed, pulled her wet blond hair back into a tight braid, and slid on slacks and a thin blouse, then her shoulder holster. She poured some dry food into Mouse's dish and added water to his bowl on her way out of her downtown loft, and was in her car twenty minutes after Simone's furious call.

She dialed her boss at his home. He answered quietly, probably so as not to wake his wife. "Richardson."

"Megan here." She told him what Simone told her.

"And?"

"That's all I have. I'm on my way to the morgue to see what we can do."

"We probably won't be able to stop them. They have jurisdiction over their soldiers, dead or alive."

"It would be much better if we worked together on this."

"If anyone can convince the army's CID to share, it'd be you, but I'm not holding my breath." He sighed as if to emphasize the point. "I'll call Olsen's office." Olsen was the U.S. attorney who oversaw their district. "Let me know what you find out. It may not be worth fighting them for."

"Sir, Price is connected to two other murders. Did you read my report? I emailed it last night. We need the evidence to track down a serial murderer, CID and their rules notwithstanding."

"Point taken." He hung up, and Megan wasn't sure if he was fully on her side.

While military investigations were essential in keeping order among the armed forces, Megan simply couldn't see what benefit there was to the Criminal Investigation Division taking over the murder of an AWOL soldier when his death most likely had nothing to do with his being AWOL.

Unless the other two victims were AWOL.

She called Richardson back.

"Sir—"

"I'm about to shower, since you woke me. Can I have ten minutes?"

"Did you find out about the other two victims? If they were veterans?"

"No. I sent an alert to headquarters about the possible connection."

"I'm going to follow up on that. Maybe there is another connection—"

"That they were all AWOL?" he guessed what she'd been thinking. "Let me know." He hung up.

Texas was two hours ahead of California, but it wasn't even seven a.m. there. Still, she called and left a message for the detective in charge of the Duane Johnson homicide. She did the same thing for the Dennis Perry homicide in Las Vegas. Then she called Matt.

"I need—"

"Good morning to you, too, Meg."

"Sorry, I—"

"I know. I've had an earful from CSU. I got you a temporary restraining order, but I don't expect it to hold up. It'll just delay them, and probably not for long."

"Enough time for me to convince them that they don't want to take our victim and evidence."

"Good luck. I'm not holding my breath." He hung up.

Megan appreciated the legal system. Laws were there for a reason. Even military laws. But she wanted to solve a murder. Find a killer, build a case, and hand it over to the U.S. attorney for prosecution. She wanted to punish the bad guys. She only wished she was better versed in such situations like dealing with CID, but she would wing it. After all, they were on the same side.

When she pulled up in front of the morgue, there were two army jeeps and a black sedan with military plates. A soldier in uniform stood sentry. She drove around back and saw the crime scene unit's van. An ambulance was bringing in two corpses from a local hospital for processing when Megan walked in. She didn't see Simone, but heard her voice echoing in the sterile building. Megan cringed. She flashed her badge though the intake pathologist didn't pay much attention, or so Megan thought. She started walking toward the voice when the gal behind the desk snapped "Grab some booties," and pointed to a box on the wall.

"Thanks." Megan slid them on her flats and continued to walk toward the voice.

"What about 'restraining order' do you not understand?" Simone said, hands on her hips, as Megan rounded the corner into the cold storage room. Rows of bodies on steel gurneys, most of them covered with sheets with only their feet showing, lined the huge refrigerator.

Megan was surprised to see that Matt had beat her to the morgue. She nodded to her brother, and to the pathologist who was standing next to Simone.

All eyes went to her. Megan quickly assessed the situation and realized that she was likely the ranking opposition, for lack of a better word. She extended her hand to the man in the suit—military lawyer, she pegged. "Hello, I'm Supervisory Special Agent Megan Elliott with the FBI. I think we can work something out where we all get what we want."

The lawyer said, "Lieutenant Paul Stork. Your victim is our primary suspect in an attempted murder case. Private First Class Price has been AWOL for five years. And, as I was explaining to the district attorney, section—"

Megan cut him off. "I understand, Lieutenant. And I respect your need to investigate your own crimes. May I suggest that we find common ground so we—"

Stork interrupted. "There is no common ground, Agent Elliott."

Megan appealed to his sense of justice. "Price was the victim of a serial murderer who has killed two other men—in Texas and Nevada. The evidence is crucial not only to this investigation, but to those investigations. We need to make the link—"

Stork put his hand up. Megan realized the gesture was the same one she often used when she wanted someone to stop talking, and it irritated her intensely. She vowed she wouldn't do it again, and planned on apologizing to her ex-husband at her first opportunity.

"Agent Elliott, if there is any evidence pertinent to the Sacramento Police Department's investigation into this homicide, my office will forward it to"—he looked at his notepad—"Detective John Black."

"I think we can do better than that," Megan said.

Stork's phone rang. He answered it without excusing himself. He listened, then said, "Thank you," and hung up.

"If—"

He put his hand up again and Megan wanted to slap it back down. Stork motioned for the two soldiers standing sentry over Price's body to move him out.

"That was the DOD," Stork said. "I have confirmed authority to take over this investigation. The FBI does not have jurisdiction in this matter, as I'm sure both you and the district attorney are aware." He turned to Simone, who was red-faced. The pathologist had a hand on her shoulder, his knuckles white as he restrained her as subtly as possible.

"Ms. Charles, I have sent over a team to collect the evidence stored at the Sacramento Police Department. If you make this difficult, I'll have you taken into custody for obstruction of justice." He said to the pathologist, "Mr. Ward, if you would please retrieve all clothing, evidence, and material you removed from Private First Class Price's body, post haste."

Post haste? Who spoke that way?

"It's logged in with—" Ward began.

"Please bring it to me. I have a busy day ahead and need to arrange transport of the body to our facilities."

Ward didn't bat an eye and left the room.

"Nice try, Mr. Elliott," Stork said. "I assume you were trying to help your wife out, but you should have known better."

"Sister," Megan and Matt said simultaneously.

Matt added, "This is still my county, and that man, AWOL or not, was murdered in my jurisdiction. I will likely be prosecuting his killer at some point—before or after you. I hope you'll consider that when you process the evidence and ensure that Ms. Charles and Detective Black have a copy of all your records and files."

"We'll provide what we can," Stork said, noncommittally.

"You jumped on this real quick," Megan said. "We've had the case for less than twenty-four hours."

"Your office contacted the army," Stork said.

"Excuse me?" Then Megan remembered. "When we were confirming his identity and seeking next-of-kin records." Dammit, her diligence got her case yanked.

"The CID still moved faster than I've ever seen the army move," Matt said. "Who's Price's victim? A general?" Megan noted the sarcasm in her brother's voice.

"Price is wanted for the attempted murder of his commanding officer."

Ward walked back in and handed a sealed box to the soldier Stork indicated.

"Thank you, Mr. Ward. You have been very helpful." He nodded to them, then motioned for the soldiers to leave with him. "Have a nice day."

Simone didn't restrain her scream of frustration as Stork left with their victim. "Asshole!"

Matt said, "I know Stork's type. He can make your life hell if he wants to."

"I've never been in the military," she snapped. "I don't take orders well."

Matt turned to the pathologist. "Good to see you again, Phineas. Have you met my sister, Megan Elliott?"

"I have now." He shook her hand.

"I can't believe we're just standing around here doing nothing!" Simone said. "That's my body they're taking. You can kiss any prosecution good-bye."

"Don't take it out on the D.A.," Phineas Ward said. "He delayed them long enough."

"What does that mean?" Megan asked.

Ward shrugged. "When we process the body, we take certain samples. I forgot that I'd put the vials in the lab, and the lab director is already processing them."

Simone wrapped her arms around him and kissed his cheek. "You're wonderful."

"It still won't help with a prosecution," Matt said. "Without physical evidence for the defense to test independently, most judges will throw it out."

"But it can help with victimology," Megan said, admiring Phineas Ward's foresight. "Was Price on drugs? Drunk? Did he have any illnesses? Did the killer drug him in any way? There's a connection between Price and the other two victims, and this is one way, albeit small, that we can try to figure it out."

"Exactly," Simone said. *"And,"* she added smugly, "the security tapes didn't come in yesterday. I'm supposed to get them at nine a.m., and the damn CID will already be back on their base or in Hell or wherever they're going."

Megan turned to Ward. "Did you inspect the body? Did you see anything strange?"

"Other than collecting blood and hair samples, I only performed a visual examination, weighed, and measured him. Six feet tall, one hundred seventy pounds, forty-five to fifty years of age. I don't have a positive I.D. on him, other than the identification on his person. But

I collected fingerprints and already sent them off for processing."

"So at least we'll be able to confirm his identity," Megan said. "You remembered those details?"

"My mind is full of useless trivia."

"Not so useless," Simone said, taking notes.

"I don't think he died from the bullet in his skull."

"What?" Megan and Simone said simultaneously.

"There wasn't enough blood. Was there a lot at the crime scene?"

"He lost a lot of blood when his hamstrings were cut," Simone said.

"But that didn't kill him. The blood was clotted behind his knees, and you'd be surprised at how little blood can come from a wound like that. It tears the muscle but doesn't hit any major arteries. The blood would clot quickly, yet the victim would be completely incapacitated. Not to mention being in intense pain.

"There was no clotting around the head," Ward continued, "at least I didn't see any. There might have been contamination, or perhaps a postmortem ritual of cleaning the body, but I think I would have noticed something like that." He shrugged. "It's just a guess."

"The victim's hands were very clean," Megan remembered. "Compared to what I would expect from a homeless man."

"Actually," Ward said, "now that you mention it, the body was relatively clean. I see a lot of the homeless in here, and few take regular, or even weekly, baths. His clothing, however, was quite ripe."

"Abrahamson," Matt said, snapping his fingers.

"Who?" Megan asked.

"Detective Greg Abrahamson. He was undercover on

the streets last year while investigating a series of murders. Found the killers and I have the trial coming up next month, so I've been working with him. I wonder if he knew the victim."

"It's worth a shot," Simone said. "I'll talk to Black about it."

"You're trying the case yourself?" Megan asked.

"It's very complex. I just won the motion to try the two juveniles as adults, but the battle wasn't pretty. Our office is going to be under scrutiny." He didn't have to explain why—California's entire criminal justice system had taken a huge public slap last year for sending an innocent man to death row.

Megan knew exactly what kind of pressure Matt was under. When his knee got shot out in Desert Storm—the same war that killed their father—he turned to a law degree, became a prosecutor, then a state senator, and eventually the district attorney. Putting criminals behind bars meant more to Matt than playing politics. The events of last year had put Matt back in the political spotlight, and he hadn't liked it.

"I'll call Black about Abrahamson," Simone said.

"And let me know when the security tapes come in," Megan said. "Maybe we can put a face on the killer."

"Killers," Simone corrected her.

Naked, Ethan stood in the middle of the forest.

The darkness was complete, the earth and his mind. Black. Bottomless. He breathed, but he was not alive. He spoke, but he did not think. Sucked dry by the needles that controlled his nerves, an empty shell of a man told him what to feel and when. The pain, the pleasure, the pain, the nothing.

Nothing.

He'd wanted to die. Death meant nothing. He wasn't really alive, was he?

He raised his bare arms toward the towering canopy of trees, a sliver of early light fighting its way in among the leaves. Arms outstretched, legs spread, he begged for lightning to strike him from above.

The phantom smell of charred flesh rushed through his nose, on his tongue. He snorted and moaned. The pain of electricity surging through his body, now a memory.

He looked down at his limp penis, but instead of the dank earth below he saw himself suspended by ropes, his feet barely touching the packed dirt floor. Rubbing his hands together, he felt the scars on his wrists, faint now, there for him to see and feel but no one else knew.

His body jerked as if he were on a string. He watched the needles that had pierced him years ago sink into his flesh. Wires this time, wires connected to a battery—what he thought was a battery. He looked straight ahead, the tree limbs holding the device, the wires crawling out for him.

You are mine you are mine you are mine.

Wires slithering as snakes, boa constrictors, wrapping around his ankles, knees, thighs, penis, down his throat . . .

Kill me God damn you kill me damn you KILL FUCK NO NO NO NO.

The pain tore all pleas from his mind, his throat, his scream suspended in midair. His body jerked violently from the electric jolt, a brief jolt that kept him bobbing long after they were done.

The room had been dark. The room had been bright. Hell. Heaven. Laughter. Laughter bubbled out of his scream-scarred throat. There was only Hell, Hell on earth, and all he wanted was nothing. Nothing. Empty, painless, nothing . . .

Dropping to the ground, he buried his face in the dirt, burrowing in the leaves. He would escape, run, hide.

They would find him.

She would find him.

He was being watched.

The cold hit him first. He shook uncontrollably. Raw earth assaulted him. He breathed in and coughed up dirt. His mouth was coated with the damp, moldy soil. He rose, resting on all fours, barely able to breathe.

"Ethan."

Salty tears mingled with dirt on his tongue.

"Wa-water." He could hardly speak. Where was he?

"Shh."

It was his angel of death, the one who'd saved him. Over and over. She didn't leave, didn't desert him, leave him to the enemy, leave him to be tortured. She raised him from the dirt, draped a blanket over him. He was naked. It was so cold, where were his clothes? How did he get here?

"Walk with me."

He went with her, her arm around him. He remembered tearing his shirt. His chest stung. He'd scratched himself. How bad? It hurt. She would take care of him.

"Kill me," he begged, his throat raw.

She didn't respond. He wanted to cry.

"I hurt myself," he whispered, his throat raw.

"I'll fix everything."

She would. His angel would fix everything.

"Kill them."

"Of course."

"I will kill them. I will kill them. I promise you I will *kill* them."

And she murmured in his ear, "Yes, sweetheart, we will."

CHAPTER
FOUR

Jack had been in San Diego for two hours, and in Patrick's hospital room for the last thirty minutes, and now he wanted to leave. Hospitals and anything medical made Jack antsy. He'd spent enough time in triage to cringe at the sights and smells and sounds of the sanitary building.

Unfortunately, Patrick saw that in him. The kid had an uncanny sixth sense, like Dillon. Jack didn't like to be psychoanalyzed by either his kid brother or his twin.

"You don't want to be here," Patrick said.

"I wanted to see you, make sure Dillon wasn't jerking my chain when he said you woke up as if nothing happened."

"Slight exaggeration. My muscles are weak and I remember everything. Up until the explosion," he added quietly.

Two years ago, their eighteen-year-old sister Lucy had been kidnapped and Patrick, a cybercrimes cop with San Diego P.D., had gone with a team of FBI agents to an island off Baja California where they believed she was being held captive. The trap had left Patrick barely alive; life-saving brain surgery put him in a coma. The only life support he required was a feeding tube, his body went through all the rituals of breathing and blood pumping on its own. Twenty-two months later he woke up without fanfare. Jack didn't believe in miracles, but Patrick's recovery was the closest thing to one he'd ever seen.

Patrick reached for a five-pound weight on the table next to the hospital bed. Jack resisted the urge to help him when he saw the strain cross his brother's face. Patrick did three curls then put the weight down, winded.

"Dillon came by earlier. You just missed him."

Jack hadn't missed his twin. He'd avoided him. He had plans to meet up later with Dillon and the rest of the Kincaid clan, but for now he wanted to focus on Patrick and adjust to being home.

"Thanks for coming," Patrick added.

Jack nodded. "I'm glad you made it."

"Nearly two years." Patrick frowned and stared at the foot of his bed. "Looks like they'll let me go in a few days. I'll have P.T. daily, but at least I won't be in here anymore."

"Good."

Jack didn't know what else to say. He stood. "I'll let you rest."

"I don't want to rest," Patrick said. "Did you come to San Diego to spend five minutes with me, only to go back to Texas or Mexico or wherever it is you live?"

"Pretty much."

Patrick picked up the weight again, this time in his left hand. "I'm sorry, I didn't mean anything by that, it's just . . . two years and nothing has changed."

"Everything has changed."

Patrick raised his eyebrow. "I missed so much. Dillon said you'd gone to D.C. a few times to visit him and Lucy."

"I have." Jack's trips to D.C. had given him back the family he'd let his father deny him.

You didn't have to follow the Colonel's orders to steer clear.

It was obvious that Patrick wanted to say something. "Spit it out, Patrick. What's going on?"

In a rush, he said, "Did I screw up? Did I fuck up the investigation in Baja? Tell me the truth, Jack. You're probably the only one who will."

"In Baja? Hell no. That bastard set a trap and you were caught in it. I should have gone. Maybe I could have seen it coming. I'm used to booby traps. I could have—" He shook his head, clearing the webs of guilt that continued to spin. "But I'd been certain it was nothing, that you'd been sent on a wild-goose chase. At first I was glad you'd left, thought it would keep you out of harm's way. I didn't like being responsible for everyone. Dillon was enough. But I was wrong." And that didn't sit well with Jack. Not in situations like that.

Jack stood. "I need to go. I just wanted—" He paused.

"I know."

Jack squeezed Patrick's shoulder. "Glad to have you well. Take care of yourself, kid."

The door opened as Jack spoke. Rosa and Pat Kincaid walked in, Rosa saying, "Patrick, we have great—"

Then his mother saw Jack. Without hesitation, she rushed him into a tight hug. Jack accepted his mother's warm embrace, but his eyes never left his father's cold face.

"Hello, Mama." He kissed the top of her head.

"I didn't know you were coming. You'll come to the house for dinner tonight. Everyone will be there."

"I have to go."

"No. You will have dinner—"

"Let him go," Pat said, standing ramrod straight.

"I will not. Everyone is home for the first time since—" She didn't say it, but Jack knew the last time all seven Kincaid children had been in the same room was for his nephew's funeral thirteen years ago.

Jack had no intention of spending any more time in the same room as his father. But two years ago, he'd asked his mother to forgive him. This woman had given him life, raised him, never once turned her back on him. When he returned home, she welcomed him as if he were the prodigal son. Jack had been the one to let his father get between him and the mother who bore him. She had no part in what had happened two decades ago.

"What time?" Jack asked.

She beamed, hugged him again. "Six." She turned to Patrick with a bright smile. "That's the good news I have. The doctor said you can come home for the evening. By Friday, you will be released for good."

"You mean they're letting me leave?" he grinned. "For real food?"

"I'm making all your favorites. I have Nick helping because his wife is no good in the kitchen." She shook her head. "How could I raise a daughter who can't cook?"

Letting his mother babble to Patrick, Jack stared over her head at his father.

Pat stared back for five seconds, then turned and left the room.

Jack followed.

Pat stood in the middle of the brightly lit hall. He waited for Jack to approach.

"I'm not turning my back on my family again."

"You made that choice twenty years ago, Jack."

Jack suppressed his rising anger. "*You* made the choice. You gave me an ultimatum I couldn't agree to. If I had had the balls back then I would have ignored you and never cut off contact with Mom."

"You owe me an apology. I saved your career."

"I didn't ask you to."

"Dammit, Jack, you're stubborn and shortsighted. You would have been court-martialed!"

"I was willing to take that chance." He would have risked not only his career but his life twenty years ago in Panama to save the family who had taken a stand against Noriega. He found them hiding, with hardly any food or water, and he'd extracted them, brought them to an American base. Against orders, but should he have let them be slaughtered? The area hadn't been secure, they were the only civilians in the small outlying village, trapped because one of the children was handicapped and couldn't make the journey to safety fast enough.

Pat fisted his hands. "I couldn't watch you lose everything. Jeopardize the entire mission, embarrass the army, embarrass me—" He stopped.

"This was about embarrassing you? People were killed because you pulled me out. The mission was never in jeopardy. I was risking only *my* life and *my* career."

"You can't save the world, Jack."

"But I could have saved them!" He slammed his fist against the wall. Pictured the Ortega family when he found them a week later, executed. Father, mother, children, grandmother. A family of nine murdered in cold blood because their father had taken a stand against the criminal Noriega and his thuggish cronies.

"You don't know that. They were safe where they were. How do you know that your impulsive decision to move them didn't lead to their enemies finding them when I sent them back home?"

Turning his back on his father, Jack stepped into the staircase. He ran up the thirteen floors and stood at the top, unable to exit to the roof. He pounded his fists on the locked door, then put his hands on his knees and breathed deeply.

He didn't know if he was to blame for the Ortega family being slaughtered. Jack had lived with that guilt for twenty years.

CHAPTER
FIVE

By the end of Tuesday, Megan had exhausted all avenues she could think of to regain control of the evidence and Price's body. She finally decided to break ranks and call an old friend. If J. T. Caruso, one of the principals in the local office of Rogan-Caruso Protective Services, couldn't find the answers she needed, no one could.

She was one of the select few who had J.T.'s private cell phone number—courtesy of her brother who had been in the navy SEALs with J.T.—though she rarely used it.

"Caruso," the deep voice said.

"It's Megan Elliott."

"Meg," J.T. said warmly. "How are you doing?"

"Personally, fine. Professionally . . . well, I have a situation I need your advice on."

"Does it have to do with the dead veteran you pulled yesterday?"

It always unnerved Megan how J.T. seemed to know everything. "I swear you're a psychic."

He laughed honestly, seeming to surprise both himself and Megan. "Sometimes I wish I were. Truth, Mitch mentioned it to me this morning. Do you need to borrow him? I know your squad is spread thin."

She hadn't even talked to her ex-husband, Mitch

Bianchi, but he still had a lot of friends on the squad. Half the time Megan wished she had never encouraged him to take the job offer from Rogan-Caruso last year. The best agent in fugitive apprehension, Mitch's exceptional instincts and abilities were sorely missed. However, Megan had to admit that Mitch was better suited to private investigation than following the rigid rules of federal law enforcement.

"Thanks, J.T., but I really need you on this one."

"What can I do?"

"You were in the military police, weren't you?"

"Navy."

"My victim was AWOL from the army. Their CID took my evidence and my body. I want them back."

"That won't be possible. The army—hell, the entire military—doesn't like to share. If CID has flexed its jurisdictional muscles, you're out of luck. Though I'm surprised they acted so quickly."

"That's what I thought as well, but the vic attempted to kill his commanding officer. At least that's what they told us."

"Okay, that makes more sense. If he was simply a deserter they'd probably have been satisfied with positive identification and the coroner's report."

"Price is the third in a string of murders with the same M.O. Two dead men in two other states killed by the same people."

"There's more than one killer?"

"Evidence suggests there were at least two on scene."

"How common are serial killers working in pairs?"

"Not rare, but not common. There've been several high-profile cases—the Hillside Stranglers; several male-female partnerships, where the woman lures the victim into the trap; Bittaker and Norris, who were prison buddies and started a killing spree when they got out. There's usually a dominant and submissive— Why am I telling you this?"

"It's interesting."

"You don't need me to teach you Forensic Profiling 101," Megan said.

"I don't usually draw such violent cases."

It was Megan's turn to laugh. "Perhaps not serial murderers, but don't forget I've known you for a long time."

"I could never forget that," he said, perhaps too seriously, or maybe because Megan was on pins and needles. "What would you like me to do?"

"If I can't get the evidence back, do you think you can find out what's going on? I am particularly interested in the autopsy report and any trace evidence report. The Sacramento Police Department isn't letting go; the detective in charge is digging into the victim's background, his last few weeks, trying to put together some sort of victimology profile, plus following up on one lead we had before the CID took our case. But without the autopsy report, a weapon analysis, and a comparison of the needle marks with the previous victims, it'll be hard to tie him into the other two murders. I need to be sure we're dealing with the same killer, or the joint investigation could be compromised."

"Why? If you have two other victims, why is this one so important?"

"If there are three known victims attributed to the same killer, where the M.O. is similar and there is a cooling off period, that puts these killers into the serial murderer category and they're most likely to kill again.

It frees up staff and resources at the federal level, and when we're competing with other, higher-priority squads like counterterrorism and counterintelligence—"

"Say no more. I know someone at the DOD. Let me see what I can find out. What information do you have on the victim?"

Megan shared everything she knew, and thanked J.T. She felt immensely better knowing that she was at least working the case.

Her BlackBerry rang and it was an out-of-state number. She took the call.

The caller had a Texas drawl, definitely southern with a slight accent that sounded Hispanic. "Miz Elliott? This is Detective José Vasquez with the Austin Police Department. To what honor do I owe speaking with the FBI?"

Megan couldn't tell if Vasquez was being sarcastic or not. Her office had a terrific relationship with local law enforcement; other regional divisions didn't. She glanced at her watch. It was after eight in the evening, putting Vasquez in Texas two hours later.

"Working late," she said.

"So are you."

Okay, no small talk. "I'm working with Sacramento Police Detective John Black. He told me he spoke with you briefly yesterday about a homicide two months ago in your jurisdiction."

"Yes. He had a similar M.O. And the FBI is involved?"

"Three cases, similar M.O.s, and Black called me in early. We've worked together before."

"What do you need to know?"

"My victim was in the military. Army. I'm trying to

track down any connection among the three victims, but so far other than their gender, that they lived alone, and were roughly middle-age, we have nothing."

"I sent Detective Black a copy of our files."

She'd read them. "There was nothing about a military record. Did you run a check?"

"No need to. I didn't see anything in the house—well, he had a POW sticker on his truck. Lotta people have them."

"I need his Social Security number to look up his records through the online military personnel system." She'd put in the name and current address, but that wasn't enough. "I have a copy of the autopsy report, but it's a fax of a copy and the numbers are unclear." She'd been surprised they were handwritten. Most records were typed or computer-generated now.

He rattled off the number. She wrote it down, then logged into the online military database and typed in the search parameters. She couldn't access detailed records without a specific request that needed to be approved by the military, but she could pull up basic information like name, rank, last-known address, and status.

"What do you think is happening here? As I told Detective Black, the trail went cold mighty quick. No witnesses, no other like crimes. Our lab has been going over trace fibers, but so far nothing we can use. I was thinking revenge."

"Revenge?"

"Oh, yeah. Guy was hamstrung then had all these needle marks. Couldn't see them until the autopsy. Reggie, the coroner, called me in to see them, he didn't believe it. Hundreds under the skin, but a needle so thin it didn't leave a visible mark unless you looked real close."

"Revenge?" It didn't make sense on the surface, but it felt like that to her. Personal. She cringed. She was beginning to sound a lot like her ex-husband. She preferred dealing with facts. The fact was that there was no evidence of revenge, unless she could find a specific connection among the three victims, something more specific than the possibility that they were all military.

She asked, "In your investigation, did you come up with a connection to Dennis Perry, the mechanic in Las Vegas?"

"Name ain't familiar 'cept from the hot sheet. When I saw it, I went through my notes. Name didn't come up. Wish I could be more help."

Her records search online was complete. She couldn't suppress the excitement in her voice as she said, "Detective, I think we have our connection. Johnson was in the U.S. Army from 1986 to 2006, honorably discharged. Price was in the U.S. Army from 1978 to 2004, when he went AWOL."

"That's near a twenty-year overlap."

"But it's something I didn't have before, and maybe Dennis Perry's records can narrow it down further. Thank you for your help."

"Call me if you need anything else. Keep me informed, all right?"

"I promise."

Thirty minutes later, Megan had Perry's service record and now a nine-year window—Perry was in the army from 1995 to 2005.

She grinned tightly. She had something! A slim thread, but it was more than she'd had this morning.

She picked up her phone to call Detective Black when

her BlackBerry trilled again. She answered, "I was just about to call you."

"The security tapes came in. Completely worthless."

"Why?"

"Someone blocked the signal from seven p.m. until three a.m."

"And no one noticed?"

"No one monitors the cameras. They operate automatically, more as a deterrent than anything else. And if someone gets his car vandalized, he can get a person on tape. But for practical or preventive security? Worthless."

"Dammit," she muttered. "What about the van?"

"Not on the camera before seven. That gave them an hour to drive in and disappear before security came through."

"All tapes? Even the stairwells?"

"It's all the same system. So what did you want to tell me?"

"I have a connection among the three victims." She told him about their U.S. Army records.

"Were they stationed together?" he asked, excited.

"That's going another level in, and I need more time. I can't get it without a formal request. I'm giving it to one of my best analysts and I'll let you know if anything comes up, but it won't be tonight." And it probably wouldn't be tomorrow. Or the next day. Unless orders came down from high up the food chain, the army wasn't going to jump immediately. And Megan didn't have enough juice to go all the way to the top.

"I have plenty to do. By the way, I spoke to Greg Abrahamson, the detective who was undercover downtown. He knew Price. Not by name, but when I mentioned the clean hands Abrahamson knew exactly who I was talking about. Said he was obsessive about keeping clean. Washed his hands constantly, was known to bathe in the river regularly. No sicko ritual there for the killer."

"Thanks for checking."

Megan hung up and called J.T. back, only to get his voice mail. She left the information she'd learned about the three victims. There was no way she could get their military records quickly through traditional bureaucratic routes. But she might be able to get the information through other, faster channels.

She feared that if she didn't figure out the connection soon, another veteran would die. She'd do everything in her power to stop it.

Jack had checked the Cessna Caravan's instruments and now inspected the weather report in the small open office inside the private hangar. The sun was quickly disappearing and Jack wanted to get back to Hidalgo tonight. His trip had been troublesome on many levels, though it was good to see Patrick awake.

He heard footsteps and looked up to see Dillon approach. "Ma wasn't the only one upset you didn't come by the house."

His twin brother knew just how to twist the knife. Jack shrugged, continued to look at the weather report but didn't see anything new. "I called."

"What happened between you and Dad today?"

Jack had never told anyone what had happened between him and the Colonel, and didn't plan to break that silence now.

"Dammit, Jack, I thought we were beyond this martyr crap."

"Is that *Doctor* Kincaid speaking or my brother?"

"Take your pick."

Jack assessed his brother. They weren't identical—Dillon was fair-skinned like their father, his hair light brown, his eyes green. Dillon and Colonel Pat Kincaid had a lot in common. Honor. Rules. Society.

But it was Jack—the dark-haired, dark-skinned, dark-eyed son—who'd worshipped their dad for the first nineteen years of their lives. Dillon was the smart kid; Jack was the kid expelled for fighting. Dillon prided himself on straight A's; Jack prided himself on pitching no-hitters. Dillon went to college on full scholarship; Jack enlisted in the army the day he graduated from high school.

Jack had wanted to be his dad.

Now he wanted to be anyone but.

"Take off your shrink hat, Dillon. I'm not open for inspection."

"I've never tried."

"Bullshit."

"Shit, Jack, you make this so hard sometimes."

"Don't go touchy-feely on me."

Dillon laughed, but it didn't reach his eyes. "Every time we make headway, you pull out the fact that I'm a psychiatrist. I specialize in violent killers, not stubborn mercenaries."

Jack leaned against the half wall of the office and gave his brother a wry smile. "How's Kate?"

Dillon tensed. "If you think baiting me is going to work, you're shit out of luck, Jack. And if you think I haven't figured out what happened, you must think I'm an idiot."

Jack picked up his overnight bag. He didn't need Dillon's lectures or disdain.

"I have friends at the hospital," Dillon said quietly.

Jack didn't say a word. His eyes closed. He didn't want to explain.

"Tell me," Dillon pushed.

"It's none of your fucking business."

"Is family so unimportant to you that you're just going to turn your back on us again?"

Again. That stung.

"I never suspected that the reason you disappeared was because of Dad."

"We all thought he was a saint," Jack said, surprising himself. He took a deep breath and faced Dillon. He didn't know what he was expecting—his father, a saint, or a shrink, but what he saw was his brother. The brother he once had. The brother he could have again if he wasn't such a "stubborn mercenary."

"He's human. So are you." Dillon caught his eye. "I think."

Jack didn't smile, but the tension dissipated. "Tell Ma—" He stopped. What should he say? That his father had disowned him? That her son may have been responsible for the deaths of an innocent family—or that her husband had been responsible? Could the family live with the fact that the Colonel had placed Jack's *career* above the lives of civilians?

"I can't go back, Dil. Not now."

"What happened?" he asked quietly. "Jack, you and me. What happened?"

Jack shook his head. He had promised himself twenty years ago that he would never talk about his father's betrayal with anyone, especially the family. Ma loved him, and Jack wouldn't hurt her again for the world.

"Dad disowned me," Jack said, staring straight ahead. "And that's it."

"Don't leave it at that—"

"I realized tonight that twenty years isn't long enough. I also realized that I shouldn't have let him sever ties to my family. He thought that if he took away everyone I cared about, I would come back and tell him he was right and thank him for showing me the error of my ways and saving my career." He grunted. "It's clear now. I made a new family in the army and I didn't need—I didn't think I needed—you or Ma or anyone."

Jack faced Dillon, jaw tight with restrained emotion. "You're my brother. I—" He paused. "I want my family back. But I no longer have a father."

"You don't—"

"I do mean it, Dillon. He told me never to come home. No more. He no longer exists to me. He disowned me twenty years ago, but he still controlled me all this time. Now I'm free. And if you can't accept it, that's you."

Dillon frowned. "You know this isn't over."

"Yes, it is."

They stared at each other in silence for a long time. Dillon's phone beeped. He read a text message. "Everyone is at Connor's place. Come back with me. One night."

The radio buzzed behind him.

"Kincaid, you're cleared. The thunderstorms moved northeast."

Jack stared at the radio. Dillon didn't say another

word. It was on Jack now. Did he want his family back? Could he turn his back again?

Could he live with himself if he did? Would they call him if they needed him, or would they disown him as well?

"5-A-Z-1-1-1-3-4, copy."

Did he want to turn into Scout? He loved the man, but Scout had nothing outside of their team. No family. No wife. No kids. And while a wife and kids were out of the cards for Jack, he did have a family. Brothers and sisters, and maybe a few nieces and nephews down the road. Could he turn his back on the future?

Did he want to?

He picked up the microphone. "Thanks, but I have a change of plans. I won't be leaving until oh seven hundred."

"Roger, oh seven hundred. I'll have the Cessna ready."

CHAPTER
SIX

Frank Cardenas was a priest.

Why hadn't Karin known? She'd had his name and address, but they hadn't scouted Hidalgo. It was a small Hispanic town, they were white and stood out. It had already been risky going to the bar to get the lay of the land, but she couldn't send Ethan in there, with or without her. He'd become too unpredictable. It was better when she acted alone, when she was disguised.

She'd had his address, the small house next to the church. She hadn't known it was a rectory. For all her plans, the way she arranged each murder, stalking the victims, she'd gotten arrogant in her success. Ethan was pushing to finish, though; she could have held him off a couple extra days to do further research. But after finding him naked in the dirt, she realized she didn't have much time before Ethan's mind permanently snapped.

She could tell Ethan that Frank Cardenas had moved. Or it was the wrong Frank Cardenas.

She couldn't kill a priest.

What do you mean you can't? You can kill anyone. He's guilty, just like the others.

Father Cardenas locked the church doors at midnight.

The night was balmy, the air still. The silence and calmness made her antsy.

He walked toward the rectory and saw her. She couldn't avoid him now.

"Father?" she said.

He approached, face impassive. But his eyes scanned the area discreetly. Paranoid? "May I help you?"

"I need to make a confession."

"Reconciliation is an hour before every Mass," he said. "Tomorrow I open the church at six a.m."

"I have to leave early in the morning."

The priest offered to arrive thirty minutes earlier.

"I have to leave at five." Was that a lie? Not really. They did have to leave early. As soon as they killed two men. . . .

"Dear Lord," Cardenas mumbled.

Had she heard correctly? Was that a whisper of Heaven in the air? More likely the gloating of Hell.

"Let's go into the church, child."

Father Michael used to call her "child" in a warm, endearing voice. Before he'd been murdered.

But she had found him justice. She had punished the wicked. An eye for an eye. That was her calling.

"Thank you."

He walked alongside her. She was leading him to the slaughter. Her limbs grew heavy. She put her hands in the pocket of her windbreaker, felt the syringe with the mild tranquilizer. Only if necessary. Ethan was waiting at the house, but he'd see them. He'd come here.

They approached the church. She had to buy time. Maybe within the church there would be answers.

"I haven't seen you here before," he said.

"I'm visiting a friend."

"And you're Catholic."

"Yes, Father. Born and raised."

"But—?"

She laughed bitterly, but it ended in a sob that she quickly swallowed. "I haven't been to Mass in over twenty years."

"Let's save this for the confessional."

"It may take awhile."

"Sleep is overrated. What's your name?" He walked toward the main doors.

She stared at the side of the church, eyes wide. "Is that the Passion?" Small lights shone behind the narrow stained-glass windows that lined the walls. "They're beautiful." She was awestruck, walking slowly along the side of the old church.

The glasswork's eyes accused her. She imagined Pontius Pilate sentencing her to death. But unlike Jesus, she was guilty.

Don't feel guilty!

She hadn't killed anyone who didn't deserve it. Criminals who slipped through the system. Predators who deserved to die for their crimes. Murderers. Rapists. Child molesters. The world was a better place because of Karin.

But a priest? She couldn't. Wouldn't.

She had to. If she didn't, Ethan would, and he'd hurt him first. Make him suffer. She liked that part, but not a priest. Not Father Cardenas.

She could kill Ethan first.

No, she hadn't finished her training. There were still things she needed to learn. She'd have to speed it up because Ethan wasn't getting any saner. The guy was combustible.

She could "accidentally" kill Father Cardenas. So he wouldn't suffer. Whatever he'd done to Ethan in the past, maybe . . .

"They're old," Father Cardenas said. "Over two hundred years, except for the weeping women, which was broken by vandals shortly after I came here."

"It looks the same as the others."

"The artisan is very talented."

"Are you from Hidalgo?"

"No."

"The church sent you here?"

"Yes, but I asked to come."

"Why?"

"It's a poor town, but spiritually strong. And it was a good place to come for redemption."

He looked at her. In the dim, yellowed outdoor lights, he seemed to glow. Like an angel. "Isn't that why you're here?"

She nodded. She couldn't speak.

He unlocked the door.

"The confessional is across the way, in the chapel," he said, letting her step inside first. The lights were on, though dimmed. The church was old, with worn pews, old statues, and a simple altar. To the left was a small alcove where several wooden kneelers faced the statue of the Blessed Virgin on a pedestal. More than half the one hundred and ten candles behind her were lit, their low flames dancing faintly with the stirred air.

She dropped a handful of coins into the donation box, the metallic clink of change thumping when it hit the wood bottom. She took a long match from its holder and lit it from a low flame, stared at it, head bowed as if in prayer.

On the one hand, Frank Cardenas had left Ethan to be tortured and die. On the other, he was a priest and had been forgiven by a higher power. Would killing him be true justice?

Ethan wanted to kill them all. But that was because she had planted the idea in him. It had been her plan from the beginning, Ethan simply embraced it. Wholeheartedly. He couldn't see anything else. He wouldn't understand her hesitance because Cardenas was a priest. She could lie. She sometimes did, and usually got away with it.

This time, Ethan would know.

The priest walked toward the chapel on the opposite side of the church.

Dammit, I don't know what to do!

Father Francis turned on a low light in the confessional, leaving the brunette woman to gather the courage to confess. He'd seen the struggle in her eyes. The fear of giving up the pain, the guilt, and the sin to God. He'd been where she was. He hadn't gone to confession in the fifteen years he served in the army. Because he knew he couldn't promise not to commit the same sins again.

He still had a gun, but he never touched it. He kept it in a box in his bedroom, in the closet, high on a shelf. He opened the lid only when he needed to remember, to repent, to beg for mercy and forgiveness. He had nearly put a bullet in his head with that gun.

"What a way for you to call me, Lord," he mumbled as he closed the curtain of the confessional.

Francis had come to Hidalgo for many reasons, but primary among them was because Jack had settled with his crew here on the Rio Grande, and Francis owed Jack more than his life. He doubted Jack understood the impact he'd had on Francis's life—and the lives of so many others. And he worried about his old friend, letting the past eat him alive. Jack didn't see it. Francis didn't see much else.

He knelt, crossed himself, and said his own prayers, holding the rosary his grandmother had given him on her deathbed. He'd been nine.

"You will be a priest, Frankie. But first you have to walk through purgatory."

He hadn't understood back then. He hadn't wanted to be a priest, and purgatory was for dead people.

Now, he accepted that his grandmother had been a prophet, a personal prophet for him.

Francis heard a voice. The woman—she hadn't given him her name—might be lost. Maybe she hadn't paid attention to him when he pointed toward the side chapel.

A door closed.

He walked out. The church was empty, he sensed it before he searched and realized no one was inside. Just him.

Francis glanced up at the crucifix behind the altar. "And you, Lord."

He hoped the woman found what she needed, but feared her demons were too great to battle alone. The encounter was odd enough that Francis walked through his church, checked the tabernacle, the altar, the sacristy. Everything looked in order.

"Francis," he muttered to himself, "why are you so apprehensive?" It was the woman, he decided, the odd woman who wanted to confess, then left without forgiveness. Usually, those returning to the church for redemption had committed what they felt was an unpardonable sin, and had some sort of brush with death where they began to search their souls.

"I don't know what she did, Father, but please have mercy on her."

He put the woman from his mind, putting the lost sheep in God's hands.

On his way out of the church, Francis walked past the prayer candles. None were lit. The sight should have enraged him—why would she blow them out? But instead, he felt a deep, deep sadness. And fear.

Ethan slapped her. Again. Three times. Tears of rage stained his face. Karin had betrayed him.

She pushed back at him. "Don't *ever* hit me!"

He grabbed her hair, pulled her to him. He didn't see the woman who'd saved him. Instead, he saw fangs and horns and laughing eyes. She wanted to hurt him.

"You changed the plans! You were supposed to bring him around to the house. We had it planned!" He was a grown man, but he sounded like a petulant brat. He shook her to prove he was a man. Inside, he was hollow. He watched from above. Was that him?

Kill her.

No. No no! Ethan needed her. His heart raced. He was going to die, his heart was going to run away without him. He turned his head, saw the beating organ running on legs down the street. Was that his heart? He blinked. Nothing. There was nothing. It was the middle of the night, there was nothing. Dark, empty, black.

"You didn't tell me he was a priest," she said.

What was she talking about? "I don't understand."

She pulled away from him, took two steps back. "Dammit, Ethan! I can't kill a priest. I can't. I can't."

"But he hurt me."

His voice was a whisper; he didn't know he had spoken.

She put her hands on his shoulders. "Maybe he is one of the few who is sorry."

Ethan's laugh sounded like the growl of a lunatic hyena, a combination of psychotic glee and rage. It stopped as suddenly as it began. That wasn't him laughing, was it? Yes. No. He didn't exist anymore. Did he?

"You know what they did to me."

She caressed his face. He didn't feel her hand, but then she skimmed her nails down his neck.

"I can't kill a priest."

"What if he's sticking it into little boys? Could you kill him then?"

"That's different."

"How do you know he's not?"

"If you take him out, I'm done."

"You can't be done. That's not how it works." *Don't leave me. Don't desert me. They'll hurt me again.*

He was shaking uncontrollably. "We agreed," he whined.

"This was my plan in the first place!" she shouted. "The whole thing! I gave it to you, you'd never have done anything but complain and try to kill yourself!"

He didn't need the reminder. She always told him the same thing. *I saved you. You're mine. You're mine and we'll find vengeance. You deserve it. Everything will be fine when they're dead. Everything will be perfect.*

"I know." His voice was a squeak.

"I always have a backup plan. We'll do Bartleton now."

"We have to do both."

"No."

"You're the one who hates changing plans midstream."

"I learned something while staking out the bar earlier," she said.

"What?"

"Bartleton is a drinker. He'll be out of it, at least enough to slow his reaction time." She glanced at her watch. "We don't have much time. He'll be walking home from the bar any minute, and we need to get into place."

It felt to Ethan like she was manipulating him. He was confused and panicking. He needed to kill the priest. If they changed the plan, nothing would be right again. It felt out of order. Something was missing. An itch he couldn't scratch.

Karin watched the psycho closely as he dug his fingernails deep into his palms. He was so close to the edge, but she couldn't lose him now. He had to finish teaching her. When she'd used Ethan's techniques on Perry, she'd failed. She couldn't afford to fail when it mattered. She *wouldn't*. She needed more practice. She'd use Bartleton. They didn't have many more on the list.

While Ethan was thinking, she remained silent. She would not kill Frank Cardenas. When she looked in his eyes, she didn't see a predator. She didn't see a killer. She saw redemption.

Fool. He's a good liar. They're all liars.

Not him, not the priest.

"There's always hope, child."

She bit back a cry. It was as if Father Michael had whispered in her ear.

"I want to die," Ethan whimpered.

"I know."

"Why don't you kill me?"

Because you're a lousy teacher! "I love you, Ethan."

His face softened. "What do we do now?"

"Bartleton."

"I can hurt him."

"Yes. But you need to let me do it this time. Show me, Ethan. Teach me right this time."

"I promise."

She didn't know if he would or wouldn't. His psychosis was a minefield. She had to tiptoe carefully.

But she'd saved the priest. Maybe it would buy her time.

Ethan smiled unpleasantly.

"This will be fun, right?"

"Right."

Fun. This wasn't fun anymore, it was work. She shivered as they walked in the shadows away from the church, toward Lawrence Bartleton's house.

Karin did not look back.

CHAPTER
SEVEN

Loud knocking startled Megan from a deep sleep. For a split second, she opened her eyes and forgot she was at her loft. Mouse jumped from her lap with an irritated *meow* and papers and photographs slid to the floor. The privacy blinds in her fourth-floor loft apartment were only half drawn; dawn crept through Sacramento to the east. She'd fallen asleep in her living room for the second night in a row.

The pounding resumed and she walked to her door, looking through the peephole and seeing the young attorney who lived across the hall. He worked in Matt's office and had been the one who told Matt about the new lofts when Megan moved to the city four years ago.

She opened the door. "Jesse."

He was dressed for work. "Sorry to wake you up, Agent Elliott, but I have an early court hearing and this came for you yesterday. I signed for it."

He handed her an overnight envelope. It was so light Megan wondered if anything was inside. She moved it right to left. Something small and thin shifted to the side. The label came from a shipping company out of Reno, Nevada. She didn't think she knew anyone in Reno, at least no one well enough that they would have her home address.

"Thanks, Jesse. I needed to get up anyway."

"I didn't want to leave it on the doorstep in case it was valuable. They *claim* this is a secure building." He shook his head. There had been two robberies in the past year.

"I appreciate it, Jesse. And don't call me Agent Elliott. I told you that."

"Can't help it," he answered, sheepishly. "Gotta go. Bye."

She closed the door and yawned widely. She started coffee, fed Mouse, who made his hunger loudly known, then picked up the envelope again. Reno . . . She glanced at the return address, squinted to read the small handwritten letters. Sacramento. 4800 Broadway.

Her heart raced and she dropped the envelope on the counter.

Broadway . . . the morgue.

There was no reason the morgue would send her a package at her residence. None. She hardly knew anyone at the morgue. Phineas Ward, the supervisor, was a mere acquaintance. He obviously knew Matt, though . . . would Matt have given him her home address? Never. He was as security conscious as she was. And why would it have been shipped from Nevada? It made no sense.

She ran to her bedroom and opened her emergency Evidence Response Team kit. She extracted two plastic gloves from a box and slid them on, and put a simple cloth and elastic mask over her nose and mouth—worthless in a gas attack, but she could avoid breathing in any fine particles, like anthrax. She closed her door, locking Mouse inside so he didn't inadvertently contaminate potential evidence or get hurt.

At her small kitchen table, she picked up the envelope and examined it more carefully. It didn't appear that there was anything bigger than a business card inside, but she wasn't taking chances. The anthrax scares after 9/11—while she'd still been an agent out of D.C.—had her expecting the worst. She felt like a fool. But better a fool than dead.

Holding her breath, she carefully opened the cardboard envelope with her Swiss Army knife.

Almost immediately she ascertained that there was no biological contaminant. In fact, the envelope was empty. No . . . there was a small weight at the bottom.

She took a sheet of paper from her notepad and carefully tapped the contents of the envelope onto the paper.

A small metal plate fell out.

An identification tag. The stamped metal landed upside down and backward, but she could read the name nonetheless.

PRICE, GEORGE L.

Less than thirty hours after Jack Kincaid left Hidalgo he returned to the small private airfield outside the city limits. He regularly used the unmanned strip for his operations. He didn't have his own plane, but Scout had been the pilot for so long that Jack didn't think he'd ever need one. He had a nest egg stashed away for his retirement— and in this line of work, he had only a few good years left before age defeated him. When he was ready, he had a friend who'd sell him a nice little Skyhawk at a good price.

The idea of retiring came more often now—ever since Lucy's kidnapping and rescue and Patrick's near death. He had a plan to set up a private soldier training facility.

He didn't know much else except for being a soldier, but he saw a need, especially to protect missionaries and other do-gooders who thought they could change the world. Too many were dying. Jack couldn't protect them all, but he could train up a force to do it.

He landed and decided to poke fun at Scout. He called his cell phone, half expecting Scout to pick up, though he'd probably have a hangover. He tended to drink heavily after a mission because Jack forbade drinking on assignment.

Scout's voice mail picked up.

"Leave a message if it's important."

Jack grinned. *Scout.* "Buddy, it's Jack. I'm having a bit of a problem with the Caravan. Don't know what happened, can you call me back?"

He hung up, then remembered that Scout had plans with his girlfriend and her two sons. Good. Jack liked Rina, she was good for Scout. Maybe he would finally cut back on the drinking and take some personal responsibility. Since Padre had retired from soldiering, on the job Jack trusted no one more than Scout. But personally, Scout didn't care much about anything except hitting the bar.

Jack took his truck to his favorite diner just outside Hidalgo on the interstate. It served up a real breakfast—eggs, bacon, toast—cheap. Nothing fancy, but everything tasted great. Jack could cook, but he didn't care to. He kept it simple and functional when he was home; out on assignment, meals weren't his responsibility.

It was eleven when he hit town and drove past Scout's house on his way to talk to Padre at the church. A police car was stopped in front of Scout's place. The chief of police himself was getting out of the driver's seat as Jack passed. That couldn't be good.

Jack pulled his truck over and jumped out. Scout's drinking was usually under control, but sometimes . . . he'd gotten into a fight last year. Had to pay restitution and do a bit of community service. Swore to Jack it wouldn't happen again. And then of course that bar fight with Perez's deputy . . .

As Jack approached, he took in everything around him. Art Perez. Rina, standing across the street with her boys and a couple other folks. They all looked worried. Another police car turned the corner. And Padre was standing on the porch, pale, but looking more like the warrior from yesterday than the man of God he was today.

"Kincaid, stop—" Art began.

Jack walked past him. "Padre—"

"Don't." His eyes were sharp. "Scout's dead."

The truth sunk in instantly. Jack had no denial. He'd seen dead men before. Friends. Men he took orders from, and men who took orders from him. He'd seen women and children raped and murdered. No denial, but that didn't stop the hot anger from flooding through him, or the raw pain that filled him.

"How?"

"Jack." Art followed him up to the small porch. They were three large men; it was crowded.

Jack didn't look at him.

Padre said, "He was murdered."

Surprise lit Jack's face. "Murdered. At the bar?"

Padre shook his head, glanced through the window.

Jack stepped inside as Art exclaimed, "You can't! This is a crime scene."

Jack ignored him, but didn't touch anything. The foul,

familiar scent of death—blood, urine, feces—sat heavy in the hot, thick air. He walked through the bungalow—living room on one side, two small bedrooms down a short hall to the right with a bathroom between them. The sunroom Scout had built himself a couple years back where he spent most of his free time watching sports was in the back of the house, behind the kitchen and dining room.

Scout lay prone on his kitchen floor, eyes open, dried blood pooled around his head and the back of his knees. Instantly, Jack knew that Scout had been hamstrung—he'd seen it before, in another country, another life.

Flies had already found the body—it was ninety degrees at noon. Scout was naked, but he'd soiled himself. The smell was worse in here.

A chair was on its side. Cut duct tape still attached to the armrests. Blood on the chair and on the terra-cotta tile floor. Jack had helped Scout put in the tile when he bought the place years ago.

"Jack." Padre spoke quietly.

"Who?"

"We don't know. But—"

Jack turned. "What do you know about this?"

"Come to the rectory with me."

Jack shook his head. He pinched the bridge of his nose and took a deep breath through his mouth. "Tell me."

Art Perez spoke. He could be a boisterous, uncouth bastard, and he and Jack had had it out more than once; this morning, however, he seemed to understand that professionalism went a long way.

"Rina's sons came over this morning because Lawrence had offered to take them into Brownsville for a special Toros game. He was supposed to pick them up at ten, but didn't show and Rina told the boys to go over and wake him up." Perez frowned. "She's torn up about it. Juan found the body."

The body. Scout was a body now.

"Juan called me," Padre said. "I came right away, called Art, then Rina. Jack—"

Jack didn't have anything to say. Scout had been murdered. The method was vicious, cruel. How had he been surprised? Why was he naked? Had he been with a woman? Had a *woman* done this to him? Scout wouldn't let himself get conned, but he was known to turn his head toward a pretty face. Why, dammit? Why had Scout been killed? Jack mentally reviewed their most recent assignments. He didn't know of anyone or any organization who would do this . . . like this. It looked both personal and like an execution. Had Scout known his killer?

Perez said, "You need to leave. My men will process the scene, collect evidence, and remove the body."

Hidalgo had its unfair share of murders—Perez had investigated enough of them—but this was wholly different from a drug hit or a barroom brawl. Not something Art Perez could handle. Hell, he could barely handle being chief of police on a good day.

"Call the Rangers," Jack said before he thought about tact and diplomacy. "This isn't a random act of violence."

Perez reddened. "Don't tell me how to do my job, Kincaid."

"Jack—" Padre began, and Jack put up his hand.

Jack would find Scout's killer. He would call in every favor, every chit, spend every dime he had to do it.

"I will find out who killed Scout," he said, his words clipped to stifle the emotion.

"Stay out of my way, Kincaid. You're already pushing it. Don't think I won't lock you up. Just give me a reason. One fucking reason to put you behind bars."

Jack stepped forward and said in a low voice, "I'll be watching, Perez. Don't fuck this up."

Jack looked back at Scout's body. Rage and sadness battled and his teeth clenched.

"Rest in peace, friend."

When I find who did this to you, they won't walk away.

CHAPTER
EIGHT

Wednesday morning, less than two hours after she had opened the overnight envelope, Megan sat in SAC Bob Richardson's office with two other agents, Detective John Black, and the speaker phone. Richardson had contacted Assistant Special Agent in Charge Hans Vigo at Quantico. Hans had been a friend and mentor to Megan since he'd recruited her into the FBI while guest lecturing at Georgetown, where she'd been studying law. Hans was a profiler, though he had declined a post in the prestigious Behavioral Science Unit. He was often sent out into the field to consult, and Megan had immediately thought of him when Price's dog tag fell from the express envelope. This murder had taken on a whole new importance.

She'd finished briefing Hans about the case as she knew it, with the only known connection among the three victims being their time in the army. "Bob has made a request with the DOD to pull their military records, but you know how slow they are. By the time we get them, if at all, more people could die."

"Will die," Hans said. "Three dead in two months. The first victim was on February 11. The second on April 2. Price early on April 13."

"They're escalating," Richardson said.

"Possibly, but more likely they have a plan. They are exceptionally well-organized for sadistic killers."

"Sadistic? Is there a sexual component in the murders? There was no evidence of that at any of the crime scenes." Megan pulled out her reports, worried that she had missed something important.

"Sadistic doesn't necessarily mean sexual gratification, though the killers likely received sexual gratification either in the planning of the murders or after the fact. The actual murders were methodical, well-planned, but at the same time reckless."

"Non sequitur, Dr. Vigo," Richardson interjected.

"Bear with me, Bob. Let's look at the actual murders. Two people come together to kill a specific target—their victims are not random, they were selected because of who they are or what they represent. Victimology in this case is critical: if they were killed because of something they did or didn't do, it'll be much easier to identify potential suspects, particularly if all three victims were involved in the same event. If they were killed because of what they represent—the military, or the army specifically—it will be more difficult. In the latter case, you'd probably be looking for a soldier or former soldier who felt he had been treated unfairly by the military or his unit. Possibly suffering from post-traumatic stress disorder and reliving a horrific event, accompanied by some sort of psychosis that leads him to believe killing other soldiers will relieve his anxiety. But I don't see this type of killer as working with a partner or going through the elaborate ritual."

Megan leaned forward. "So you think the killers knew the victims personally?"

For a moment, Hans didn't say anything. "Possibly, or at least knew *of* them if they had never met them before. They were singled out specifically, and that's why I want you to meet me in Austin."

"Austin, Texas?" Megan asked.

"There's far more going on here than the reports indicated. I need to talk to those who knew Duane Johnson. He's the first known victim, and the killers waited nearly two full months before killing again, which makes me think they were waiting for something."

"Like what?"

"Could be for the second victim—Perry—to be in a position where they could get to him, or because they wanted to see what the police would do, or because they feared they'd screwed up somehow."

Megan took notes while shaking her head. "I can't go to Austin, I have to get Price's body back, work with the CID on the evidence and autopsy—"

Richardson interrupted. "They're not going to give you a thing, Megan. And we have a far more important situation here."

Hans said over the speaker, "I agree. How did the killers know you were on the Price case, Megan?"

Megan had been thinking about that since she opened the package. "I don't know. Maybe one or both of them were observing us Monday morning at the crime scene? Our office gets a lot of attention, especially after the O'Brien case last year. I did that interview—" She frowned at Richardson. She hadn't wanted to talk to the press, but her boss felt that having her on prime-time news would help with public relations. "They could have picked up on my position on the Violent Crimes Squad."

"Why you and not the SPD detective? Or the media?"

"Okay, I'll bite. Why?" She wasn't sure she wanted to know the answer.

"I don't know."

"Great. If you don't know, how does that help?"

"It could be nothing—the killer taunting police—and because the FBI is considered the higher law enforcement agency—no offense, Detective Black—the killers would want to taunt the FBI. But they had your home address, Meg."

"I know," she said quietly.

"I think it's a good idea to get out of town," Richardson said. He used the intercom to ask his assistant to book a flight ASAP for Megan to Texas.

"I'm not running away."

"I'm not suggesting you do. Dr. Vigo wants your help and the FBI has already determined this is a serial murder investigation. We have the authority to go in if we need to. And you can't do anything here that SPD can't do—I have confidence that Detective Black will keep us informed if anything important arises."

"Absolutely," Black said. "And," he added, "the information you bring back from Austin and Vegas can help us here because we have next to nothing after losing the evidence to CID."

"Is this connected to Price being AWOL?" Megan asked the group. "Price was living on the streets; how did the killers know him? Know where to find him?"

"Aw, that's the million-dollar question." Hans said. "If you can figure that out, I think you'll have a much greater chance of capturing them. They have inside information—suggesting that they personally know these men or have access to their records."

"But CID didn't know where Price was until he was dead and we flagged his record."

"Which narrows their information source exponentially. We have to learn everything we can about Duane Johnson and Dennis Perry. One or both of them could have known where Price was."

"Agent Vigo," Black interjected, "you said that the crimes were both methodical and reckless. Can you expand on that?"

"Sorry, I got sidetracked. Methodical in that they were well planned. They waited for their victim, hamstrung him to prevent escape, restrained him, and tortured him with needles for an indeterminate length of time, but probably between one and five hours. Then they executed him."

"It sounds more like playtime," Megan said. "Pulling wings off butterflies."

"Excuse me?" Richardson said.

"You're right on the money." Hans was proud. "I hadn't thought of it like that, but yeah, they were playing. Torturing the victim as much to make him suffer as to derive satisfaction and pleasure from being in control of another's pain."

"And then they get tired and shoot him in the head. Quick and efficient, when there's nothing quick or efficient about human torture."

Hans said, "I think the dynamic between these two killers is critical. Which is the dominant personality? Which one decided the targets and how to take them out? Who pulled the trigger?"

"Metaphorically?" Black asked.

"Literally. Whoever pulled the trigger is the dominant killer. He may be the person torturing the victims, or both could be involved, but whoever uses the gun is in charge."

"Essentially, playtime is over. Pick up their toys and go home."

"Right."

"Is there always a dominant killer in a partnership like this?" Black asked.

"In my experience," Hans said. "Two dominant personalities would not last long together. One would kill the other, or they would go their separate ways. Someone has to make the rules, someone has to follow orders. This is a partnership in that the submissive partner does what the dominant partner wants. If the weaker of the two acts out, the dominant will slap him down."

The intercom buzzed. "SAC Richardson, I have Agent Elliott on a ten-twenty flight to Texas."

Megan glanced at her watch. "That's barely an hour."

"You'd better get going."

Hans said, "I'm taking a military transport, I'll meet you there. Be careful, Megan. I really don't like the idea that the killers have your home address."

"Neither do I." Megan stood, then asked Hans before he disconnected, "What are the chances we can find them before another man dies?"

"You don't want to know."

Jack didn't particularly want Padre tagging along, but it wasn't like he'd tell the priest to back off. Scout had been his friend as well, and seeing him dead and naked would stay with Jack for the rest of his life. Scout had been family, closer than blood.

He asked Padre, "You okay?"

"Been better. Watch your back with Perez."

"Fuck Perez and the jackass he rode in on. Dammit, Padre, you know Perez can't handle this."

Jack slowed his truck as he neared the rectory. "You want off here?"

"No."

Jack hadn't expected Padre to bail, and he pressed the accelerator. Driving too fast, he halted in front of El Gato, the bar on the city/county border where Scout had been last night.

Jack jumped out of the truck and his friend followed. Padre wanted to talk, but he couldn't talk now. Not about Perez, not about anything. He focused on finding out what happened the night before, when Scout left, who he left with, and who he may have had a confrontation with.

The Hernandez family owned El Gato. Cece worked six days a week; her brothers Pablo and Carlos worked nights. They reluctantly shut down on Sunday as a nod to their devout mother, who had given her children the seed money to open the bar from the insurance settlement after her husband died on a construction job.

Cece's eyes were rimmed red as she poured a draft for two men at the bar. "Señor Jack, Father," she said when they came in. "What happened?"

"I need to talk to Pablo." Jack didn't care for Carlos, the youngest and laziest of the three siblings. He'd brought drugs into the bar and Jack quickly put an end to that. Still, he was wily and sly enough to keep dealing, just more carefully. Jack preferred to deal with Pablo. Though Pablo didn't speak English, Jack was fluent in Spanish.

"Upstairs. He doesn't know anything."

Jack walked to the back of the bar and through a door that led to the apartment where Pablo lived.

It was noon and Pablo was sleeping. Jack didn't fault him—the bar owner worked until two every night, but Jack had little patience for anyone today.

"Pablo." In fluent Spanish, Jack said, "Wake up. Time to get up."

Pablo moaned. Jack saw him reaching under his pillow. He had a hold on his wrist before Pablo could draw the gun.

The paunchy man rolled over and glared at Jack through eyes framed by overgrown brows and a face stubbed with a day's growth of beard. "You should have said you were Señor Jack."

"Scout's dead. I need answers."

Honest surprise lit Pablo's face, telling Jack he didn't know anything about it. He released the barkeep's arm and stepped back.

"Señor Scout? How?"

"Someone broke into his house and killed him." Jack didn't go into details. "I need to know everyone who was in the bar last night. Regulars and strangers. *Everyone.*"

Pablo sat up, the sheet sliding away revealing thick legs and dirty boxers and a stained undershirt. He scratched his thick head of hair and said, "I can make a list."

"Good." He searched the room for paper and pen, not caring what fell to the floor.

Padre added, *"Mucho gracias."*

Jack wasn't in the mood for diplomacy. He knew enough about criminal investigations to know that if they didn't catch a whiff of Scout's killer soon, he would disappear. The more time that passed, the harder it would be to solve the case. And frankly, no one gave a shit about the poor citizens of Hidalgo, Texas. Jack knew Chief Art Dipshit wouldn't call in the Rangers. He'd rather keep his jurisdiction intact than ask for help, even when he desperately needed it.

Pablo rose and shuffled to the living area where he found a torn envelope that had once held a utility bill, and started writing names. "All the regulars," he said, "except Sam and Juan, and Juan Cristopher, Jorge's son. They caught a job in Brownsville, could take two weeks." He thought, wrote down a bunch of names. Xavier, Bella, Miguel. "Miguel. He only comes if Bella comes, and with the kids getting in trouble, she's steering clear of my place. But that lousy husband of hers took the boys camping and she had a free night."

It was common knowledge, except to Bella's husband, that Miguel and Bella were having an affair. At this point, Jack didn't care about their infidelity.

"Anyone else?"

"Tuesday night, mid-month. Slow time. Wait until May first, we'll be packed for a week."

"Strangers?"

"We always get a few here and there. You know, we got a good location, right off the highway, people going down to Reynosa, coming back up."

"How many?"

"Last night—college boys. UTSA, from their I.D.'s. I

carded them. Fucking gringos, paid in pesos and laughed. What am I going to do with pesos?" Pablo waved his hands above his head.

Probably coming back from a long weekend of whoring in Reynoso. Idiots. But if they were drunk enough, they might have thought it sport to murder someone. Thrill kill.

"How many? Were they drunk?"

"Three, and they didn't drink more than two or three *cervezas* each. But I think they had a little"—he sniffed loudly—"happy powder."

Carlos. Jack knew it like he knew his own name. Bastard. "What time did they leave?"

"Midnight." He motioned side to side with his hand. More or less.

"What about Scout?"

"Just before closing. I make sure he don't drive, just like I promised you, Señor Jack. No driving if he has more than two. But he walked here, and he walked home. I think he left alone. I didn't see any of your other men."

Lucky stayed in Reynoso with his girlfriend, and Mike lived in Brownsville with his wife and daughter. His other regulars didn't live nearby, flying or driving down when an assignment piqued their interest—or the money was good enough. He had someone he could call in San Antonio to follow up on the college kids.

"What were the UTSA boys driving?"

Pablo knew cars. "Convertible Caddy, Eldorado. Late nineties."

"Color?"

"Silver."

Jack asked, "Anyone else?"

"A couple tourists."

"What did they look like?"

"How am I supposed to remember? All gringos look the same to me. Cars, I remember. People, fuck— Don't, Jack—"

Jack had stepped forward. He didn't touch Pablo, but his fists itched.

"The tourists?" Jack repeated.

"Gringos. They came and left early. One couple, older. Gramps. Took pictures, had bottled water, left. The other, a woman, came in about the same time, had Jack straight up."

"When did she leave? Or was she with the couple?"

"I thought she was their daughter, but she stayed longer. Maybe left at nine."

"What did she look like?" Padre asked.

Jack glanced at him. He had almost forgotten the priest was in the room. He didn't look well.

Pablo muttered under his breath. "I don't remember. I swear, maybe someone else will remember. She had a ball cap on. That's all I know. I swear. She could have been twenty or fifty, for all I know."

"What was she wearing?" Padre asked.

"Clothes."

Jack leaned forward.

"I don't know!" Pablo exclaimed, pushing his sloppy handwritten list at Jack. "I don't remember. Nothing that stands out. Jeans, maybe."

"Did she talk to anyone?"

Pablo looked worried and relieved at the same time. "Carlos brought her the drink. Maybe he talked to her some. She was there, then she wasn't. I don't keep my eyes on everyone all the time. I have work to do, bills to pay, stock and cleaning. I'm not a babysitter. Talk to Carlos, talk to everyone. I'm real sorry about Señor Scout, but I don't know anything else. I swear, Señor Jack, I know nothing."

CHAPTER
NINE

Wednesday morning was a whirlwind—Megan barely had time to pack an overnight bag and arrange for her neighbor Jesse to take care of Mouse—and by three p.m. central time, Megan landed in Austin, Texas. Hans had called for a liaison to meet them from the FBI's Austin field office. Renny Davis was a tall, thin man with a complexion and sharp features that suggested part Native American heritage.

"Thanks for picking us up," Hans said after introductions.

"My pleasure," Davis said. "I've heard great things about you. I'm signed up for one of your classes in the fall—advanced victimology—as part of ERT training."

"I look forward to seeing you in class," Hans said.

They made small talk as they walked to Davis's car. As the Austin agent drove, Megan asked, "Have you been involved with the Johnson homicide from the beginning?"

"Nope," Davis said. "No need to be. I didn't even know about it, other than a cursory news program, until headquarters issued the hot sheet."

Megan looked at her notes. "That was issued on Friday. Three days before Price was killed. Vegas ran the M.O. and up popped Johnson, so they contacted their local FBI office about a killer crossing state lines. That was . . . last Wednesday."

"I contacted José when I got the sheet. He's the detective in charge, I've worked with him before. He told me they had shit—excuse me—and were hoping that Vegas would come up with something more. You headed there next?"

Megan glanced at Hans with raised eyebrows. "Are we?"

"Yes. If we get what we need here, we'll be on a plane tomorrow night. The Vegas file is pretty thin. Either there was no evidence or it hasn't been processed. We might be able to help expedite on that end."

Davis asked, "Do you think he'll strike again so soon?"

"*They* will most certainly kill again," Hans said, "and sooner rather than later." He explained his theory to Davis about why the killers waited a longer time between killing Johnson and Perry than Perry and Price. "That's why it's doubly important to scrutinize this crime scene even more carefully."

"They could have been waiting for a specific day," Megan said, "or they didn't have a good opportunity. Perry had an on-again/off-again girlfriend. There's nothing here about whether they were on or off and for how long. Just that she hadn't seen him in two days."

"Exactly," Hans said. "They want their victims alone."

"What did local police think happened?" Megan asked Davis.

"For a while the thought was organized crime. The hamstrings, the torture—restraint. As if he knew something or hadn't paid up, or maybe screwed around with another man's wife. But nothing connected. Even his ex was shocked and had nothing but good things to say about him."

"Then why'd they divorce?" Hans asked.

Megan knew there were many reasons to divorce, even if you liked your spouse.

Davis shrugged. "José might know. Johnson was well-liked by friends and family, thought to be moody, and had a few friends from his army days who took his death pretty hard. But no one with a beef, no one who knew of a problem, no disgruntled customers."

"We'll need to talk to his friends from the army," Megan said.

Davis pulled up in front of the main Austin police station. He slid an official business placard on his dash and they got out.

José Vasquez was much younger than Megan had thought after speaking with him on the phone. He looked about twenty, but being a detective, Megan figured he had to be closer to thirty. He was short and wiry, completely antithetical to his deep voice.

He and Davis knew each other, and Megan could tell that having the local fed with them was a big benefit.

"I found you a conference room," José said, "and all my files are there. Got photos, the coroner's notes you asked for, Agent Vigo, witness statements, evidence reports. The whole nine yards."

"Can we get out to the crime scene?" Megan asked.

"It's been cleaned out. Everything was left to Johnson's kids, and his ex is selling the place and putting the money into a trust for them. Probably best thing, I wouldn't be too keen on keeping a place where someone I cared about was killed."

"But we can still access it, right?" she asked.

"I'll get us in, just takes a call. Why don't you sit down, make yourselves at home—coffee is right around the corner." He left.

Hans sat down, full of nervous energy. Very unlike his usually easygoing demeanor. "Something up?" Megan asked casually.

"There's something off. I don't know what. I need more information, as much as I can get, and maybe I'll figure out what's bothering me."

"We got the parking garage security tapes back. Someone scrambled the digital code."

"And no one noticed?" Davis asked.

"They're not monitored twenty-four/seven. They're supposed to be a deterrent."

"Seems like the killers would have had to know that, otherwise they wouldn't have been comfortable sitting there for hours. What about the switched license plates?" Hans asked. "Is Sac P.D. following up on that?"

"Yes," Megan said, then explained to Davis about the security guard making rounds in the garage and taking note of the license plates of cars left overnight. She then said to Hans, "What I don't get is, they obviously knew all about the security at the garage, but how did they know Price would be there? The guy's homeless."

"Maybe they picked him up. Or have been following him for a few days, finding out where he liked to walk or sleep. Where was he attacked?"

"In the stairwell of the garage."

"Could he have been sleeping in there?"

"It's possible," Megan said. "Black and his people are talking to the victim's friends. But the homeless don't like talking to cops. So far he's not getting a lot out of them."

But it made sense that the killers had watched Price, just like they knew when Duane Johnson would be coming home from work.

"I haven't studied homeless psychology in detail," Hans said, "but many who congregate in an urban environment like this have mental problems, often including drug addiction."

Megan nodded. "But here's Price, who didn't appear to be an addict, who was AWOL and even the army didn't know where he was. So how did these two killers rout him out? He was a specific target. How did they find him?"

"That's a damn good question."

Megan pulled out her cell phone and dialed Detective Black. She posed her question to Black, and added, "There may be a witness. Someone who saw something, maybe someone following Price."

"The homeless in this area have had regular skirmishes with the local police. They're suspicious by nature. They're not talking to me. I've been trying."

"What about your friend Abrahamson? The guy who went undercover? Pose the dilemma to him, maybe he can come up with something."

"Good idea. When will you be back from Texas?"

"Anyone's guess. I'll keep you in the loop."

"Appreciate it."

Megan hung up and told Hans about the conversation. He was deep into reading the files. She picked up the evidence report and pored through it. The victim, Duane Johnson, had left his restaurant, Duane's Rib House, at just before eleven Wednesday night, February 11. This was habitual, the restaurant stopped serving at ten, according to his employees, and they were always out by eleven. Duane worked every day except Mondays and had an assistant manager who opened five days a week.

It was this assistant manager, Joanne Quince, who began to worry when Duane was late on Thursday. *"Duane always comes in by four—I have to pick my kids up no later than five from the sitter. He's never been late."*

At four-thirty, she called his cell phone, then his house phone, then his ex-wife, Dawn. Joanne left one of the waitresses in charge, picked up her kids, then left them with a neighbor and drove to Duane's house. Dawn was already there, crying, and on the phone with the police department.

"We couldn't live together, but I loved him. He was a great father. Never missed a child support payment. We had dinner together every Sunday, for the kids."

When the police arrived, they found evidence that someone had picked the garage door lock. Duane didn't have an alarm system, he lived in an attractive middle-class rural neighborhood—everyone had a couple acres, the modest ranch-style homes were set far back from the road, and a flood canal separated the front yards from the street. There were no fences, but no one would have been able to see inside the house. The blinds were all closed.

Johnson had been attacked in the garage after pulling in and closing the door behind his truck. The garage light had been loose, and while no fingerprints were on the bulb or surrounding assembly, the dust had been disturbed, indicating that someone had deliberately disabled the light. Johnson's hamstrings were cut in the garage, then he was dragged into the house and duct-taped to a chair.

"Here," Hans said, tapping a toxin report. "He had trace amounts of a tranquilizer—benzodiazepine class. He was a big guy. I wonder if he fought back even after being sliced."

"Or," Megan said, "maybe he saw someone. It says in the report that there was a disturbance and possible scuffle in the garage—two paint cans and a box of screws had been knocked over."

"Did you get a tox report before CID took Price's body?"

"No, but there are blood samples at the morgue and the pathologist sent them to his lab."

Megan finished reading the reports, viewed the crime scene photos. The killers were precise. They knew their target and why they chose him. They had all the necessary supplies—knife, duct tape, needles to torture their victim. The attack and murder were well planned and well executed.

"I know what's been bugging me," she said.

"Shoot."

"The evidence here—the plan. The methodology. This wasn't their first kill. At least one of them had to have practiced, wouldn't you think?"

Hans weighed her statement. "It's a good bet that Johnson wasn't their first victim, but there're no other like cases in the country that have been reported to the FBI. I scoured the databases. I have an analyst on it full-time as well, contacting smaller local agencies who don't regularly report or where the information was incomplete. Maybe something will pop—"

"But it might not be exactly the same. Maybe the first victim wasn't hamstrung."

"I've taken that into account."

Megan looked at the photos but didn't really see them. She wasn't articulating her point well. "Where would someone learn how to use needles to torture? It's like acupuncture, but with pain as the goal instead of relief."

"A doctor. A trained acupuncturist. Anyone in the medical field or with some anatomy training." Hans wrote rapidly on his pad. "I can't believe I didn't think of that before. But it makes sense. I'll talk to my analyst and see what she finds after adding in that information. Perhaps an army medic."

"But we don't train our soldiers to torture like this," Megan said.

"I wouldn't know."

"What if they practiced and then hid the evidence?"

"Such as destroying or burying the body?"

"Yes. Or allowing the wounds to heal. The coroner wrote in his notes that he almost missed the punctures, they were so small and many had already started to heal. I think we should be looking for executions."

"Executions?"

"People killed with a bullet in the back of the head."

"Ballistics would have matched Johnson's with anything in the system. I have the ballistics report right here."

"The detective in Vegas said they didn't have their report back yet." Ballistics could take weeks, sometimes months, to run through the system and find all crimes where the same gun was used. Unlike television, they couldn't pop the bullet in a machine and yield every crime in which a particular gun was used within an hour, primarily because of a backlog of work. Expediting such tests and analysis was certainly something the FBI could help with.

All ballistics reports eventually ended up in an FBI database, but it was a product of time and manpower. The system was as up-to-date as possible, but still there were thousands of local law enforcement agencies sending in their records. A clearinghouse, yes, but nothing happened overnight.

"Maybe we should put out a call for execution-style murders within the last . . ." Megan paused. She wasn't sure how long these two had been operating.

"Let's go back twelve months to be safe," Hans said. "Once they perfected their system, they would want to get started right away. I'll call in the information. Good thinking, Megan. I should have thought of it earlier."

The farther they drove away from Hidalgo, the more upset Ethan became. Agony tore at his gut. His intestines slithered around: snakes, twisting, tightening, poisoning him with sharp fangs. He'd fucked up. He let one get away. The overwhelming urge to turn around and cut the priest's heart out had him whimpering.

She said, "It's over, Ethan."

"We can still go back."

"No."

Ethan slammed his head hard enough on the steering wheel that they swerved into the next lane.

"Don't," she said.

He slammed his head again. "I have to go back."

"We stick to the plan. We're halfway to Santa Barbara. There is no turning back."

He cried out. "I can't let him go. I can't let him go. You changed the plan. It's your fault!"

"You're tired. Let me drive."

"No!"

"Ethan, honey, listen to me. If we turn around we won't be in Santa Barbara by Friday, and then we'll have to wait a month. Do you want to wait an entire *month* to punish General Hackett?"

"We'll do it the same way as the others. In his house—"

"He's married."

Ethan snorted, then he laughed so hard she had to grab the wheel to stop them from hitting an eighteen-wheeler head-on.

"Dammit, Ethan! Pull over."

He did, still laughing. He didn't know what was funny anymore. Or even if it had been funny. He just felt like laughing, the sound bubbling out before he could stop it. His sides hurt, those vile snakes slithering around, but he couldn't stop.

She got out of the car and paced, swearing. Ethan couldn't hear her words, but he recognized the body language, her clenched fists, that look on her face that said, *I could kill.*

It made him laugh harder.

His door opened.

"Move over."

He couldn't talk. Tears ran down his face. She unbuckled his seat belt, pushed him over, and got into the driver's seat. "You bastard! Driving like that, you're going to get us pulled over. Stupid fool."

She pulled back into traffic. Ethan's laughter began to subside when he pissed in his shorts.

"Whoops," he said, giggling.

"We're staying in Benson for the night. You need sleep. I need sleep."

"Let's go back to Hidalgo and kill Cardenas."

She didn't answer.

"I don't need you." He pouted and crossed his arms. He stared straight ahead. The endless road widened and shrunk in front of him. The cars passed and he kept turning to look. His fingers began to tap. He shuffled in his seat, rolled the window up and down. Up and down.

"I have to drive."

"We're almost there. Less than ten miles."

"I can't sit. Not here. Not doing nothing. I have to drive. Please. And we'll go back to Texas."

"Ethan, I'm not missing this opportunity with General Hackett. It's all set up. We can go back to Hidalgo after."

"Really?" He brightened. "I can poke the priest?"

"Yes."

"I knew you'd see it my way. We can't leave the job undone, right?"

"You're absolutely right, Ethan."

Karin stared at the road, trying to tamp down on her anger. She wanted to kill Ethan in the worst way. She couldn't look at him. He was almost over the edge permanently. She'd saved his life at least a half dozen times over the past two years, three of them in the last six months. His hold on reality had been diminishing, though it had been tenuous from the moment they'd hooked up.

She'd been working in a gym in New York City, trying

to forget how screwed up her life was, when Ethan came in. He'd been ordered to exercise by his doctor to work the muscles that had weakened while he'd been tortured. At the time she didn't know what had happened to him, had assumed he'd been in some sort of accident. But she quickly saw in Ethan a quiet lunacy that she could use. And when she learned of his skill with needles . . . a plan was born.

She gradually pulled him away from his shrink, away from his doctor. Karin became Ethan's caregiver. She gave him everything he needed—someone to talk to, someone to fuck, someone who cooked for him and cleaned up after him, someone who stopped him from killing himself. She gave him a purpose: torture those who had left him to die. *"An eye for an eye, Ethan. You do to them what was done to you. Then you'll be healed."*

He had believed her. And all he had to do was believe her for two more days. Once they took care of General Hackett, she wouldn't need him anymore.

And Karin would kill him before letting him go back to murder Father Cardenas.

CHAPTER
TEN

"What was with the questions? Do you know something?" Jack asked Padre as they drove to Carlos's house outside of the city limits. If Hidalgo had a pricey area, this would be it. Everyone had a small yard that they watered and kept green behind chain-link fences and broken sidewalks. Carlos had three cars when his brother couldn't afford even one. Oh, yeah, he was dirty. Jack would take care of him later.

"I had a visitor last night at the church as I was locking up. A woman. White. But . . . I don't see the connection."

"What did she look like?"

"Long dark hair. Medium height, maybe five foot five. Pretty, but a little thin."

"How old was she?"

"Forty, forty-five. I'm not as good with ages. Clean appearance, clean clothing. Dark slacks and a white blouse. A dark windbreaker."

"And?"

"She wanted to confess."

"You take confessions at midnight?"

"If someone needs it. If you came to me at three a.m., I'd listen."

"Don't wait up for me," Jack said, but he was thinking. Picturing Scout dead on the floor, hamstrings cut, bullet to the back of the head. Not a female touch, but they say the sexes are getting closer.

"Was she driving?"

"On foot."

"Then she had to have a place to stay."

"Or a car parked elsewhere."

"The church is a good two miles from El Gato. A white woman isn't going to walk through town at midnight, alone or not. She was alone?"

"I believe so. I didn't see or hear anyone else. She didn't act like anyone was waiting for her. But, well, she didn't confess."

"I don't understand."

"I brought her into the church, she wanted to pray, and I gave her privacy. Then she left."

"Did you check the silver? You're not a softie, Padre. You left a stranger alone in the church?"

"I was in the chapel, waiting for her. And yes, I walked through the church. Nothing was taken or vandalized. The prayer candles were extinguished. I sensed that she'd been walking, saw the church, saw me locking up, and thought it was a good time to confess, but then got nervous. People don't like to talk about their mistakes." Padre glanced at Jack. "Do they?"

"What mistakes?" Jack got out of the truck and strode up to Carlos's front door. Two pit bulls, chained to a lone tree, barked ferociously at the men. Padre approached more cautiously.

Jack pounded on the door. "Carlos! Open up. It's Jack Kincaid and we need to talk." He heard shuffling inside. "Now, Carlos."

A minute later a young woman—if she was eighteen, Jack would eat his hat—answered the door. The security screen was still locked, but through it Jack could see she wore a bra and shorts and nothing else.

A distraction.

Before Jack even heard the car start, he was running across the lawn full speed. Carlos put the car in drive at the same time Jack grabbed a chunk of his hair through the open window and pulled. Carlos tried to drive, but Jack held tight and Carlos slammed on the brakes as Jack pulled open the door. He yanked Carlos from the driver's seat. The car rolled forward and Jack barely noticed Padre jump in and put the car in park before it rolled into the street.

Jack pushed Carlos to the dirt and straddled him, slamming his palm against the side of his head. "What are you running from, asshole?"

In rapid Spanish, Carlos said, "I don't know what you're talking about, Kincaid. I was just going to the store for my girl and—"

Jack pulled him up by his black T-shirt and slammed him back down. "Don't fuck with me, Hernandez. Scout is dead and I want to know what you know."

"Scout? Dead?" He tried to sound like he hadn't heard, but Jack wasn't buying it.

"I said don't fuck with me."

"I'm not! I swear I'm not!"

The girl from the house came running out, pulling on a T-shirt. "Let him go! Let him go!"

Then she saw Padre and her eyes widened. "Father Francis, I—"

He stared at her with narrowed eyes. "Emilia. I am

sure your mother doesn't know you are skipping school, does she?"

"I—no, I—" She turned and ran back into the house.

Jack silently thanked the power of Catholic guilt and focused his attention on Carlos Hernandez.

"Tell me about the boys from San Antonio."

"I don't know—" But he looked Jack in the face. "Look, it was nothing, a onetime sale, just—"

"They're your mules, aren't they?"

"I don't— You're fucking with the wrong person, Kincaid. You think you're a saint? You think you're the morality cop of Hidalgo? You're an outsider, no matter how much money you throw around or how many kids you send to college. Your money is a drop in the bucket. Just because you got the priest on your side don't think you're indispensable. Or him."

Jack changed his position, pinning Carlos with a knee firmly planted in his groin. Carlos twisted in pain, but the more he moved the more it hurt.

"Do not threaten me, *puta*. Tell me about Scout. Now."

"I didn't do nothing to him. I don't know nothing about it. I swear to God, in front of your fucking priest, I don't know nothing that happened to him."

"Did you talk to a woman in the bar last night? Gringo? Thirties, wearing a ball cap?"

"Maybe—" Jack pushed his knee higher, and Carlos's voice rose a pitch. "Yeah!" He was breathing faster. "Just passing through."

"What did you tell her?"

"About what? It was chitchat. About owning a bar, shit like that."

"Did she ask about Scout?"

"Naw, she didn't ask questions, maybe how's it going and crap. She bummed a cigarette off Enrique Roscoe. Yeah, right before she left. I swear he holds those cigs in tight fists, so she must have winked at him or something. Maybe he knows something. I don't know, I just didn't say nothing about no one, and you'd better get off me or I'll call Perez and have you thrown in jail. And if you think I can't, you're a fool."

Jack suspected Carlos was blowing smoke, but he didn't want to test it. Perez would be livid when he learned Jack was asking questions about Scout's murder. Delaying that revelation as long as possible was to Jack's advantage.

He pushed off Carlos, who scrambled up and moved away while adjusting his aching dick. "Keep your bitch in line, Padre," he said as he got back in his car and sped away.

"Jack—" Padre said.

Jack walked off his anger. Carlos Hernandez wasn't worth it, but the asshole was messing with the wrong people if he thought he could be a major player in the drug trade. The kings down in Mexico would eat Carlos for breakfast. Jack could care less about the jerk, but he feared collateral damage. Naïve girls like Emilia.

"You might want to turn up the fire and brimstone in your homilies," Jack said. "Too many people are turning the other cheek—for the wrong people."

Jack got back in the truck. "Let's find Enrique. Maybe he can give us more information about this wayward Catholic brunette."

*   *   *

It was after six that evening when Detective Vasquez drove Megan and Hans to Duane Johnson's house.

Hans walked around the house alone while Megan stood in the garage and tried to put herself in the killers' shoes. Waiting for their target to come home. It took a patient killer. Someone who planned. Three murders, no evidence yet that pointed to any specific suspect. Generalities only—likely someone affiliated with the military—current or in the past. Someone with a grudge against the army specifically, and possibly Duane Johnson and the others individually. Someone who had access to information about the veterans and where they lived, worked, their schedules.

The killers had to have stalked Johnson before killing him. And Dennis Perry. How had they traveled? Plane? Car? She could pull flight records for specific flights, but to pull multiple flight records without knowing the specific airline, both the destination and the origin, or the date of travel . . . it would be virtually impossible to find out if an UNSUB had been on flights to Austin, Las Vegas, and Sacramento. If Megan had only a name, they could get the information, but it would still take time.

It bothered her more than she'd let on to Hans and her boss, Bob Richardson, about receiving Price's dog tag at her apartment. The killers had to have been watching the crime scene, otherwise how could they have identified her? She wasn't a spokesperson for the department, though she'd had her moments in the limelight. Last year the *Sacramento Bee* had done a huge article on the serial killer she'd killed who buried his victims alive. Richardson had thought it had been a great idea for her to do an interview with the press; she had hated every minute of it. Her brother Matt, the district attorney, handled the press much better than she did. But it had been good P.R. and Richardson was all about the image of the bureau. And that led to the television interview and that would have led to a national spot, except Megan told her boss no more. She couldn't do her job if she was too high profile, and she didn't want to be the public information officer.

Vasquez joined her in the garage and said, "Find anything?" in a tone that said he thought being at the crime scene two months after the murder was a waste of time.

Megan walked over to where the garage floor looked bleached. "Is this where the paint can spilled during the scuffle? Where Johnson was hamstrung?"

"Yes, and I know what you're thinking."

"You do?"

"That the killer stepped in the paint and left nice footprints to identify. The killer may have done just that, but they scrubbed the floor before leaving."

"Scrubbed?"

"There may have been footprints, but someone came in and used Johnson's shirt to rub the paint over any possible prints."

Megan frowned. "I didn't see that in the report."

"If it wasn't there, I forgot. But it didn't give us anything, except that the killers tried to clean up."

She stared at the door. "The house was cleaned."

"Of course."

"There still might be—" She opened the garage door and called out for Hans.

He came from the back of the house. "Find something?"

"I don't know. But the killer stepped in the paint. It could have been tracked all over the house, maybe invisible to the naked eye."

"The house has since been cleaned by a biological clean-up company," Vasquez said.

Megan sighed. Good biohazard companies wouldn't have let anything slip by. "It was worth a try."

"I'll call the crime scene supervisor. Tell him what you're thinking and see if he has any ideas."

"We appreciate it," Megan said. She was grasping at straws. She wanted a break, *something* that pointed to a suspect. She'd worked hundreds of murder investigations over her fifteen-year FBI career, so many that her boss in D.C. had suggested she get a job with local law enforcement. *"Violent crime isn't our priority,"* he'd said in 2002. *"You may be happier in a different agency."*

But she loved working in the FBI, and she thrived in the Violent Crimes Squad. She didn't want to do anything else. It had taken her three more years before she was transferred into a supervisory role and moved to Sacramento.

"Agent Davis said something about friends of Johnson who were in the military with him. Veterans?" Hans asked.

Vasquez nodded. "They had a weekly poker game over at the VFW Hall. I'll take you there. They didn't have anything to add to the investigation." He glanced at his watch. "Happy hour is just ending. I don't know if you'll get anything useful from them, but honestly, I don't think they know anything."

*   *   *

It took Jack until the dinner hour to find Enrique Roscoe. Seemed he'd "just missed him" at his four regular hangouts. Padre had to go to church for Mass. Jack knew his friend was worried, but he couldn't think about that right now. Jack wasn't going to do anything stupid, and he was relieved when Padre was no longer riding shotgun.

Jack returned to El Gato at seven that night, circling back to the first place he looked for Enrique. There he sat, a beer belly at twenty-five. Jack slid onto the bar stool next to him.

"Tell me about the pretty gringo you talked to yesterday," Jack said, voice low. He ignored Pablo whose gesture asked if Jack wanted his usual.

"Fuck off."

Jack grabbed Enrique by the collar. The kid smelled of beer and marijuana. His red eyes blinked rapidly, and he worked his mouth without speaking.

"Carlos told me you had a nice chat with her. I want to know what you said, what she said."

"Let him go," Pablo said. "I don't want trouble. Please, Señor Jack, just talk."

Jack let go of Enrique's shirt. "Spill it."

Enrique shrugged, rolled his shoulders, picked up his beer. "She bummed a cigarette off me."

"I want the pack."

Enrique barked out a laugh. "That was two packs ago. Check the landfill."

"Did she use your lighter?"

"She had her own. She lit mine." Enrique reached under his waistband and did an elaborate show of adjusting his dick.

"Name?"

"Didn't say."

"Carlos says you chatted her up."

Enrique shrugged. "Whatever."

"Did Scout talk to her?"

"Dunno."

Jack's fists clenched. He resisted the urge to deck the bastard. "Did she talk about Scout? Friends or family in town?"

"Why? You think she killed him?"

Jack didn't answer. He stared at Enrique.

Enrique shrugged again, drained the rest of his beer, and motioned for another.

"She didn't ask anything. Just talked about how much she liked traveling and sitting in local bars. I asked her to dance, she said no, that was it."

Jack didn't know what to make of the information, and he knew there was more to it than small talk. "Carlos said you talked to her for quite some time."

"Fuck Carlos, he's a liar. He came up when I was just about to get a peek down at her tits. She had these nice"—he cupped his hands—"C cups. Smaller than I like, but her shirt was cut to here"—he touched his chest—"and there was this nice tan line."

"What color shirt?"

"White. She was too skinny for me; I like some meat on my women." He made a motion like he was grabbing ass. Jack bit back a comment, and asked, "Hair? Eyes?"

"Dunno. Two?" He laughed at his own pathetic joke. This was going nowhere. "Carlos talked to her?"

"He came over and hit on her. Told me to scram. I told him to fuck off, then went to take a piss. Came back and Carlos was gone. She was there, paying. I went over, she said she had to go. Early appointment or some such garbage. I thought she might be meeting up to screw Carlos, but ten minutes after she left, Carlos comes back in with his boys." Enrique leaned over and said in a stage whisper, "I think he was just feeling her out to see if she was a cop."

"Cop?" Jack raised his eyebrow. "You thought she was a cop?"

"Hell no, but you know how paranoid Carlos is."

"Shut the fuck up, you drunk fool."

Jack pivoted on his barstool. Carlos stood behind them with two of his punks—both bigger than the youngest Hernandez.

"You told me you didn't talk to the woman." Jack slowly rose from the seat.

"I don't have to tell you anything, you fucking half-breed."

Jack stood his ground. "How long was this woman around here?"

"She left. Early. Long before your drunk *gringo* comrade."

Jack stepped forward, wanting too much to slam his fist in Carlos Hernandez's nose. "If I find out you're lying to me, Hernandez . . ."

"You going to tell the priest on me?" he mimicked. "He your boyfriend?"

The three laughed. Jack started to walk out. He was too close to letting loose. Too close to letting the demons out. And Carlos wouldn't survive.

Art Perez walked into the bar, a deputy at his side. Could the chief of police not go anywhere alone? Jack stopped when Perez blocked his path.

"I hear you've been sticking your nose into my investigation," Perez said.

"I'm not interfering with your investigation."

"You dragged Pablo Hernandez out of bed, then beat up his little brother in the middle of the street."

"Damn straight," Carlos said from the bar. "Arrest him, Officer!" He laughed and everyone around him joined in.

Jack said, "Scout was one of my men. I will find out what happened."

"Maybe you brought trouble back with you from Guatemala." Perez glared. "Yeah, I know all about you and the other soldiers of fortune here. I also know a bit about your good friend Frank Cardenas. You might want to think about that, Kincaid. Frank's history may not go over well with some of the people here, and if enough of them flood the diocese with complaints—well, let's just say he may find a nice post in the cold Alaska diocese after I'm done."

Jack had always known that Perez was a bastard, but this was low even for him. The police chief was baiting him, waiting for Jack to throw a punch so he could arrest him. Waiting for him to react. Jack froze. He would do Scout no good in jail.

"Stay out of police business. I know how to do my job." Perez stepped forward, toe to toe. Jack didn't budge. He barely breathed. "And leave Carlos Hernandez alone, or it's war. Ten years living here is nothing, Kincaid. You're still the outsider, and I'm still the hometown boy made good."

Perez left. Carlos and his two cronies followed. Jack turned back, glared at Enrique, and slapped his hand on the bar, rattling every glass underneath.

Pablo slid a Tecate over to him. "On me. Sorry about Scout, Señor Jack. Really." He ambled off down the bar.

Jack breathed out slowly. He took a long swallow of the beer, tasting nothing. He glanced up at the television. There was no sound, but the tag on a photo of some capitol building read "THREE DEAD SOLDIERS."

"Pablo!" he shouted. "Turn up the TV!"

Pablo obliged, and the ancient Zenith TV behind the bar blasted into life. The fuzzy channel at least had clear sound.

The reporter was saying, "So far, three men in three different states, all U.S. Army veterans, have been found dead—execution style." Pictures of three soldiers in uniform flashed on the screen, but the images weren't clear enough for Jack to make them out. He could tell, however, that Scout wasn't one of them.

"According to the Austin Police Department, the Federal Bureau of Investigation has taken an active role in the case, sending two agents from Washington, D.C., to assist local authorities in tracking who may be the first serial killer targeting our armed forces. . . ."

Serial killer? *Scout?* Jack didn't want to believe it, but he couldn't deny that Scout was killed execution style. Except the report said nothing about hamstringing. Jack knew the police routinely didn't share all details of a crime with the public.

The reporter continued. "If anyone has information about these crimes, please contact Detective José Vasquez with the Austin Police Department at . . ."

Jack left. Austin P.D. be damned. He was going straight to the top.

He sat in his truck and called Washington, D.C. His

brother Dillon was living with a fed. And dammit, Jack would pull every string and make any promise if it led to justice for Scout.

For the first time since he'd seen Scout's body, Jack believed he had a decent shot at finding his friend's killer.

CHAPTER
ELEVEN

The VFW Hall that Duane Johnson had frequented every Monday night for a poker game was located on the dilapidated side of the Austin business district. As José Vasquez drove Meg and Hans across town, the scent of thunderstorms hung in the air even though the colorful, sunset-hued sky was clear. Megan was exhausted. This was their last stop before checking into a hotel Agent Davis had secured for them.

The hall was more than half full, with the majority of patrons in their late fifties and sixties. Vietnam era, Megan thought. Still, a decent number of men were in their thirties. And while women had a larger role in today's armed forces, there were only a handful in the establishment.

Taking the lead, Vasquez led Megan and Hans over to two men sitting at a table on the far side of the back room. Two of three pool tables were in use.

"Reggie, Norris, meet Special Agent Elliott and Dr. Vigo from the FBI. They're here to help find Duane's killer."

Reggie was as white as Norris was black. He was tall, skinny, around forty years of age; Norris was tall, linebacker-wide, and at least sixty, if not older. He also had only one eye, but it didn't miss anything. Both were drinking draft beer.

"Hmm," Norris said.

"Skeptical?" Hans asked.

Norris shrugged. "Been a couple months."

Megan sat down next to the men. "Sometimes it takes awhile, but neither Hans nor I are backing down."

"Yep."

Megan tried a different tack. "Where were you stationed?" she asked.

"Fort Meade," Reggie said. "Spent three years in Iraq."

Norris stared. "Ord." He sipped his beer.

Meg nodded. "California. I know it."

Norris raised an eyebrow. "It's closed."

"Right. In 1994. I lived there when I was ten. My father moved around a lot."

"Army brat."

"One of the brattiest."

Reggie chuckled. "Somehow, I don't see that."

"Just ask my brother. He was so fed up with army brats that he joined the navy." She rolled her eyes.

The men laughed, and Megan breathed easier.

"You really think you can catch Duane's killer?" Norris asked doubtfully.

"Yes," Megan said. "I don't give up."

"Easily?"

"I don't give up." She had a few cold cases on her desk that she still worked. She hated to lose; she hated more to have a killer walking free while his victims were six feet under.

"We told the detective everything we know."

"My partner, Hans Vigo, and I have some questions. They might sound strange."

"Did Vasquez say you're a doctor?"

Hans shrugged. "Depends how you define 'doctor.' I have a Ph.D." Hans had three, but Megan didn't elaborate. "I might be able to save you if you start choking on peanuts, but if you need emergency brain surgery, you're dead meat."

The men laughed again, and Hans sat next to Megan.

"What do you want to know?" Reggie asked. "We told Vasquez everything about Duane. He plays poker with us on Monday nights—that's when his restaurant is closed. He's known for his ribs, but it's the hamburgers that bring me out on payday."

"We're a tight bunch here. We'd notice strangers hanging around," Norris said. "Nothing bizarre or out of the ordinary for as long as I can remember. Duane was a good guy. Paid his taxes. Loved his kids. Hell, he even loved his ex-wife. Dawn was a good woman, they just couldn't live together, you know?"

"They were still getting it on," Reggie said.

"Shut up, kid," Norris said.

Reggie waved his hand in the air. "Duane wouldn't care. What do you think, that Dawn had something to do with his murder? Not a chance."

Megan said, "What I'm really interested in is Duane's military background."

Both men grew serious. "Why?" Norris asked.

"Have you seen the news? Two other veterans have been murdered in a similar manner."

"You mean that homeless vet in Sacramento?" Norris said. "Just saw that tonight, before you walked in. There wasn't much to the story. Just that police thought it might be connected with Duane's case, but they didn't give us shit in the report. Same as we been hearing for the last two months. No offense, José."

"None taken."

"So you remember the news story?" Hans asked, one eyebrow raised.

" 'There, but for the grace of God, go I,' " Norris quoted.

"I was at the crime scene," Megan said. "George Price is my case."

"And that's connected to Duane?" Reggie asked. "How?"

"There are three victims, all were army, all with multiple tours, and thus far there are about ten years of overlapping enlistment. We're trying to find any common posts or assignments."

"It wasn't just a random act of violence?"

"No," Megan and Hans said simultaneously.

Hans added, "Someone is targeting specific veterans. He will kill again if we can't figure out the connection and stop him."

Reggie and Norris drank their drafts simultaneously. "What do you want to know?" Norris finally said. "We don't just sit here and talk about our lives like this is Oprah's studio."

Megan nodded. "You probably know where Duane served."

Reggie nodded. "He did basic at Fort Bragg."

Megan made the note. "1982."

"About right. If that's what his records say, that's probably right," Reggie said. "He did a tour in Desert Storm."

"Do you remember when?"

"First year—ninety. I enlisted that year, but didn't get over there until ninety-one. He was gone by then."

"He was in Afghanistan for a spell," Norris said. "Went back voluntarily."

"A lot of the guys do," Reggie said.

"Somalia," Norris said. "He was Delta."

That was a revelation. Special Operations. Were Price and Perry Special Ops as well? Megan made a note to find out.

"Fort Bragg?" Hans asked.

"That's what I said." Norris said it in such a way that Megan was certain Norris knew for sure. There were only two or three bases the army's elite Delta Force operated from.

"Did Duane mention either Dennis Perry or George Price to either of you?"

Reggie shook his head. "If he did, I don't remember. But if you're in the same unit, most guys don't use the name your mama gave you. I was Apollo from day one."

"Apollo?" Megan asked. "I don't think I've heard a Greek god used as a nickname before."

"Not everyone gets shot in the foot first day in basic," Reggie said. "Fucking big-city prick never held a gun before in his life—*bang*—takes out my big toe." He slipped off his shoe and showed everyone his four-toed left foot.

Norris shook his head. "He gets a kick out of that story. I still think you shot yourself in the foot."

"Fuck you," Reggie said in a jovial tone.

"One more question," Megan said. "Can you remember anything Duane might have mentioned about an operation gone bad? Something that might have generated bad will?"

"Nope," Norris said. "He took an honorable discharge in 2004. Had near twenty years, I think. Good pension, opened up the restaurant. If he had a bad op—and I sure had one or ten, we all did—he didn't talk about it. Duane was one of the good guys. Fought for his country, didn't whine about it, had a nice family, ran his business, and did some charity work for . . . what group was it Reggie?"

"An at-risk youth group. I don't remember the name. But he'd go speak at high schools about joining the military instead of gangs or dropping out of school. There was even a write-up in the paper about him a year or so ago—nice spread, too."

Megan thanked them for their time, got their numbers in case she or Hans had follow-up questions, and they left. Vasquez dropped them off at the hotel. Hans and Megan sat in the nearly empty restaurant before they checked in, both of them famished.

While waiting for their meals, they discussed their notes and observations, but their meals had just been served when Hans's cell phone rang.

He excused himself and left the restaurant. Megan thought it was odd, but dug into her meal realizing she hadn't eaten since a quick pastry at the airport as she boarded the plane before eleven. It had been another long day.

Her phone rang. It was a restricted number. "Hello," she answered.

"Megan, J. T. Caruso."

"Got news?"

"Price was stationed at Fort Bragg and attached to Delta Force, Special Operations."

"I know about Delta." She dropped her fork and

grabbed her notebook. Her heart raced as she said, "The first victim was Delta out of Fort Bragg."

J.T. continued. "Price went AWOL when his commanding officer, Lieutenant Kenneth Russo, charged him with assault and attempted murder. He hasn't been seen since."

"Attempted murder?"

"It was nasty and political. From what I've heard—and this is not public information, and the army will deny it, so it's FYI only—five years ago, Russo was assigned an operation to extract a Taliban leader who was quietly seeing a prostitute outside Kabul. Price was assigned to his team."

"I thought the purpose of Delta was to create teams of men who worked together and trained together, not put together randomly."

"Generally, that's true. I don't know the details of this operation, I just know this was the first time Price was under Russo's command." He paused. "I put out a message for Kane to see if he's familiar with either Russo or Price or that operation, but it may take him a couple days to make contact."

Kane Rogan, one of the three Rogan partners in Rogan-Caruso, worked out of the country extensively on sensitive projects for business and governments. Megan remembered he'd done time in the military, but she had no idea in what capacity.

"I appreciate it," Megan said.

"A few months after they returned stateside from this failed mission," J.T. continued, "Price and Russo got into a fight in the barracks. Price supposedly pulled a knife, stabbed Russo, and ran. Russo was in surgery for a couple hours, and when he recovered, he retired."

"And now Price is dead."

"So is Russo."

"What?" Megan straightened. "When?"

"Last summer. Robbery. Shot multiple times."

"Where?"

"When he retired, he moved to Florida. I'll email you the stats."

"You're incredible."

"So I've been told. Do you think there's a connection?"

"The first victim was stationed at Fort Bragg. I'm waiting to hear on the second victim. But I'm putting my money on the same background."

"Oh, I almost forgot."

"I doubt that."

"Price didn't die of a gunshot wound. They did the autopsy. He had a heart attack. He was dead or close to it when he was shot."

"Then why shoot him?" Megan pondered.

"That's your arena, darling. I just supply the facts. Maybe they didn't know he was dead, or thought he might recover if someone found him quickly."

"Would you know he was dead?"

"I'm special."

"These killers would know."

"If you say so."

Megan frowned. How did it all fit together? "Thanks, J.T."

"I'll let you know if I hear from Kane, but I don't know if he'll be able to shine any more light on the situation."

"I owe you one."

"I think we're up to twenty-two, but who's counting?"

"Ha."

"Anytime, Meg. Watch your back." He hung up.

Megan shut her cell phone. J.T. walked a fine line between legal and illegal security work, but he was her brother Matt's closest friend. Megan didn't know everything that had happened between J.T. and Matt, but they would move heaven and earth for each other, and that included helping her out.

Hans sat down and Megan told him everything in a rush. "We need to contact the Orlando FBI office and have them look into the circumstances of Russo's murder. That may be the beginning. He may have been the first victim."

"We should do that," he said absently, and Megan said, "You didn't hear a word I said."

"I did. Sorry. That was a friend, Dr. Dillon Kincaid. He's a civilian consultant with the FBI and I've worked with him on several cases."

"He's helping us on this?"

"Now he is. His brother just contacted him. We might have another victim."

"Who? Where?"

"Former Sergeant Major Lawrence Bartleton, now a soldier for hire based in Hidalgo, Texas. Dillon's brother Jack runs a small mercenary group focused on rescue missions and foreign hostage situations. Jack was Delta, as was Bartleton. This is our first real lead, with people who have an in with the victims and might give us something tangible we can work with."

"Did the local police call it in?"

"There's a bit of a problem with the local police."

"Dammit, we can't just walk in there and take over. It's just not done that way anymore. And they don't have to give us anything."

"True, but the police chief isn't pursuing the same investigation. He's following a personal vendetta against Kincaid's group by running with the idea that one of the rebels Kincaid ticked off in Guatemala or some such country is behind the murder. Kincaid saw the news report on the other victims, and made contact. He's willing to help us. We need it."

Megan didn't like the idea of walking into a small town and taking over an investigation, officially or unofficially, but as she learned from J.T., she had no easy access to the military and their methods. How could she find out how these men were connected without inside information? While she could get name, rank, and serial number—and not much more—through proper channels, any personnel records would take time—a commodity they didn't have. It had been less than seventy-two hours since George Price was killed in Sacramento. The killers had escalated exponentially. Two months, two weeks, two days. Having a real in, someone like this Jack Kincaid, might be their only hope to stop two killers who had killed four, maybe five times, with impunity.

"When are we leaving?"

Hans grabbed two rolls from the bread bowl and stood. "Now."

CHAPTER
TWELVE

It was dark while Jack sat in the cab of his truck outside El Gato watching who came and went, waiting for Dillon to call back about the possible serial killer. Jack called a Delta buddy Scott Gray, who now worked for the Rangers, and filled him in on the murder in Hidalgo on the Q.T. While local authorities could work their own murder investigations, generally the small towns like Hidalgo would call in either the county or, more commonly, the Texas Rangers to work the case. Scott confirmed what Jack suspected: Art Perez had not contacted them about Scout's murder.

"But we're interested," Scott said. "I'll pass this up the chain of command, but I suspect someone will be down there tomorrow."

"I'm having some problems with the chief of police," Jack said without further explanation.

"I got a call from a reporter," Scott said with a wink in his voice.

"Thanks. Let me know if you need anything. I contacted my brother, who's affiliated with the FBI. I'm waiting to hear how they're involved."

"If it's the Hamstring Killer, the feds are all over it. I heard two agents were in Austin today."

Jack thanked Scott for his help and hung up. He

watched Deputy Ripa leave the bar. As usual, he'd drunk too much and was ripe for conversation. Jack had gotten some of his best information from Ripa after a night out. He needed to find out what evidence, if any, had been collected at Scout's house. This mysterious brunette had captured Jack's interest, especially if it was the same woman who'd approached Padre. Had she been sent to make sure Scout was alone? To keep Padre occupied? The priest often went to El Gato near closing to take care of Scout and any others who had drunk too much. Or were they not connected at all? Was Jack reading too much into the situation?

Right now, he needed to gather intelligence so he could create a plan. Intelligence, plan, execution.

He opened his truck door quietly and said, "Ripa."

"Go away, Kincaid. You're going to get me in trouble with Perez." The deputy still wore his sidearm. Guns and alcohol were a dangerous combination. Jack kept his guard up.

"Perez is doing nothing about Scout's murder. Where's the evidence?"

"The station. And he is working it. He traced Scout's last week. He says you brought the trouble to Hidalgo, it's not on his head."

"Do you watch TV?"

"What?" Ripa swayed a bit, squared his feet. "I gotta go. If Perez hears I even told you to fuck off, he'll be in my face. I don't need that shit. I got an ex-wife and kid to support."

"What happened to Scout had nothing to do with Guatemala."

"I don't care. I just don't want trouble." He burped loudly.

"Where'd he send Scout's body?"

Ripa blinked. He hadn't expected the question, and it was obvious to Jack he wasn't lying when he said, "I don't know. I guess Edinburg, or McAllen. Why?"

Jack didn't trust Perez with the investigation into Scout's murder, but he'd follow proper procedures with Scout's body. There was no morgue or coroner in Hidalgo; they generally sent autopsies to the county seat. Jack would go up there first thing in the morning and talk to the coroner. He hoped the feds didn't screw it up. Jack usually got the information he wanted, but he knew that the FBI and other government bureaucrats went in with attitudes that sometimes didn't go over so good down here in south Texas.

Jack told Ripa, "I've been all over town and back and talked to everyone at the bar last night. Where has Perez been? Who's he talking to?"

"I told you." The bar door opened and Ripa said loudly, "Get out of my face, Kincaid, or I'll arrest you."

"On what charge?"

Two of Perez's cronies came out. *Abbott and Costello,* Jack thought.

"Arrest him, Ripa," the tall jerk said. The squat one laughed.

Jack's cell phone vibrated in his pocket. He ignored it and said, "Thanks for nothing, Ripa." Though he confirmed what he suspected: Art Perez was doing next to nothing to find out who killed Scout; worse, he was mucking up any legitimate investigation by not sending the evidence to the Ranger's state-of-the-art lab. Jack knew why: Hidalgo City would be charged for the services, and Perez ran the police department on a tight budget. The chief of police would wait until the Rangers came on their own. Suddenly, it was clear to Jack: it was all about the money. If the Rangers came in and took over the case, Perez wouldn't have to pay for it. If he asked for help, half came out of the city coffers.

Jack mentally berated himself for not figuring it out earlier. But now he had a card to play.

He got in his truck, ignoring the stares of Ripa and the Abbott and Costello lookalikes, and drove off. He missed his call, so he retrieved his phone and hit Send. It was Dillon.

"What do you have?"

"The two agents in charge of the Hamstring Killer investigation are currently in Austin, Texas. I talked to my friend Hans Vigo. He and Agent Megan Elliott are flying to McAllen as soon as they get to the airport. He figures two hours."

"I'll be there."

"I gave Hans your cell phone number."

"Fine."

"He's good. He was part of the FBI effort to identify Lucy's kidnapper. Just—" Dillon didn't say anything else.

"I won't be pushed aside."

"That's what I told Hans. He's fine with it, Jack. He said they need an in. You can trust him."

"Hmm."

"You can trust him like you can trust me."

"And this Elliott?"

"Don't know her, but Hans says she's good."

"Thanks, Dillon."

"I can come down."

"Not necessary."

"If you need another set of legs or just to run a theory past, call me."

Jack would normally deflect any offers of help. He had his team, men he'd trained or retrained to suit him, and he didn't want or need anyone else. But already he had two feds on the way, and Dillon did have an expertise that Jack didn't. More than that, Dillon was his brother. Jack had to remember family helped each other, both ways.

"I will," he said. "Thanks."

"Anytime."

Jack hung up and made a U-turn. It was less than thirty minutes to McAllen, so Jack had time to stop by Scout's. Jack had been a soldier long enough that he could read a scene as well or better than any cop. Perez wasn't sharing information with him, so Jack had to find out what happened on his own.

It was ten at night with thunderheads obscuring the moon, minimizing the chances of anyone seeing him. If a neighbor spotted him, Jack was fine. If Perez had a patrol out on Scout's street, Jack might have some trouble.

He parked around the corner from Scout's house and walked casually along the street. Crime scene tape had been woven around the porch railing. There was a seal on the front door. No patrol car in sight. Jack walked around back while slipping on gloves.

There was a police seal on the back door, but Jack knew that Scout didn't lock any of the sunroom windows. The police hadn't even checked. Jack was inside in less than ten seconds.

The smell of Scout's violent death hung in the stifling house, retaining the heat of the day. Jack looked around the sunroom, didn't see anything out of place, and walked the house with a flashlight.

Scout was a patriot through and through, and did whatever Uncle Sam had asked him to. It was that blind loyalty, however, that Jack was certain had led to some actions that Scout couldn't deal with, and that had led to his drinking. Yet when Jack told him to sober up, they had a job, Scout did just that. Maybe it was Jack's fault. He'd let Scout do what he wanted when they didn't have an assignment—maybe he should have ordered him to stop drinking or he was off the team. Maybe he should have showed him some tough love.

Shit. Nineteen years and Scout was gone. If it had been in the field, Jack could have handled it better. Scout always expected to die doing what he loved. Maybe took too many risks because of it. But to die with a bullet in the back of the head? Naked and hamstrung? Jack wanted to snap the neck of the bastard who did it. Who took away Scout's dignity before he killed him.

Still, something about the scene had bothered Jack from the minute he walked in earlier that day, and now he hoped to figure out what it was.

He went to the front door. The blood spatter told Jack that Scout had been hamstrung just inside his living room. Enough time to walk in, close the door . . . There was no sign of a struggle, save for a broken lamp near the door that could have fallen if Scout tried to grab on to something when he fell. Jack followed the trail of blood to the kitchen, where Scout had been duct-taped to a chair for an unknown length of time, before the tape had been cut. Scout had been pushed or fell to the floor. Shot in the back of the head. The sight was burned into Jack's head.

Scout had been drunk. His reaction time may have been slow, but his instincts always stayed sharp. Like Jack, he wouldn't walk into a dark house, even his own, without caution. Pausing. Listening for a breath, a heartbeat. Sensing movement, heat, the faint expel of air from an enemy's lungs. Sniffing for adrenaline, cologne, the smell of something *different*.

Jack closed his eyes and used his other senses to try and figure out what had bothered him earlier in the day.

The stench of death that Jack had been ignoring came rushing in. Death and fear. He walked through the small house. If he were a killer, he would have secured the building, made sure no one was inside.

Ten minutes later, Jack was frustrated. He went back to the kitchen and stared at the dried pool of blood on the floor. "Dammit, Scout. Who did this?"

He pictured Scout lying on the floor. He had avoided looking at his friend's dead body as much as possible. But now he couldn't get it out of his mind.

And suddenly he knew.

Scout hadn't been wearing his dog tags. He always wore them, even in the shower. Or, Jack should say, *it*. The second tag had been torn off on Scout's last mission when he'd broken his back and couldn't walk out. He was left for three hours before his team could return to him. *"I only have two lives, Jack. I used up one."*

To verify that Jack wasn't imagining it, he went to Scout's bedroom and bathroom and shined his light around on the off chance Scout had taken the chain off and forgotten it. Nothing.

Jack left the way he'd come in, taking care not to disturb anything. He didn't know what this meant, but he hoped that Dillon's feds could use the information.

He heard a car drive up. Another. By the sound, police cruisers. Shit. He couldn't slip through the backyard, too much light from the streetlamps, and if he were seen it would make him look guilty of something. He'd just talk his way out of it. As long as Art Perez wasn't around, Jack was confident he could be leaving for McAllen to pick up the feds in the next five minutes.

He walked around the side of the house, hands in view.

Art Perez stood there, in civilian clothes, a cat-ate-the-canary grin on his face.

"I knew you'd show up sooner or later."

Megan had grown frustrated thirty minutes ago when their ride was a no-show. It was after midnight, she was tired, hungry, and crabby, and stuck in a small, empty airport thirty miles from their destination.

"Have you tried him again?" she asked Hans. Hans had left a message, told the ride where they would be waiting.

"Yes."

"Are you sure he's coming?"

"Yes. Dillon talked to him only a couple hours ago." But even saintly Hans Vigo was beginning to sound irritated.

Thunder rolled through the sky, the clouds were thick with the threat of a downpour, though there was no rain yet. The humidity was enough to make Megan miss the dry heat of Sacramento.

The sound of the Jeep came before they saw it.

The driver pulled near them, but didn't get out. He was a Hispanic male about forty years old with short-cropped hair and wearing a priest collar. "Your friend's brother is a priest?" she asked.

Hans shook his head. Megan didn't like the unknown situation, and had her hand on her gun.

"Dr. Vigo?" the driver asked. "Agent Elliott?"

"Yes."

"I'm Father Francis Cardenas. Jack Kincaid sent me for you. I'm sorry I'm late. There's been a situation. Jack's in jail, and we have to get him out or he'll be dead by morning."

He was strapped to a cot. Naked. His eyes burned and he couldn't see. The room was too bright, too bright, too much light, God help me help me help me die.

The door opened and he began to shake. Not from cold, the room was too hot, the lights too bright, to be cold. The fear. The pain. No, no no no no no no . . .

No words, no explanation, and the needle went in, at the back of his neck, and every limb screamed in pain, as if he'd been zapped by a lightning bolt. There were no tears, no voice to the agony that rippled through his body, wave after wave after wave . . .

They'd left him. They hated him and left him. Not to die, they didn't want to give him anything, they wanted him to suffer. Maybe he was dead. Maybe this was Hell. It couldn't be that he was alive.

Another needle and the pain put him over the edge. . . .

"Ethan!"

He blinked. Every finger in both hands was on fire. He stared at them in the dim light of the cheap hotel room they'd rented somewhere in New Mexico. New Mexico? He didn't remember. Not for certain . . . his fingers weren't on fire. They were there. Right there. He moved them, watched them glide right and left and right and left . . .

"Ethan, it's me."

The female voice had a panicked sound.

"Ethan, you're okay. I'm right here. You're okay."

He looked at her and didn't recognize her. Why was this woman in his bed? Another trick? Another perverse, sadistic torment? Let him glimpse a goddess, then snatch her away?

He reached out to touch her face. She didn't flinch or disappear. He remembered her. Familiar. Pain and love. Hot and cold. She hated him. Loved him.

"They left me," Ethan croaked.

"I know, baby. I know."

Ethan's nightmares—memories?—now occurred nightly. Karin didn't know what that meant, but it wasn't good. His slips were more frequent, like going into the woods and burying himself in dirt. But there was nothing she could do about that now. And when he was like this, Ethan was more forthcoming and patient with her training. Karin was almost there. After last night . . . she resisted the urge to gloat.

Instead, she hugged Ethan close, his head to her breast. The tension started to leave his body. He began to shake violently, then fell back into a deep sleep so suddenly, became so still, that for a moment she thought he'd died.

She felt his pulse. Strong. She stared at Ethan as he slept, this time without the memories, the real nightmares that had turned him into . . . into what?

A killer like you?

She swallowed. She had good reasons for what she needed to do. Karin always had good reasons.

You turned him into a killer. Without you, he would be locked up in a padded room, or maybe someone could have helped him. What do you think of that? That you turned this pathetic, tortured man into a sadistic killer?

What was sadistic about killing those who hurt others? If it weren't for those soldiers, who were supposed to protect the innocent, who were there to make sure no harm came to Ethan, he would never have been a hostage and tortured for months.

It's not your fight. You're using him. You're killing him.

Perhaps she was, but she didn't start it. And Ethan wanted to die, anyway. He'd tried it enough times.

She was confident in the rightness of Ethan's cause. When she'd killed before, it was for the justice of others. Never herself. When General Hackett died, she would finally be able to kill for herself.

It would be a righteous kill.

CHAPTER
THIRTEEN

Megan walked into the Hidalgo Police Department with Father Francis Cardenas while Hans worked on getting a warrant from the presiding U.S. attorney to remand Jack Kincaid into their custody if she couldn't sweet talk the chief of police into releasing him. Because it was so late, Megan wasn't holding her breath on either count. But the priest was certain that Kincaid was in grave danger and Megan couldn't *not* at least try and figure out what was going on and see if she could fix it.

She felt out of her element in the border town, blond hair, green eyes, and boobs, which the desk sergeant stared at instead of the badge that was clipped to her belt. She grabbed her badge and put it directly in his line of sight. "Supervisory Special Agent Megan Elliott, Federal Bureau of Investigation. I'm here to speak to a witness in a homicide I heard you have under arrest."

"And who might that be?"

"Jack Kincaid."

The sergeant grunted. "Sorry, it's after hours. Unless you're his attorney."

A loud *thump* and *slam* against the back wall made Megan unconsciously jump.

"Is that the jail?" she asked, gesturing toward the

door in the back with the words *Authorized Personnel Only.*

"So?"

Megan felt as if she'd walked into the Twilight Zone. "Sergeant, I think you have a fight in your jail."

Father Francis said, "Jorge, you don't want to be party to Art's vendetta against Jack."

Jorge hesitated a second.

A body was slammed against the wall, making the room shake. Megan strode past the sergeant without waiting for an invite. Someone was getting the shit beaten out of them, and Megan feared it could be fatal.

She tried the door. It was locked.

"Key. Now!"

The sergeant hesitated, then pressed a button that released the door.

Megan opened it, holding it only briefly so Father Francis could join her. "Stay back," she told him.

Inside the jail were two small cells on the left and one large "drunk tank" on the right. Megan quickly assessed the situation—three against one—in the larger cell. Oddly, or not, considering the priest's fear, the cell door was ajar.

Megan drew her Glock and held it steadily on the men. "FBI. Put your hands behind your head and get down. Now!"

They stopped, all four registering surprise.

The priest stepped forward. "I told you to stand back," Meg said. Though Father Francis looked fit, she didn't want to bring a man of God—or, frankly, any civilian—into a potentially dangerous situation.

He ignored her. "You okay?" he asked a tall, dark-haired, olive-skinned man.

He—Jack Kincaid, most likely—nodded slightly, never taking his eyes off his three attackers, none of whom had obeyed Megan's orders. Megan saw a flash of steel in the palm of one man. He had a knife.

"This isn't your business, Padre. Take your girlfriend and go. Five minutes."

"You'll need more than five minutes to kill me," Jack said, voice low. "You've been trying for ten."

What was this, Megan thought, *the Wild West?* Didn't these guys hear her? "FBI!" she said again. "Drop your weapons, *now!*"

The wiry guy with the knife lunged for Jack. Dammit, the situation had rapidly deteriorated. "Knife!" she shouted. She aimed for the attacker's hand, pulled the trigger, and the bullet clipped his wrist. He dropped the knife, clutching his hand to his chest, and backed away against the wall.

Jack kicked the knife out of the way and stepped toward Megan, eyes still on the other men.

"Fucking bitch shot me!"

Megan gestured to the other two men. "Hands up. Up where I can see them. Now!"

Jack was two feet from her. She wasn't sure he wasn't dangerous as well. He certainly looked it, especially with the blood around his nose from the fight and a cut along his neck. At second glance, she realized it was a knife wound. They'd gone for his throat. Father Francis had been right. They'd fully intended to kill him. He was favoring his right side. Had he been stabbed? Did he need medical attention?

"Kincaid?" she asked.

"Yes."

"You okay?"

"Fine." His voice was casual, laced with a hard edge.

Out of the corner of her eye, she saw one of the two uninjured men pull a switchblade into a throwing position.

The priest said, "Paul, put the knife down. It's over."

Jack stepped toward Megan in a protective move.

The slam of a door had Megan glance toward the entrance. A tall, bulky man in a Stetson entered with the desk sergeant who'd ogled her breasts.

Everything else happened fast.

"Down, Kincaid!" Stetson shouted, a Taser in hand.

Megan's badge was on the front of her belt, clearly visible, and she again identified herself.

"Megan Elliott, FBI. Blue shirt has a knife." She didn't want to shoot another man, but a knife thrown this close could kill. She inched in front of Jack, who was unarmed and obviously the target. Why these thugs wanted him dead Megan had no idea, but it was clear neither her gun nor her badge panicked them even with their friend down.

"All fours, Kincaid," Stetson said again.

The priest said, "Art, don't." Megan was perplexed but didn't have time to reflect on it.

Jack stepped in front of her. Did he have a death wish? She turned her body to be a bigger shield, but Kincaid wasn't making it easy. He was injured and bleeding and she was the one with the gun and the badge; why didn't he stand back and let her do her job?

At the same time Jack moved, Stetson aimed the Taser not at the man with the knife, but at Jack.

The *zip* of the Taser C2 cartridge being depressed registered at the same time as two lightning bolts of pain hit

Megan in her right shoulder, radiating instant fire through her entire body, blinding her. Her gun fell from her grasp and she hit the ground at the same time.

She'd been told what to expect if she was hit with a Taser and what options she had, but for a full minute—or longer, she didn't know—she couldn't think, couldn't focus, couldn't stop her body from convulsing. Breathe deep. Control her gun. Focus, dammit!

She heard voices, shouts, a lot of swearing. She pulled herself up on all fours, her vision returning, but she couldn't see her gun. She felt around for it.

A low, deep voice so close to her ear that she could feel the brush of his lips on her earlobe said, "Relax, Blondie. It'll pass faster if you relax your muscles."

"Kincaid has the gun!" a voice shouted. She felt a hand on her back, and the weight of her gun in her holster. She relaxed as best she could and felt her body rising from the floor. Her vision cleared and she was staring into black eyes only inches from her face.

"Put. Me. Down." Her words were faint and her throat raw.

Jack Kincaid smiled with half his mouth. "I don't think you have your sea legs yet."

Hans Vigo, a man who never raised his voice or swore, thundered, "Chief Perez, you'd better explain what just happened or I'll have the DOJ on your ass so fast you won't be able to shit."

Jack carried her out of the cell and Hans rushed over. "You okay, Meg?"

She nodded. "Put me down," she said quietly.

Jack set her on her feet and she swayed, legs shaking. He stuck his arm behind her, holding her up.

"You have no jurisdiction here," Perez said. "Kincaid

disarmed the woman, took her gun. She had no business being in here. It was a prison riot. We should have been in lockdown." He glared at the desk sergeant, who was looking at the floor.

"That's bullshit," Jack said.

"You shot a federal agent," Hans said, his voice still vibrating with emotion.

"She intentionally stood in front of Kincaid. She should know better than to walk into a brawl and get herself disarmed. Maybe you'd be in your element, little lady, kicking off those shoes and staying in the kitchen."

Megan's generation was rarely confronted with out-and-out explicit male chauvinism and she didn't know what to say, if she could say anything. Her legs steadied and she took a deep breath.

"I wasn't disarmed. I didn't drop my weapon until you Tasered me, you bastard."

"That's not how it looked to me," Perez said.

Father Francis said, "You allowed three men with knives in a jail cell with an unarmed man."

"I allowed nothing. I wasn't even here. I'll mount a full investigation. Back in the cell, Kincaid. You're still under arrest for breaking and entering."

Jack didn't move.

"My hand! Dammit, Art, she shot me!" the first knife-man was sitting against the wall, his T-shirt, now bloody, wrapped around his wrist.

"You're lucky you still have a hand," Megan snapped.

Hans said, "I have a warrant to take Mr. Kincaid into protective custody as a material witness." He handed it to the police chief. "I've also contacted the Rangers who said you hadn't informed them about Lawrence Bartleton's murder, which I believe is standard procedure.

They'll be here first thing in the morning to assist in the investigation."

"Standard procedure my ass," Perez said. "There's no mandate to call in the Rangers or the sheriff."

"But they should have been informed of the homicide," Hans said, not backing down. "And because this is connected to an ongoing federal investigation, I'll be talking to the U.S. attorney and the state D.A. about jurisdiction."

Perez clearly wanted to argue. Megan watched the veins in his neck throb. Rubbing her head, she felt an intense headache coming on. She was still shaking, but she had her wits about her.

In the end, Perez didn't say anything as the four of them walked out of the jail, through the lobby, and outside. The night breeze felt like heaven as Megan took off her blazer. Distant lightning lit the sky, followed by the roll of thunder.

"Sit," Jack told her, pushing her into the back of the Jeep in which Father Francis had picked them up at the airstrip. He slid in next to her.

The priest turned the ignition as Hans got in the passenger seat.

"What the fuck happened, Meg?" Hans turned to her as the Jeep sped away. "What were you doing in the jail cell? I told you to wait until I got the warrant."

"I heard a fight." She took a deep breath. "Do you have water in here?"

Jack reached into the small back storage of the Jeep and retrieved a water bottle. "It's warm."

"I don't care." She tried to unscrew the cap. "Damn."

"Your strength will come back." He took the plastic

bottle, opened the top, and handed it back to her. "Drink slow or you'll throw up."

She sipped. "You've been Tasered?"

"Once or twice."

"Why were you arrested?" Megan asked. Focusing on questions and answers kept her mind off the pain that made every nerve in her body throb.

"Perez thought I was breaking into Scout's house."

"Were you?"

"He didn't catch me."

"You did." Megan couldn't believe it. She felt like some sort of rebel, breaking a criminal out of prison.

"Would you like me to lie to you?"

"Why were those men trying to kill you? Don't they disarm prisoners before they put them in jail?"

"They weren't prisoners. They were Carlos Hernandez's goons."

"Who?"

"Carlos is a midlevel drug runner I pissed off."

"Where are we going?" Megan asked, looking at the scenery passing by. "Isn't that the church?"

"I'm taking you out to Jack's place. It's in the county, more private."

"I need to file a report," Megan said. "I discharged my weapon, and then—"

Hans interrupted, "I'll file the report. I'm the senior agent."

She felt belittled somehow, and Hans wasn't looking at her. What had she done wrong? She'd followed protocols—okay, she didn't wait for him, but she had reason to believe the life of a civilian, a potential witness, was in danger, she had to act. Hans would have done the same thing. Hell, he had *trained* her at Quantico; he would have been the first through the door had he been in her position.

"Hans, I didn't do anything wrong."

He pivoted and stared at her. "You nearly got killed."

"It wasn't that bad—"

"Dammit, Megan." He turned away from her again.

Hans was upset, but so was she. She didn't understand why he was treating her like this, why he sounded so angry. A life had been in danger, she acted. That was Megan's job. Perez's comment about being barefoot and in the kitchen made her tense again. Hans wasn't like that; he'd never treated her differently because she was a woman. At Quantico he demanded as much from her as from the men. He didn't let her slack off, and he respected her. Or so she'd thought.

She wished it was just her and Hans right now so she could get him to tell her why he was so upset. He'd been the closest thing to a father to her after her dad died. . . .

She was shivering. The air was warm, electric with the pending storm. She couldn't stop shaking and didn't know why she was so cold.

Jack reached over and rubbed her shoulders. "The tension isn't going to help you get over the shock. We have a twenty-minute drive. Relax, close your eyes. Let it go."

Relax? How could she relax with Hans angry at her? With Jack Kincaid sitting so close to her she could smell the soap he'd used in the shower. She felt the heat radiating off his body. His thigh pressed against hers in the small Jeep. She wanted to move away from him—she wanted to move closer. Put her head on his broad shoulder. His body was rock hard—all muscle, no fat. His face—dark, eyes probing, a day's growth of beard making him look even more dangerous. When he saw her looking at him, he winked. She turned her head and frowned.

Jack Kincaid's presence was overwhelming. Smart, sexy, confident. Too damn sure of himself. He'd almost gotten killed, and he was sitting here in the back of the Jeep, his arm draped over the back of her seat, as if nothing had happened—nothing too unusual anyway. She blamed her strange reaction to him on weakness—she'd been hit with a bolt of electricity. She absently rubbed her shoulder where the probes penetrated her skin.

Her problem was she liked confident men. She liked the smart guys. No, she told herself, Jack Kincaid was beyond confident. He was arrogant. Cocky.

He shifted in his seat and pulled the edge of her blouse from her neck. "You'll have a nasty bruise," he said, inspecting the punctures. "But you'll be back in action after a good meal and a night's sleep."

Attentive and sexy.

Don't think about him.

"You're shaking." Reaching into a box in the back, he pulled out a wool blanket. "Not a satin sheet, but it'll do the job." He wrapped it around her body, touched her hands. "Damn, Blondie, your hands are like ice cubes."

He brought her hands to his mouth and blew into them, then rubbed them in his large, very warm hands.

It was hard, impossible, to ignore Jack Kincaid when he was blowing hot air into her hands, when their bodies rubbed against each other as the Jeep bounced over the rough road. She tried to scoot away, but with every jolt of the Jeep, she was pushed back against him. He wrapped an arm around her and stuffed her hands into his leather bomber jacket. God, he was hot. Literally. A furnace . . .

She pulled her hands out as if they burned; he grabbed them again, turning stiffly in his seat, a faint grunt in his chest. Megan remembered his injuries. She'd been thinking about Jack the man, instead of Jack the victim. What was wrong with her?

She pulled one hand from his grasp and pushed up his chin, inspecting the cut. "They went for your throat." That ticked her off. Someone needed to answer for the attack on Jack Kincaid. "It doesn't look too deep."

"It's not."

She tore a small piece from her blouse, poured some of the water from her bottle onto it, and dabbed away the dried blood. She then wiped the blood from his face. His jaw tightened.

"Sorry," she said.

"It's not you, Blondie."

Blondie. "We weren't formally introduced. Megan Elliott."

"Jack Kincaid."

She nodded. "Were you stabbed?" She put her hand on the front of his shirt, feeling around for a wet spot that would indicate blood.

"No, but feel free to inspect anywhere you want."

She pulled her hand away and put it in her lap. "You were favoring your right side." She sounded like she was accusing him of something. She breathed deeply. *Megan Elliott, he's just a man.*

Jack Kincaid was not *just* anything.

"Paul got a jab in there, his fist, not a knife." He shifted again in his seat, obviously uncomfortable.

She was going to regret this, but she couldn't help herself. Jack was like her brother in that he'd never admit he was hurting. Matt had cracked a rib during a high school football game, and if it wasn't for her, he'd never have gone to the hospital until the bone had broken and punctured an organ or worse.

She pulled up Jack's shirt; he let her. She saw a bruise forming, but no blood. She ran her hands around his stomach to make sure there wasn't a life-threatening injury elsewhere. In the dark, with his darker complexion, she might not see any blood. His abdomen molded a perfect six-pack. She jerked her hand back, averted her face. What was she thinking?

Are you serious, Megan? You think Jack Kincaid would sit so casually if he were seriously injured? This man knows how to take care of himself.

Jack leaned over, his breath warm in her ear, sending first heat, then chills through her body. She blamed the sensation, and the distant memories it aroused, on being hit with a Taser. This was not normal. Not for her.

He wrapped the blanket tighter around her, holding her close to his side.

"I would have survived," he whispered. His lips touched her ear. On accident? On purpose? "But thanks for the backup. I'll have fewer scars because of you."

CHAPTER
FOURTEEN

Jack checked his perimeter and was satisfied that no one had been out here since he left two days ago. San Diego seemed so far away—the confrontation with his father, seeing his family again. Even his call last night to Dillon that brought the two feds into his world seemed long ago.

While some people went with high-tech security measures, Jack was old school. A string in the doorway, seemingly random props that weren't so random to see if anyone had rifled through his stuff. And a good old-fashioned safe, no computers to store important documents.

He brought out several bottles of water and beer to the table and watched Megan Elliott carefully. When she'd walked into the jail and announced herself as FBI, he had almost laughed—it seemed so Hollywood. While he hadn't liked the three-to-one odds, he was at his best when using his wits, and the three idiots Carlos had sicced on him would have been dispatched without the one-woman cavalry.

He touched his tender nose. Swollen, not broken. So he'd missed one or two well-aimed punches; the bastard broke a finger because he didn't know how to throw a punch in the first place, well worth the bruising Jack had.

The bridge in his mouth had been knocked loose, and he'd have to go see someone to fix it, unless he could convince Padre to pull out his old field kit. Padre could fix damn near anything, organic or mechanical.

The senior agent was angry and worried, and at first Jack thought there was something going on between Vigo and Megan, even with the fifteen-year, give or take, age difference. But he quickly ascertained that Agent Vigo was protective of Agent Elliott like a father would be to a daughter. Good.

Not good. Jack had no time to dally with a fed. Frankly, he hadn't had time for a personal life in years, and he didn't care to start up with someone who played too close to the rule book he'd tossed twenty years ago. Most feds followed those damn rules as if they were a sacred text. Otherwise, they walked, or ran, away, like his brother's girlfriend.

Megan Elliot was something else. She'd been damn scared when she walked in and saw the fight. All female cop—hip-hugging slacks and tailored blazer, her badge flashing, pinned to her slender waist. Long, long legs . . . tight ass . . . perfect tits. How the woman could look so damn sexy in clothes that concealed all that incredible, silky skin he didn't know.

Though scared and facing an unknown situation, she held her ground, exuding confidence and control. Taking charge. She'd told Padre to stand back. Jack smiled. Lieutenant Frank Cardenas, Delta Force. *"Stand back, Father!"*

Her unexpected arrival had given him a few precious

seconds to recover from the knife attack and had tipped the scales in his favor. A good gunner could do that, and she'd hit Jorge in the wrist without hesitation when he lunged with the knife.

God, he liked a woman who could shoot.

Beauty and brawn. What a combination.

He went to the bathroom to wash out the cuts that Blondie had tried to clean in the Jeep with her torn blouse and water. He wished she'd have gone lower than his abs with her soft hands . . .

The antiseptic wash burned enough to send all thoughts of the sexy fed and her roaming fingers from his mind.

"I'll do it."

Padre stepped into the bathroom and bandaged the cut. "Why'd you let him get so close?"

"Three against one."

"You're getting old, Jack."

"I didn't see you stepping up to the plate."

"I would have if I thought you were in real danger."

"Having my throat sliced and my nose whacked isn't enough?"

"It's a shallow cut, and your nose isn't broken. What's going on with Perez? Did he let Carlos take over?"

"Hell if I know, but I can't worry about the drug trade or Perez or Carlos when Scout's killer is out there."

"What's going on here? Serial killer? It doesn't make sense. How did Scout get on his radar?"

"I don't know. The feds may have the law on their side, but that's not going to help them if a soldier has gone off the deep end."

"You think one of ours did this?" Padre asked, shaking his head.

"I don't know. I don't know the other victims, but we need to find out how they connect to Scout. Because they do." Jack lowered his voice. "We find out what's been going on, then deal with it ourselves."

"Then why'd you call your brother for help?"

"Because he's the only one I could get information from about this so-called serial killer. Dillon thinks Vigo walks on water or something. Don't know anything about the woman, but I'll find out."

Jack made it a point of knowing everything about the people he worked with. Even when he planned on ditching them.

The FBI wouldn't be able to do squat about who killed Scout. They had strict rules, and all it took was one idiot and an entire conviction could be thrown out. They needed evidence, they needed to build a case, and while Jack believed in the system in principle, it didn't always work. He'd make sure the system worked this time. No one would get away with killing Scout, or the others.

As a soldier for his country, Jack had fought on the front lines for the rights of criminals as well as victims. Fighting for a country he believed in never used to bother him because he was a patriot first. Even with all its problems, it was still the best damn country in the world.

But because what was broke couldn't be easily fixed, Jack preferred his new approach: taking jobs where there was a clear bad guy, where he could make a difference—and he had the authority to do what was needed to protect the innocent.

And he was damn good at it.

After Padre patched up his neck and Jack took care of the minor cuts, he went back to his living area—kitchen, dining, and living all in one, with a bedroom and bath off to the side, and a loft upstairs where he preferred to sleep. Simple and functional.

Blondie had cleaned up well, he noted, using his kitchen sink. She'd taken off her blazer and her blouse, revealing a little creamy camisole that was too modest to be considered underwear, but sexy nonetheless, hinting at curves and peaks without showing anything. She'd taken her hair down from the twisty knot, and while she'd pinned the sides back, he was surprised at the length. Straight, very blond, and so silky it shimmered under the lights.

She caught him staring, and instead of blushing or averting her eyes she said, "If my attire bothers you, I'll put on my blouse, but considering it's wet—I washed out the blood before it stained—it might end up bothering you more."

"Nothing you wear, or don't wear, would bother me, Blondie."

"Megan," she said.

"Where are you from, Megan?" Padre asked.

"California. Sacramento."

"Sacramento?" Jack raised a brow. "You're a long way from home. I thought feds stayed in their own territory. Is this akin to doctors making house calls?"

"I had the third victim, but he was snatched from me by the military police. Because I have a familiarity with this case, and I have a background working serial murders, I was brought in to liaise with the individual FBI offices and the local police in order to collect evidence and track these killers."

"Well, that's—" He paused. "Killers?"

She nodded. "Two."

"How do you know that?"

"Evidence. Should we start at the beginning, or are you just going to ask me questions?"

Testy. And tired. Dark circles rimmed her eyes. Agent Vigo put a cup of coffee in front of her and a bowl of Frosted Flakes with milk. "You don't have a lot of food," Vigo said.

"I'm rarely home."

"You didn't have to—" Megan began.

Vigo interrupted. "Just eat. You were given a decent jolt, you need to keep your strength up. Considering we skipped dinner when Dillon called, this is probably your first meal since last night."

"I had something at the airport this morning," she grumbled, but ate the cereal. She smiled. "I haven't had Frosted Flakes since I was a kid."

Jack felt mildly uncomfortable having his provisions teased. He strode over to the coffeepot, where Vigo had made a very strong brew. He poured a cup, added sugar, and drank.

Vigo asked Padre, "How far are we from town? Twenty minutes?"

"More or less. Why?"

"We need to get a room. While Meg fills you in, I'll call for reservations."

"I don't know that you're going to find a room in town; there's only one motel I could even half-recommend. I'd offer the rectory, but it has only one guest room."

"You're all staying here tonight," Jack said. "It's not safe in town, though Perez is going to realize he made a huge mistake messing with the feds. I don't know if he let Carlos bring in his thugs, or whether Carlos is just getting cocky. Did you really call in the Rangers?" he asked Megan.

"Damn straight. Did you really break into the victim's house?"

"He didn't catch me breaking into anything," Jack evaded.

She said, "What did he catch you doing?"

"Walking on the grounds. He assumed I was going to break in."

"But you did enter," she said. "Before he got there. Why?"

He winked again.

Megan didn't know what to make of Jack Kincaid. He was unlike anyone she'd dealt with. More arrogant than her brother, which was quite the feat, but just as loyal. He needed to be in charge, she saw, and had probably been a leader in the military, though Hans said Jack had been enlisted not a career officer. Started with the Army Rangers, moved to Special Operations, then the elite Delta Force. He'd been honorably discharged ten years ago, but still trained with the Reserves. And he was a soldier for hire, something Megan knew a bit about through her brother's friendship with J. T. Caruso.

Hans said, "Okay, what's said in this room stays here. We're not here to arrest you, but I have to know that you're going to tell us the truth. These killers are targeting specific men—and so far, all known victims served in the U.S. Army. Two, at least, have been Delta Force trained. Not easy men to kill."

Megan pulled out a thick folder from her briefcase,

opened it. Turned the first photograph around. "Duane Johnson, served in the U.S. Army, rank corporal, 1986 to 2006. According to his friends, he was Delta, but we don't have military confirmation on that."

"You may or may not get it," Jack said.

She nodded. "I figured. I'm trusting his friends at this point, at least to the extent that we need to come up with a victimology and suspect profile. Johnson is likely the first victim, though there is some question on that. We're looking into a fatal home robbery in Florida as well—it may or may not be connected.

"Johnson was killed two months ago in Austin, Texas, hamstrung in his garage when he came home from closing his restaurant. No suspects, no prints, no DNA, no witnesses. Trace evidence is at the Texas State lab, but so far nothing has popped. They've agreed to send the trace to Quantico. Las Vegas agreed as well, and our scientists will work on connecting the evidence to the same person or persons.

"Johnson was tortured prior to his execution-style murder." She showed the crime scene photo of Johnson with the bullet to the head. "The coroner believes he was pierced with acupuncture-style needles, and although he can't say for certain, he believes that the locations were chosen to cause intense pain by stimulating specific nerves. There were one hundred nineteen known punctures on his skin, though there may have been more. These types of very small holes heal quickly and are also easy to miss in an exam."

She slid over the next photo. "Dennis Perry, 1995 to 2005. Both men were stationed out of Fort Bragg for all or part of their enlistment. We have confirmed that

Duane Johnson was Delta—as best we can because the military hasn't been forthcoming with information—and I suspect that Perry was as well. Las Vegas is our next stop. Same M.O.: hamstrung when he was entering his apartment, then tortured. He had something stuffed in his mouth, most likely to prevent him from calling out or screaming. There was a note on the report that some puncture wounds were from possible drug use. A low level of barbiturates were found in Perry's system, but no mention of multiple acupuncture-type markings. Doesn't mean they weren't there, but I don't know that after this long we'll be able to determine anything. Still, he was hamstrung, tortured in some manner, and had a broken nose. Then he was shot in the back of the head like Johnson. FBI ballistics now has the evidence, and we should get a confirmation in a day or so whether the bullets came from the same gun.

"Finally." She opened a second folder. Much thinner, mostly handwritten notes—hers. She showed the few pictures that she'd taken with her cell phone. "George Price. Homeless veteran in Sacramento. Early Monday morning, I got a call from Sac P.D. about a murder that matched an FBI hot sheet connecting the Johnson-Perry homicides. I run the Violent Crimes Squad, so I went to the scene.

"Price's murder had the same M.O.: hamstrung, but he was homeless and attacked in an alley late Sunday night. Downtown Sacramento rolls up the sidewalks at night, and after midnight on Sunday, no one is out. At least no one with honorable intentions. Price was carried—this is how we know there were at least two people involved—into a parking garage, where we believe he was tortured in a similar manner to Johnson and Perry."

"Carried? How did you figure that?" Jack asked.

"From the drops of blood. They were consistent with the victim being carried by two people," Megan said. "The size and spacing of blood evidence, plus the scrapes on his bare feet, indicated that he'd been picked up by the armpits and carried.

"It's a theory," she added, backtracking a bit. "But it's supported by the evidence we have."

"I'm not questioning your theory," Jack said. "Just curious how you came to the conclusion."

Megan nodded, but wasn't sure exactly what anyone was thinking. Was she wrong about the two killers? Had she read the evidence incorrectly? Been swept away by Simone Charles's confidence? Saw what Simone saw, and nothing else?

Hans spoke. "There is at least one key difference. Price was AWOL since 2004, wanted for the attempted murder of his commanding officer. When we ran his I.D., CID came down on us hard. Took the body and evidence."

"You have the photos."

Megan shrugged. "I saw something and the photographer had moved on."

Jack raised an eyebrow, and Megan ignored him. She said, "I learned through a friend with contacts at CID that Price didn't die from the head shot. He had a heart attack. Either the killers knew he was dead, and shot him to make his murder identical in M.O. to the others—meaning that they want us to know they are choosing these victims, laying down bread crumbs so to speak—

or it was overkill. They had to do it because they are obsessive-compulsive. Complete the cycle, execute the plan to the letter."

Hans nodded. "I think the shooter had to follow through, the exact same way. He couldn't do anything but."

Megan shook her head. "I think the shooter did it because he wants us to know that Price connects to Perry and Johnson. And now your friend."

"Why?" Hans said. "It's classic OCD behavior. The killer had to perform according to the script. Like you said, execute the plan to the letter."

"Yeah, but . . . the dog tags." She looked at Hans, then turned to Jack. "The killers sent part of Price's identification plate to my attention. They want to make damn sure that we know Price is part of the puzzle. It's a message, and when we figure out the code we'll know who did it."

"And Scout was just another victim."

"I'm sorry about your friend," Megan said. Jack was staring at her, and the pain of his friend's death hit her in her heart. Jack Kincaid was more than an arrogant soldier, he was also a compassionate soul who'd lost someone close to him.

"Father?"

When Hans spoke, Megan and Jack both averted their eyes and turned to Father Francis. He looked stricken.

Jack questioned, "Padre?"

Megan raised her eyes at the concern in Jack's word. "Father Francis, what's wrong? Do you know any of these men?"

He looked from Megan to Jack. "I knew all of them."

CHAPTER
FIFTEEN

Jack ran a hand over his face, walked over to the window, and stared into the darkness. The storm that had been threatening all night had just started to drop its load of rain. It would come down hard for an hour or two, then stop. Dawn should be clear, though another storm was heading their way. As he listened to Padre talk, Jack knew Padre was on the kill list. All he could think about was what had happened to turn someone against an entire special forces team.

"I've known Scout for nineteen years—same as Jack," Padre said. "Jack and I were in the Rangers together, both of us young and stupid."

"I wasn't stupid," Jack said automatically, though there was no humor in the joke he'd repeated a hundred times.

"Met Scout two years later when he transferred in from Virginia."

"With the dog," Jack said.

Padre nodded. "Scout had a thing for dogs. That mutt almost got him court-martialed."

"Scout tried to convince our sergeant that the dog just showed up one morning."

"Hannibal didn't believe him, but he let the dog stay."

"Drew the line on letting the mutt come on tour."

Padre smiled sadly. "I didn't know Duane until after Jack left. I was thinking of going as well . . ."

"But?" Hans said.

"I was fighting the call."

"The call?" Megan asked.

Padre pointed heavenward.

She blushed slightly and glanced downward. Jack would have been more intrigued by her embarrassment and blush, and wondering how else he could bring color to her pale face, if he wasn't so worried about Padre.

"Ten years ago. I moved to another unit, hooked up with Johnson and Perry. Duane was solid. Perry had a drug problem. Could be an asshole, but when push came to shove, he always came through. Thornton was also on the team."

"Thornton? Where can we find him?"

"He's dead. Died during an operation five years ago. We'd been on at least two dozen missions together, but when Thornton died that was my final mission. I asked for a discharge, got it, and joined the seminary. Rejoined, I should say. I'd been in for two years before but that's another story."

Jack squeezed Padre's shoulder. "Price?"

"Scout knew him well. We called George Price 'Princeton' because he dropped out of some Ivy League college to enlist. He and Scout worked together before."

"Was it just six of you?"

"Eight. Last I heard, Jerry Jefferson was still overseas. Afghanistan. Re-upped four or five times."

"And?"

"The team leader, Ken Russo."

"Russo?" Megan dropped a set of papers on the floor, then gathered them up.

"He's dead, isn't he?" Padre said.

"I'm sorry," Megan said. "It may not be connected."

"You think it is," Jack said.

"It could be a coincidence, but in light of everything else . . . we're going to pull all the files and ballistics reports. He died ten months ago during an apparent home robbery. No one was charged."

"I need to warn Jerry," Padre said.

"Of course," Hans said. "Better coming from you. Do you know how to contact him?"

"Yes. I'll take care of it."

"Wait," Megan said. All eyes turned to her. "Are you sure Jefferson is still in Afghanistan?"

"Last I heard," Padre said.

"What are you implying?" Jack interrupted.

"Other than Father Francis, Jefferson is the only member of that Delta unit who is still alive. He may not be a potential victim."

Padre shook his head. "I will vouch for Jefferson. He wouldn't kill in cold blood, not his people. Not Scout."

"We have to consider every possibility," Megan said.

Hans added, "I don't have to tell either of you that soldiers have the highest incidence of post-traumatic stress syndrome—"

"No!" Padre slammed his fist on the table. Jack turned his head. The priest rarely lost his temper. Conflict and anger gave his hard-lined face an ominous expression.

Jack didn't want to agree with the feds, in fact, he didn't agree with them, but he also understood that they had a job to do.

"We'll do our job, Padre. They need to do theirs."

"What do you plan to do?" Padre asked, biting down on each word. "Not warn him?"

"Of course not," Megan said. "He could be in danger, but if he's still in Afghanistan he's probably safer there than here. We need to look at his movements, however, and if he's in the States . . ."

She didn't have to finish. Jack nodded curtly while Padre quietly tamped down on his temper. "I'll find him," he said.

"Did you know any of the other victims, Jack?" Megan cleared her throat. She was upset that Padre was distressed, but she didn't back down. Jack liked that.

"Just Scout." Jack looked squarely at Padre. "Frank, I'm calling in Tim, Mike, and Lucky. None of them were Delta, so they're not targets—if I can believe you," he glanced at Megan and Vigo, "which I'm inclined to do on this point."

"Don't call," Padre said. "I know there's a threat, I'll watch my back."

Jack's voice dropped and he said through clenched teeth, "I'm not going to let you die like Scout."

"You didn't let him die."

Padre didn't understand. Scout had been Jack's responsibility. He should never have stayed the night in San Diego. If he'd returned sooner, he could have stopped it.

"Don't push me, Frank. You're not going solo. The guys will skin me alive if I don't call them in. We're still brothers; that's never going to change."

When Padre gave his silent assent, Jack sighed a margin of relief.

"I'll go back to the rectory with Father Francis," Vigo said.

"No." Jack didn't want to offend the FBI agent, but he looked about fifty, had a bit of a belly, and frankly, Jack didn't know him. Could he even protect himself, let alone a Delta-trained sniper like Frank Cardenas?

"Then I'll go," Megan said.

"Don't be ridiculous." Who did she think she was? Wonder Woman?

"I get it." She started putting her files together and shoving them back in her briefcase.

He expected her to explain herself, all women did, often ad nauseum. He had three sisters. He knew a bit about women.

She didn't explain. She grabbed her blouse, felt that it was still wet, and stuffed it unceremoniously into the side pocket of her briefcase. She pulled the blazer over her camisole, and somehow, the entire process only made her look sexier, when her purpose was clearly to show she wasn't going to be manipulated or placated.

"Father, the three of us will go back to the rectory. We need you to write down every operation you worked with those seven men. Every place you went, any other people you worked with, failures as well as successes. Your friend Jefferson is probably a target; we need to contact him immediately and see if he can fill in any blanks. But if he's in the States, we need to bring in a team to find him."

"No," Jack repeated. Didn't they get it? "You're all in danger: Padre from a serial killer, and you two from Perez."

"Perez has cooled down," Megan said. "He's not so stupid as to send anyone after two federal agents, and he doesn't have a death wish to do it himself." She turned to Padre, ignoring Jack. "You are the only one we know who has information we need to help figure out why these men were targeted."

Vigo nodded. "Between official and unofficial channels," he nodded toward Megan—and Jack couldn't help but wonder if maybe Blondie wasn't the straight-laced, rule-playing fed he'd first thought—"we should be able to piece together the victims' service records and find any common points. They were selected for a reason, and when we know *why* we'll know *who*."

"Thank you for the cereal," Megan said and started toward the door. "Father Francis, we can put you in protective custody while we work on this. There's no reason you should feel threatened or—"

Jack shook his head, laughing. "Oh, this is rich. The feds putting a Delta-trained sniper in protective custody."

"Jack," Padre snapped.

"They have rules and procedures. How the hell do we know we can trust them or anyone in their office? How did the killers find those men? How did they trace a homeless guy who went AWOL? The killers have too much fucking information about our people. Someone has been talking or one of the killers is someone high up the food chain. High enough to know where Price was hiding out. The feds have no idea who to trust. Dammit, I'll go with you. I'm not letting you out of my sight unless someone *I* trained is covering your back."

Padre turned to him. "Jack, you want to find Scout's killer as much as I do. What I know can help."

"Stay here," Jack said.

"I have Mass in the morning. I can't stay." He held his hand up when Jack tried to protest. "And don't suggest for one minute that I cancel Mass. I know it was on the tip of your tongue. I'm going to do my job. You do yours. Work with them. Agent Elliott did a good job covering your ass tonight; I think they'll be fine."

"Blondie doesn't know who she's up against."

Megan dropped her briefcase on the wood floor. "First, do *not* talk about me as if I am not in the room. Second, you may call me Meg, or Megan, or Agent Elliott, or Your Royal Highness, but do not call me Blondie." She turned to Vigo. "*You're* the senior agent; what are we doing?"

Jack could see that asking anyone what to do got under Agent Megan Elliott's skin. She was used to being in charge, making the rules, not following them. Well, so was he. And he wasn't going to relinquish command to a feisty blond cop. Though it would be fun to watch her try to wrestle control away from him.

Hans looked a bit sheepish. "Meg, I'm sorry, I only said that because I was worried about what happened in the jail—" He stopped as he saw that he was digging himself farther into a hole that Megan's silence was widening. Her silence and her piercing green glare.

Yowza.

Vigo glanced at his watch. "It's two-thirty in the morning. What do you think, Meg?"

She took off her blazer and draped it over a chair. "We'll crash the Jeep in sheer exhaustion, though I'm sure the Delta studs here"—she jerked her thumb in Jack's direction—"will claim that they don't need sleep, food, or water and are still functioning human beings. We'll leave at dawn, in time to get Father Francis back for his obligations—if that's okay with you, Father."

Padre nodded. Jack shot him a look. Ten minutes ago

he had everything under control. How had he lost it to Megan?

Yet he was getting exactly what he wanted: the four of them under his roof so he could protect them and monitor the situation.

"As soon as Mass is over, we need to sit down and start on that list," Megan continued. "And when the Rangers arrive, we'll make contact and get a copy of the evidence, autopsy report, and witness statements regarding Scout's homicide. Someone saw something. These killers aren't invisible men."

"Good plan," Vigo said.

Jack realized that if he wanted to regain control and protect those he cared about, he'd better earn the respect and the ear of Agent—Supervisory Special Agent—Megan Elliott.

"Fine," Jack said. "Then I guess the only question is where everyone is going to sleep. Ladies choice: where would you like to bed down, Your Royal Highness?"

Ethan hadn't slept well. The cheap motel room's laboring air conditioner made the hot air only more humid. The nightmares had been followed by an odd lull, a peace he should have enjoyed but instead it terrified him.

Dawn came too bright, too fast, in the rearview mirror. Hours ago they'd left Benson, Arizona, passed through Tucson, and were now . . . where? He didn't know. I-10 was endless, a ribbon of asphalt in a bleak, dry desert. Another time he would have appreciated the contours and colors, the vastness and the vistas. Now he wanted to bury himself in a hole and die. Take a handful of pills and disappear forever.

He needed to die. But the fucking *bitch* stopped him every time he had a gun to his head, a knife on his wrists, ready to fade away, painless, thoughtless. She said she cared. He started laughing again.

"Ethan?"

He swallowed the laughter, but it squeaked out in a feminine giggle. "What?"

"What's wrong?"

"Nothing." What *wasn't* wrong? He stared at his hands on the wheel of the truck. They looked foreign to him. Were these *his* hands? Had they given him new hands? Hands that could hurt, torture, kill? Maybe the restraints they'd used had cut off his hands at the wrists, and they sewed on his tormentor's fists. That's why he knew where to poke, where to press the needle into the flesh. A fraction of a millimeter off and the pain was only as irritating as a bee sting. But when the nerve was stimulated just so . . .

He screamed and let go of the wheel.

"Ethan!"

He barely heard her voice. He was drowning, his lungs unable to draw in air. His scream continued, he was helpless. He couldn't stop. They were killing him . . .

Real pain cut through the vision. His mouth shut. Her hands were on the steering wheel, keeping the truck in their lane. His foot was on the accelerator flat to the floor. They rapidly approached the rear of a minivan.

He glanced at the odometer. Death at 110 miles per hour. Yes. Sixty more seconds and splat, all over the desert. Him and her, gone instantly. Just. Like. That.

She turned the wheel and put them into the eastbound lane, barely missing a collision with the minivan. The car they passed honked at them. Ethan glanced over, saw the kids in the back of the car. The infant seat.

They didn't care about him. Not when he was imprisoned, not when he was freed. He was nobody.

His foot eased up on the accelerator—100 mph . . . 90 mph . . . 80 mph. He hovered between seventy-five and eighty miles per hour and only then did Karin take her hands off the wheel.

Biting his lip—he didn't notice how hard until he tasted blood—he glanced at her. She'd dyed her hair again. When? She was dark blond when they'd met. Then brown. Now . . . blond. How had she done that? When? In the motel? He didn't remember. She was prettier as a blond. Softer. As a brunette, she looked unreal, like everything he saw, as if in a dream. Now she was crisper. Real. Not a figment of his imagination.

Or was she? Had he made her up? Where had she come from?

"Let's get breakfast," she said. "There's a diner on the other side of the California border. Quiet. Thirty minutes."

He shrugged. If she was real, she didn't understand him. If she was unreal, he didn't understand himself. He would have laughed, but deep sadness overwhelmed him. Tears burned his eyes. She should love him, but she didn't. She said she did, but she was using him. The thought came to him so clearly, he had a flash of sanity. For one minute he remembered who he was deep down, who he had been before. It was like watching the *Wizard of Oz* change from black and white to Technicolor. Vivid, clear, awesome . . . frightening.

For him, horrifying.

He blinked rapidly, the color giving way to shades of

gray, then to nothing. Nothing but the steering wheel and the endless road.

"Ethan, it's okay."

He drove in silence. What would she do if he tied her down and really hurt her? He knew things he hadn't shown her. Places on her body that would bring her such pain she would beg him to kill her. And he wouldn't. He would let her suffer as she let him suffer. Alive.

"I'm sorry, " Ethan said.

"It's okay, baby. It's okay." She touched him like a lover, fingers soft on his skin. She kissed his cheek. "It's going to be okay. Exit up ahead. You need a good meal."

He followed her orders and stopped at the roadside diner in Blythe. Ethan didn't talk as they ordered. The woman—Ethan wasn't quite sure what her name was—talked about nothing while they ate.

"When are we going to be in Santa Barbara?" he interrupted.

"Five, six hours. Depends on traffic."

"Okay."

She said, "You have to be extra careful. We're almost done. What if the minivan driver you almost hit took down our plates? Called the cops? We're too close. I can't risk screwing this up."

"I'm sorry." And he was. "Don't hate me."

The woman touched his hand. Ethan didn't feel it, but he saw her fingers rub his palm. Why didn't he feel them?

She's not real, right?

"I don't hate you," she said. "I love you, you know that."

He nodded.

As they were leaving the diner, a man approached. He was short, stocky, balding, and wore small wire-rimmed glasses. The stranger pushed Ethan in the chest. Ethan took a step back and looked down at the man. "Hey."

"You should have your license revoked!" the man yelled.

"I'm so sorry." Ethan looked at the blond standing next to him, apologizing profusely. Did he know her? Of course. Yes.

"My husband has been driving all night," she said, "and I was supposed to keep him awake, but I fell asleep. I know we should have pulled over, but my mom . . ."

Tears slid down her cheeks. Ethan had never seen her cry. She looked like a sad angel. His angel. He wanted to protect her, take care of her. He put his arm around her. She put her face in his shoulder.

The man glared at them, but stepped back. His wife, a pretty woman devoid of makeup, took his arm. "Don't make a scene, Ned. It's okay."

"No, it's not," the blond wept.

"Where are the kids?"

"Eddie is with them. It's okay." She smiled nervously at Ethan. "We're sorry to bother you."

The blond said—What was her name? Carrie? Annie? Kelly? No, nothing like that. Ethan couldn't remember. She was a stranger.

"No, I'm sorry. Mom had a heart attack yesterday and we've been driving all night from Houston. I have to see her before—" She took a deep breath.

Ethan thought her mom was already dead. She wasn't a stranger. He squeezed his temples. His head pounded like he had a hangover.

"Let's go, honey. The coffee will keep us going until we reach San Francisco."

"I thought we were going to Santa Barbara."

She squeezed his arm so tightly he would have yelped, except it felt too good.

"San Francisco." She shook her head and said to the strangers, "My mom moved last year. John never liked her, and—" More tears rolled out. "John, I need to go. Please."

Who was John?

She pulled Ethan out of the restaurant and back to the truck. She had the keys.

"Get in the backseat and close your eyes. You are screwing everything up!"

Ethan obeyed. There was a blanket on the floor. He pulled it around him. He was so cold.

He fell asleep before they reached the interstate.

CHAPTER
SIXTEEN

Megan called J. T. Caruso at seven Thursday morning while Hans was on the phone with Quantico and Father Francis was celebrating Mass in the church. At that moment, she didn't know where Jack Kincaid was, and that was probably a good thing. She was too aware of his presence, of the way he looked at her, of his quiet arrogance and intense loyalty. The latter two reminded her too much of the men she respected more than anyone, her father and her brother. She'd instantly felt an odd kinship with the mercenary; yet at the same time was acutely aware that he was *not* related to her.

"It's five o'clock in the morning," J.T. answered unceremoniously.

"I know." She'd forgotten about the time difference. "It's important, and I don't have a lot of time."

"Now you really owe me one. I'm going to be off-stride for the rest of the day."

She doubted that. "I'm sorry."

"Tell me."

She filled him in on what she knew—and what she didn't know. "I need information on Jack Kincaid, Francis Cardenas, and Jerry Jefferson," she concluded. "I need to make sure that what I know is accurate."

"Don't you have paid staff to run background

checks? I know budget cuts are hard, but I didn't realize how bad."

"Please, J.T. The wheels of the bureaucracy grind slowly. I need this information before I retire."

He let out a brief laugh. "Kincaid. Common name. Jack. Even more common. Jerry Jefferson? Really, Meg. I'm good, but I need a little more."

She looked at the notes she'd written when Hans had filled her in on the plane trip down the night before. "Jack Kincaid, thirty-nine, father is Patrick Kincaid, Senior, retired colonel, U.S. Army. His brother Dr. Dillon Kincaid is a civilian consultant for the FBI at Quantico. Jack enlisted when he was eighteen, based in Texas— Army Rangers. I don't have anything about his service, except that he went to Fort Bragg at some point and trained for Delta Force. He left ten or so years ago and is now a soldier for hire based in Hidalgo, Texas."

"What type of mercenary work?"

"Primarily hostage rescues in Central America, according to what I've learned, but I don't have independent confirmation. He's at least bilingual—Spanish and English—and I suspect he might know other languages."

"Suspect?"

"He has a lot of books, not all in English and Spanish, and I don't think they're for show."

"One of the Rogans should know of him. Why?"

"He's a potential victim of our killer. And he has weaseled himself into my investigation." She didn't honestly believe Jack was a possible victim, though she suspected Francis Cardenas was in danger. But it sounded better than her simply wanting to know everything about Jack Kincaid because he'd gotten under her skin.

Besides, she was running a murder investigation. She had every right to know about Kincaid.

"Anything else?"

She gave him what little she knew about Father Cardenas and his friend Jerry Jefferson. "Jefferson is supposedly still enlisted and stationed in Afghanistan. I need to make sure. If not—"

"He's in danger."

"Or a killer."

"Is it always black or white with you?"

"Are there other colors?"

"You think a priest is involved?"

"I think he's a target. I want to get him into a safe house, but he refuses to leave his church. Somehow thinks that because he's a big bad former Delta warrior he's invulnerable."

"All of us special forces 'warriors' are invincible," J.T. said. "I thought you knew that."

She sighed. "Right. You bleed just as red as the rest of us, J.T. The four known victims were all Delta trained, I remind you. I don't suppose you've heard from Kane yet."

"Not yet. I'm on it, Meg. Be careful. Matt is ticked that you've been calling me and not him."

"I'm thirty-eight years old, I don't need to call my big brother every day."

"But you'll do it because he'll worry."

"Right, as soon as I can. Thanks, J.T."

She hung up.

"So who has the privilege of giving my life a rectal exam?"

She jumped and whirled around. Jack Kincaid stood against the wall, trying to look casual yet was anything but. He was angry. She was embarrassed that she hadn't noticed he was standing there. Talk about stealth . . .

"You're a potential target, and—"

"Bullshit. All you had to do was ask me."

"I don't know *what* to ask."

"You sure knew what to ask J.T. J.T. who? Some snot-nosed desk nerd at Quantico running me through his fancy computer database?"

"That would be Harrison Ng," she retorted. "I decided to keep this off the books."

"Off the books?" He took a step toward her. "Dragging my name, and my life, through some slimy private investigator? A former cop maybe? Your lover?"

"What's with the attitude, Jack? You'd do the same thing in my shoes. And I'm not going to apologize for doing my job. I'm not going to violate your privacy."

"You already have."

This was important to him, Megan realized. His privacy, his anonymity. He lived in the far reaches of a distant county next to a depressed border town where he was smarter and sharper than the entire police force put together. She couldn't help but wonder why he chose to live here, why he had become a soldier for hire, why he'd distanced himself from mainstream society.

"J. T. Caruso. He's a principal with Rogan-Caruso Protective Services, and a good friend of the family. He and my brother were Navy SEALs together. When I say this is off the books, it's way off the books."

Jack's anger faded away. Not just because he had heard of Rogan-Caruso—and had taken a few assignments from Kane Rogan—but because Megan was sincerely contrite, flatly honest, and she didn't back down. This was her job. He had to remember that. Her job was going to come first. It was helpful now, but later . . . later he would have to re-evaluate.

"I called in Lucky, one of my team members. He's going to sit on Padre twenty-four/seven. Tim is coming down from San Antonio as well, and I even got Mike coming in. They'll be here tonight. It's probably a good thing, with Perez showing his true colors yesterday, and Hernandez sending his goons after me."

He stepped closer to Megan. She had changed clothing, but he couldn't tell much difference. Another blouse, another cami peaking out, tailored slacks. Low-heeled boots. He liked the shoulder holster she wore. Most female cops he knew wore their guns on their belt. Her hair was tied up in the back, like she'd had it yesterday when she burst into the jail cell to save him. He had no idea how she got that much hair to stay in place. He'd like to watch her put it up sometime. And take it down.

His eyes betrayed his thoughts. Megan flushed slightly, her red lips parted to reveal straight white teeth. Her green eyes darkened, then glanced almost demurely downward. She blinked, then looked at him, expertly hiding her reaction to his close proximity.

Before she could say anything snappy or formal, Jack touched her on the shoulder where the Taser darts had penetrated. "I noticed you were bruised last night. Does it still hurt?" Jack wanted to deck Perez for firing the damn Taser at Megan. Not just because she was a fed. Not just because she was a woman. But because she was . . .

What? What exactly is Megan Elliott to you, Jack?

No one. Blondie was no one to him, and he needed to remember that.

"Not much. Funny thing was, I've never been hit with a Taser before, and I swear, it hurt more than the time I was shot."

"Shot? Where?" He'd seen a lot of her skin the night before. White, creamy, perfect. He hadn't seen a bullet scar.

Her face changed, dramatically, from light to very, very dark. Bad memories. He recognized the transformation and wanted to know the circumstances of the shooting.

"Kidney," she said quickly, her hand unconsciously moving to her lower right side. "But God gave us two just in case someone shoots you in the back, right?"

She was trying to lighten it up, but Jack saw that her mind was years in the past. He wanted to know who shot her and why. Was she on the job or not?

Padre came into the kitchen. "I saw a Ranger's truck drive past as I was leaving the church. They were headed toward the police station."

"That's my cue," Megan said. "I'll find Hans and gather as much information as we can about Scout's murder, and then come back here and talk about what you remember, Padre."

Jack stole a glance at her. Did she even notice she'd adopted the nicknames of his friends? He didn't think she did. She spoke smoothly. He actually liked it, she'd personalized the case, which meant, at least to Jack, that she cared about the people involved. Even Scout. A drunk, but a loyal soldier. A friend. Damn. Jack didn't want to think about him being dead.

"Agent Elliott—" Padre began.

"Call me Megan, okay?"

"Can you find out about Scout's body? I want to have

a funeral and arrange for his body to be transported to Arlington."

"Of course."

Jack said in a rough voice, "He wanted to be cremated."

"I remember," Padre said.

"I'll let them know," Megan said. "There should be no reason you can't have the body by the weekend."

Hans drove Father Francis's Jeep to the police station and parked next to the Ranger truck. He hadn't said anything to her the entire ride, and Megan couldn't help but worry that she'd overstepped her bounds last night or this morning or . . . when?

"Are we okay?" she asked when they stopped. She looked up at the sky. A dark blanket of clouds blocked out the sun, but still no rain since the brief downpour last night. A flash of lightning made Megan jump, and the responding thunder had her grabbing the dashboard.

"I should be asking that."

"I'm fine." She hated storms. She'd spent two months in New Orleans after Katrina. Her experience in Kosovo identifying the remains of the dead had been invaluable in Louisiana, and while she'd been good and much in demand at that distasteful job, it had been emotionally and physically devastating. Ever since, she dreaded storms, knowing that floods and levees breaking and high winds created not only property damage, but extensive human casualties.

"Meg?"

"I just need to know that we're okay."

"Of course we are."

"You acted like I was a dumb rookie last night. What did I do wrong?"

"I don't know, I wasn't there—"

"But you assumed I did something wrong." It hit her hard.

"No. That's not what I meant."

"Then what?"

Hans ran his hand through his thick head of salt-and-pepper hair. "I was scared to death. I care about you, Meg. Too much, I know. It's more than a partnership."

Meg's stomach churned and her face burned. "Hans . . . I . . ."

He laughed, took her hands. "Oh, God, Meg, you should see your face." He squeezed her hands and said, "I love you like a little sister. Hell, I'm almost old enough to be your father."

"Hardly. You'd have been a very young dad." But she smiled. "Okay. As long as we're good."

"I overstepped last night, and I'm sorry."

"No apologies. I understand. I would have done the same if the situation was reversed."

"I don't know if I would have had the courage you showed last night."

"Courage? I don't know about that." She'd been as scared for herself as she was angry at the sheriff as she was fearful that she'd have to use lethal force.

"Courage doesn't mean you're not scared."

"I know," she said firmly, though she wasn't quite sure about that. "I've run the scene through my head a dozen times and I can't see any other way to have done it."

"Then you did it right. Besides, even if you did think of a better way, you can't go Monday-morning quarterbacking your split-second decisions. You're one of the best on your feet, Meg."

She jumped when the thunder rolled again. "Let's go in and talk to the Rangers."

They got out of the Jeep and she added, "I called J. T. Caruso and asked him to quietly look into Jack and Father Francis. I don't think there's anything suspicious about them, but I need to cover all the bases."

"I've already talked to Quantico about them." Hans sounded contrite.

"You had to."

"Jack's brother Dillon is a good friend. I don't like going behind anyone's back."

"Well, I didn't. Jack overheard part of my conversation, so I told him exactly what I was doing." She paused. "What do you think of Jerry Jefferson? Did you find him?"

"Working on it. I'm going off Father Francis's knowledge that he's in Afghanistan. I should know exactly where within the next couple hours."

"If he's not there?"

"Then we'll find him."

The two Rangers were standing outside the main entrance, one smoking a cigarette. Hans extended his hand and flashed his badge. "Assistant Special Agent in Charge Hans Vigo, FBI. My partner SSA Megan Elliott."

The Rangers tipped their hats. "Pleasure." The smoker was Rich Barker; the quiet Ranger was Ted Hern.

Hans glanced at the station, then pointed to the threatening sky. "Is there a problem here? Where's Perez?"

"Hasn't come in yet," Barker said, taking a drag on

his cigarette. "So the Hamstring Killer hit Hidalgo. You sure?"

"As sure as we can be without seeing the evidence or the body," Megan said. "We're going off a witness who saw the body and recognized the M.O. from a news report."

"Ain't surprised Perez didn't call us."

"Problems?"

"Territorial."

"Have you had problems with him in the past?" Megan asked.

"Here and there. We keep a close eye on the town. It's a border town. There's a strong drug trade, other issues. Perez isn't part of the real problem, but he sure ain't part of the solution.

"So we just wait?" Hans was getting antsy; normally he was the patient one.

"We had the desk sergeant call Perez. He should be here any minute."

Megan said, "Unless he wants to make you wait, just to flex his muscles."

"He'll be here. We have jurisdiction; we can walk in when we want. We're just playing nice."

Hern said, "You came all the way from D.C.?"

"Quantico," Hans corrected. "Megan's from Sacramento. She pulled the third victim. The killers are escalating."

"We read the hot sheet y'all sent over," Barker said. "Ted, you were Delta, right?"

Ted Hern nodded.

"Did you know any of the victims?"

"Only Scout. Bartleton," Hern said. "But not until he moved here to join Kincaid's men a few years back."

A truck turned onto the street and sped into the lot. Art Perez, in uniform, jumped out and put on his hat. "Rangers, this wasn't necessary."

"Art," Ted tipped his hat. "Let's go look at what you've got on the Lawrence Bartleton homicide."

Perez looked from Hans to Megan and back to the Rangers. "As I told Lieutenant Gray last night, I'm certain that Bartleton was taken down by one of the Guatemalan rebels Kincaid's group has been battling. They just returned from an unofficial operation not three days before the murder. And—"

"Gray? You mean Scott Gray?" Barker nodded to Hern. "Were Kincaid and the lieutenant at boot camp together, or was it Desert Storm where they hooked up? No matter, Scott tells the story to anyone who'll listen, how Kincaid, then just an Army Ranger, saved his ass when he walked into the middle of a minefield without detonating a single one, but got trapped. Damnedest thing, really, but Kincaid hotwires a Chinese chopper, never even flew one before, and lowered a rope for Scott to grab on to. The bastard almost got himself killed in the process, but hell, they all came away without a scratch."

Hern nodded. "I don't see Kincaid leaving loose ends in Guatemala."

Perez reddened. "Kincaid isn't a saint. He was arrested for obstructing justice."

"How so?" Hans asked.

At the invitation to expand, Perez went off. "He's been all over town asking questions as if he were a cop. Talking to everyone who was at El Gato, where Scout was drinking the night he was killed. He even had one of his mercenaries track down three college kids from UTSA and interrogate them! He's been asking everyone about this woman who was in the bar, he attacked one of the bar owners, and he threatened one of my deputies. I've been saying since he came to town that Jack Kincaid is dangerous, but just because he's friends with the *priest,* no one listens. I caught him red-handed at the crime scene after the fact. He wouldn't tell me why, and it supports my argument that he brought back trouble to Hidalgo from Central America, and he's trying to cover it up." Perez was red in the face when he was done, but satisfied that he'd finally gotten his thoughts off his chest.

Barker said, "Hidalgo has plenty of trouble all on its own."

"What woman?" Megan asked. "Have you followed up with the bar owners? What did they say—"

"Go ahead and talk to them yourself. My reports are all filed." Perez opened the door and said to the desk sergeant, "Jorge, let them have the Bartleton files and anything else they want to see." He glanced at Megan, then turned to the Rangers and said, "You think Kincaid is a saint? Go pull my file on him."

"If you had anything on Kincaid, he'd be in jail," Barker said.

Perez stared at Megan. "He was." Then he left.

"He certainly doesn't like Jack," Hans said thoughtfully.

"Was anything he said true?" If Jack knew something that would help in this investigation, why didn't he say something? Megan didn't like being deceived or manipulated.

The desk sergeant led them to the evidence room and put the files in front of them.

An hour later, Megan stood up and stretched. Perez

had spent more time tracing Jack's steps than following his own investigation. And Jack had done what she'd have done were she investigating the murder. But he wasn't a cop, and he had overstepped his bounds. Perez had some justifiable reasons to arrest him, though certainly not to allow three armed men in to attack him. Meg wasn't sure the chief of police hadn't known about that.

"There's not much here," Barker said. "Perez was more interested in following Kincaid; that's where all the info came from. We should talk to him."

"He's at the rectory," Hans said. "We've been working with him."

But he didn't share this information with us. She didn't know what, if anything, Jack had learned about Scout's murder, but she had a few choice words for him. If he didn't answer her questions right she'd put him in jail herself.

Barker stuffed a piece of gum in his mouth and said, "Perez fucked up the collection of evidence. How could he let so many people contaminate the crime scene? The kid, the kid's mother—"

Hern said, "She was Scout's girlfriend."

"—the priest, Kincaid, a half dozen cops. I swear, half of Hidalgo walked through that house before Perez sealed off the place."

Hans said, "My boss has given us priority use of the trace evidence lab, just let me know what you need. They're already working on two of the other murders and maybe something will come from this one that will help.

Hern said, "We appreciate the help."

"There's no autopsy report," Megan said. "Wouldn't the autopsy have been done by now?"

"I'll ask the sergeant," Barker said and left the evidence room.

"Is the body here?" Megan asked.

"Probably up in Edinburg, at the morgue. Twenty minutes or so north."

Megan glanced at Hans. "We need that report. I'd like to talk to the supervising pathologist as well. Compare the marks on Johnson and Perry with Scout."

"Agreed," Hans said. "Would you like to join us?" he asked the Ranger.

"One of us will," Ted said. "We'll also want to follow up on the witness statements from El Gato. And no one talked to the girlfriend or her kids."

"Do you want to follow us back to the rectory, then we can split the interviews?" Hans asked. "Meg and I are headed to Las Vegas tomorrow morning if nothing breaks here. We have a meeting with the coroner and investigating officer."

"I didn't know the FBI sent teams around the country. I thought you folks were regional."

"Special circumstances," Hans said.

Barker returned. "No report. I called the morgue and they haven't done the autopsy yet. I told them to hold until we got there, unless you don't need to see it. For us, we can take the report."

"Same here," Megan said, "but I'd like to observe."

Hern said, "We'll meet you at the rectory in thirty minutes."

They shook hands, and Hans and Megan left. When they drove up to the rectory, Jack stood on the front porch looking at the sky. "The rain finally came," he said.

The first fat drop fell from the sky as Megan got out of the Jeep.

"Did you learn anything?" he asked.

"Plenty," Megan said. "Were you going to tell me about the interviews you conducted, or was I supposed to learn about your private investigation from the police chief's reports?"

Jack raised an eyebrow. "I didn't learn anything that you can use."

"What were you expecting to find? Fingerprints? A receipt from the local motel? And how do you know what I can use? How many murders have you investigated? How many have you solved? This is my responsibility, not yours, and I will not allow anyone to withhold information without serious consequences."

Jack stepped forward. Within seconds the rain turned from fat droplets to a downpour. "Scout is *my* responsibility. Don't think for a minute that I'm going to back down. If I thought anything I learned was important, I'd have—" He stopped.

"What?" Megan demanded.

"Scout's tags."

She blanched. "How do you know about the dog tags?"

"What do you know?"

She raised an eyebrow and didn't say anything. If this arrogant soldier thought she owed him any explanation or information . . .

Jack said, "For what it's worth, I planned on telling you about the missing tag, but with the events last night, it slipped my mind."

"Tag? One tag was missing?" Just like Price.

"Scout had only one tag—the other was pulled when he went down four years ago on his last mission. Fell off a cliff, broke his back. They couldn't move him without a chopper, so pulled a tag just in case. So he wore only the one, and it wasn't on his body. No chain, no tag. Is that the same as the others?"

"Not exactly. Price was missing one of the two tags, and the killers sent it to me. But Johnson and Perry— Johnson's sons have his tags, and I'm still trying to get word from Vegas about Perry."

"Why would the killers take Scout's identification? To dehumanize him?" Jack tensed.

"Maybe they're planning on sending it to someone else. Or to me." She frowned. "Hans, what's going on here? I'd think they were keeping souvenirs, but they're not. They're using them for something."

Hans said, "We're getting drenched. Let's talk about this inside." He walked into the rectory, expecting them to follow.

Jack and Megan stared at each other in the rain.

Her anger had dissipated, surprising her. Jack was used to being in charge, but it didn't bother her because even when he was pushy, he wasn't manipulative. So much like her father, her brother—she felt as if she already knew Jack Kincaid and how his sharp mind worked. It was comfortable, like meeting up with an old friend after years apart.

"I'm sorry," Jack said. "I should have told you last night. I meant to."

"I'm sorry I snapped. I know you feel responsible for Scout, but we're on the same team."

"Truce?"

"Truce."

Her smile faltered when Jack reached out and brushed back strands of her hair that had fallen out of her knot. Her breath caught in her throat as she looked in his eyes. His dark stare was so intense, so powerful, that for a moment she was mesmerized, caught in a trap she didn't want to escape. His rough fingers skimmed her face, down her neck, a light touch that made her shiver in anticipation of more.

When his hand dropped to his side, Megan could finally let out her breath.

Jack said, "I'll fill you in on everything I did yesterday. I don't know if it's going to help, but it's worth a shot."

CHAPTER
SEVENTEEN

Ethan woke to nothing.

No movement, no noise. He froze and listened. Distant cars moving fast. Birds chirped and squawked. A motor, but not the truck.

He sat up, looked around. Where was she? She'd left him. Deserted him. Just like the army.

The gunfire was so loud but unreal at the same time. Pop-pop-pop. Poppoppoppoppop. A machine gun spewing out bullets. One nicked Ethan in the arm. He looked down and saw blood. Just a bit. Nothing to worry about.

He was in the middle of a firefight! He wished he had a camera, but on this clandestine mission cameras were forbidden. Adrenaline rushed through his veins. His first real firefight. He pulled out a notebook and rapidly jotted down words and phrases. 103 degrees. Dry and dusty. Arid. Flashes of gunfire. Brows beaded with sweat and tension. A precision team. Well oiled. Well trained. America's elite. Fighters. Killers. Comrades. Oh, that was good!

"What the fuck are you doing?" one soldier hissed. "Stay put! You already almost got us all killed, dipshit."

He nodded, eyes wide, and went back to his hiding spot. They didn't like Ethan, he had known it from the beginning. Didn't want him to be here, didn't want to see the truth in print. Continuing to write, he thought of an opening line.

The first gunfight of the day was right out of a Hollywood movie. Heat, heroes, and panic. Special forces were brave, but fear ate at their resolve like . . .

Like what? Come on, think!

He stayed hidden, writing, the gunfire moving farther away. Shouts, then silence with the occasional report of a rifle. He liked that phrase; he had to be wary and not use it more than twice in the article.

Pulitzer Prize, baby, it was within his reach . . .

Silence.

Ethan peered out from the cavity of the rocks. The air reeked of gunpowder. And blood.

The soldier, he couldn't remember his name, who had been assigned to "babysit" him (as he lamented), was dead. There was too much blood for him to be alive. And his head . . . half of it was gone.

Ethan swallowed and looked around.

Where were the others?

They'd left him? Left him with a dead body?

He heard a helicopter in the distance, coming closer. He relaxed. They were coming back for him. He stepped out of his hiding place and looked skyward, ready to wave them down.

They came out of the woodwork like termites. Dozens of them, men wearing traditional Taliban headdress, holding guns. Rifles. Handguns. Knives. These were not Americans. They were the enemy.

Ethan thought he was going to die. He put his hands on his head and waited for the bullets to penetrate his body.

Make it fast, God. I don't like pain.

He didn't learn until later what pain really was.

*   *   *

They were going to punish General Hackett for sending Ethan on that mission in the first place. For assuring him, and his editor, that he would be safe. Protected. "It's an easy mission," Hackett had said. "In and out."

Where was that woman?

Ethan got out of the truck. The sun burned and he began to sweat as he started toward the bathrooms. A semi with insignia from Arkansas or Alabama—Ethan couldn't tell from the distance—was parked on the far side. Fear clawed at him, constricting his throat. He went back to the truck and reached under the passenger seat for the gun the woman kept there. It snagged on the metal wires and he pulled hard.

Bartleton's dog tag fell to the ground.

Dammit, he'd told her not to do it again. He didn't know she'd grabbed it, but there was the proof, wrapped around her gun. Lying bitch.

He picked up the tag, tossed it into the cab, and slammed the door shut.

Behind the restrooms were half a dozen picnic tables. The woman—Kate? Christina? Carmen?—hadn't seen him. She was sitting at one of the tables. Was that her? She'd changed; he remembered now. She'd cut her hair in the motel. All of it, off. Put a different color on. Told him it was part of her disguise. But he knew her now from her build, the way she moved, her eyes. She couldn't change her eyes. *Karin.* Her name was Karin.

He skirted the building and walked around to the far side where she couldn't see him approach. He'd scare her. Serve her right.

Then he heard the voices. For a minute he thought they were in his head. They weren't. It was Karin, and she was talking to a man. The trucker? Ethan peered around the side of the building. Looked like a trucker. Jeans. T-shirt. Skinny kid. Twenty, twenty-two maybe. The building shielded Ethan, but he could hear their conversation.

"Are you okay?" the trucker asked Karin.

She didn't say anything, just shrugged.

"Are you here alone?"

"Yes."

She glanced toward the truck and Ethan smirked.

"Are you sure? You're looking kind of skittish. I'm not going to hurt you."

"I know."

"It's going to be okay," he said. "Do you want me to call someone?"

"I'm just getting a breath of fresh air."

"Do you have a name? I'm Thomas. Let's pray, okay?"

What was this kid doing? Praying for Karin? Did he know how many men she'd killed? Didn't he know that she wanted to kill him? Ethan could see it. She'd fuck him and kill him. She'd done it before, had told Ethan all about it. Why couldn't this kid see that? *Why was he praying for her, the spawn of Satan?*

"Thomas?"

A woman's voice from behind him startled Ethan. When he whirled around the woman screamed.

Panic spread to every nerve in his body. He pressed the trigger. A reflex. He didn't plan it.

The woman fell to the ground.

"Loretta! Dear Lord, Loretta!" Ethan heard the shouts from the picnic table, but the noise barely registered.

He stared at the woman. She was dead. It was obvious from her eyes that he had killed her. Her hands were on her stomach. A large, round stomach.

An agony-filled cry bellowed from behind Ethan. He turned and saw the praying Thomas now rageful. He was running toward Ethan. Ethan fired again. Then two more times. Thomas dropped to the ground, his chest a bloody mess.

"What have you done?!?"

Roxanne? Rachel? Regina? Whatever her name was—Ethan couldn't remember—she panicked. She screamed at him. Her eyes were wild. Maybe she had changed her eyes. He couldn't remember her name. He should know it. He frowned. It was right there minutes ago.

"Shit! Shit! Oh fuck, Ethan, you're crazy!"

She snatched the gun from his hand. He let her. Why didn't he shoot her, too? Why didn't he just stop it all now? Shoot her, then himself. But now he had no gun.

She pushed Ethan. He stumbled backward. "Dammit, Ethan, why? Why did you kill them?"

"I don't know."

She screamed in rage and slapped him, then grabbed his wrist and pulled him toward the truck. "Get in, I'm driving. We have to get out of here right now. You're ruining everything. You fucked up again, Ethan. How am I going to get out of this?"

He opened the passenger door and clamored in, slammed it shut, and she drove off, yelling at him. Then she stopped and the silence was bliss. Then it was Hell. Total silence, just the purr of the truck and the woman's sniffles. She was crying. Why was she crying? They didn't talk about what happened. He didn't know whether to be worried, scared, or elated.

He didn't feel guilty.

Thirty minutes later he asked, "How long until Santa Barbara?"

Megan and Hans listened to Jack go over yesterday's events. The more she listened, the more she realized she would have done almost the exact same things, except she wouldn't have tackled a known drug smuggler in public, nor would she have broken into a secure crime scene to look around. The former action was all testostrone; the latter could jeopardize the legal case.

Scout's missing dog tag was an important bit of information that was not in Perez's reports, and something that easily could have been overlooked. But that was not the case with the mysterious brunette who may have been at both El Gato and Father Francis's St. Ignatius. If Perez had been doing his job right, he should have made the connection, and not gone off on the wild theory that some rebels in Guatemala crossed the border for retribution against Jack and his team.

"Are you certain it's the same woman?" Megan asked.

"Almost certain," Jack said. "From Padre's description and two people at the bar, she appears to be the same. There're not a lot of non-Hispanic women in town. She'd stick out whether she was white, black, or Asian."

"Could be completely unrelated," Hans said. "But it's a good idea that you called in your men to stick by Father Francis for the time being, until we have better intel about the motives of the killers."

"We need to get a sketch artist here," Megan said. "Have Padre describe the woman while she's still fresh in his mind. We can call her a potential witness, nothing about being a possible suspect."

"And it may have nothing to do with this case," Hans said.

"And it may have everything to do with this case!" Megan shot back. "It's the only thing we have right now. There's no forensic evidence to help us narrow down a suspect. We have a stranger in town, a woman who shows up at a known hangout for two men who were on the same Delta Force team, a team that is systematically being slaughtered."

"Father Francis is alive," Hans said.

"And that means what?" Jack said, his voice low with anger. "That he's involved?"

"That's not what I said."

"But you thought it."

"He has an alibi for the first three—"

Jack pushed back from the table. "Don't."

"It's part of our job," Hans said. He was uncomfortable, but he held Jack's glare. "We have to rule out everyone. Including you."

Hans's BlackBerry vibrated on the table and he picked it up. A few seconds later he said, "First Lieutenant Jerome 'Jerry' Jefferson is confirmed in Afghanistan. Last leave was four months ago, which he spent in Hawaii."

"Which means what?" Megan asked.

"The killers can't get to him." To Jack, he said, "Sit down, Jack. We need to work through this."

Jack continued standing.

Megan said, "We don't know how many killers there are, we only suspect two. There could be three, ten, an entire conspiracy."

"Meg, I think you're stretching it—"

She put up her hand, then winced when she remembered how much she hated it when the jerk from CID did it to her. "Yes, to illustrate a point. We have *no idea* who is behind these killings. We have very basic victimology—they were all U.S. Army Delta Force soldiers who worked together for a period of two years on dozens of missions. But we don't know which mission triggered the killer, why he—they—are acting now, or why they've chosen to kill in such a brutal manner.

"So until we know *why*, we don't know that Jefferson isn't in danger, or that he isn't the one spearheading the attacks. And this woman might have information. Maybe she's a battered girlfriend or wife—"

Hans interrupted. "This crime is too masculine."

"Why? Because it doesn't have a sexual component?"

"Most male-female killing pairs are enacting sadistic sexual fantasies, or the female is bait, luring the victims for her dominant male partner."

"But this isn't sexual sadism, this feels like revenge. Whether directed toward these men because of who they are, or what they represent, I don't know. But why not a woman? A wife or sister of a dead soldier?"

"I don't know. There hasn't been any hint—"

"Except for the female stranger in town. Profiling is based on statistics, Hans. You taught that in Criminal Psychology 101. If four out of five serial killers were abused as children, that still means that twenty percent *weren't* abused."

Hans nodded. "Okay, we follow that trail. I'll ask the Rangers to send a sketch artist for Father Francis to work with."

"Sketch artist?" Padre said as he stepped into the kitchen. "For what?"

"The woman you saw at the church late Tuesday night," Megan said. She glanced at Jack. He was still standing at the table, but the tension and anger had left his stance. He seemed intrigued and contemplative. He caught her eye and gave her a slight smile. She turned away. "Do you have the list of missions?"

Padre put a notepad in front of her. "Here." He looked defeated.

"Thank you, Padre." Megan read his notes. All the missions where the dead had worked together were in Afghanistan. "All eight of you were on each mission?"

"No. I also included missions where I didn't go as part of the team, or Jefferson didn't go. Since we're both still alive."

"What type of missions?"

"They're classified."

"I can't work with something that's 'classified,' " Megan said. "If something that happened on one of these missions is somehow de facto responsible for these men being targeted, then I need to know."

Padre seemed to have changed overnight. More hard edges and temper than the priest who had picked up her and Hans the night before at the airstrip. Megan ached that the man had to cough up his past demons, but she also knew that if he didn't, more people would die.

"Some of the missions were assassinations. Some were extractions or liberations." Padre left it at that.

Jack asked quietly, "How successful?"

"The third mission was a disaster. Our intel was wrong and we nearly got ambushed. Aborted and re-grouped two days later. The last mission was also a failure. We lost a man. Thornton. I told you about him last night."

"Orders?" Jack asked.

"Seize a high-ranking Taliban member. He was a weak link, had a regular mistress. High security, but no change in habits. We'd been gathering intel on him for months. We went in, but—" He stopped.

"And?"

"The P.R. department had us bring a civilian with us. Open-door policy."

"A civilian? On a Delta mission?" Jack couldn't keep the shock out of his voice. "They've sent reporters and cameras to the lines, which is foolhardy, but on one of *our* missions? That's insane."

"Another reporter, a big guy, had done it the year before with great success, according to the powers that be. But I found out later that that reporter had spent three years in the Marines. He went in because he'd gone to basic with a guy who could get him in. He had experience and could take care of himself. We didn't know any of that, of course, only that afterward the Marines had a lot of favorable press and write-ups, lots of backslapping and goodwill toward man." Sarcasm hung in the air.

"Your civilian was a reporter?"

Padre nodded. "An idiot. He screwed up the mission, and worse, he got Thornton killed."

"What?" Megan asked when Padre didn't continue. "Is he dead, too?"

"Barry Rosemont didn't do what we told him to do. We knew we were being surrounded, and there was no way to get out. We had to call in an extraction team, breaking radio silence, which alerted the Taliban to our exact location. Russo ordered us to split into two teams and left Thornton with Rosemont in what we believed was the most secure location. They were supposed to stay in the rocks, radio silence, no matter what they heard until the Blackhawks arrived.

"Rosemont panicked, exposed himself. Thornton sent Morse code that their position had been compromised, and we did everything we could to get back there, but by that time it was too late. Thornton was dead and the Taliban had Rosemont."

"They took him hostage?" Megan asked.

"We didn't know that at the time. Then, we assumed he was dead and they took his body and Thornton's to parade over the airwaves and demoralize us. It would have worked. We'd been making great inroads in Afghanistan, something like this would have really damaged our position."

"But he wasn't dead."

"No. They held him hostage for three months. Another Delta team extracted him and brought him back to the States."

"Do you know where he is now?" Hans asked.

Padre laughed humorlessly. "I don't want to know. The bastards desecrated Thornton's body. I blamed Rosemont. It was hard to forgive him. I did—I had to— but I don't want to think about him. Thornton was a good man. He had a family."

Padre excused himself and left the rectory.

"Do you want to go with him?" Megan asked Jack.

"He needs to be alone." The concern in Jack's eyes for his friend was heartbreaking.

Megan's cell phone rang, and caller I.D. showed an

unfamiliar Sacramento number. She answered. "Megan Elliott."

"You'll never believe it!"

"Who's this?"

"Simone. We have the body."

"The body?"

"The John Doe. Price."

"You've lost me."

"The dead guy in the alley? CID just dumped him back at the morgue. They ran his prints. It's not George Price."

Megan's stomach flipped. "But we had his prints. Why didn't we know immediately?"

"We don't have access to the military database. Only criminal and DMV databases. The guy's prints didn't show up, but we weren't concerned. If he had no record, no reason to be in the system, we wouldn't have them. We would have naturally checked the military next, but they had the body. They didn't tell us until this morning!"

Megan was in shock. "But it's the same M.O., the I.D., we have a connection with the other victims—"

"I don't know what's going on, but I thought you should know. CID gave us a photograph of Price—the one they've been flashing on the news was Price at eighteen. But they had a photo that's only five years old. There's no way in Hell our John Doe is Price. Both white, six feet tall, basic build, similar coloring, but obviously not the same man. I'll shoot an e-mail with the pic off to you . . . done. You have more contacts and resources. If you can find the real George Price first, more power to you. In the meantime, Black is trying to find out who our John Doe is and how he came by Price's dog tags."

Megan hung up the phone, perplexed.

Why did the killers think the homeless John Doe was Price? Had they never actually seen him before? Or was it so long ago they didn't exactly remember him?

Or did this mean that George Price was part of the killing team?

"The victim in Sacramento isn't Price?" Jack asked.

Megan shook her head. "This changes everything. We need to find the real George Price."

"If he's still alive," Hans said. "Or wants to be found. He's been AWOL for five years. He could have a new identity, be out of the country, in hiding. He's not going to come forward knowing he'll be prosecuted by the army for attempted murder as well as desertion."

"What if he's involved?"

"First Jefferson, now Price?" Jack said. "You're really stretching it. Why would Price put his own identification around a man he just killed?"

Megan fumed. "How do I know? To stage his own death?"

"He'd know the prints wouldn't match," Jack snapped.

"At least I'm trying to figure it out! We don't know what's going on, but George Price was dead three days ago, and now he's not. He's still AWOL, but that man was killed by the same people who tortured and executed three other Delta Force soldiers who had all worked together for two years in Afghanistan. You tell me there's not a connection somewhere. Maybe the homeless guy found the tags in the garbage, for all we know. But then how in the world did the killers mistake him for Price?" She couldn't figure it out, and it was eating at her. Deductive reasoning was one of her strengths, but nothing in this scenario made sense.

"I'll call Quantico and have them start looking," Hans said. He shook his head and Megan felt his disapproval. "I'm surprised that you of all people made such an amateur mistake."

Before she could respond to Hans, Jack said to her, "Maybe you should call in your friend from Rogan-Caruso—the one you have investigating me. Because he seems to be able to get information out of a magic hat. Though he didn't get the goods that Price wasn't Price."

Megan's brows furrowed. What was Jack saying? J.T., yeah, he would be a good contact. But Jack almost sounded jealous. What a ridiculous—ludicrous!—idea. She really was exhausted.

"Good idea," she said absently. Jack mumbled something under his breath, but Megan didn't hear the words. She watched Hans walk away and realized he was angry with her. She ran through everything that happened Monday—yeah, they made the assumption the victim was George Price; they took his prints to verify . . . but when CID came and took the body, Megan didn't even question the man's identity. Of course it was Price, why else would the army take him?

But she'd made an assumption that, though based on circumstantial evidence, was false. The entire case was in jeopardy.

Except that the homeless John Doe had been killed in the same manner as the other victims, and therefore Price's tags must have deliberately been put on the body. Price was connected somehow. This was no coincidence.

She looked around for Hans to explain, but he was

across the room talking quietly on the phone, his back to her. And Jack was staring out the window, his back also facing her. She felt as if she would explode. She needed to talk it out, analyze every angle.

Someone rapped on the rectory door and Jack answered. "Hern, right?"

"Right. Good memory, Kincaid."

Ranger Ted Hern came in, taking his hat off. "Dr. Vigo, Agent Elliott. Glad you're both here. We may have a break."

Hern's expression was dour while he waited for Hans to wrap up his call. "Two dead bodies at a rest stop outside Blythe, California. And in the parking lot, the highway patrol found a military identification tag for Lawrence Bartleton."

CHAPTER EIGHTEEN

Hans said to Megan as he punched buttons on his cell phone, "I'll get a military transport out of McAllen. We should be in California in a couple hours."

Jack said, "I have a plane. I'll take you."

"That's not necessary," Hans said, putting the phone to his ear.

Megan caught Jack's eye. He was a hard man, but he wasn't too hard to read. He'd go with or without them. Scout was his friend, he felt responsible. Megan understood that all too well. "Jack's contacts may come in handy," she said. "And we can leave now."

Hern said, "The victims were a young truck driver, twenty-three, and his wife. She was pregnant."

"Any witnesses?" Megan asked.

"I don't know. Barker and I can stay here and follow up on the autopsy and potential witnesses in the Bartleton investigation."

"Father Francis may have seen a potential witness, or possible suspect, at the church Tuesday night. Can you get a sketch artist to work with him?"

"We'll jump on it," Hern said.

"Appreciate it," Megan said. "My e-mail is on my card, and I can receive images on my BlackBerry. Get it to me as soon as you can." She looked at Hans, who was on hold, and then asked Jack, "You have a plane that can fit all of us?"

"Yes."

"How long to Blythe?"

"Three hours in the air, plus or minus."

Megan glanced at Hans again. Why didn't he want to use Jack? He wouldn't have been her first choice, but right now the fastest way to Blythe would bring them that much closer to the killers. They'd been at a rest stop. Someone had to have seen *something*. There had to be a witness. Even if they didn't know they were a witness.

Hans said into the phone, "Sheryl? Sorry to bother you. I found transportation. . . . Thanks anyway. I appreciate it." He hung up and said to Jack, "I guess you're our pilot."

Jack found Padre kneeling in front of the statue of Our Lady of Guadalupe in the St. Ignatius chapel off the main church. He didn't say anything for a long minute. While he often came to church because of Padre, he hadn't really thought about the reasons, if there were any. Today, he took in the old, lovingly cared for stained glass, antique statues, worn wooden pews, simple altar with the polished brass tabernacle behind it, the candle in the sconce proclaiming Jesus was present. He'd given a lot of money to Padre's church, but he never gave a thought to what it went to. In the back of his mind guilt spread. He was trying to buy off God.

Jack was no saint. He blamed God for most of the wrongs in the world. Blasphemy, he was sure. After all, God let Satan roam free. How else could a pregnant woman and her husband end up murdered at a roadside water hole? Where was God in that?

"I can feel your anger and frustration, Jack," Padre said without turning around.

"I'm taking the feds to California. They have a lead on Scout's killer."

"Good."

"I just talked to Tim. He'll be here in half an hour. Until then, Ranger Hern will be around."

"Hmm."

Jack sat in the pew behind Padre. "Frank."

"It has to be related to Thornton."

"Excuse me?"

"That last mission. It was . . . a disaster. I've gone through every mission on that list, and that's the only one that was major-league fucked. Unless you count the assassination of a family of terrorists. Including their fourteen-year-old son."

"Don't do this to yourself."

"Go, Jack."

"I need to know that you're okay."

"I'm okay."

"You're not."

They stayed there for several minutes, Jack sitting, Padre kneeling.

Jack asked, "What do you know about George Price?"

"Quiet guy. Dedicated. Career soldier. I was surprised he'd gone AWOL."

"He's not dead."

Padre looked over his shoulder at Jack.

"The victim's prints didn't match Price. The feds think he's alive, and either hiding or a part of this."

"I'll find him."

"No. What if he is part of it? What if he snapped? He attacked his lieutenant."

"You're not my commanding officer, Jack. Never have been."

Jack's jaw tensed. "Frank—"

"I'm careful. Five years in the priesthood isn't going to erase sixteen years as a sniper."

"Keep Tim in the loop. I—" He didn't know how to say it. He couldn't lose Padre like he'd lost Scout. How do you say something like that?

"Same here," Padre said, as if reading Jack's mind. "Get going. Find whoever killed Scout. I'll find Price. I can't imagine he'd be part of this, but I've been surprised before."

"I'll let you know what happens. And . . . let me talk to Price when you find him. Please."

"All right."

Jack rose, put his hand on Padre's shoulder, and squeezed. He turned and left. He didn't have anything else to say and prayed his friend would be safe.

They arrived in Santa Barbara at two that afternoon. Ethan could hardly contain himself. The sand! The ocean! It was beautiful. He laid down in the sand and smiled at the bright, bright blue sky. He loved the beach. Volleyball, chasing seagulls, finding seashells. He sat up and started digging in the coarse sand and found one. It was broken, but it was still really cool.

"I can't believe you got us a place on the beach!" He clapped his hands together. "I love the beach." He dug around for more shells, grinning. He pulled out another and it was perfect.

She didn't say anything, and Ethan tried to remember

why they were here in the first place. Vacation? No. They were meeting someone.

"Is he here?" Ethan blinked. Who was he waiting for? It was important. Very important, but he couldn't remember.

"Not yet," she said.

"Good." He smiled at the waves, at the seagulls' squawk-and-dive routine, turned his face to the sun. Still smiling, he said, "Let's go swimming."

"As soon as you teach me one more trick."

He pouted. "I want to play. Please."

"I need to know now. It's important, Ethan. Very important."

"*Please* let me play in the sand. Just *five minutes.*"

"Show me what I need to know, and you can play the rest of the day."

"What do you want to know?" he whined.

"The needles, Ethan. Snap out of this idiocy. I have questions and you have the answers. You will tell me. Then you can come back to the beach. I promise."

They stayed in their cabin for two hours and Ethan answered all her questions. He used his own body as an example, the pain breaking through his happiness of being young again. He wasn't young; he wasn't a child anymore.

He left her happy—giddy with her killing knowledge—in the cabin and walked back out onto the sand. He didn't know what to do. Why was he here? He hated the sand. It reminded him of the desert. He went back to the cabin and found a small pile of seashells near the door. He took a rock and smashed them.

He wished he was dead.

But the bitch had taken his gun.

CHAPTER NINETEEN

The bodies had long ago been taken to the morgue when Megan arrived at the crime scene. Thirty miles east of Indio, California, it was near the highway leading to Joshua Tree National Park. The entire rest stop had been taped off and dozens of law enforcement officers from the California Highway Patrol to National Park Rangers to the Riverside County Sheriff's Department scoured the area for evidence that would point a finger at whomever had shot and killed a young pregnant wife and her husband.

The man in charge was Assistant Sheriff Red Warren. Megan introduced herself and Hans, then Jack by his military rank of staff sergeant—easier than explaining who he was and why he was here.

"You sure came quickly," Warren said.

"We weren't far," said Megan. "This may be connected to a serial murder investigation," Hans added. "Can you walk us through the crime scene?"

"We'll start over there." Warren gestured to a big rig on the far side of the lot. As they walked over, he said, "According to the male victim's driving log—Thomas Hoffman—he stopped at the rest area at oh three hundred hours. The Highway Patrol drove through the rest stop at oh seven hundred hours and the rig was here, no activity. CHP noted the plates and went on. We've put a call out to the other big rigs in the area—" He gestured toward the opposite end of the rest stop where three eighteen-wheelers were lined up, and another was pulling in, being directed by a CHP officer where to park. "We asked who had been in communication with Hoffman in the last twenty-four hours. They started showing up—it's a tight community. Last word we had is that Hoffman told another trucker that he was getting a late start, but planned on making his destination— Portland, Oregon—by midnight. It's about fifteen hours, taking mandatory rests, so he couldn't have planned on leaving much after nine this morning."

"What time was that?" Hans asked.

"Eight-thirty this morning."

"When were the bodies found?" Megan asked.

"Ten-ten. An older couple stopped to use the facilities and found the bodies."

"Any other witnesses?"

"Not that we've found. This stop doesn't see a lot of traffic during the week."

Warren opened the cab of the truck. A simple wood cross hung from the rearview mirror. A well-worn Bible rested on the center console. Knitting needles attached to a half-made white and green blanket stuck out of a needlepoint bag with a Thomas Kincade design and the phrase "With God All Things Are Possible" embroidered in fancy script.

"Where were the bodies?" Megan asked, her voice sounding unnatural. She should know better than to get emotional. But this double homicide hit her unusually hard. She should have been able to stop it. What had she done wrong? Had she missed something? Could she have been able to save the lives of these two young married lovers and their unborn child?

"Behind the facilities." Warren led the way.

Jack was behind Megan. He put his hand on the small of her back, so lightly she wasn't sure if it was intentional or not. She glanced over at him; looking straight ahead, he applied more pressure on her waist. She took a deep breath and pushed aside the unexpected emotion.

"Why did they park so far from the building?" Hans asked.

"Privacy," Warren replied. "The restrooms are open twenty-four hours. Headlights from oncoming cars could be distracting. And over there, where the Hoffmans parked, big rigs often park overnight. It's not technically legal, but we never rouse them. I'd rather have them rested and living on the cheap than exceeding their limits."

"Were they the only rig here last night?"

"We're trying to find out. Probably not, there are usually a few on any given night." He shook his head in disgust. "We've never had any problems here. Never had a serious crime. Nothing more than simple vandalism. Nothing like this."

The assistant sheriff stopped in a clearing behind the restrooms, approximately fifty yards from the truck. There were half a dozen wooden picnic tables cemented to slabs of concrete surrounded by hearty grass and low-maintenance evergreens.

"We've had our best people out there going through the entire area with a fine-toothed comb," Warren said. "The M.E. is performing the autopsies today, so we can extract the bullets and rush ballistics; half my off-duty cops are asking to work on their own time. The sheriff has the word of the attorney general that this case is a priority, but when I found out your people were involved, I was hoping we could ask for a bit of forensic assistance. Your ballistics capabilities are the best in the world, from what I've been told."

Hans said firmly, "I'll fly the bullets to the lab tonight and personally assure you that we'll have a report in less than twenty-four hours, if I have to return to Quantico and do it myself."

Hans's raw voice surprised Megan. She glanced at him, saw that he was staring straight ahead, eyes dry but red. She'd seen him angry, she'd heard him express sorrow and frustration over victims or the system, but she'd never seen him emotionally involved at a crime scene.

He'd been quiet during the plane ride, but Megan thought he'd been asleep. Now she wondered.

Megan noted the evidence markers—one to the left of the facilities, one halfway between the picnic tables and the first victim. "Was the husband at the tables approaching his wife or here moving away?"

"We believe that the husband was at the picnic tables and his wife was here, near the facilities. Evidence in the restroom suggests she'd used the facilities to freshen up. A small trash bag was next to that table," he gestured, "and we think they'd had breakfast, then Mrs. Hoffman entered the restroom. We don't have a good indication as to which victim was shot first, and no idea why. The female victim was shot once in the chest at close range; her husband three times."

"Robbery?" Megan asked.

"Not that we can tell. Mrs. Hoffman had her purse, with about forty dollars cash and two major credit cards. Mr. Hoffman had nearly two hundred dollars, credit and gas cards. The rig was unlocked, nothing appeared disturbed. My men have already printed it."

"Where did you find the dog tag?" Megan asked.

Warren gestured for them to follow. Thirty feet from the building was another police marker. He said to one of his deputies, "Grab the dog tag. It's in the van."

Warren pointed to the ground. "Right there, on the asphalt. We were hoping initially that they belonged to the killer, but when we ran the name we learned he was recently murdered."

"The killer took the I.D. off the body," Megan said, glancing at Jack. He'd been so quiet she would have forgotten he was there except for his stalwart and commanding presence.

"It could have been another sign," Hans said. "A sick way to connect these murders with the previous. Was Mr. Hoffman or his wife ever in the military?"

"I wouldn't know, but I'll have one of my deputies check immediately."

Megan frowned. She didn't want to disagree with Hans in front of anyone, but cautiously she said, "It doesn't make sense. While these killers take risks, I don't see them shooting someone and tossing evidence like garbage. If they'd planned on leaving the tag, it would be more purposeful, like when Price's tag was mailed to me. They wouldn't have dropped it here as if by accident. It would be with the bodies."

"We can't assume anything," Hans snapped. "Sheriff, have you printed the bathrooms? Male and female? The dog tag? What about the picnic tables, looking for anything that might belong to the killer? Quantico has state-of-the-art facilities to help with trace evidence. Does your CSI unit have a forensic vacuum?"

Hans's unusual brusque manner had Megan both concerned and irritated.

"Let me walk you through what we've done, Dr. Vigo," Warren said, straightening his back, "and you can let me know if I've forgotten anything."

Megan watched Hans walk off with the assistant sheriff. Jack said, "What do you think?"

"I think—" She stopped. She was committing an investigational sin, snap theories that could cloud her impartial judgment.

"We need more evidence," she said.

"But you have a theory," Jack prompted.

"I don't have proof."

"Lay it on me."

Megan looked around. The rest stop—unseen from the road. The picnic tables—obscured, but not completely hidden, from where the killer's car was presumably parked.

"The killers stopped here. To rest, to use the bathroom, to look at a map. It's secluded and they would have the expectation of some privacy. With robbery as a motive pretty much ruled out, I don't see why they killed the couple. For the thrill?"

"The thrill," Jack said flatly.

"They're not dumb criminals. They've killed too often and left too little evidence to be spontaneous and undisciplined. Maybe they heard a car approach and got out of the lot fast. Or panicked because the murders weren't planned. Maybe the Hoffmans witnessed something or overheard the killers talking about murder. Our killers feared a witness. Something made them pull out fast. I'd stake my career on the theory that they didn't know Scout's dog tag was left behind."

"Aren't most criminals caught because they do something stupid? Wasn't Ted Bundy pulled over for speeding or something?"

"Exactly. And that's why I think they didn't know about the dog tag. It's a screwup, and let's hope for more of them. They may well lead to our perps. We know much more about them now."

"How so?"

"We know that they were in Hidalgo Tuesday night and killed Scout, and then here, near Joshua Tree, Thursday morning before ten a.m. That's less than thirty-six hours. There're not a lot of routes they could have taken here in that short time. The most likely route is I-10, which means we can contact all the motels immediately off the interstate, restaurants, gas stations. It might not yield anything, but it's more than we had yesterday."

"But we have no descriptions," said Jack. "Nothing to show people."

She sighed. "It's still a thread to follow. With high-profile murders, we can call in extra people and resources and scour security tapes. Especially if we narrow it down."

"How?"

"That there's a woman involved."

Jack thought on that for a moment. "You think the brunette who came by the church is involved?"

Megan took a deep breath. She didn't like running forward on a hunch, but her ex-husband had told her time and time again to trust her instincts, and she'd recently been trying to do just that. It wasn't just her gut feeling, it was the circumstantial evidence. . . .

It had been circumstantial evidence that had her wrongly identifying the body in Sacramento as George L. Price.

"I don't know," Megan mumbled.

"But you think she's part of it?" Jack pressed.

"It's the only thing that makes sense with what we know," she said, qualifying her comments. She glanced over to where a tight-lipped Hans was standing, writing down everything the assistant sheriff was saying.

"They would have made it more obvious," Megan said to herself. She put her hand to her mouth and looked up at Jack, heart pounding with the realization. "That's it!"

"What?"

"Price. What if the killers had Price's tags—and put them on the homeless John Doe?"

"Why would they do that?"

"To connect the murders." As she spoke, Megan knew she was on to the *something* that had been eluding her for the last four days. "We now know John Doe in Sacramento wasn't George Price, but for a couple days, we assumed he was until CID said the prints didn't match."

Meg had bought into the assumption the killers wanted her to. She had ignored her years of experience and training, which taught her that no matter what you thought, assumptions were not facts supported by evidence. One of her Quantico instructors told the class, *"If you walk into a crime scene and see red drops on the floor, ninety-nine times out of a hundred it's human blood—but it's the one time it isn't, and you assume it is, that's going to jeopardize your entire case, embarrass you, and put the entire FBI on the hot seat. It's not blood until you prove it's blood."*

"Why would the killers want us to think the homeless victim was Price?"

"We may not know until we find them. But I do know that it would have taken us longer to make the military connection between the victims. The tags gave us a clue to pursue, and sending one to me was another big arrow telling us that it was important. It's the *why* that stumps me."

"They're taunting you. Mocking. Showing their superiority. 'You,' meaning the police in general."

Megan nodded. "I think you might be right."

"How do you know the homeless guy didn't just find the tags in the garbage?" Jack said.

"I don't. And up until CID took the body, I'd considered that possibility, but I screwed up. When CID came in, I labeled him Price and didn't question his identity any further."

"So is it a coincidence or not?"

"Not. Price was in the same unit as Padre and the others. His tags were found on a dead John Doe. Scout's tag was taken from his body, and dropped at this crime scene—accidentally or not, it came from Hidalgo, which means the killers were here. Whether they were planning to send the tag to the police again, or planned on leaving it on another body, we don't know, but we definitely have a connection."

Her cell phone rang and she glanced at the caller I.D. J.T. She didn't want to take it, knowing he most likely had a report on Jack's background for her. She almost sent it to voice mail, when Jack said, "Answer it." He seemed to sense the nature of the call.

A tic throbbed in Jack's neck as he walked past her, toward the far end of the rest stop.

She answered the phone. It was J.T. "You're not going to believe the latest," she said.

"That the victim isn't Price?"

"Dammit, J.T., how do you know these things?"

"From the same guy who told me about the autopsy. CID knew yesterday, by the way. They kept it to themselves. What does that mean on your end?"

"It means I need to find George Price."

"Thought so. I put some feelers out, but so far not even a nibble."

"Father Francis Cardenas, the priest I told you about, used to be on Price's Delta team and is trying to track him down. Considering he's been AWOL for five years, he could have taken a new identity or left the country. For all we know, he's hiding out in Mexico or Canada. Anyway, right now I need to get back to work. I'm at an ugly crime scene."

"Aren't you interested in the background check you asked me for?"

She looked around for Jack and couldn't see him. She wanted the information, and she didn't. She felt like a voyeur, spying on Jack Kincaid's life. Did she really need to know who he was and what he'd done?

Yet he was a witness. Jack Kincaid had a relationship with at least one of the victims, and he was their pilot for the time being. She needed to know who she was dealing with, especially if it got really messy.

You're kidding yourself. You know exactly who you're dealing with.

She found herself trusting Jack in ways that surprised

her, but her training told her she had to be cautious. And she was curious.

"Abbreviated version," Megan said. "I really don't have much time."

"There's nothing that sends up red flags for me, so you can rest easier. Now, the government might have some issues with him, but he had an honorable discharge, several major commendations, and saw some heavy combat. Most of his records are sealed so tightly that even I can't sneak a peak. Frankly, I wouldn't mind having a man like Jack on my team."

That made her feel marginally better, but she'd also dealt with some of the men J.T. employed and contracted with. They were hardly saints.

"Jack enlisted in the army when he was eighteen. Army Rangers. Made it out—most don't last through training. Missions across the globe, most in Central and South America. Ten years ago he retired and has been living in Hidalgo ever since, hiring out his services. I don't know him, but I ran the name by Duke Rogan and he says it's familiar. Probably through Kane—he's been known to bring in mercenaries when needed. There're no public photos of Kincaid that aren't military issue, no public articles or interviews. He does the job and keeps his mouth shut. He's exactly the type of man I would want for liberation and rescue operations. But—"

She waited. "But what?"

"He's a bit of a maverick. I get a sense that he's a bit of a fixer."

"A what?"

"Fixer. Kane and I use it to describe people who want to right wrongs, who stand for the underdog even when the underdog is about to get his brains bashed in. I don't have a list of all his ops, Delta or private, but the ones I found support this. I did hear that last week he led the rescue of a team of medical missionaries from the University of Mexico, and not only returned them to the embassy unharmed, but retrieved most of their supplies. Penicillin, hydrocortisone, prednisone. All extremely valuable on the black market."

Megan almost wished she was writing this down. "Thanks, J.T."

"You don't have any questions? How unlike you, Meg."

"You've been immensely helpful. Now if you can find George Price for me . . ."

"I'll see what I can do."

"I owe you another one."

He chuckled and hung up.

Hans approached her. "I'm going to the morgue with the assistant sheriff. He said there's a decent motel just outside Indio. His deputy will give you directions."

"I'll go with you—" she said.

"No," he cut her off. "Stay here and see if they come up with any witnesses. I'll meet you at the motel later."

"Hans—"

He'd already turned his back to her. She watched him get into a sheriff's car and drive away.

Why in the world was Hans so angry with her? He hadn't been himself since he learned about the mistaken identity. Didn't he see that the dog tags actually helped them? She frowned. Why would the killers intentionally point them in the *right* direction? If she could sit down with Hans and try to talk it out, she knew they'd find something to go on.

Terrific. Both Jack and Hans were ticked off at her, and she hadn't done anything to warrant it.

"Hey, Blondie. Meg."

Her stomach jumped into her throat and she whirled around. "You scared me!"

"I know." Jack had no remorse, but a faint hint of humor tinged his voice. "Padre just called. He thinks he found Price. I can talk to him if you need to stay here—he's in southwest Colorado. Two, two-and-a-half-hour flight."

"Are you sure it's him?" Megan was skeptical. "How did Padre find him so fast? The guy has been hiding from the military for five years. I find it hard to believe your friend found him in less than twelve hours."

Jack shrugged. "They served in the same unit. Padre probably had a better idea where to start looking than anyone in the military bureaucracy."

"I'll go." Megan looked at her watch. It was nearly five. She dialed Hans's cell phone. His voice mail picked up. "Hans, I have a lead on George Price. I'm going to follow up on it with Kincaid. I don't know when I'll be back, but I'll call you tonight." She pocketed her phone. She couldn't worry about Hans right now. She only hoped that Padre had really found Price and this was not a wild-goose chase.

CHAPTER
TWENTY

Jack could sleep anywhere, anyplace, anytime—except during take-off and landing.

Megan didn't have that problem.

She'd fallen asleep as soon as he leveled off after taking off from Joshua Tree. Two hours, fifteen minutes later, he'd landed near Cortez, Colorado, and she was still sleeping.

The quiet flight time had given Jack the opportunity to reflect on more than Scout's murder and his brother Patrick coming out of his coma. Jack also spent a lot of time, too much time, watching Megan.

There was something about her . . .

Her curves. She had one of those tall, hourglass bodies. The kind of curves that a man could dip in and out of. The kind of breasts that begged to be touched, kissed, squeezed.

Long, long legs. Legs too long for her torso, long and muscular. Megan wasn't fat, but she had the shaped body of an athlete. Hard and soft. Hard muscles covered by soft, soft skin. He pictured her legs naked, moving up and down his legs, uncontrollable.

And damn, but was she smart. It was almost sexy that she didn't realize how good she was, but it bothered him that she second-guessed herself so often. He didn't even think she noticed it, it was so ingrained in her. Maybe that was part of being an FBI agent. You weren't allowed to think for yourself. Sort of like being enlisted in the army. You implement orders. That was your job, your vocation. And if you think too much, you're screwed.

After they'd landed, he couldn't resist pulling the clips from her hair. He did it slowly, so as not to wake her. Nothing happened, but he suspected when she sat up, her hair would fall in silky cascades down her back. He touched the bun. Soft. So white. His hands looked nearly black against her hair.

Jack had turned forty last month and in all those years he had never been in love. He'd slept with women, had what might pass as a relationship, and for a time he had a fantasy that his brother's girlfriend would turn to him instead of Dillon. Not that he wanted Kate. She was too much like him.

But Megan was like him, too . . . and completely different. She was a bulldog, pushing, thinking, probing . . . but she also played by the rules. She worked within the system. Jack hated the system. The tired old rules that had forced him to leave innocent people to die.

Megan Elliott was one of *them*. She may not have made the rules, but she sure as hell followed them. And no matter what Jack saw in her, the internal light that told him she would—she *could*—be her own person, he suspected that when push came to shove Agent Elliott would sacrifice anyone and anything, including herself, to preserve the damn system.

Yet she had come with him to talk to Price. She had left her security blanket—Dr. Hans Vigo—and joined Jack on a trip into the unknown. She'd attempted to ask for permission, but when it wasn't forthcoming, she'd made her choice. She might follow the rules, but she was willing to forge her own path.

Jack swallowed uneasily and focused on the controls, double—triple—checking the gauges and system.

Twenty-four hours ago Megan had burst into his life, gun drawn and hackles raised, and now Jack never wanted her to leave.

Shit. What was he thinking? He wasn't, and that was the problem. He wanted to screw her. That's all it was, he hadn't had a good lay in months. Years! The last few women had been . . . nothing to him. He didn't even seek out companionship anymore. If someone was willing and able, sure, he'd oblige, but he didn't pursue any woman.

He wanted Megan in the worst way. He wanted to kiss those pink lips. Top and bottom. He wanted to put his mouth on her breasts, suck her nipples until she squirmed and moved beneath him. Jack wanted to hold her hips as he moved in and out of her, bringing out her passion. He saw in her a fireball ready to combust if he touched just the right spot.

He stifled a groan and willed his dick to settle down. He was only horny because he had a smart, sexy woman sleeping in the cockpit next to him, her lips slightly parted, her lacy little camisole peeking out from under her blouse.

Man, he was in deep shit.

"Wake up already."

Megan groaned and tried to roll over on her side. Her elbow hit something metal and she jumped, sitting straight up.

It was dark. She looked out the window and saw her reflection. Her hair had fallen out of her bun. She must have been in a rush, her hair never fell out when she put it up. She glanced around, feeling out of sorts.

Jack smiled her way, his dark eyes unreadable.

"I'm sorry. I shouldn't have fallen asleep."

"We're here."

He rose from the pilot's seat and walked stooped over to his small overnight bag sitting on one of the seats.

She rubbed the sleep from her eyes and glanced at her watch. Seven-thirty. "Wow, you made fantastic time."

"Scout kept the Caravan in great shape."

She hadn't realized they had been using Scout's plane. She should have put the plane into evidence, or logged it as part of the victim's estate, but she didn't say anything.

She turned in her seat. Jack had pulled off his shirt. His back was to her, marked with scars. She sat on her hands when she almost reached for his deltoids. She swallowed, needing water.

You just woke up. You're dehydrated.

Right. More excuses. *Admit it, Megan, what warmblooded woman wouldn't want that hard body next to her in bed?*

He pulled on a body-hugging black T-shirt, strapped on a shoulder holster, then donned his bomber jacket. Covering up the goods didn't slow her racing heart. He looked as dangerously sexy clothed as bare-chested. "Do you have a jacket?" he asked.

"What you see is what you get," she said lightly.

He turned and frowned. "We're at sixty-two hundred

feet. While this area is nice and warm during the day, it gets cold when the sun sets. It's fifty degrees now, with an expected low of forty-four."

"You should have told me before we left," she snapped. "I asked the deputy to take my bag to the motel back in California."

"I assumed you'd have known that the Colorado mountains weren't south Texas in April."

She bit back a response. "I'm fine," she said through clenched teeth.

"Take my jacket."

"I'm *fine*." She whipped out her cell phone to dial Hans. She couldn't get a signal.

"Try later. We're in the middle of nowhere."

"Where is nowhere?" she asked as they left the plane.

"A small unmanned airstrip outside Mesa Verde."

"How'd you land?" There were only two landing lights on the runway she could see.

"I'm good."

"Where are we going? Should I call the local field office and have someone pick us up?"

Jack laughed. Meg stopped walking and crossed her arms. Damn, he was right. She was freezing.

"Give me your jacket," she said.

He did. She almost felt bad, except that he was still laughing as he handed it over.

She wished she hadn't taken his leather jacket. Sure, it was warm, but it smelled like Jack Kincaid. All male. She wanted to sink into his jacket and close her eyes, feeling as if Jack himself was wrapped around her.

"I have it all taken care of." He walked across the

dark airstrip. Megan wanted to protest and demand information; instead she followed.

They'd walked in silence half a mile and came upon a four-wheel-drive pickup. Jack stopped just out of sight of the pickup, then nodded. "It's Princeton."

"Who?"

"George Price. Princeton is what Padre called him."

Megan stopped walking. "He could be a killer. You should have warned me."

"The killers were in Riverside County this morning. In a vehicle. They couldn't have driven here in ten hours."

"Maybe they had a plane!" She didn't like being brushed off, and she really hated not knowing the game plan. "You should have told me the plan."

"Padre talked to a mutual friend of Price's who said he hasn't left the mountain in years."

Megan said, "I'm not taking any chances, Jack."

"Trust me on this one."

She didn't want to trust Jack. He wasn't a cop, he wasn't a federal agent, and she was the one responsible for stopping these killers before they hurt anyone else.

"I have your back, Blondie."

"Be careful," she said.

The corner of his mouth tilted up. The half-smile on Jack's hard-lined face almost made her heart melt. *Almost.* She could withstand his overwhelming sex appeal.

That's what she told herself as she quickly looked away, flushed, and approached the man who might be the real George Price.

Jack reached the truck first, opened the door, and used it as a shield. "Princeton?"

Price looked more or less like the photo the army sent this morning but bald instead of a standard military cut. He sported a gray mustache and trimmed goatee and wore a diamond stud in his left ear, which had certainly not been there five years before.

"You're not Frank."

Price had a gun in his hand fast; so did Megan. She aimed it at Price's head. He had his gun aimed at Jack through the window.

"Don't even think about it, bitch."

Jack said, "Jack Kincaid."

"Kincaid," Price murmured. "I know of you. And the cop?"

How did he know she was a cop?

"Megan Elliott," Jack said. "I give you my word no one will know you're here."

"I've already packed up," he said, gesturing toward the back of the pickup. "I'm on my way to Timbuktu. You have five minutes. That is, if the cop puts her gun away."

"You first," Megan said.

Price didn't move.

Jack hit Megan's wrist and disarmed her. She wasn't expecting it—her entire focus was on Price. She felt betrayed and hurt.

And genuinely pissed off.

Jack had her gun and held it butt out to Price. The AWOL soldier nodded with a half grin, and Jack returned the gun to her. "Put it away, Megan."

"Ten minutes," Price said. "Only because I like her."

Jack and Megan got into the pickup. She found herself sandwiched between two Neanderthals.

"Sorry about the war games," Price said as he started up the vehicle. "I can't be too careful."

"I understand," Jack said, then added, "but next time you pull a gun on me or mine, I'll break every fucking bone in your hand."

CHAPTER
TWENTY-ONE

Ethan's head pounded. The six ibuprofen and four Tylenol he'd taken over the last two hours had done little to diminish the pain. He needed to sleep, even if his sleep wasn't real. Sleep for him was a movie of the past. It left him not only unrested, but panicky.

"You're a fool." She slapped him. *Slapped* him. "Hold on, Ethan. It's almost over."

"Where's Hackett?"

"He's coming," she said. "Trust me." She looked around the rented cabin, foot tapping, angry at him. Ethan didn't know why.

He took one of his needles and absentmindedly pushed it into his palm. The accompanying pain masked the ache in his head. He pulled the needle out, rolling it between his fingers. "We should have gone to his house. I told you we should have gone to his house."

"I shouldn't have to explain to you again why that's impossible. Too many people, a good security system. Hackett comes here every third Thursday. This is the best place to take him."

"It's too open. Too public." He looked out the window toward the beach.

"He always gets a cabin, not a room in the main lodge."

"That doesn't matter. It's still too public."

"We'll stuff a rag in his mouth like the guy in Vegas," she said. "You just have to focus. No more mistakes, okay?"

He crossed his arms. The sun was setting. He could hear the ocean, but couldn't see it under the reflecting shimmer of the light. He didn't want to be here. He wanted to go home to Pennsylvania. Would his mother even recognize him? He hadn't talked to her in five years. When he came back from Afghanistan, she'd cried. He couldn't handle her tears. Her pain. Any pain, except his own.

"This is the end, Ethan. You know that, right?"

"There's more."

"No there isn't." She kissed his neck. He barely felt it. "After Hackett, you'll finally have peace."

"They aren't all dead."

"That's okay."

He pushed her away. "It's not okay!"

"Can you do this? Or are you backing out now?"

"Of course I can do it," he snapped, rubbing his temples. "Too much sun. I hate the beach."

She shook her head. He didn't know why hating the beach made her look at him with contempt. Was it important?

"I need to be able to trust you, Ethan. This is the last one."

"We left Frank Cardenas alive."

"We've talked about this."

"I'm not done talking."

"I am." Stepping toward him, she touched his face softly. A caress. "Honey, I need to know that you're with me. That you're ready. This is the riskiest of them all."

"I'm ready." He nodded to emphasize how ready he was.

She started toward the door. "When I call—"

"What?" he asked. Where was she going? "Don't leave me."

"I have to. He'll be here. Do not leave this room. Okay?"

She smiled and Ethan blinked rapidly. Did he see fangs in her mouth? No, it had been a trick of the light.

She said, "It won't be long. Be ready when I call."

He straightened. "I will be."

His head pounded. Something wasn't right, but he didn't know what. Maybe it was just him. He was wrong. He was very, very wrong. He laughed, then squeezed his eyes shut with the pain.

She was still in the room. "Don't do anything, go anywhere, talk to anyone. Not until I call you."

Ethan picked up a vase and aimed for the wall, but she grabbed it out of his hands and slapped him. The familiar sting comforted him as much as the sound of her palm hitting his flesh.

"You've already jeopardized everything! Don't cause a scene just because you can't have your way."

"I didn't do anything wrong." He didn't think he had. She'd taught him to think on his feet, and he always did. Those people at the rest stop could have identified them, so he'd taken care of it.

"Don't go there, Ethan."

"They were witnesses. And you were listening to that fool." He stared out the windows. The sun had disappeared. Maybe it had drowned in the ocean. All that was left was bleeding pools of orange, pitiful remnants of the dead sun.

"Do you know how many times I begged for mercy?" He didn't know he'd spoken out loud until he heard his voice ringing in his ears. Still, he doubted. Had his lips moved? Had his throat vibrated?

"Do you know how many times I cried out for the God my parents told me, *promised* me, was there? I turned to Satan, hoping at least he was real and would deliver me. I didn't care about my soul; I just wanted it to stop."

And Satan had come, complete with tits and ass. Ethan turned away from the darkening sky and looked at his master.

She wasn't a god or a devil. She was real, yes, in the flesh. His penis twitched, wanting her to touch him, to hurt him. Make him want to die. She could kill him. She wore a sexy red dress. Like Satan would wear if he were a woman.

"There is no God," he whispered to her. "There is no Satan; there is nothing but humans slithering around the world much as they slithered out of the ooze millions of years ago. And you were buying it. You were *listening*. He would have told someone about you. Remembered you. *You* taught me to be careful. *You* taught me to cover our tracks, to wear disguises, to prevent evidence from building a case against us. It's *working,* and then you turned into a quivering mass of pathetic, crying *Jell-O* when some idiot starts to pray for you. It's your fault he's dead."

Her face was livid. "He caught me off-guard. But you killed him! You didn't have to kill him."

"What was your excuse with that fucking *priest* who left me to die? I should never have listened to you."

"Don't bring the priest into it. The fact remains, you

shouldn't have shot them. Ballistics, you asshole. You used the wrong gun!"

He didn't know what she was talking about. He didn't know much about guns, only what she'd taught him. Yet she looked at him like he'd made a big mistake. He hadn't! But she didn't like him anymore. Despair washed over Ethan.

"I—"

"Just forget it. Forget it," she barked. "They won't be able to get the ballistics report overnight. Forty-eight hours, and that's stretching it. They'd have to pull out all the stops to get anything that fast. I already got rid of the gun, we're going to be okay, I hope it's okay." She shifted nervously on her high heel shoes. She was worried about something. He should remember what, but he couldn't. He squeezed his temples again, the pain blinding.

"It could have been so much worse, Ethan. Get it together and don't do *anything* without my express permission."

His lip quivered and he bit it. "Okay."

"I'll call you when he gets here," she said. "Then you'll have to get ready. Can you do that?"

He nodded.

Karin stared at Ethan and worried that he was going to screw up her entire plan. There was too much riding on this for him to go totally bonkers on her. She'd been managing his psychosis for two years through manipulation, pain, and sex, but none of that seemed to be working anymore.

He didn't look well. She couldn't do anything about that now. She refused to feel guilty for what he had become. He had made his own choices, twisted mind and her manipulations notwithstanding.

She patted Ethan gently on the cheek, still red from her most recent slap. "I need you to be strong. We're in this together. When we're through, you'll be back to your old self. You believe me, right? You know that this was the only way for you to reclaim your life?"

He nodded. She smiled and kissed him. "Good boy. Wait for me."

She closed the door on him and took a deep breath, the evening air fresh and salty, a bit crisp. This was it. Everything she'd been working toward for the last year was riding on tonight.

As long as Ethan stayed in the cabin and waited for her call, her plan would work.

She pulled off the clear latex gloves she'd been wearing and stuffed them in her large purse. She'd had an excuse for Ethan had he questioned her about them, but he hadn't noticed. She wondered if he even really saw her. Most of the time he didn't remember her name.

Which was good, but she couldn't count on it. Like she couldn't count on Ethan not noticing that she hadn't brought any of her personal belongings into their beach cabin.

She stopped far enough away so if Ethan was looking out, he wouldn't see her. She pulled out her compact, inspected her new hair color. She wished she didn't have to cut more hair off later, she kind of liked this in-between length.

She applied another layer of makeup, popped in brown-colored contacts, and fluffed her bottle-blond hair. She'd curled it earlier. She never wore her hair all primped and perfect. It would be a great cover. As soon as she got it wet, it would go straight.

She walked across the resort grounds and into the main hotel and sat in the bar to wait for General Lyle Hackett.

He preferred blondes.

Price took them to a dark biker bar on the outskirts of Cortez, Colorado, fifteen minutes from the airstrip. Megan didn't like feeling intimidated, but she clearly stood out in this environment. She resented Jack for putting her in this situation when they could easily have talked back at the airstrip—or met Price on neutral turf. As it was, everyone in the bar knew Price by name. They called him "George," not much of a new identity.

Price took a bottled American beer; Jack ordered the same. Megan asked for water. Everyone looked at her.

"Get her a beer." Jack leaned over and whispered, "Loosen up. He's okay. But everyone here was suspicious of you the second you walked in, and you announced you were a cop when you ordered water."

"So what?" she snapped. She *was* a cop. A *federal* cop. She didn't want to show Jack how nervous she was out of her element, but he knew. He tugged on her hair, kept his hand on her back. Protective. She didn't need protecting. But she grudgingly admitted to herself that it felt nice.

"So you thought I was dead," Price said after draining half his beer in a gulp.

"Yes," Megan said. "Have you ever been to Sacramento—"

Jack cut her off. "You heard about the Hamstring Killer."

"Not until my pal called me after talking to Padre." He used his bottle to gesture toward the wide-screen television. A baseball game played on the screen. "This is the only television I watch, and it don't play nothing but sports."

The stupid act was just that: an act. Megan tried to ask another question, but Jack squeezed her leg. She bit her tongue and sipped her beer. She resisted the urge to wrinkle her nose. She'd never liked the taste of beer. Wine, sure; margaritas, any day. But beer? Never. Still, she had to do something; otherwise she'd give Jack Kincaid a dressing down he'd never forget. Forced to trust him, she didn't have to like it.

"Scout was one of his victims," Jack said.

Price sipped his beer. "Sorry, Kincaid. That sucks." He sounded genuine.

"So were you."

Price shook his head. "Not me."

"A guy in Sacramento was killed wearing your dog tags."

Price continued shaking his head. "Don't know anything about that. I tossed them five years ago. The day I walked out on the army."

"Where?" Megan interjected.

"Excuse me?"

"Where did you toss them? In the garbage? Gave them to a friend?"

"Why?"

"My victim had them around his neck."

Price shrugged. He glanced left and right as if waiting for someone to jump him. "Don't know, don't care."

Jack said, "He could go after Padre next. It's connected to one of your missions. I think it's related to the one with the reporter. Your team disbanded after that."

"Don't *fucking* bring up that little *prick*." Price slammed the empty bottle down on the bar. Without asking, the bartender brought another.

"We have to catch this guy. Padre gave me the players, and the only people still alive who were on that mission are you, Padre, and Jerry Jefferson. Jefferson is still overseas."

"And Rosemont," Megan added. "We're looking for him right now." Hans said he'd put in a call after getting the list of operations from Padre, but Megan hadn't been briefed.

"I hope he's dead." Price snarled.

Megan didn't like George Price. "How did you feel about the rest of your team?"

He leaned forward almost imperceptibly. Jack tensed beside her, but Megan held her own. She wasn't going to have either of these men bully her, lie to her, or manipulate her. She had too much riding on this case. Justice for the dead, for one. But more important, stopping the killers from claiming another victim.

Price's voice was low. "Let me make it perfectly clear, *Miz* Elliott, Barry Rosemont was never part of my team. He was our fucking *albatross*. He killed Thornton as certainly as if he'd pulled the trigger himself."

Jack said, "Padre said it was a trap."

"You can call it a trap. I call it a setup. They were waiting for us. Because Rosemont couldn't follow orders. He wandered off, was seen by one of their spies, who reported it. By the time we realized we were being followed, our target was long gone and we were surrounded. Thing is, Rosemont *knew* he'd been seen. He didn't tell us because his assignment was to write about a Special Ops mission from planning through execution."

Price was so tense Megan thought if she touched him he'd blow. She stayed silent; this was Jack's world.

"I was in Somalia," Jack said quietly. "The media really fucked us over there."

"I don't blame the assholes in the media as much as the damn politicians thinking that every battle should be broadcast live so the world can watch. And the military leaders who went along with them. Public relations. Fuck that. War ain't pretty, never was, never will be."

"Who had the bright idea to send a reporter on a covert mission?" Jack asked.

"Hackett." Price practically spat his name. When Jack didn't say anything, Price added, "He's retired. He should be dead, too." Price stared straight ahead. "Joe Thornton had two boys. Little kids. He had four more months and then he was out. Was going to be a cop, was already accepted to the police academy."

The pain in Price's voice hit Megan hard. Her dad had come home melancholy at times, looking a lot like Price did now: hard, defeated, hopeless. But Dad had always come back to himself, had always been a solid, noble role model. Price was no role model, but Megan didn't think he was a cold-blooded killer either. Nor was he a torturer. If Price killed anyone, it would be the person he held responsible for the failed operation, not his compatriots.

"Scout had a girlfriend," Jack said, surprising Megan. "Rina had two boys. Thought he'd finally settle down a bit."

"Sometimes it's not in the cards for men like us," Price said. "Sometimes it is." He looked pointedly at Megan. She resisted the urge to shift in her seat, but couldn't stop herself from straightening her back.

"Why'd you attack Russo?" Jack asked.

"Haven't you wanted to deck your commanding officer now and then? When they were stupid?"

"I never did."

"You're a better man than me."

"You didn't deck him. You stabbed him."

"That was an accident. I just wanted to beat the crap out of him. It got out of hand. And it was his knife. He pulled it first."

That was news.

"Why?"

"The interview he did. Five years ago, right after we brought Thornton's desecrated body home. He went on one of those twenty-four-hour news programs and blamed *us* for what happened. He was there, he knew *exactly* what happened and what Rosemont did—and didn't do. Yet he told America that it was his fault, him and his team. That Rosemont had been our responsibility, and we lost him and Thornton because of an error in judgment."

Price slammed his hand on the bar. "I was like an uncle to Joe's boys, but I haven't seen them in five years because their mother thinks I'm the reason their dad is dead. When I saw the program, I snapped. Russo had excuse after fucking excuse, but the fact was, he felt guilty that we didn't go back after Rosemont. When he gave the interview, he'd just gotten word that the reporter was a hostage, not dead like we'd thought. The Taliban was between us and them. We called in reinforcements and waited for a couple Blackhawks so we could return and extract Thornton. But they were hidden, as secure as possible under the circumstances."

Price closed his eyes. "Thornton radioed, said Rosemont had panicked. Compromised their position. His radio was on when the bastards shot him." He drained his beer. "Twenty-two minutes. The prick couldn't sit still for the twenty-two minutes it took the choppers to rendezvous with us and return. Joe died a *hero*. That's what Russo should have said."

Twenty minutes later, Price dropped Jack and Meg back at the airstrip. "You don't have to disappear," Megan said. "I'm not going to turn you in."

Price nodded. "I appreciate that. But I'm outta here. Sometimes people do things they don't want to do. You'd feel guilty about it, but you won't lie if you're asked a direct question."

"But—"

Price shook his head. "I'm a good judge of character. That's how I've stayed a free man for the last five years."

"What happened to your dog tags?" Megan asked.

"I thought Russo was a dead man. I didn't mean to stab him, but I didn't want anyone else taking the fall. I dropped them on his body and disappeared. Haven't seen them since."

CHAPTER
TWENTY-TWO

One thing Karin's mother taught her was how to gather intelligence. If you learned your target's strengths and weaknesses, you could better strategize.

This lesson was particularly important when you were playing double agent, so to speak. That she'd been using Ethan didn't bother her; that she intended to seduce Lyle Hackett bothered her even less.

When she'd started planning Ethan's revenge, she'd had to locate their targets. That wasn't so easy, and Ethan wasn't a lot of help.

But because of his public comments and the attack on his life, Lieutenant Ken Russo had been the easiest to track down. He'd retired to Florida where he lived off disability and worked part-time as a bartender. It had been no problem to move to Orlando and seduce him. Easy to engage him in pillow talk. Easy to search his computer, his files, his memories for the information on all of his team members. He'd been right about everything—except Frank Cardenas.

"Cardenas. He's down in south Texas with Bartleton and some mercenaries."

She had known Russo had a drinking problem, and she'd exploited it. Got him talking about the operation where Ethan was taken hostage, about the men and what had happened to them since. What he didn't know she was able to find once she uncovered their full legal names in Russo's records.

But she'd assumed that when he said Frank Cardenas was with Bartleton, that he was a mercenary as well. It had never occurred to her that he could be a *priest,* even though Russo said his nickname was *Padre.* Until she saw him the other day. He might as well have had a damn *halo* over his head.

She sat at a small table in the bar of the resort hotel and ordered a chardonnay. What she really wanted was something stronger. Cardenas reminded her too much of Father Michael. Not in appearance—Father Michael had been Irish, sixty, and jovial. Like Santa Claus.

Until he was dead.

But she'd claimed vengeance for him. It was only right—he hadn't deserved to die. She was to blame. . . .

No! It wasn't your fault. You couldn't stop her. But you avenged Father Michael. You took care of it when you had the opportunity and the means and the alibi.

And she had made it look like an accident. Suicide.

But Father Michael was still dead, and the fact remained that if she hadn't told him the truth, he would still be alive.

All she'd wanted to do was get her mother out of her life. She wanted to see the bitch behind bars. And would she gloat! She imagined visiting hours, saying to Crystal, "You're stuck here and I'm free and don't have to listen to you anymore."

She'd never felt guilty for any death until Father Michael's. And she hadn't even pulled that trigger.

She sipped her chardonnay and looked around. Hackett was late, and that bothered her. She wasn't going to be able to hold Ethan together for much longer. She might have to change her plan and find another way to get rid of him . . .

Then retired general Lyle Hackett strode into the bar and glanced around. He did a double take when he saw her, then sat at the bar on a stool—where he could watch her—and ordered his usual double Chivas on the rocks.

Research had paid off. When Hackett's wife had her monthly Bunco games, he came here. Had been doing so for more than two years. For the next twenty minutes she discreetly flirted from across the room. For a sixty-two-year-old retired general, Hackett was good looking. He still had a flat stomach. And while his hair was salt-and-pepper gray, he had most of it, trimmed neat and short. He fit the image of retired military.

The bartender brought over a chardonnay. "Compliments of the gentleman at the bar."

She raised her glass to Hackett. He raised his in response.

She said to the bartender, "Tell him he's welcome to join me."

Less than a minute later, General Hackett sat next to her. She raised her glass in a toast. "Thank you."

"A beautiful woman like yourself shouldn't drink alone. Here on business?"

"Yes," she said. "It's just such a beautiful resort. I wish there was more time for pleasure." She smiled, sipped her wine, and added, "My boss put me up in a cabin right on the beach. I could stay there the entire week, leaving only to walk along the ocean at sunset." Karin sighed.

"Sounds nice."

"It is. I'm Rose," she lied smoothly.

"Lyle. Very nice to meet you, Miss Rose."

"Likewise, Mr. Lyle."

She had him on the hook. All she had to do was reel in the line, all the way back to the oceanfront cabin where she'd drop the sinker. Two fish, one bait.

While Jack checked the plane and weather reports, Megan walked up and down the airstrip trying to get cell phone reception.

"Damn, damn, damn," she muttered. The Hamstring Killer had to have killed Ken Russo. There was no other explanation for how a homeless John Doe had George Price's dog tags around his neck. And the killers had to know he wasn't Price, yet they still sent her the tag. They wanted to make sure there was no mistake, that her homeless victim was connected to the other victims. Why?

But she couldn't get anyone on her cell phone—not the Florida FBI office, or Quantico, or Hans in California.

Jack called to her, "Meg, we've got to go. There're thunderstorms from the southeast moving this way."

"Do we have time to go back to town so I can find a phone? I need to call in this information. If the police can look again into Russo's murder we might finally have a suspect."

"If we go back to town, we won't be off this mountain until morning. It's now or not tonight, Meg."

"Fine, we go now." There was no way she wanted to be stuck in Colorado when the investigation was going full force in California. She glanced at her watch. She'd changed it to Pacific time that morning—eight-thirty. They'd be settled into the motel by midnight, but as soon as they landed she'd be on her cell phone to Florida about Ken Russo. And she wanted a copy of that interview Price said had been the impetus of his attack on Russo. And find out if Hans had been able to locate the reporter, Barry Rosemont.

She felt a tinge of worry that she was letting a criminal get away, but at the same time, she couldn't very well have arrested Price and dragged him back to California with her and Jack on the Cessna. And he had provided important information. They were getting close. The key was Russo's murder. Completely different M.O. Why? There was something there, something at the crime scene or Russo's background that the killers didn't want authorities to know about. Otherwise, why not kill him in the same manner as the others? Why not torture him? In addition to Russo's murder being nearly a year ago, it had been set up as a robbery. Was that so the police wouldn't link his death to the others? Possibly.

"Relax," Jack said.

"I am."

He reached out and snatched her cell phone from her grip. She hadn't realized she'd been twisting the phone around in her hands until he took it away.

"You can try again when we get airborne, or we can use the radio."

"Okay. Good. Thanks."

"Let me get the bird off the ground. I need to stay ahead of the storm."

"Right. Of course."

She had a million things on her mind, from the investigation to Hans's strange behavior at the crime scene to her guilt that she'd messed up at the beginning. But now she had a huge break, a major lead. She couldn't wait to work it.

She glanced at Jack when he started the plane, his profile momentarily taking her breath away. Her stomach fluttered and she turned away, flushed, remembering how Jack had touched her face earlier.

Maybe it was that she was still wearing his leather jacket, wrapped in his scent and warmth. That was it. She'd known him only twenty-four hours. Why did it seem so much longer than that?

Jack double-checked the gauges. Then he said, "Ready?"

"Yes."

"Meg?"

Turning, she opened her mouth to respond and his lips were on hers.

All thoughts vanished, all reason gone, her lips melted into Jack's. His hand held her jaw, keeping her facing him, in just the right position for a kiss that was so perfect, she forgot every mouth that had ever touched hers.

Her lips parted unconsciously, her body reacting, unable to control her physical response. Her mind was mush, full of Jack and all the possibilities that lay between them. At that moment, she couldn't have given directions to her apartment even if she'd been in front of the building.

When Megan's lips opened, she released a sigh and

the spontaneous kiss took on a life of its own. Jack didn't know what he had been thinking, just that she looked too good, too *kissable,* sitting in the co-pilot seat, a frown on her lips because she couldn't use her cell phone, her bottom lip protruding in a slight pout that made him want to suck it. He'd planned to give her a quick peck—for luck or some such excuse—but when he'd tasted her, he wanted more. That she felt the same, that she opened to him and put her hand around his neck as if to keep him right there against her lips, made him want to lie to her, tell her the storm was imminent and directly in their path. Then he could take her to the back of the plane and make love to her.

He was halfway out of his seat, pulling her up with his hands, before he realized what he was doing. What he'd been thinking—or not thinking. He let go of her and sat down, his breathing labored. Her skin was flushed, her lips swollen and red, turning Special Agent Megan Elliott from a no-nonsense federal cop into a soft, warm, and incredibly sexy woman.

Her eyelids slowly opened and for a moment he pictured a siren, the way her green eyes had darkened, beckoning him, her lashes long and thick, her lips parted. His cock twitched and he shifted, but failed to alleviate the discomfort.

He coughed to mask his lust and focused on the gauges. "Buckle up, Blondie, it might get bumpy."

Megan looked straight ahead as she obeyed, but he didn't miss the confusion on her pretty face. He felt the exact same way.

Watch out, Kincaid. You like Blondie way too much.

* * *

Ethan waited to the left of the door. Waited. Waited.

She'd called fifteen minutes ago and said she was coming back with Hackett.

He wasn't good at waiting. He was barely able to hold off the panic, the overwhelming sense to flee, that had gotten him captured in Afghanistan in the first place.

It was their fault! They left you!

They were coming back. Thornton had said they were coming back to get them. Thornton had kept whispering, *"Shut up. Shut up."*

Ethan whimpered as if he was still trapped in the rocks. *Something crawled over his foot. He looked down, saw the scorpion as if he were right back in the rocks. He shook his foot violently.*

"You're going to get us killed!"

He looked around the room, expecting to see Thornton. His heart raced. Where was he?

Voices. Oh, God no, he was going to be killed.

A woman's laugh. Odd. What woman traveled with the Taliban? Waves crashed across the desert . . . Ocean waves. He wasn't in Afghanistan.

Santa Barbara.

Ethan looked at the knife in his hand. He remembered what he had to do.

"Whoops!" A female voice said outside the cabin door. She giggled. "I dropped my key."

"I got it," a man said.

Ethan frowned, clutched the knife. What was she doing? Too much noise.

Shut up! Shut up! You're going to get us killed.

He stayed flat against the wall, silent.

He had to trust her like he hadn't trusted Thornton. Had he just listened, not panicking, not screwing up in the first place, he'd never have been held hostage. Thornton would never have died. Ethan couldn't have done any of this without Karin. She was the brains. He knew it. It was all her plan, to help him get better. But he didn't feel better. Instead he felt cold. He was so cold.

"Rose, God woman, you're driving me crazy."

Rose? Who was Rose? Was Ethan in the wrong room? No, this was his room. He'd taken it using his fake I.D. Ethan Rose. Rose. Rose.

The door opened.

"Lyle," the woman said. "You've made my whole week worth it."

"And we haven't gotten to the good part."

Lyle Hackett. It was him. Ethan's target.

The door swung shut. In the dim light, Ethan saw her eyes staring at him over Hackett's shoulder. She nodded as Hackett kissed her neck. Her head tilted back. She mouthed *now*, then wrapped her arms around the general's neck.

Smooth and swift, with more confidence than anything else he had done in the last five years, Ethan brought the blade down hard across the back of General Lyle Hackett's hamstrings.

Hackett screamed, but it was stifled when he fell to the floor.

"Gag him!" Ethan exclaimed. "You were supposed to drug him so he couldn't make any noise!"

Hackett was dragging his body toward the sliding door that led to the beach. He was howling, a fierce, pain-filled bellow that could summon the devil himself.

Ethan grabbed a gag from his black bag and stepped toward Hackett. Out of the corner of his eye, he saw movement. And something . . .

She had her gun out. The gun she'd told him she got rid of. That's when he saw the shine of the plastic gloves as her hands gripped the weapon. And finally Ethan figured out what had seemed so wrong and out of place earlier.

She'd been wearing gloves the last time she was in the room.

She aimed the gun at Hackett.

"No," Ethan said. "Not yet—"

She fired the gun twice, in Hackett's back and his skull. *Bang bang.* His body convulsed, then was still. Blood seeped from under his body and spread wide, a dark burgundy as the thick beige carpet absorbed what seemed like a huge amount of blood. She must have hit his aorta. Ethan hadn't ever seen that much blood, even when Thornton's body had been riddled with bullets.

"What are you doing?" he cried. "Someone will hear."

She pointed the gun at Ethan.

He stared at her. Her eyes looked different. Darker. Her disguise—she didn't look like the woman he'd met two years ago, or the one he'd left Texas with two nights ago.

"You fucked up yesterday, Ethan. You killed without a plan."

He shook his head. "This isn't about yesterday." The gloves. The gun. In a clear and terrifying flash of sanity, *he knew.* He'd been set up.

"Thanks for the lessons. I'll put them to good use."

He stepped toward her at the same time the fire

alarms went off. Someone must have heard the gunshots and pulled the alarm. Ethan made a move for the gun, knife in hand. She dropped to her knees and now he was over her, knife raised in a stabbing motion.

"You fucking traitor!" The pain and rage and hurt overwhelmed him. He saw clearly, and in the brief moment before he sliced her he realized this had been her plan all along.

She pivoted at the last second and the knife went into her arm.

She grunted and scrambled away. Ethan went after her. She had to die. He wailed, a foreign and forlorn sound. He kicked her and she stumbled, then rolled onto her back, right next to the dead general. He brought the knife down again, ready to plunge it deep into her black heart.

"You. Set. Me. Up."

He felt the searing pain before he heard the gunshot. His body jerked again. Again. He saw Thornton in front of him, his body full of holes, his brain a bloody pulp.

I'm sorry.

Ethan fell to his knees. Reached for his savior, his executioner. She crawled away. Then everything went black.

Finally.

The scent of death permeated the room, the blood cloying, the warm fragrance of gunpowder tickling her nose. She tossed the gun toward Ethan's body and picked up the knife. Her arm stung, and she was furious that he'd gotten a jab at her. She shoved it into her bag.

She ran out the back door, a quick glance at the digital clock on the desk of the cabin. She'd killed two men in two minutes. There had to be a record in that.

But she wasn't free yet.

She slipped off her spiked heels as soon as she hit the sand and ran down the beach, away from the cabin, toward the pier in the distance. She paused half a minute to pull her red dress off and stuff it into the side pocket of her oversized purse. She wore a one-piece red swimsuit underneath. It was dark and moonless and no one was this far down the beach, though she heard a group of people in the distance. The tide was coming in, wetting her bare feet.

She bent down and scooped up the ocean water with her arms, splashing it over her body, wetting her hair, washing the blood off her hands and face. She rubbed the saltwater all over her. A larger wave crashed right in front of her, drenching her, and she laughed at the night.

Sirens whirled in the distance. She looked back at the resort hotel, the entire place ablaze with light as the floodlights snapped on. She'd run farther than she'd first thought. A distant whirl of police lights caught her eye as they stopped near the row of cabins.

Her heart raced, her mind awhirl. It had worked out even better than she'd planned. She'd been able to seduce Lyle Hackett instead of drugging him. The thrill of seducing a man to his death exhilarated her.

When she'd first conceived of this plan, she'd felt a bit guilty that the trained psycho had to die, but after Ethan had killed those people at the rest stop, she lost that guilt. He should have been dead years ago. His botched suicide attempts were pathetic. If he'd *really* wanted to be dead he could have done it.

She pulled a sealed gallon-sized plastic bag from her

purse and removed a black-and-red-flowered sarong. The plastic had kept blood and evidence off her clothing. She tied the skirt around her waist, draped the bag over her shoulder, and walked casually toward the pier. Toward freedom, toward revenge and final justice.

It was time to start the endgame. This was the part of the plan she'd never told Ethan about. She had known he'd be dead before it started.

CHAPTER
TWENTY-THREE

When Megan checked into the motel she had a message that Hans wanted to see her ASAP. She glanced at Jack, uncertain about what had happened between them on the plane. He avoided her eyes and for a moment she thought she'd imagined the whole thing. Or that she had been the aggressor and Jack was embarrassed.

But the truth was he'd kissed her and she kissed him back. And then some.

"I need to talk to Hans," she said, her voice thick. She handed him his jacket.

He took it, but didn't seem to know what to do with it. "I'm going for a run."

He looked like he wanted to kiss her again, then he stepped back. "See you in the morning, Blondie."

She watched him pick up his duffel bag and walk out of the lobby without looking back. She released a pent-up breath. How could one kiss leave her so disoriented?

Little sleep, lots of work.

Right, Megan, lie to yourself all you want.

She walked through the same doors. Jack was in the room right next to hers. Hans's room was across the corridor. She was not going to chase after Jack. No matter how incredible that kiss had been, it was just one kiss, and she had work to do. She glanced at her watch. It was nearly midnight.

Maybe Hans was asleep. She'd done everything she could since leaving Colorado—called Quantico's Assistant Director Rick Stockton himself about Price and Rosemont after getting his home number from her boss, who she quickly briefed. Richardson also had news from Detective Black in Sacramento—the van, where John Doe had been tortured, had been found abandoned in a remote area of Placer County, off Interstate-80.

Which made sense to Megan. Price's dog tag had been sent to her from Reno. I-80 went through Reno. The killers could have gone almost anywhere after that, but instead took a straight course down to south Texas and killed Lawrence "Scout" Bartleton.

So far, no useful evidence had been collected off the van, but it was being processed in the FBI garage by their trace evidence experts.

When Megan finally talked to Stockton, he assured her that he would take a personal interest in reexamining the Russo case and pull the tapes from the interview Price mentioned. He would also get a warrant for Rosemont's medical records. He ordered her to sleep. "An exhausted agent makes mistakes, Agent Elliott."

Except she hadn't yet connected with Hans, and he'd left her the message. She'd slept two hours during the flight to Colorado. She could spare another hour.

Hans opened the door seconds after she knocked. He held the door open for her to enter, but said nothing, shutting it firmly behind her. He walked over to the desk where papers and crime scene photos were spread, but he didn't sit down.

The cliché "death warmed over" fit Hans. His skin was too pale, his eyes bloodshot, and he seemed to have aged ten years since she'd last seen him.

"What's wrong?" she asked.

"What did you think you were doing tonight?"

"Excuse me? Didn't you get my message? Rick Stockton said he would call you and—"

"Yes," Hans interrupted, "but that doesn't excuse you for going after a suspect on your own."

"Jack Kin—"

"I don't care!" Hans crossed over to the dresser and put his palms down on the top, not looking at her. "You know better than this. What about a warrant? What about backup?" He turned and stared at her. "You've fucked this up from the beginning."

She blinked. Hans didn't swear. Not like this. Did he really think she'd screwed up the case?

She had assumed the first victim was George Price, but the more she'd thought about it that night, the more she realized that if she thought he was a John Doe from the beginning, they'd never have made the connection to the army or Delta Force or the dead soldiers so quickly. Jack had concurred. With the incompetent police chief in the Bartleton investigation, and the lack of communication between the different agencies until the FBI showed interest, they certainly wouldn't have teamed up with Jack and Padre and had the information about the Delta ops that led to a possible suspect—the reporter, Barry Rosemont. And no way would they have found Price without Padre's connection. At least not tonight.

Yes, she made a poor assumption, but it had ended up being beneficial.

"Warrant?" she said, not knowing what part of Hans's verbal attack to address first. "I didn't need a warrant. I was talking to a potential witness—"

"Witness? Is that what you're calling killers these days?"

"You've lost me, Hans. Where do you think I've been?"

"Hunting down George Price. And if he's—"

"He's not the killer."

"And you know this how? Because he told you?"

Her mouth dropped open. "I— He didn't have motive or opportunity."

"And you were able to ascertain this in a few hours?"

Megan didn't know what she'd done to warrant such a dressing down. She straightened her back and said, "Let me explain from the beginning. I think you must have misinformation or something—"

"I talked to Father Francis. He tracked down George Price like that." Hans snapped his fingers. "We find out the real George Price isn't dead, and less than twelve hours later the only other surviving Delta team member hands you his location on a silver platter?"

"It's a close-knit group. They know people. I don't understand your point."

"Maybe Frank Cardenas isn't the good priest everyone thinks he is."

"This doesn't sound like you—"

"You don't know me, then."

Hans might as well have slapped her. Megan had met Hans three months after her father was killed in Desert Storm. She'd been a senior in college. A visiting lecturer, Hans had recruited her into the FBI. Became a friend, a mentor, someone she'd confided in. He'd been the best man at her wedding, and while her marriage to Mitch Bianchi hadn't lasted, her friendship with Hans had. They'd spent six weeks in Kosovo together, and afterward she didn't consider anyone else a closer friend or confidant than Hans Vigo.

"Price told us that—"

He cut her off. "You found him?"

"Yes. It was arranged."

"And you didn't arrest him?"

"For what?"

"He went AWOL five years ago and disappeared. You found him, and let him go? You used to believe in the law, Megan. You used to believe in the rules. The system."

"I still do. I didn't do anything—"

"You let our primary suspect in seven murders get away!"

Megan's voice cracked when she said, "Price didn't have the opportunity. He's not a suspect. He's no saint, but if you were there you'd have heard his testimony and known he was telling the truth."

"I wasn't there. You left without me."

"You didn't answer my call."

"The interview could have waited."

She didn't agree, but simply said, "It's my case."

"I'm the senior agent."

He was pulling rank again. Her stomach flipped. She pressed on when all she wanted to do was run away—or scream at Hans. Something strange was going on with him, and she didn't know what it was.

But his words niggled at her. Maybe he was right.

Maybe she shouldn't have let George Price walk away. Maybe her judgment was completely off.

"Price told me he left his dog tags with Russo's body after he accidentally stabbed him."

"He *accidentally* stabbed his commanding officer?"

"Price said the knife was Russo's. Russo had gone on a news program and blamed his team for a failed mission in Afghanistan that resulted in a civilian being taken hostage. Rosemont—Padre mentioned him."

"The same ex-soldier who miraculously located an AWOL sergeant in less than a day."

Megan had had enough with Hans. "I don't know what is wrong with you, Hans! I followed a lead and it paid off. For years you've been telling me I need to trust my instincts more, and when I do you tell me how wrong I am. I'm telling you right now that I believe everything Price told me. He had nothing to do with these murders. He's been living quietly in the mountains of Colorado for five years. If he had anything to do with it, he would never have agreed to meet with me. He didn't know it wasn't a trap; he came willingly because Padre asked him to."

"And you believed everything he said. He could have been laying out a nice false trail so we didn't go looking for him. To throw us off track."

"We'd have never found him! If CID couldn't find him for five years, we wouldn't have. He's off the grid."

"If I were you, I'd spend tonight writing up a detailed report of what you did and said and heard. You're going to need it."

"What?"

"You fucked up, Megan. I wish things were different, but I'm going to have to file a report with the Office of Professional Responsibility. So you'd better be damn sure that you followed proper procedure or you'll be lucky to have a job next week."

CHAPTER
TWENTY-FOUR

Jack ran hard for five miles, but the workout did little to curb his appetite for a certain lanky blond fed who had legs that went up to Heaven and lips that begged for sin. He'd have to take a cold shower if he was going to get any sleep tonight.

He jogged up the path leading to his room and glanced toward the pool. It was closed, but maybe a quick jump in the deep end would get rid of the ache in his groin. Not the ideal way to ease his hard-on, but he didn't think slipping into Megan's bed would go over too well.

Jack wanted to drown the little devil sitting on his shoulder telling him to go to Megan, consequences be damned.

The pool was gated, but the gate wasn't locked. He approached the edge of the pool and removed his shirt, then saw a lone figure sitting at the opposite end, feet in the water, hands back, face upward.

He'd recognize her silhouette anywhere. *Megan.*

The breeze was warm and dry even at one in the morning. The underwater lights were dim, framing her curvy, athletic frame. Jack walked around the pool and sat next to her. "Up for a little skinny dipping?" he teased. *Why did you say that? What are you planning on doing?* "Everyone else in this place is sleeping," he added.

"Umm," she said, averting her face.

He touched her cheek to turn her face to his; it was wet.

She batted away his hand, wiped her face with her shirt. "Why aren't you sleeping?" she asked, her voice cracking. She coughed into her hands and cleared her throat.

"I went for a run."

"At one in the morning?"

"I needed to release some energy."

She didn't say anything and he realized she knew exactly why he was in discomfort.

He asked, "What's wrong?"

"I'm okay."

"I didn't ask if you were okay."

Of course she was okay, she was a cop. They had to be okay with senseless death and violence. In many ways, cops and soldiers were alike. They saw the worst of mankind and they continued to do the job. The dead and dying; the helpless and hopeless. Dead women, dead children, dead soldiers and cops. Jack had seen more than he'd ever wanted, or expected. He'd been raised by a military father, but he didn't know what that meant at the time. Not until he saw his first corpse. Buried his first friend. Killed his first enemy.

Megan explained, "Fifteen years ago I graduated from Quantico. I hadn't wanted to be an FBI agent. I didn't know what I wanted to be. I'd never been close to my mom, and although I know I romanticized my father as perfect, especially after the divorce, he was still my hero. When he was gone . . ."

Her voice drifted away. Jack stuck his feet in the water and watched her toes stretch and relax, stretch and relax. Her toenails were painted dark red. What was that on the big toe? A flower? Jack couldn't imagine Megan sitting still long enough to allow someone to paint her toes. Maybe he didn't know her well enough. Yet.

"One of my professors had a family emergency," she said. "We had a substitute for two weeks, a guest lecturer, Hans Vigo from the FBI. I thought that was silly for a psychology class, until I listened to him. I was hooked. He recruited me and the rest is history. I can't imagine being anything other than an FBI agent. This is what I am supposed to be. I'm nothing without the job. I *am* the job."

She looked out at the ripples that their feet made as they moved lazily in the cool water. Her eyes were still bright, but there were no more tears. Jack breathed a silent sigh of relief, though her words pained him. They were familiar and foreign at the same time.

"Before I left the military, I couldn't see myself in any role other than soldier," he said quietly.

"You're still a soldier."

"It's different when you can walk away when you want."

"But can you? Really? Just walk away and never do what you know, what you love? What if it was taken from you?"

Before Jack could say anything, she continued. "I had a kidnapping my first year in Sacramento. A five-year-old girl. At first they thought her father had snatched her because he and the mother had been in court fighting over custody ever since the girl had been born. But we quickly realized he hadn't, that a child predator had grabbed her.

"I knew the statistics, that if we found her alive, she would have been . . . hurt. But I also knew that if we didn't find her fast, she'd be dead. My team worked closely with the sheriff's department, analyzed every tip, every trace of evidence, and based on a small flower, we tracked them to Amador County, east of Sac. We talked to everyone about our suspect's black van. We found them. In eight hours, forty-nine minutes. And the little girl was not only alive, but untouched."

She smiled. "Melody. Her name is Melody and she's nine years old now. And it's her and everyone else I can save—and can't save—that keeps me going. If there's a victim, I want to catch the perp. If there's a crime, it needs to be solved. I hate loose ends."

"But."

"Most crimes I understand. Melody's kidnapper, he was a repeat sex offender. I *understand* that. He needed to be stopped, but at least I could look at the victim and look at the criminal and figure out who and what and why. But those folks at the rest stop? Where's the why in their murders? Why them? Why did they die? It was senseless and wrong. Hell, if they'd been *robbed* I could understand it! Hate it just as much, but at least there would be a *reason*. But the killer just shot them and walked away. Let a family die for nothing. And the baby . . . oh, God, I haven't felt this helpless since Kosovo."

"I didn't know you were there."

"After the war. I was part of the evidence response team that dug up the mass graves and identified the remains of those slaughtered. Another senseless crime, on a far bigger scale."

"You couldn't have stopped what happened in Kosovo just like you couldn't stop what happened to that family yesterday."

"But that's the thing: I know I couldn't have done anything about Kosovo, and at least giving families a body to bury, answers to their questions, kept me going. But how do you know I couldn't have stopped Thomas and Loretta from dying? Hans thinks if I hadn't jumped to the conclusion that George Price was a victim, the Hoffmans wouldn't have died. I should have brought Price in for questioning—"

"Stop, Megan. We already talked about this. If you didn't think your victim was Price, we wouldn't even be this far in the investigation."

"But the killers wanted it like this. Why?"

"I don't know."

"I feel manipulated when I realize that it's because of the killers that I'm here at all. They're jerking me around, pulling me along on a chain, keeping me far enough away so I can't stop them, but close enough so I can almost see them . . . then they slip away. I feel so damn helpless! And now Hans is furious that I spoke to Price without a warrant and didn't bring him in."

"He spoke to us because Padre assured him he was safe."

"I didn't ask Padre to do that. I have the laws of this country to follow. I should have brought him in. What if I'm wrong *again*? What if he *is* involved somehow?"

"You don't believe that. If you believed he was guilty, you would have arrested him in Cortez."

"What if I missed something? What if I overlooked evidence, or ignored a witness, or—"

Jack put his finger to Megan's lips. She sucked in her breath, startled by the touch. One finger, but a wholly intimate gesture.

"What happened tonight with Hans?"

Two tears escaped her eyes. Jack's jaw clenched. He wanted to hit the man who had made Megan cry.

"It's me," she whispered. "I messed up."

His voice was deeper than normal when he spoke. "I don't have to tell you what you know in that sharp and beautiful head of yours. Shit happens. People like us stop it when we can, but most of the time we're cleaning up other people's messes. You didn't do anything wrong. You followed your head, and it led you to information that *is* going to lead us to answers."

"You believe Price is innocent, right?"

"Do you?"

"I don't know anymore. What if I let a killer get away?"

"Is that what Hans said?"

"He may be right. But it's out of his hands, and mine." She turned her head away from him, wiped her eyes, stared at their feet in the water.

"What do you mean?"

"He's filing a report with OPR. Sort of the FBI's version of CID."

Jack put his hand on her jaw and forced her to look at him. "Why?"

"I don't break the rules, Jack. But since Monday I've completely disregarded every rule out there. And if my assumptions led to the Hoffmans being killed—"

"Stop."

Megan wanted to look away, but Jack held her gaze. He was holding her face too tightly, but in the way he stared at her, she saw the war battling beneath his skin. The same war within her.

"You are not responsible for anyone dying. You did not pull the trigger, and neither did George Price. You know it, I know it, Hans knows it, too. I don't know what happened today to get his panties in a twist, but tomorrow he'll think differently."

"I hope so," she whispered.

He dropped his hand from her mouth, skimmed her thigh with his fingertips.

This time when Jack kissed her, Megan knew what to expect, but her heart still skipped a couple beats, her blood heated, her breath came heavier. He was intoxicating, and she was an addict. She'd never get enough of Jack, his lips, his tongue, his hands as they moved up her thigh, skimmed her pelvis, landed solidly on her waist. His fingers kneaded her, as if he were a cat getting comfortable. *Tom Cat.* Jack wasn't the sort of man to build a relationship, a life, or start a family. Megan knew that in her head, but her heart, and her libido, told her head to stop thinking.

Then she had no room for thought at all. Jack's kiss was anything but timid and hesitant. His hands moved from her waist, firmly skimmed her breasts, then fisted in her hair, kneading, as he held her head right where he wanted it, his mouth open, his tongue searching for hers. Her senses breathed in his rich, intoxicating aroma of sweat from his run and lust from their embrace. She'd never imagined such an instant passion, a white heat that devoured her, making her yearn for someone, making her want Jack.

He kissed her thoroughly, her lips wonderfully swollen, her body hot and needy. She pushed away thoughts of the future, of how wrong it was to be here with Jack, someone she shouldn't want and couldn't have. Megan simply enjoyed the intense heat and mutual deep attraction. Simple? There was nothing simple about Jack Kincaid, and nothing simple about how she felt about him.

He slipped into the pool and pulled her in with him. She gasped as the cool water soaked her clothes. He seemed unaffected. He looked at her, his face inches from hers. Just looked. Her mouth parted. He rubbed his index finger around her lips, up her face, to her eyes. He closed her lids lightly, kissed them with a feather of a touch.

"Come here." His voice was low and as rough as the whiskers on his face. Without waiting for her to come, he pulled her to him, neck deep in water, holding her up with little effort. She wrapped her legs around his waist, her wet body rubbing against his hard chest. His hand went up under her cami, his thumb rubbing her nipple. She gasped into his mouth and he kissed her hard, his hands stroking up and down her back, her face, her hair.

"It's time," he whispered into her ear.

"For what?" She licked his jaw, up to his earlobe and he clutched her tighter.

"To make love."

She pulled back. "Here?"

He shot her a smile. "I'd love to, but I was thinking more along the lines of a bed. This time."

This time.

His hand rose from the water and he was holding a key. The number on the plastic tag was 115.

"That's mine."

"It was in your pocket." He grinned as he kissed her, then swam over to the edge of the pool, holding her close to him. He lifted her out, sat her on the edge, then pulled himself out with the grace and sex appeal of a champion swimmer. The water poured off his body and she couldn't avoid staring.

He held out his hand. She took it and he pulled her into his arms. Jack didn't take his eyes off her as if fearing she'd change her mind.

She may have lost her mind, but she had no intention of changing it.

They walked to her room, but Megan didn't notice anything except Jack as he unlocked the door and they slid inside. As soon as it closed, he backed her against the door, his mouth on hers, her arms around his neck. She shivered, from the heat of passion and the cold dip in the pool. He turned her around, walked her over to the bed as if they were in the middle of an intimate dance. His leg was between hers, her leg was between his, and she felt through his wet shorts how this tango was going to end. The thrill coursed through her body, a surge of both lust and apprehension.

"Jack—" She could say no more because he was kissing her again.

"You're cold." He pulled off her cami in one motion. His hands cupped her bare breasts, warming them, and she gasped at the extremes, the heat and the cold.

Jack's hard body radiated a thousand degrees of heat, and Megan's chill disappeared, filled instead with something she hadn't felt in . . . forever. No thought, no responsibility, no doubt, no regret. She opened her arms to Jack, offering everything she had, knowing he would take it all and more. Knowing he would give everything, and then some.

What happened to his shirt? He wasn't wearing one. He'd left it at the pool. He stepped out of his wet shorts and he was naked. In the dim light, she saw his silhouette, a perfect Cuban god. Her breath caught—*Breathe, Megan! Breathe!*

She swallowed, her mouth dry, and stepped forward. Her hands rested on his chest, she ran her fingers up and down, back and forth, massaging his chiseled muscles. He leaned into her, and she felt the edge of the bed against the back of her knees. And still he moved forward. Pushing her down, his hands on her hips, tugging her pants and panties off together.

"Megan," he whispered in her ear, then nibbled on her lobe, his tongue darting in and out and around, his hands on her breasts, her shoulders, her head. His hands moved in a rhythm they created together, seeming to touch her everywhere, but not enough. She wanted more, more of him, as much of Jack as she could have.

She grabbed his hands, held them tight, and arched her back so she could kiss his neck. His day's growth of beard was both rough and incredibly erotic as it scratched her cheeks and lips. Her tongue came out, licked him like he was a chocolate ice cream cone, up to his lips, where she claimed them as hers. At least for now, at least for tonight.

Jack had known from the moment he kissed Megan in the plane hours earlier that he would be in her bed tonight. One kiss did not satisfy him; he'd been tasting her ever since. He was intoxicated with the need, on the verge of losing control. He never lost control. Not in life, not in the field, and not in bed with a woman.

But with Megan, he felt that hard-wired control slipping away, her body both sexy and timid, arousing him beyond reason. He wanted her now, all of her, without hesitation. Her skin was soft, her muscles hard. The contrast was as sexy as the woman herself. She had no idea how he'd craved her, no idea that the minute she burst into the jail cell when Carlos Hernandez's goons were trying to kill him that he'd wanted her just like this. Naked. With him. In bed.

Her hands were everywhere, his head, his back, squeezing his biceps. Her legs moved as well, up and down his calves, her back arching whenever he eased up, trying to catch his breath, trying to slow things down. Slow things down before he couldn't. But slow meant being in control, and his last thread of restraint snapped.

He didn't want slow. He wanted *now.*

He put his hand between her legs, damp from the pool, damper with desire. She gasped when he pushed his finger into her. He leaned up, watched her face. The way her flushed face glowed. Her lips red and swollen from his relentless kisses. Her hair was wet and loose around her head, tangled and wanton. Her eyes were half-closed, and she licked her lips, her breath heavy, her fingers clutching his shoulders as she sighed.

"Look at me."

She opened her eyes at his command. He kissed her softly, his tongue and lips trailing up to her ear and back to her mouth. He stared into her eyes, so dark green and so deep he could drown in them.

This moment in time was perfection.

He forced himself to enter her slowly, easily. She gasped and wrapped her legs around his calves. For a moment they both froze, as if they'd reached a juncture and didn't know which way led to safety, which way to destruction.

"I want you, Megan." He sank into her, not knowing which path this union would ultimately take, but willing to fight for them, this primal possession unfamiliar but real. More real than anything Jack had felt or believed in for a long, long time.

He wanted her, yearned for her, needed her. He couldn't articulate it, he couldn't fathom how he could have Megan in his life. It was an overwhelming sensation of rightness as he wrapped his arms around her, holding himself deep inside her, wanting to go slow, to savor her touch, her smell, her tightness, her trust. But slow wasn't in the cards, not this time, as the blood rushed from his head and Jack could no longer think, and all patience disappeared.

Megan lost her ability to reason as Jack began to move deep inside of her, slowly, the muscles in his neck tense with forced restraint. She put her hands on his tight backside and held him inside her, wanting to stay like this forever, but needing to rush the explosion that was building rapidly within her. It was as if all the energy in the room, in the city, in the entire state, had merged within them, combustible, waiting for the blast.

"If you touch me like that I'm going to lose it."

"I. Am." She couldn't finish her sentence. She *had* lost all common sense and reason when he touched her at the pool. She knew then that they'd only be able to appease their desire in bed. It was lust, pure animal lust.

But it felt so much bigger than simple sex. She didn't want to think too much for fear their connection would slip away.

His slow strokes moved faster and dove deeper. She

gasped, her hands running up his back, squeezing, to his shoulders, her short nails digging in as she felt the last of her energy rushing to the spot where their friction generated combustible heat.

They were in sync, their bodies moving together for the mutual benefit and need to pleasure the other, skin slick with perspiration. Meg closed her eyes again, the sensation of their flesh together so dominate, so volatile. Her hands gripped his shoulders.

"God. Jack."

He kissed her, his lips moving in rhythm to their hips, and she cried out into his mouth as her body turned inside out, releasing her lust, her mind, and her heart to Jack.

When Megan's body shook beneath him, Jack let go. It had been an inner battle to hold on as long as he did. He wasn't a teenager anymore—what was with this insatiable need? He'd gone in too fast, unable to stop himself. He didn't lose control.

Until now.

He rolled over onto his back, bringing her with him. Kissed her over and over again. Her skin tasted of salt and chlorine.

"Now," he said, "I can do it the right way."

"If that was the wrong way, I like the wrong way."

He smiled and kissed her.

"I want to make love to you."

"And what was that?"

"That, darling, was sex. Pure lust. Now I'm going to make love to you." He kissed her. "Slowly." He brushed her hair away from her face and licked her forehead. "Very slowly." His heart still raced and he felt hers pounding against his chest. His hands caressed the side of her face. "You're beautiful, Megan."

His hands ran down her body as she rested on top of him, breath heavy and satisfied on his chest. He loved the taste of her, especially now, her body hot and slick and relaxed. She seemed to melt all over him, as relaxed as a purring cat.

His fingers trailed down her spine, to her waist, and over rough skin. Feeling . . . what was that? He circled his hand over the unexpected texture of her flesh.

She tensed and tried to roll away. He didn't let her. He pulled her back. "This was where you were shot?"

"Yes." Her voice was clipped.

She didn't want to talk. Jack wasn't going to let her remain silent. The light was dim, but he sat up and wiggled her around until he could see the wound clearly.

The scar was large, part of it round, part an incision from where the surgeon had gone in to remove the bullet. But it wasn't a small invasion. It had been major surgery to remove her damaged kidney.

"I know, it's ugly."

He kissed her scar. "All better."

She'd turned her head away from him. He turned her head back. Her eyes watered. Oh, God, no. He couldn't take tears. Not these kind of tears.

"Sweetheart, if you think a little scar is going to bother me, you don't know me."

As he said it, he realized that they didn't know each other. Not the details. He didn't know where she was born, where she grew up, if she had brothers or sisters, why she and her mother didn't get along.

But he knew her heart and her mind. He could predict with relative certainty what she would say or do. He knew the important stuff. Her compassion was endless and her sense of right and wrong well formed. She was worthy of love. To love and be loved. Jack didn't know if he was worthy of her.

Megan stared, eyes probing his, and he kissed her. He didn't care, he would do anything to keep her in his life.

He might not know everything about her, but he knew that she fit with him. He wasn't good with emotions or explaining his thoughts and feelings. That was why he'd been estranged from his family for so long. He was a man of action. Do it, don't talk about it.

But something about this scar bothered Megan deep inside. She'd been flip yesterday when she told him about being shot in the back. But she wasn't flip about it now.

He kissed her lightly on the cheek, and adjusted their bodies so that she was spooned closely against him, his arms tight around her, his lips on her ear.

"Tell me."

"I have one kidney."

"I know."

It took her a minute to speak. He didn't move. He wasn't going anywhere. Neither was Megan.

"I was ambushed. I wasn't watching my back when I should have been. And took a bullet. It's only one kidney, and it's gone, and yeah, it still bothers me, but I'm fine."

The way she said it made it sound like a betrayal, but Megan didn't say more. She took one of his hands, the one that had been lightly caressing her breasts, and kissed his palm. Her tongue sent jolts of lust down to his hardening cock.

"You were going to show me the difference between having sex and making love."

"I am."

He kissed her neck, turning her on to her back so he could have easier access to all her soft skin. Lips to lips, lips to neck, lips to breast. His hands kneaded her shoulders, her arms, her thighs.

"There is not going to be an inch of your skin I don't taste," he whispered, his voice rough. "From your head . . ." he kissed her eyelids, his tongue trailing down to her ears, then to her neck. "To your painted toes."

He slid off the bed and Meg groaned from the sudden chill. Then his mouth was on her toes and she gasped. Electric bolts jolted her body as Jack sucked her toes, licked the bottoms of her feet, kissed her ankles. The backs of her knees. And higher.

True to his word, Jack tasted every inch of her flesh. Slowly.

And slowly, they brought each other up and over the edge once again.

After killing Ethan and Lyle Hackett, Karin walked a mile to the hotel she'd checked into the day before under one of her aliases, Erin Hunter.

She'd always liked that name. Hunter. It suited her. Erin *the* Hunter. Erin. Hunter. *Huntress*. She grinned.

It was late, but the hotel was brightly lit and she wasn't positive that her late-night dip in the ocean had washed away all the blood. She slipped in through a side door, using her card key, and rode the elevator up to the penthouse suite. She deserved the penthouse. She'd ordered champagne when she first arrived, asking the staff to deliver it while she was gone. It was still cold, sitting in a stainless steel cooler filled with cold water.

She stripped, shoving her bathing suit and sarong into the black bag. The bag had to be disposed of, but she needed to destroy the evidence first. A heavy dose of bleach, then toss it in the ocean or a lake. She hadn't wanted to take the knife, but after Ethan cut her, she had no choice. She worried about her blood on the floor, but hoped either the crime scene investigators didn't test the small square where the knife had fallen, or that there was so much contamination they couldn't differentiate her blood.

Even if they were able to test it, her DNA wasn't in any database. Still, she didn't want it to be, and now she would have to be far more careful in her work.

First things first. She had her own vengeance to seek. Then she could go back to business as usual.

She showered and scrubbed her body under water as hot as she could stand it. Shampooed her hair twice. When she stepped out, her skin was pink and she felt fabulous. She stared at her reflection, took out scissors, and cut her hair yet again. She wished she didn't have to do it, but hair grew and having a straight, short bob instead of shoulder-length curls would help with the disguise.

Next, she took brown hair dye and colored her hair again. The dye wouldn't stay as well on the blond she'd used yesterday, but all she needed was to change her overall appearance and this light brown was closer to her natural color.

The end result was pretty good, a golden sort of brown. A little lighter than she wanted, but different enough from the woman—*Rose*—who'd been seen drinking in the bar with Lyle Hackett.

She slipped into a luxurious white hotel bathrobe, the logo embroidered in gold on the lapel.

Time to celebrate.

She popped the cork off the champagne, poured herself a glass, and walked out onto the balcony. It was chilly on the coast this late at night, even in southern California, but she didn't care. She breathed in the salt air, the breeze raising goose bumps on her damp skin.

She'd take these hours to rest, and then she'd watch the police and the FBI run around in circles. And when the time was right . . .

. . . she'd finish the job. She had Ethan to thank for her new skills. She could hardly wait to use them.

"To Ethan," she said to the ocean and drained her champagne.

CHAPTER
TWENTY-FIVE

Megan was awakened by the hard, naked body wrapped around her.

Jack's arm was draped over her, the blankets were on the floor, and the sheets a tangle around them. She would have been freezing if she wasn't lying next to a self-charging heater.

"Your phone's ringing," Jack said. "I didn't think I should answer it."

She jumped up and found her phone in her purse, which she'd dropped on the small desk when she first came in the night before. Before the spontaneous swim, before making love to Jack.

She missed the call. It was from Hans. Suddenly, she was mindful of her nakedness.

"You're blushing," Jack said.

"How can you tell?" she asked, looking around for her shirt. She found the cami she'd worn the night before; it was still damp from the pool. She opened her small suitcase.

"You're beautiful."

Her skin heated even more. At the rate she was going, she was going to look like a cooked lobster inside of two minutes.

"Don't be embarrassed," Jack said.

"I . . . we . . . it's complicated." Megan pulled on a T-shirt.

He chuckled. "If you mean to say that you and me having sex complicates things, yeah, maybe a bit, but I like complications. Especially one like you."

He stretched like a satisfied cat, his long, hard body only partly covered by the sheet. She turned her back on him. She couldn't look at him, not like that, without remembering exactly what they'd done together last night. How he made her feel not only during sex, but after. How he'd held her. Kissed her. She'd never felt so comfortable with a man, never felt so alive, so sexy, so desired.

She pressed Send on her phone to return Hans's call. He answered immediately. "Meg?"

"Sorry, you woke me and I couldn't find my phone."

"General Hackett is dead. We're going to Santa Barbara."

"Hackett? Dammit, we sent agents to his house to warn him."

"I spoke to the Los Angeles office. They said they called and Mrs. Hackett said her husband was out of town for the evening."

"And they didn't follow up?"

Hans paused. "They assumed that if he was out of town, the killers wouldn't know where. See where assumptions can lead?"

Megan blanched. Hans was still angry, but she was more confident that her actions were right. "I'll be ready."

"You should also know that Barry Rosemont, the reporter Frank Cardenas told us about, was also murdered, and his partner is still at large. The gun that killed the two men was left at the scene, but the knife that cut Hackett's hamstrings is missing. The detective in charge will meet us at the airport, fill in the details, and walk us through the crime scene. But the gun is the same caliber—nine millimeter—as the firearm that killed the Hoffmans. And," he added, "same bullet casings."

"What did—"

Hans interrupted. "We need to leave."

"Jack can fly us. It'll be faster, especially during morning commute time—"

"Ask him."

She paused. Did Hans know Jack was in her room? "Okay. What about Rosemont's partner? He just skipped out?"

"No sign of the partner at all. We don't know if Rosemont or the UNSUB killed Hackett, but it's clear that Rosemont was murdered. The police are going through all security tapes and are interviewing staff and guests. We'll know more when we get there."

"But—" She felt Jack behind her, his hands on her shoulders.

"Thirty minutes, meet me in the lobby."

"Yes, but—"

He hung up before she could say anything else.

"What?" Jack asked, massaging her muscles.

"Barry Rosemont. He's one of the killers, apparently." She turned and faced Jack. "I'm so sorry. About this, about your friend, Scout. And General Hackett, he's also dead. We couldn't warn him in time. I feel awful."

"It's not your fault."

"Hans is still mad at me. I don't know what's going

on with him, but he's not acting like himself. And we still don't know who Rosemont's partner is."

"Maybe by the time we land in Santa Barbara the police will have answers."

"I hope so. Thank you."

"Don't thank me. I'm part of this until the end. You know that, right?"

She nodded. "We're leaving in thirty minutes and I need to shower—"

"*We* need to shower." He kissed her. Her lips were sore from last night's passion, but his caress was gentle, kind, loving. He picked her up and carried her to the bathroom. "Thirty minutes should be just enough time."

On the way to the airport, Hans was in front with the taxi driver, talking quietly on his cell phone. Megan had hoped that because she and Hans were working together on the case, he had rethought his comments from the night before, but if his icy reception this morning was any indication, he was in a worse mood now. Any other time she would have called him on it, but he wasn't himself so she tread lightly.

Jack squeezed her knee. He leaned over and was about to say something when Megan's cell phone beeped, indicating a high-priority e-mail. She glanced at it. "It's from my office." She opened the e-mail and added, "It's about the van in Sacramento."

She skimmed the report. "It was wiped down with Clorox Clean-Up. Bleach. There were bloodstains, but they were contaminated. No prints so far, but they're still going through it. However, there was a pair of shoes in the middle of the back of the van. Worn sneakers with blood. It's our John Doe's blood." She tapped Hans on the shoulder. "Did you hear me?"

Hans turned, and pointed to the cell phone he held to his ear. She leaned back and sighed. "So we know where he was tortured, and they found two long, thin needles that appear to match the marks on the body. They sent one to the morgue for verification."

"And nothing else?"

"No."

Hans was on the phone the entire drive to the airport, and finally shut it off when Jack was taxiing the plane for take-off.

"That was Rick Stockton," he said.

"And?"

"The Orlando field office is reviewing all the evidence in the Russo murder and will get back to me. He also pulled the Russo interview from CNN and ordered a transcript, which will be e-mailed to us as soon as they get it. But it was pretty much an apology for screwing up a mission. Russo took the blame. Or, as Rick said, he shared the blame with the whole team."

"Prick," Jack said.

Sitting behind, Hans didn't respond.

"What do you think happened in Afghanistan?" Jack asked Hans.

"I don't know."

"I can tell you that Frank Cardenas doesn't lie. If he said the reporter jeopardized the mission, then the reporter jeopardized the mission."

"Soldiers tend to support each other," Hans said. "When one speaks out—"

"They usually have an ax to grind," Jack interrupted.

"We take care of our problems internally. We don't share them on Oprah."

"A lot of good your internal solutions have been."

"Your point?"

"The military is notorious for covering up failed missions. This time, they couldn't."

"You're not going to get an argument from me on that one," Jack said, "but failed missions are caused by many things, and leading the failures is bad intelligence, followed by assholes in public office who think they can run a battle from behind a desk and jerks like General Hackett who want to stroke the media and open our missions like a ride at Disneyland."

"Hackett's dead," Hans said coldly.

"I'm sorry he's dead, but that doesn't mean he was right."

"Hans," Megan interjected from the co-pilot's seat, not liking the direction the conversation was going, "can we get Rosemont's medical records? Anything the military has? He must have been debriefed, hospitalized, maybe on medication."

"The military isn't going to share—it's most likely classified. Rick already put in the request yesterday when we got his name, but doesn't expect them to be forthcoming. As far as medical records, we need a warrant."

"We should be able to get one," Megan said. "There could be something important there."

"I'll make sure it's put in. But it's not going to bring Hackett or the Hoffmans back to life."

"What is going on with you?" Megan demanded, turning around in her seat so she could face Hans. They were thousands of feet above the earth; no way he could avoid her this time. "You're testy and snide and being an asshole."

He glared at her, face hard, eyes unreadable. "I don't have to answer to you, Agent Elliott. The only reason you're on this plane to Santa Barbara is because Rick Stockton didn't agree with me that you fucked up. But he's looking into it so don't think you're in the clear yet."

Megan turned away from Hans and blinked back the threatening tears. She didn't know what to say; what could she say? His reaction to her wrong assumption about the victim in Sacramento was over the top. Something else had to have happened, and it was obvious Hans wasn't going to tell her. Did he tell Rick? Was there something he wasn't saying?

Did Hans know about her and Jack? Did he think she'd been unprofessional? Maybe she had been. It wasn't like she'd planned to have sex with Jack Kincaid. And she didn't regret it. She hadn't jeopardized the case, or slept with a witness or suspect. Jack was essentially a civilian consultant. Hans thought she screwed up the case, that was it. But she couldn't talk to him about it now. He wasn't open to anything she said.

She saw her best friendship disintegrating and she couldn't do a damn thing to stop it.

Santa Barbara Detective Grant Holden was in his early forties and reminded Meg of the blond cop from the classic show *Adam-12*. After introductions, he drove them to the hotel and filled them in on the double homicide.

"The chief of the forensic unit is handling the evidence himself. He's methodical and in my opinion the best in the state. You'll want to talk to him when we get there; he can walk you through the crime scene. Frankly, the whole thing is a circus."

"A circus?" Megan asked. She was in the back of the car, Hans was in the front. Jack stayed at the airport and said he'd take a cab—he needed to arrange to have Scout's plane refueled.

"Media is all over it."

"How'd they find out?"

"Police scanners. Hotel staff and guests. But it's not that they're simply on scene reporting a murder at the resort—they know Barry Rosemont is the Hamstring Killer."

"That's not good."

"We think the info came from Hackett's widow, but how can we accuse her right now?"

"Good point."

"Because it leaked out, we decided to use it to our advantage. We've released a photograph of Rosemont to the media and have asked anyone who believes they have seen him in the last forty-eight hours to contact my office. We're hoping if a witness comes forward he or she can describe Rosemont's accomplice."

Megan said, "Good. Let us know how we can help get the word out."

"I do have more information than I had earlier this morning when I spoke with you, Agent Vigo," Holden said. "Apparently, Hackett was getting chummy with a woman last night in the bar."

Both Megan and Hans turned to Holden. "A woman?" they said simultaneously. Megan added, "Brunette?"

"Blond. Attractive, late thirties to late forties. Not a registered guest."

"Name?"

"The bartender who worked last night is on his way to meet us at the resort. He's the only one who talked to her."

"What about the crime scene?" Hans asked. "You said the room was registered to Ethan Rose, but the manager identified Barry Rosemont as the individual who reserved the room and paid."

"Correct."

"And he came in alone?"

"Yes. We've been looking at the security footage and have seen Rosemont on tape only briefly—when he registered he entered through the main entrance. Yesterday early afternoon, one thirty-seven p.m. Alone. Asked specifically for a cabin on the beach. They weren't going to rent it to him because they were booked for the weekend, but he wanted it only one night. Said he was passing through."

"Driver's license?"

"Ethan Rose. We found his false identification. Quality fake. He also had an expired New York driver's license under the name Barry Ethan Rosemont, which we've learned is his real name. His prints came back as Barry Ethan Rosemont. Criminal record. He'd been arrested while a student at Berkeley, eighteen years ago."

"For what?"

"Breaking and entering. He was working for the student newspaper and broke into the security office to pull reports of rape that had been filed by students. He was doing an exposé of the administration covering up on-campus assaults. Charges were dropped."

"Did he run the story?" Megan asked, curious.

"Not that we know."

Hans said, "Any leads on Rosemont's partner?"

Holden shook his head. "Nothing so far. We've dusted the entire room, printed the staff, and are going through every guest methodically. So far, nothing. But there's a lot to process. Extensive blood, spatter, angles. We're still not exactly sure what happened. Ian, our chief forensics guru, can walk you through the evidence when we get there."

He turned the sedan into the resort. He wasn't kidding—the place was crawling with media. Every major and minor California television and radio station insignia was visible, plus two national news stations.

"Nobody's talking to them, right?" Hans asked.

"Just our PIO, completely scripted," Holden assured him. "I've threatened everyone else with bodily injury or working the next ten major holidays."

"And the needles?" Hans asked. "You said you found a black bag with a couple hundred acupuncture needles."

"Yes. I have no idea what Rosemont had planned. There were also two knives, but neither one had been used on Hackett."

"How did the killer escape?" Megan asked. "He killed his partner and ran? Doesn't the hotel have security?"

"Three minutes and forty seconds passed between the first report of gunfire until the head of security arrived at the crime scene. The report of a gunshot was probably a minute or two delayed. It wasn't until after the final gunshot that someone called in. Plenty of time to escape."

"Someone had to see something," Megan said. "It's a hotel."

"Resort," Holden corrected as he stopped the car. "One hotel with two hundred rooms and forty individual cabins along the beach. All the cabins have sliding glass doors, and the unit in question has doors that open right onto the beach. They were unlocked, and a few drops of blood were found on the small patio. The killer most certainly escaped that way."

"With all the blood in the room, the killer would have stepped in it," Megan said. "Any footprints?"

"Possibly—you should talk to Ian Clark about that." He opened the door. "Ready?"

CHAPTER
TWENTY-SIX

While the Cessna Caravan was being fueled, Jack called Padre. He didn't want his friend to hear about General Hackett or Barry Rosemont from the media or anyone else. He was also concerned about Megan. He didn't want her to have professional trouble because she'd adhered to an agreement she wasn't even party to. She could have arrested Price and turned him over to local police. She could have had the local FBI pick him up at the bar or called CID with his last-known whereabouts. That she had done none of those things because she promised she wouldn't, even when facing intense pressure from Hans Vigo, told Jack that she had a backbone of steel and an inherent sense of loyalty to match any among Jack's team of soldiers.

Padre got on the phone. "Did you meet up with Price?"

"Yeah. He gave us what we needed. But I wasn't calling you about him."

"You sound grim."

"The reporter, Barry Rosemont, killed General Hackett last night."

"I know." Padre's voice was flat.

"You know?"

"It's all over the morning news. I'm surprised you didn't see it."

"I'm still at the airport fueling. So you know Rosemont is dead?"

"And there's a chance that another unidentified killer is on the loose. Yeah, I know all about it."

"And you're okay?"

Padre said nothing for a long minute, then, "It's hard."

Jack didn't have to ask Padre what he meant. Priests had to act like forgiveness was a given. And sometimes it wasn't. Even for men of God.

"Why didn't he kill me?"

Jack almost didn't hear him, Padre spoke so quietly.

"I don't know," Jack said, also quietly. "Maybe you did something five years ago that made him not blame you."

"I was a different man then, Jack."

"Not as different as you think."

"If anyone should have been spared, based on how he treated Rosemont, it would have been Duane Johnson. He was the only one who stood up for the kid. Not me. I told him he was our albatross."

The regret in Padre's voice was thick.

"It was Rosemont's choice to kill," Jack said. "Maybe he felt it was too risky to go after you so soon after what he did to Scout. Maybe he had another insane reason for killing Hackett next. But it's over."

"What about his partner? Any leads?"

"Not that I know of, but I'm heading over to the hotel in a few minutes and I'll find out. Be careful, Padre. I need you alive and well when I return to Hidalgo. If Rosemont's partner is going to finish this twisted game, you may be next. What about the sketch? Did the Rangers send over a sketch artist?"

"She arrived an hour ago, but I have a funeral Mass at one—in fact, I need to prepare, the family will be here in a few minutes."

"As soon as you're done, send it to both me and Megan. And watch your back. Both Tim and Mike are there, right?"

"Yes. We're fine."

"I'll feel better when I'm back there."

"When is that? There have been inquiries about your services. One of the major charities in Belize wants escorts when they take a Habitat for Humanity group out to a remote village next month."

Jack had put his business on hold this week, but he hadn't had a choice. Now he did. Rosemont was dead; he could go back to Hidalgo right now if he wanted. Nothing was holding him here—except Megan and Rosemont's murderous partner.

He'd become a glorified chauffeur—flying the feds around instead of driving them. While they might have needed him at first to help with the military angle, it was clear now that his expertise wasn't in demand.

While Megan had proven she could take care of herself, she was facing an enemy capable of taking down Delta-trained soldiers. Rosemont was dead; his killer was even more ruthless. Jack was concerned about Megan's safety.

"You still there, Jack?"

"Tim can take any job he wants as long as he brings in an appropriate team," Jack said, "but I'm taking a week." Jack would take as much time as Megan needed.

"A week?"

"I'll keep in touch. Watch your back, Padre. We don't know what's going on here." He hung up.

Megan hadn't asked him to protect her, and she'd probably tell him she didn't need a bodyguard. Maybe she didn't. But Jack wasn't taking any chances. She was part of his life now, and he took care of what was his.

Dr. Ian Clark was a short, cerebral-looking middle-aged forensic expert with little hair and Coke-bottle glasses that doubled the size of his blue eyes, which Megan found disconcerting.

"Put on booties and gloves," he demanded. "We're not done."

Megan slipped on the protective gear and surveyed the room. The bodies hadn't been removed, but Dr. Clark was bagging the second victim. Two technicians were collecting trace evidence. Another tech came out of the bathroom with two paper bags, one in each hand, and passed by Megan without acknowledgment. A fourth tech was outside studying the sliding glass door.

The resort beachfront cabin was one large room, comfortably sized, with a king-sized bed, desk, and sitting area with two love seats. A refrigerator was under the desk, and a small bathroom and closet were to the right of the entrance.

The first thing that struck Megan was the amount of blood. She looked around the room, saw blood soaked into the neutral beige carpet, spreading several feet across. Blood spatter radiated across the floor, indicating that someone had been shot while laying on the carpet. She said as much.

"Correct," Dr. Clark said. "General Hackett was attacked three feet from the door—hamstrung. You can see the spatter on the bathroom door. He fell to the ground, and it appears he pulled himself toward the doors at the rear of the room. He moved six feet before he was shot—twice, a head shot and once to his back. From the amount of blood, a bullet pierced a major artery. There's also brain matter and bone embedded in the carpet. We'll be cutting out the carpet for further blood analysis."

"Where was Rosemont found?" Hans asked.

Dr. Clark stood in the center of the room. "He was close to Hackett's body and fell across his legs. He was shot in the chest twice."

"Detective Holden said there was no knife found."

"Correct. We've broadened the search, but so far nothing. We've also received a limited warrant to search every hotel room, occupied and unoccupied, in the resort."

Holden said, "My officers are in the middle of that search. So far, nothing."

Clark continued. "Though I will need confirmation from the autopsy, it appears that Rosemont attacked Hackett as soon as the door closed. I inspected Rosemont's hands and he was wearing gloves. The gloves had small nicks in them, consistent with brushing against a sharp blade. We also found a medical-type bag with restraint materials and more than two hundred acupuncture needles. The needles tested positive for blood and there is multiple biological matter on them. He may have rinsed them off, but he never sterilized them."

"Prints?" Megan asked.

Clark shook his head. "Far too slender to retain enough fingerprint information for a possible I.D."

"What about prints in the room?" she clarified.

"We found several of Rosemont's prints on the main door and the sliding glass door, in the bathroom, and on the desk. There are several sets and the hotel is providing us with prints of all its employees to compare to. But the only recent prints belong to Rosemont and Hackett. Hackett touched the doorjamb, the knob, and he had a key for this room in his pocket."

"But I thought the room was registered to Rosemont under the name Ethan Rose," Hans said.

"Correct. But Hackett had a key."

Meg turned to Holden. "You said that Hackett was seen with a woman in the bar."

"Yes."

"Rosemont's partner."

Hans turned to her. "We don't know that."

"Why else would Hackett have a key to this room? Females are great lures."

Holden said, "One of the housekeeping staff said she saw Rosemont and a woman on the beach earlier yesterday, but she couldn't provide a description, only a blond Caucasian." His phone beeped and he excused himself.

Megan looked at the two body bags, then at the door. "Did Rosemont shoot Hackett or was it Rosemont's partner?" she asked, almost to herself. "What I don't get is why such a public place. The general must have caused a raucous when he was hamstrung. He wasn't gagged, correct?"

"No."

Hans said, "Test his blood for all barbiturates. If he

was drugged before he came in, he may not have been able to call for help."

"And the killer escaped through the back door," Megan said as she crossed over to the sliding glass doors. The beach spread out in front of her, the ocean rolling up only a hundred feet beyond.

"Look here." Clark led them to the door. "See those prints?"

"Prints?"

"Shoe impressions."

Megan squatted and looked carefully at a triangle pattern. "These are shoes?"

"High heels. There are no identifying marks, but we can see the impression of the spikes in a couple places— mostly by the main door. I think the killer tried to run on her toes and not put the spike part of the heel down, but sometimes she couldn't avoid it."

"You think the killer is a woman."

"I think the killer is very likely a woman," Clark said. "Hackett had lipstick on his face and neck."

"And she ran across the beach?" Megan looked out. Crime scene tape divided the beach in half.

"Yes, south. But we were only able to track her footfalls for about thirty feet before they became too integrated with the other prints."

"Heels in the sand?"

"No, she took her shoes off. Come here." He opened the door and they walked to the small patio that fronted the sand. "No prints, so she probably had gloves on—"

"Wait," Megan said. "If this is the same woman Hackett was getting cozy with in the bar, how could he have not noticed she was wearing gloves?"

"Maybe she drugged him," Hans suggested. "Or used a towel or cloth to touch anything."

"Regardless, she didn't leave prints, but there is blood on the back of this chair, and a few droplets of blood that has me thinking she stood in the sand, took off the heels, and carried them with her. We're scouring the garbage cans and beach between here and the pier, and so far nothing. No shoes, no knife, no evidence."

Holden came out to the patio. "The bartender who served Hackett and the woman last night is here."

"Let's talk to him," Hans said. "Do you have a sketch artist available?"

"Already on site," Holden said. "We also have a witness. He sounds legit, swears that he saw Rosemont at a diner outside Blythe yesterday morning. He and his family are in San Luis Obispo and I was going to send an officer up there for a formal statement, but maybe one of you would like to go?"

"Agent Elliott will accompany your officer," Hans said.

Before Megan could protest, Holden said, "Terrific. I'll call Officer Dodge and have her swing by and pick you up. It's only an hour and a half away. You'll be back before dinner."

CHAPTER
TWENTY-SEVEN

Jack couldn't find Megan anywhere in the hotel. He was about to try her cell phone again when he saw Hans Vigo walk into the main lobby with the same plain-clothes cop who had picked Hans and Megan up at the airport earlier that morning.

"Where's Megan?" Jack asked as Hans approached.

Jack had been worried about Megan, unable to reach her, her cell phone busy or going directly to voice mail.

Hans Vigo looked at Jack oddly, then walked past him and said, "She's on her way to interview a potential witness."

"Witness? Who?"

"A family. They saw Rosemont in a diner only a few miles from where the Hoffmans were killed. They said a woman was with him. It's a solid lead, so I sent her to follow it."

Jack glanced at Holden. He didn't need to say anything, but the cop understood and excused himself with a vague comment about checking on the canvass for witnesses.

"Where did she go?" Jack asked.

"San Luis Obispo. It's an hour or two north."

"On her own?"

"With an SBPD uniformed officer. What's the problem, Jack? I didn't realize I had to clear my orders with you."

The tension wasn't lost on Jack. "What does that mean, Vigo?"

"I don't have to explain myself."

"Right. Because you're the senior agent."

The federal agent's face hardened. "What do you care? Your friend's killer is dead. You can go back to Hidalgo and fight somebody else's wars for them. I'm sure you're in demand."

"And I don't have to explain myself to you." Why hadn't Megan called him? Jack pushed the thought aside. She was doing her job. He'd have liked to have known she was leaving town for the day, but she'd be back in a few hours. Still, Hans Vigo's animosity was palatable. What was his problem? Did he know that Jack had slept with Megan? Was it possible that this agent, who was almost old enough to be Megan's father, was jealous? Or was it something else? Jack didn't know Vigo well enough to decide, though Megan had said he'd been acting unlike himself recently.

"You can wait for her in—"

"No," Jack interrupted. "There's still a killer on the loose. What's going on with the search for Rosemont's partner?"

"You're not a cop, Jack."

"You can't just use me when it's convenient." Jack turned to leave, not wanting any more of a confrontation. He would keep trying Megan, to confirm she was safe, then he'd follow up with Padre and see what was taking him so long with the police artist. They needed something to go on, and right now Jack hated not having anything to do. The waiting would kill him.

Vigo asked quietly, "What's your interest in Agent El-liott, Jack?"

Slowly, Jack faced Vigo and assessed him. He couldn't tell if the question was because Vigo was jealous or pro-tective. Or both.

He simply said, "I like her."

Vigo relaxed and nodded. "I'm about to interview the bartender who served Hackett and the woman. You can join me if you like."

Megan got the call from the Orlando field office ten minutes before reaching the San Luis Obispo city limits.

"Agent Elliott, this is ASAC Todd Zarian. Assistant Director Stockton asked me to contact you regarding the Ken Russo homicide."

"Thank you. Stockton explained the situation?"

"Yes. We spoke to the local detective in charge and he opened up the files to us. I have them here in my office. Looks pretty open and shut to me. Guy comes home and surprises a burglar."

"Do you know what was taken?"

"Nothing big—television and stereo were still there. But according to friends and neighbors, a high-end cam-era was missing; the guy had receipts for an iPod and some other small electronics that were never found. Pos-sibly money—his wallet was found in a Dumpster sev-eral blocks away, no money or credit cards. The cards were used once, two hours after the murder, where the killer withdrew the daily maximum."

"Any security cameras at those sites?"

"Yeah, but the killer wore a mask and there were no identifying features or clothing. The police note that there was a lock-box in the bedroom that was busted open. It was empty and may have contained cash. We have no way of knowing."

On the surface, classic signs of a robbery. But Russo was also part of the Delta team targeted by a killer and the same individual who had possession of the George Price dog tags. If those tags weren't an obvious red flag, Megan wouldn't even be asking these questions. "Evidence?"

"None that has led anywhere. No prints. No one saw anything suspicious, but this happened between midnight and twelve-thirty. Russo arrived home at twelve-thirty and shortly thereafter gunshots were reported."

"How many times was he shot?"

"Three. Twice in the chest and once in the head."

"Three? That sounds like overkill."

"Maybe the robber didn't have a mask on when he was in the house. Didn't want to be identified. It happens a lot. We have the bullets from the autopsy and found three nine-millimeter bullet casings that match, but so far nothing has hit. They've been logged into the AFIS database, so if the gun turns up in any other investigation, it'll pop."

Zarian continued. "There are a bunch of reports, witness statements that don't seem to mean much of anything. Neighbor said she saw him leave alone at six while she was walking her dog. Another neighbor—"

"She said alone? Was she prompted?"

"I don't know. I didn't do the interview."

"Is there anything in there about a girlfriend? Wife? Friends?"

"Single, never married. Dated, but I don't have any names. Maybe he was between relationships. No one identified as a girlfriend was interviewed."

"Can you contact that witness and ask her if she knew whether Russo dated, and the name of his most recent girlfriend? Anything else she might know about such a person?"

"Sure, but—"

Megan interrupted. "It would probably be easier if I made the call."

"I'll send you the name and number."

Megan wasn't sure it would lead anywhere, but the recent seduction of General Hackett had her wondering if Rosemont's partner was truly a woman. At first, she'd been more concerned about the woman's safety—if Rosemont and his partner were surprised by two people, the UNSUB could have kidnapped General Hackett's female drinking companion, and possibly dumped her body elsewhere. But then Megan realized that wasn't possible. The cabin had been rented to Ethan Rose. The woman who brought Hackett to the cabin had been part of the conspiracy to murder. Was it possible that this woman was even colder and more calculating than Barry Rosemont himself?

Megan asked, "One more thing. Do you have a ballistics report handy?"

"There's one in here somewhere. It's in the log. Why?"

"This is a big favor, I know, but the murders I'm currently working aren't yet logged in AFIS." Not one hundred percent true—Johnson and Perry were in AFIS, but they only matched each other, not any other ballistics in the system. But Megan was convinced that Russo was connected to these murders, if only by the thin thread of AWOL soldier George Price's statement, which said he had left his dog tags with Russo. "I'd like to get the crime techs something to compare with ASAP. Can you fax or e-mail the reports to a couple different counties?"

"I'll do it," Zarian said. "Where?"

"Texas Rangers based in McAllen, attention Ranger Hern; Riverside County Sheriff's Department, attention Deputy Sheriff Warren; Santa Barbara County Forensics Unit, attention Dr. Ian Clark."

"That it?" He sounded irritated. It was grunt work, but it had to be done.

She was about to say yes, but then realized that Sacramento wouldn't have had time to run ballistics since CID returned John Doe's body. "Sacramento Crime Lab, attention Simone Charles. I'll e-mail you the contact numbers."

"Thanks. I'll get on this now. We're short-staffed right now. How can I reach you later? This number?"

"I'm on my way to interview a witness, but you can leave a message or e-mail me." She was still angry with Hans about this assignment. There was no reason she should be spending three hours on the road—ninety minutes each way—to interview a witness when it would have been easier to send a lower-ranking agent or to call the SLO sheriff and ask him to send a deputy over. Megan would have been happy to brief the officer. It was more than obvious Hans didn't want her around, and it both pissed her off and upset her. That he had gone to Rick Stockton—her boss's boss!—made her stomach queasy, and the fact that he refused to even discuss the matter made it worse.

Zarian said, "I just sent you the contact information for the neighbor, Mrs. Anne Lyons."

"Thank you, I really appreciate your help." She hung up and asked her driver, Officer Barbara Dodge, how long before they arrived. "We're in the city limits. Five, ten minutes probably."

"Thanks," Megan said and dialed Mrs. Anne Lyons. She wasn't holding out hope that Mrs. Lyons would be home, so was pleasantly surprised when an elderly female voice identifying herself as Anne Lyons answered.

"Mrs. Lyons, my name is Megan Elliott. I'm an FBI agent in Sacramento, California. I have some questions regarding your neighbor, Kenneth Russo."

"Kenny? What a nice man. A tragedy. We've always had a safe neighborhood. And then, well, many of my friends moved after that horrible incident."

"Yes, ma'am. I—"

She interrupted. "Have you found the person who killed him?"

"Not yet, but—"

"The police were very nice, very diligent, but they don't come by anymore."

A cold case robbery/homicide after nearly ten months wasn't going to keep the police on their toes, Megan knew. There were plenty of crimes to solve.

"Yes, ma'am. I'm following up on a lead—"

"All the way from California?"

"Yes." Before the witness could interrupt again, Megan spoke quickly. "My colleague in Orlando reviewed your statement and you mentioned that you saw Ken Russo come home alone the night he was murdered. Did he normally bring someone home with him? A girlfriend?"

"Kenny was a handsome retired military officer. Always helped me take my garbage out, fixed my fence when it fell down in that awful storm three years ago.

Of course there were always women who wanted to go out with him. He was a confirmed bachelor, though. Enjoyed the ladies, of course, but he liked to 'play the field,' as you kids say now."

Megan wasn't sure she'd use that phrase. She asked, "Did he have a regular girlfriend? Or do you remember who he was seeing when he was killed?"

"You aren't suggesting that one of his girlfriends had something to do with his murder! It was a burglary. They took his computer, his camera, his money—"

"You knew he had money in the house?"

"That's what the police said. They asked me about it, so I assumed he had some money."

"And his girlfriends?"

"Well, all the ladies here wanted to date him, but he was too young."

"Excuse me," Megan asked, "what type of community do you live in?"

"It's a private, gated community. Active Fifty. No minors. Joe and Liz have a college-aged daughter living with them, but—"

The community was gated? Why hadn't Zarian mentioned that fact?

"Were there any other burglaries in your community around the time Mr. Russo was robbed and killed?"

"Goodness no. This is one of the safest areas of Orlando. Well, there was Sergio Roper. He's senile. He used to go into houses at random and make himself lunch. Walked in one afternoon while I was napping. I woke up and found him eating a ham and cheese sandwich in my kitchen—"

"Mrs. Lyons, you're saying that Mr. Russo's was the only major robbery in the community?"

"Yes, dear."

"And his girlfriend?"

"Poor thing, his girlfriend broke up with him right before. They had a rather public argument, and she left crying."

"When was that?"

"Oh, gosh, I'm not sure. A week or two before Kenny was murdered. I called her to tell her, and she was heartbroken. I thought there was something special between them. But she couldn't come to the funeral. She had taken a job out of state. That's what the fight was about, apparently. She wanted him to move with her, and Kenny, he was happy with us old folks. He was only fifty-three, but he was an old soul."

"Do you have her name? Contact information?"

"In my address book. Just a minute."

Several minutes later, Mrs. Lyons came on the phone. "Hannah."

"Hannah what?"

"I don't have her last name, but here's the number."

After Mrs. Lyons recited the digits, Megan said, "That's a New York exchange."

"She's from New York, and she went back. It was her cell phone—I hear you can keep the same number no matter where you move. Isn't that amazing?" Without waiting for an answer, she continued. "Hannah had moved here to be with her parents, who were getting on in years and needed some help. Isn't that just the sweetest thing? I know so many people who have children too busy to even visit, let alone help with grocery shopping and transportation. I can't drive anymore because of my eyes."

"I'm sorry," Megan said as she finished writing down information. "Your eyes?"

"I'm blind. Well, not blind as a bat, but I can't see more than two feet in front of me even with my glasses. So you can understand why I would love to have some help, but I never was able to have children. Though some of my friends have several children and none of their kids help out—"

"Mrs. Lyons, I really appreciate your time and information. I may call you again, if that's okay."

"Yes, of course, anytime. Please."

"One more thing, how long was Mr. Russo involved with Hannah?"

"Several months. They met at a community mixer."

"How old is she, would you say?"

"Young. Forty, forty-five."

"I thought you had to be fifty to live there?"

"Yes, but she was taking care of her parents—didn't I say that? I'm sure I did."

"Are her parents still there?"

"Oh no, when Hannah left for her new job, they went to a nursing home. They were in their eighties, I think Bernard was close to ninety. He had a pretty good head, but didn't say much of anything. Millie had advanced Alzheimer's. Couldn't remember anything, bless her heart. I don't blame Hannah for moving on. Bernard never made much money working for the county, though they had a nice retirement. I think Hannah was struggling to make sure their bills were paid. Before Millie was diagnosed, she'd bought thousands of dollars of stuff she didn't need off that shopping channel. Finally, Bernard cut up the credit cards. At least, that's what I *heard*."

"Do you have the name of the home?"

"Sunny Day Adult Living. It's one of the nicer places in Orlando. If any of those places are nice."

"And their last name?"

"Rubin. Bernard and Millie Rubin."

"Was that their daughter's last name as well?"

"I suppose so. I honestly don't know."

"Thank you for your help, Mrs. Lyons."

"We're here," Officer Dodge said after Megan hung up. "Ready?"

"One minute. Let me make a quick call."

Megan dialed the number Mrs. Lyons gave her for Hannah, Ken Russo's ex-girlfriend. Her head was abuzz with questions, namely did Hannah know if Russo had been threatened or seemed distracted prior to their breakup. Megan was shocked when Mrs. Lyons told her the community was a private, gated development. Only one major theft, with a murder attached, and the police weren't suspicious of a more personal motive?

An automated voice mail system picked up and Megan debated leaving a message. When the beep sounded, she said, "Hello, my name is Megan Elliott and I'm with the Federal Bureau of Investigation. I spoke with someone who said you used to date a Mr. Kenneth Russo in Orlando, Florida, who was murdered in a robbery last year. I'm following up on the case and have a couple questions, and would appreciate a call back."

Next she called information for the Sunny Day Adult Living Center in Orlando and asked for the administrator. Unfortunately, being five in the afternoon on the East Coast, he had already left. "This is an FBI investigation that may relate to one of your residents," Megan told the manager who answered the phone. "If you would please give me the administrator's home or cell phone number, I would appreciate it."

"I'm sorry, that's against protocol, but I'll be happy to contact him if you can tell me what this is regarding."

"The daughter of Mr. and Mrs. Bernard Rubin may have information that will help in a criminal investigation, and I'm looking for a current phone number and address."

"I'll have Dr. Boswell get back to you, Ms. Elliott."

Megan gave her contact information and hung up, frustrated. Two potential leads—two good solid leads—on hold while she waited.

"Let's go," she said to Officer Dodge.

The two women exited the patrol car and walked up the short stone path to the quaint Victorian house in downtown SLO. Megan hoped Hans hadn't sent her on a wild-goose chase.

CHAPTER
TWENTY-EIGHT

The bartender at the hotel bar had been less than helpful, Jack thought. While they had a vague description of the woman, the bartender sat with a police artist for an hour and nothing came of it. If they needed a description of her breasts, no problem. The artist told a frustrated Hans that sometimes it took a few hours, but she wasn't confident that the bartender would remember enough detail to render an accurate picture.

Still, the meeting confirmed one fact: General Hackett had gone to the bar as was his custom when he arrived on the third Thursday of the month, ordered a drink, and then bought a drink for the lady in the red dress. The bartender also confirmed that the lady had invited Hackett to her table, where they engaged in conversation and another round of drinks for forty-five minutes, before leaving together. Hackett had a habit of meeting with pretty, fortysomething blondes each month.

Approximately fifteen minutes later—about the length of time it would take for a leisurely stroll from the bar to the beachfront cabins, reports of gunshots came into the reservation desk and the police station. Security was dispatched, but no one was at the cabin for nearly five minutes after the reported gunshot, largely because the security guards had all been at the main hotel, and had been uncertain where the shots came from—whether on the resort grounds or the beach itself.

Five minutes had been more than enough time for Rosemont's murderous partner to slip away.

"A woman," Jack said almost to himself as he and Hans walked back to the small conference room that the hotel had set aside for law enforcement.

"Excuse me?"

"Rosemont's partner is a woman."

"Don't leap to conclusions. She could have—" Jack raised his eyebrow and Hans stopped. "You're right. There is no other explanation."

"Someone led Hackett to that room. The bartender said it was a mutual flirtation."

"But why the elaborate plan?" Hans asked. "They were practically in public. Though the cabins are more private, they couldn't be sure that someone walking by wouldn't have heard the shot. And they would also have had to know Hackett's schedule."

"Hackett had a routine," Jack said. "The third Thursday of every month."

Hans sat down and nodded. "They knew Duane Johnson's schedule, Perry, Bartleton—" He glanced at Jack.

Jack nodded. "It's a woman. What she was doing with Rosemont is anyone's guess. But she's just as dangerous—"

"She could have been a battered partner. Females account for less than ten percent of serial murderers. In many killing pairs, the female participant suffers from domestic violence. They are too scared to leave or not do what their partner demands. Perhaps she saw an opportunity and took it—domestic violence often ends in murder. Usually, the abused wife or girlfriend, but occasionally, the abused decides murder is her only way out."

"Good in theory, but—"

Hans interrupted, "Which would support Father Francis's visitation the other night. *If* that woman, and it's not certain because it doesn't fit the M.O., was Rosemont's partner, then perhaps seeking out the priest was her first attempt at getting away."

Jack considered and dismissed the argument. "Let's take this from the beginning. Can we agree that the woman in the red dress intentionally lured General Hackett to Ethan Rose's room?"

Hans considered, then nodded. "Yes, because Hackett would have no other reason to go there. It's across the resort from his room."

"There were no prints found. If she was truly fighting for the gun and shot Rosemont out of self-defense, why aren't her prints there?"

"She may have been scared and wiped them off."

"Wiped them off, sure. But scared?" Jack shook his head. "She had four and a half minutes from the sound of the first gunshot, and just over two and a half minutes from the sound of the last gunshot, before security arrived. She wipes the gun, takes the knife, runs out the back, and disappears? She must have had blood on her, so that means she changed clothes somewhere."

"Holden's people canvassed the entire hotel. No one saw the woman except in the bar prior to the murders."

"And what's accessible from the beach?"

"Several hotels both up and down the coast, the pier,

farther up there's little commercial business, and the road access is limited. I suspect she went south."

"I don't see a panicked, abused woman killing two men in cold blood, even in self-defense, and then disappearing without a trace of evidence."

Hans took a deep breath and slowly let it out. "So she's an active and willing participant in Rosemont's killing spree."

Jack nodded. "We need Padre's sketch."

"And Megan may get something from her witnesses. I just— There's something eluding me, and I can't quite figure it out." He picked up the phone. "I know exactly what we need."

"What?"

"A fresh pair of eyes. Or rather ears. Your brother."

"Dillon?" Jack wouldn't have thought about contacting his brother, the forensic psychiatrist, but Dillon did have an uncanny way of getting to the heart of the matter, and psychopaths were his specialty.

Hans dialed the number from memory. "I hope we can track him down tonight."

Ned Stenberg was Megan's height with a comb-over and kind brown eyes behind wire-rim glasses. She wasn't surprised when he told her he was a medical lab technician at the local university—he looked the part. His wife, Jennifer, was an elementary school teacher, plump and pretty. As soon as Megan and Officer Dodge arrived, Jennifer sent their three kids upstairs.

"When Detective Holden said he was sending an officer over," Ned Stenberg began, "I didn't expect the FBI as well."

"Can I get you water? Coffee?" Jennifer asked.

Megan shook her head. "We can't stay long. We get a lot of tips when we send out a media story, but yours sounded valid. A personal visit is sometimes the best way to get information without distractions that can occur over the phone."

Jennifer led them to the living room, which was off the main entry, a tidy room obviously unused by the family.

"Would you mind repeating your story?" Megan asked the Stenbergs.

"Not at all," Ned said. "I planned on calling the police right after the incident, but—"

Jennifer said, "It didn't seem as important once they left."

"From the beginning," Megan said. "Please."

Ned began. "We were driving back from Phoenix where my brother lives. It's my spring break and we go there nearly every year for Easter and a few days. We left early Thursday morning and about an hour or so into the drive, this maniac in a truck almost kills us."

"Kills you? How? Did he exhibit road rage? Have a gun?"

"Almost ran us off the road. Had to be going a hundred twenty."

"Scared all of us," Jennifer concurred.

"Did you get his license plate?"

"Not then," Ned said. "He was going way too fast. We continued, but were all a little stressed. We usually eat brunch when we hit the Los Angeles area, but decided to stop earlier for a while and have breakfast instead. I pulled into the diner and saw the truck."

Jennifer said, "We told the kids to stay in the van and keep the doors locked."

"I was so angry," Ned said. "That was my family he almost ran off the road."

"I told him to let it go," Jennifer said.

"But I couldn't do that. Instead, I went in just as the driver was leaving."

"How did you recognize him if he went by so fast?" Megan asked.

Ned frowned. "I'm not really sure. It was more an impression. He was really tall and looked tall driving. Had dark hair. And after I said something, it was obviously him. He didn't say hardly anything, but he knew."

"And what type of truck was he driving?"

"A black or maybe a very dark charcoal gray Ford pickup."

"Make?"

"I'm not sure. A 150 or 250, I think. I'm not great with cars," Ned confessed.

"Immediately his wife came over," Jennifer interjected.

"Wife?" This was new information.

"She said his name was John and called him her husband."

"And?"

"She apologized profusely for his behavior and bad driving. Said they'd driven through the night from Houston on the way to see her mother who'd had a heart attack." Jennifer slowly shook her head.

"You don't seem sympathetic," Megan said.

"I don't know. Maybe it's just me, but if my mother

had a heart attack, I wouldn't be dying my hair to go to her bedside."

"How do you know she dyed her hair?"

Jennifer ran a finger high on her forehead. "She didn't rub all the dye off her scalp. I could see it."

"What color hair? Or rather dye?"

"Blond. She had the skin tone to be a blond, but this was very light—almost like yours, but it looked unnatural. The giveaway was the dye on her forehead. You know."

Megan shook her head. "I've never dyed my hair."

"You haven't? Oh. Well, sometimes the dye gets on your scalp and you need to rub it off. But it usually comes off after a shower or two. And then the smell, it's very strong even after a washing. She'd probably done it the night before or first thing in the morning. But it just seemed odd to me because of her mother's heart attack."

"Did either of them say anything about his dangerous driving?"

"No, just an apology from her. I don't think he said more than a word. Ned?"

Ned shook his head. "He just stared, like he wasn't right in the head." He tapped his own scalp.

Megan took out a photo sheet Holden had given her with Rosemont's photo and five other men. "Do you recognize any of these men?"

Both Jennifer and Ned tapped the same photo: Rosemont's.

"Can you describe the woman in more detail?" Megan asked.

"Pretty," Jennifer said. "And she was weepy. Probably because her husband was causing a scene."

"Even though he wasn't saying anything?" Officer Dodge interjected.

"He was just standing there looking . . . dazed."

"And the wife?"

"Taller than me, but not by much. Dyed blond hair, as I said. Blue eyes. Her hair was just below her shoulders, and her smile was nice—straight white teeth. She was wearing jeans and a plain black T-shirt, a little big on her."

Ned added, "She had small diamond earrings on. Like the ones I gave you for our anniversary, Jen."

"But no ring," Jennifer said, turning her own wedding band around on her finger. "I know some women don't wear wedding rings, but it's rare. She could have taken it off when she dyed her hair, I suppose . . ."

Megan got them back on track. "Would you be able to sit down with a sketch artist and describe the woman?"

"Maybe," Ned said. "Why?"

"I don't know how much the officer told you."

"The news report just said that if we'd seen that man, Rosemont, to call in, so we did."

"Mr. Rosemont is dead and the woman is being sought for questioning."

Jennifer blanched. "No. I . . . oh my God."

Ned put his arm around his wife. "What happened? Car accident?"

"No. Rosemont is our main suspect in multiple homicides."

Officer Dodge cleared her throat. "I'll contact the sheriff's department and see if they can send over a sketch artist."

"Thanks, Barbara," Megan said. To the couple, "Do you remember anything else about these two people? Accent? Distinguishing marks?"

Ned shook his head, but Jennifer said, "Yes. The woman said they were going to San Francisco and the husband said he thought they were going to Santa Barbara. It was really odd."

CHAPTER
TWENTY-NINE

Jack and Hans were waiting for a call back from Dillon when Detective Holden rushed in. "We got a match!"

Jack asked, "On what?"

"The bullets! An FBI agent from Orlando faxed over a ballistics report from a cold case down in Florida. He wrote that Agent Megan Elliott had requested it."

"Russo," Jack said. He couldn't help but be proud at how quickly Megan had put together the case and expedited the information.

"Right. The gun that killed Russo also killed Rosemont and Hackett."

"And," Holden continued, "the Hoffmans. The Riverside County crime lab got a copy of the same report and contacted Dr. Clark."

"What about the other victims?" Hans said. "Bartleton and Johnson and the other two men?"

"Not Bartleton," Detective Holden said. "I don't know about the others."

Hans frowned. "Can you ask Dr. Clark to contact the other crime labs and get a ballistics comparison?"

"What are you thinking?" Jack asked.

"Why change guns? Are we looking at a completely different crime?" He rubbed his temples.

Jack realized that Hans was practically asleep on his

feet. Whatever was bothering him had interrupted his sleep as well.

"Russo and Hackett were both involved, either directly or indirectly, with the mission in which Rosemont was kidnapped and held hostage," Jack said. "It would be far too big a coincidence if two separate killing pairs were targeting the same group of men."

"Right," Hans nodded. "And Bartleton's dog tag was found at the Hoffman double homicide."

"My question is, why change guns?" Holden asked.

Jack said, "So Russo's murder isn't connected to the others through ballistics."

"But it is connected," Hans said.

"No, it's not—yes, to these recent murders, but if the other three ballistics reports match Scout, then we know that a different gun was used for those victims, which makes me think that the killers didn't want Russo's murder connected with these crimes."

Holden nodded. "That makes sense. But why?"

Hans said, "Because it's often the first victim that leads directly to the killer. Can I see that fax?" he asked Holden. "I'm going to call the Orlando office and get them to overnight the reports to us. Something is in there that we can use."

The SLO sheriff's department contracted out their forensic sketch work. The woman would arrive at the Stenbergs within an hour, and had instructions to fax the sketch to Santa Barbara P.D. as soon as it was ready.

Megan asked Officer Dodge to take her back to Santa Barbara. It was getting close to four and she wanted to be back to review the ballistics reports more carefully and see if Jack could nudge his friend Padre to speed up the sketch artist. She wished she had a picture to show the Stenbergs because Megan was certain they would recognize her. Although meeting with the witnesses hadn't been a complete waste of time, Megan still felt that a local cop could have handled it just as competently.

Simone Charles with the Sacramento crime lab called to let Megan know that there was no match on the ballistics report with John Doe.

Still, just because the ballistics *didn't* match didn't mean they were different killers. Megan just had to review the evidence more closely and hope to find another commonality.

Her cell phone vibrated and she recognized the Orlando prefix, but not the phone number.

"Agent Elliott."

"Hello, this is Gerald Boswell with the Sunny Day Adult Living Center in Orlando returning your call."

"Thank you, Dr. Boswell. I won't keep you long."

"My secretary said it was about the Rubins?"

"Yes. Their daughter, Hannah."

"That's what she said, and that's why I'm calling you back. They don't have a living daughter."

"Maybe a daughter-in-law?"

"No. Their only daughter died years ago, when she was in her twenties."

"Are you sure?"

He sounded put off. "Of course. I have their file right in front of me. No living childen. I am positive."

"Does the file have the name of their daughter?"

The sound of shuffling paper, then, "No. Under immediate family, simply 'one daughter, deceased, February 1, 1960 to November 29, 1981.' Mr. Rubin was the youngest of five kids and the only survivor."

Megan almost hung up, but she remembered a case of elder abuse from her first years as an agent where an adult son moved in with his elderly and disabled parents. He spent their entire savings plus mortgaged their home, then left them destitute.

"Are the Rubins paying for your facility? Or are you a subsidized adult care home?"

"Why do you ask?"

She couldn't very well explain her vague theory without sounding paranoid and suspicious. "One of their former neighbors expressed concern over a relative of theirs who seemed to be living off their generosity. Seniors are very trusting as a group and tend to be conned quite easily."

"You're right about that, Agent Elliott," the director said, his voice decidedly more friendly. "I've seen well over a thousand cases of elder abuse and fraud in the twenty years I've been an adult care director. I don't know if the Rubins were victims, however. They bought into a plan with Sunny Day when Mr. Rubin retired from county government so that when they were in need of care, they could move in and live here rent free. Medicare and Social Security pay for their food and medical needs." He paused. "I can look into their finances for you, if you'd like. We have a board of trustees that manages the accounts for our residents. We've never evicted anyone for nonpayment. We receive donations and have many planned giving programs."

"If you can, that would be very helpful to me. Even if nothing is odd, let me know."

Megan thanked him for his time, then called Mrs. Lyons again.

"Hello?"

"Mrs. Lyons, this is Megan Elliott again, with the FBI. I have another question for you if you have a minute."

"Of course, dear."

"Did the Rubins ever talk about their daughter? Before she moved in with them?"

She didn't say anything for a long minute. "I honestly don't remember. I don't think it came up. I didn't know them well—we have more than four hundred houses and town-homes in the community. It was just because Kenny was my neighbor that I got to know them a bit, but it was only at social functions."

"Do you know if they had any close friends I could call?"

"I'm sure they did, but I don't know who. They lived on Sea Breeze Circle. Maybe the manager knows them. I'll give you her number. Paula Andrews. A darling girl."

Megan called Ms. Andrews next, but she wasn't home. She left a message on her answering machine that she was an FBI agent and wanted to talk about the Rubins who had lived on Sea Breeze as soon as possible.

"Sounds like a promising lead," Officer Dodge said as she turned south onto the Pacific Coast Highway.

"It seems clear that our female UNSUB has been an integral part of Rosemont's killing spree for well over a year. That she moved to Orlando to specifically get close to Ken Russo so she could do that. Why him? He was the team leader of the mission that Rosemont was kidnapped from. Russo was the first victim." He'd been killed seven months before Duane Johnson. How long did Rosemont and his partner plan these murders? Years?

"If he was the team leader, maybe he'd kept in touch with the other men," Dodge suggested.

Megan straightened. "And he might have their current addresses. Or know how to find them." And because George Price was AWOL, the killer stole the tags . . . why? Why was it important to the UNSUB and Rosemont to kill a homeless man and plant Price's tags on him? Contact the FBI and bring them into the case?

It wasn't common for the FBI to be involved with local homicides, but the killers *wanted* the FBI involved. If Megan wasn't already called into the investigation because of the connection to victims in two other states, she would have certainly gotten involved when she received Price's dog tag at her apartment.

The killers started in Florida with Russo. Then they did nothing for seven months before hitting Johnson in Texas. Two months passed, then they took out Perry in Nevada and "Price" in California two weeks after. *Then* they returned to Texas to kill Bartleton *two days* after John Doe. It would have been far more efficient to remain in Texas and move west. And it made no sense to kill a stranger and call him George Price.

Except to bring in the federal authorities. Except to bring Megan herself into the investigation.

Why her? She'd assumed that the killers sent her Price's dog tag because she was the squad leader of Violent Crimes and had recently been in the media because of a complex and high-profile investigation, or because they'd been watching the crime scene and saw her arrive.

But they had known where she lived.

Suddenly, a chill slithered down Megan's spine. For the first time she thought maybe there was something more going on here than simple revenge against the army and the Delta soldiers who Rosemont blamed for his captivity.

She called Hans to fill him in, but his voice mail picked up. Dammit. She dialed Jack's number. He answered after the first ring. "Kincaid."

"It's Megan."

He sighed audibly. "You okay?"

"Yes. I need to talk to Hans. Is he there?"

"We're on a conference call with a profiler. My brother."

"Oh. Good."

"I can interrupt—"

"No, I'll text him the information. I have a question for you. In February, around the tenth, were you and Scout on any mission out of the area?"

"Two short assignments, the first week of February we were in Honduras, the last week of February we were in Belize."

"Thanks."

"Why?"

"I'm just thinking about the timeline, why the killers jumped around when it would have been more efficient to kill their Texas targets first, then move to Nevada."

"What about the witnesses?"

"They I.D.'d Rosemont. I'll text Hans with the details."

"When will you be back?"

Megan asked Officer Dodge their ETA. Her driver said, "An hour, maybe a bit more because of traffic as we get closer to Santa Barbara."

"Did you hear that?" she asked Jack.

"Yes. Be careful."

"I will. You too."

Jack chuckled lightly. He wasn't a man who laughed a lot, but when he did the humor in his voice was endearing and sexy at the same time. "I'll watch my back, Blondie. And I want to watch yours, too, so get back quick. I'll feel a lot better when you're in my line of sight."

She was still smiling as she e-mailed Hans the status of her investigation, and included the information about the Rubins and the woman who had claimed to be their daughter.

"I think this is our UNSUB. I know it's a theory, but it's the only thing that makes sense right now. She befriended Russo in order to learn where the Delta team members lived, then killed him and stole Price's dog tag. The only thing I can't figure out is why they sent me the dog tag. Me, specifically. Let's talk when I get back."

She hit Send and leaned back, closing her eyes briefly. Officer Dodge said, "I just called for a traffic update. It's Friday; it's always heavy with tourists. Take a nap if you want."

"I don't think I can sleep, but five minutes to think things through would be nice."

"Feel free to bounce ideas off me. I'm pretty good with a puzzle."

"Thanks."

Megan turned her head and looked out the passenger window at the ocean beyond the cliffs, at the way the late-afternoon sun made the water shimmer like jewels. She frowned, knowing she was on the cusp of a solution, but fearing she was missing a critical piece of the puzzle.

*   *   *

Jack listened as Dillon asked questions over the speaker phone in the hotel conference room. He was impressed with his brother's quick and intelligent analysis and thoughtful inquiries. He hadn't seen Dil in action in two years, and he remembered that they were essentially in the same business. Jack gathered military intelligence to lay out a game plan; Dillon gathered psychological evidence.

"So Rosemont's partner is female," Dillon said after Hans laid out all the information they had to date.

"I'm ninety percent sure. There are no dead women in red dresses popping up, and unless there are three people involved—"

"I think you're right," Dillon said. "I have Rosemont's medical records your partner had couriered to Quantico from New York—it's the reason I was so late returning your call. I wanted to get a sense of who Rosemont was."

"And?"

"I still need more information for any substantive profile. You went over the victimology and the timeline, but I'm curious about the Sacramento victim. George Price."

"That's the thing," said Hans. "The vic wasn't George Price. He's a John Doe, homeless—was most likely a stranger to the killers."

"But this John Doe just happened to have the identification of a man who fits the profile of the victims?" Dillon asked.

"We now believe that the killer planted Price's dog tags on the victim, but I can't figure out why," Hans replied. "If the killers were more symbolic at the crime scene, it would make sense because they couldn't get to Price—he's AWOL. The military couldn't find him, and our killers probably couldn't either."

Hans continued. "That's one of the many things I'm struggling with. Price's dog tag actually led us down the path we're going, connecting the victims via their military records. No one had thought to check that with the first two victims because it wasn't obvious they were both veterans. Then Rosemont sent one of Price's tags to the FBI agent in charge of the investigation, as if to say, *'In case you haven't figured out this is important, let me shove this under your nose.'*"

"But why did they choose Sacramento of all the cities in America to plant Price's tags on a body? Wait . . . did you say that the killers sent Price's dog tag directly to one of your FBI agents?"

"Megan Elliott, supervisor of the Violent Crimes Squad. I thought maybe it was a sign that he wanted to be stopped, but . . . now I don't know."

"What about a copycat killer?" Dillon asked.

"I don't think so," answered Hans. "Rosemont was found with a medical bag of the needles he used to torture his victims. The hamstring injuries are consistent with the same type of knife, though the knife is missing and is presumed to have been taken by the accomplice. But this is the thing, Dillon: Rosemont killed two innocent civilians at a rest stop. No apparent reason, he just shot them point-blank. Now he's dead, and I can't even ask him why. A married couple. She was eight months pregnant." His voice cracked on the word.

"Hans?"

Jack watched Hans's face as it went through myriad gut-wrenching emotions, then the agent rubbed his eyes

and looked down at the table. Suddenly, Hans's odd behavior for the last two days made more sense. Jack said
nothing, but filed the information away.

"Let's retrace what happened in Hidalgo when Jack's
buddy Scout was killed," said Dillon. "Was there something different about that crime scene, inconsistent with
the first three?"

"Everything on the surface appeared to be the same,"
Hans said, "but I didn't see the crime scene. I have the
reports from the Rangers, and they read like it could be
any of the other scenes. Putting aside the rest-stop murders and General Hackett, it was the Sacramento crime
scene that was different from the others because of the
planted dog tags."

"But there was also one other thing different in Hidalgo," Jack interjected. "My friend Frank Cardenas, a
priest, had been on the mission where Rosemont was
abducted, yet Rosemont killed Scout and not Frank."

"You know this priest well, Jack?" Dillon asked.

"Yes," Jack said, his voice clipped. Everyone was suspicious.

Hans said, "Cardenas hasn't left Hidalgo in months,
and there's been no evident contact with Rosemont. Cardenas's involvement doesn't fit with what I know about
him. And it goes back to motive. Cardenas doesn't have
one. Who does?"

"After the Hidalgo murder, you noticed a change?"

"The first four murders were well planned, methodical,
disciplined," said Hans. "The last three—the two civilians and General Hackett—were rash, disorganized, impulsive. Though Rosemont came prepared to torture
Hackett, I don't see how he possibly thought he'd get
away with it, even with the privacy of the cabin. He reg-

istered under a variation of his name, was captured on the lobby security camera. After that, it would have been only a matter of time before he was identified and stopped."

"His female partner lured Hackett to the room," Dillon conjectured, "where Rosemont hamstrung him and then she shot him in the back."

Hans wasn't convinced. "That isn't consistent."

Jack asked Dillon, "How can you say that with certainty?"

"Because of Rosemont. I'll write up a formal report for you, but here's the nitty-gritty. The guy suffered from severe post-traumatic stress. He'd been tortured for three months, including needles in his nerves with the purpose of causing excruciating pain. Therefore, he wanted to cause pain to those he blamed for his captivity. He obviously couldn't go back to Afghanistan and hurt those who held him, so he turned to the Delta team who were supposed to protect him.

"He acknowledged to his psychiatrist that he didn't follow orders, and he alternately blamed himself and blamed the army. He was suicidal—had attempted suicide at least twice that the doctors knew about—and he was on medication. The psychological reports all indicated that Rosemont was a threat to himself and not others."

"That's bullshit," Jack said. "Who are these idiots?"

"Let me finish, Jack."

Jack crossed his arms. His phone vibrated and he looked down. Padre had sent a message. He clicked on it and it started to load.

Dillon continued. "But Rosemont still suffered from nightmares that were as real to him as if he were being tortured again. He also started hurting himself—cutting, poking, making himself relive the pain of captivity. I think, if he was left alone, he would have eventually been hospitalized or would have succeeded in killing himself.

"Shortly after he was ordered to start an intensive exercise program two years ago as part of therapy, he seemed to get better. But last June he disappeared and has never refilled his prescriptions."

"You can get most drugs on the streets."

"True, but psychopaths aren't going to actively look for drugs that are supposed to make them calmer."

"I thought psychopaths were born that way," Jack said.

"Some. And some are made. I think Rosemont probably suffered from mild depression growing up—like millions of people—but this incident sent him down a deadly path. I don't think revenge was his idea."

"Why?"

"He didn't have the aptitude to plan such an elaborate and detailed scheme. The two people at the rest stop? Yes, that screams an impulsive, explosive Rosemont to me. Sudden, violent, unexpected. The other murders? Controlled, well planned, organized. That's the mind of his accomplice."

"She's the instigator?"

"You're looking for a highly intelligent, extremely disciplined female between the ages of thirty-five and fifty-five. She will be attractive and a pathological liar. She is manipulative and has no remorse."

"Why would this UNSUB want to help Rosemont kill these men?" Hans asked.

"A means to an end," said Dillon.

Jack understood. "She wanted to play with his toys."

"Bingo."

Hans looked like he was still lost, so Jack added, "The needles. Torture. It takes a very specific personality to be able to torture another human being. Even if it's for the right reason, torture itself can't be done by someone who has a lot of empathy. She wanted to learn how to do it."

"I suspect that's right," Dillon said. "This woman hooked up with Rosemont around the time he appeared to be improving. Found out who he was, what he went through, and then asked him to teach her. He didn't want to, but she was very convincing, very manipulative. She orchestrated the murders and he went along with it. But don't forget he had a very real psychosis culminating in the attack against the Hoffmans. Rosemont snapped at the rest stop, and I think his accomplice realized their games were drawing to a close, that if she didn't kill him soon, he'd get them both captured or killed."

Dillon continued, "That brings us back to Sacramento. You didn't say that any other dog tags were sent to other law enforcement agencies, just the fed in Sacramento."

"Megan," Jack said, leaning forward.

"That's the key to the case."

"But the victim was a homeless John Doe."

"Exactly. But absolutely killed by the same person, right? Same M.O., same caliber weapon, same method of torture. But everything else was different. John Doe was the only one *not* killed at his residence or where he was sleeping. He was the only one who *wasn't* on the Delta Force team that Rosemont was attached to; he was the only victim who was left in a very public place to be found immediately. And he was the only victim the killer felt a need to communicate to the authorities about. But more significantly, why Sacramento? Why not a homeless guy, or anyone, in another major city? Two victims were in Texas, why not Dallas? Or Las Vegas? Or Los Angeles? Why Sacramento *specifically*? Why contact Agent Megan Elliott *personally*?"

Hans suddenly stood up. "They sent the tag to her apartment. We assumed the killers either followed her home or researched to locate her address. It isn't difficult."

"Very likely. But why her?"

"She was put in charge of the case."

"How would he or she know that?" Dillon asked.

Jack slammed his fist on the table. "You're saying that this psycho woman who wanted to learn how to torture by killing soldiers for this fucking lunatic *has Megan's home address*?"

Hans said, "I thought you knew."

"I assumed it had been sent to the publicly known FBI headquarters, not Megan's private residence!"

Jack rose from the table. Years of training had made his body rigid, but he couldn't keep his heart rate down like he did in the field. He leaned forward, fear for Megan's life making his body cold with barely suppressed rage.

He slid his phone over to Hans, showing him the artist's rendition e-mailed from Texas. "Do you know that woman? She's the woman Padre saw Tuesday night before Scout was killed."

Hans stared at the image, his face ashen. "Yes. She tried to kill Meg twelve years ago."

CHAPTER
THIRTY

A large e-mail was downloading to Megan's BlackBerry while she and Officer Dodge were stuck in slow traffic in Santa Maria, about midway between SLO and Santa Barbara. Megan was antsy to get a look, suspecting the e-mailed file was from the sketch artist working with Padre. *Finally,* she thought, eager to put a face on the woman she was certain was Rosemont's accomplice.

Her phone trilled with a call, and she almost sent it directly to voice mail when she saw the caller I.D. was from Orlando.

"Megan Elliott," she answered.

"This is Paula Andrews from the Orlando Lakeside Adult Community. I just got your message."

"Thank you so much for promptly returning my call."

"It sounded important. I knew the Rubins well."

"It's about their daughter—"

The sound of a fist hitting wood radiated through the phone. "Is that woman using Hannah's name again?"

"So you know of the woman who was living with the Rubins and calling herself Hannah?"

"Yes. I was so upset and angered by the whole thing!"

"Can you start from the beginning? Tell me about the

Rubins, and how the woman who claimed to be their daughter got away with it for months."

"Bernard and Millie were the sweetest people on earth, very private. They didn't socialize much, but Bernard took Millie for walks every day and it was obvious he loved her dearly. One day, right after Christmas a year ago, Millie comes into the social center with a woman on her arm. Introduces her as her daughter, Hannah. I'd heard Millie talking about Hannah before, but I didn't know anything about her or why she never visited. But at that point, I'd only been manager for a few months and I was still getting to know the residents.

"Hannah was fabulous. She hung out with the residents, helped them with shopping, and Millie was a changed woman. She still had Alzheimer's, of course, but she seemed brighter. Happier. The thing is, I *liked* Hannah. We went shopping together and out for lunch and I considered her a friend. There are not a lot of people my age—forty-five—in the area, so to have Hannah around was a perk.

"But then I saw her driving a new sporty car, and I started worrying that maybe this daughter was using her parents. When she took Millie to the doctor one day, I went to the house and talked to Bernard. Millie was senile, but Bernard was smart as a whip. Rarely spoke a word, but he was all there, you know? So I ask him if he's okay, if Hannah was taking advantage of his generosity. If it was true, I was thinking I might talk to Hannah as a friend, not in a confrontation, you know? And you know what he says? That this woman wasn't even Hannah. That one day Millie came home with her and *thought* she was Hannah. And Millie was so happy that Bernard didn't want to hurt her. He said, 'Millie doesn't have many years left. I want her to have her daughter back.' He said Hannah didn't want money, only a place to live because she'd gone through a nasty divorce and needed time to get her life back together."

"When you found this out, what did you do?" asked Megan.

"I checked up on her. I couldn't believe anyone was that altruistic. Call me cynical, but though Bernard and Millie were okay financially, they had money in the bank and I thought this woman was a con artist."

"So was Hannah stealing money from them?"

"I thought so, but Bernard said he was giving her a bit of spending money and had bought her the car. To me, that's manipulative. Two elderly people who lost their daughter in a tragic car accident get suckered by a woman who doesn't want to work and is happy to live off their savings. If Bernard had hired her, I wouldn't have had as big a problem, but Hannah was playing up this martyr role to the hilt. So I confronted her when I found out that she had never been married, and therefore never been divorced. I had also found out she had been a physical therapist in New York and still had an apartment there."

"Had you hired a private investigator?"

"My dad is a retired Miami cop. He knows people and found the information for me. I just wanted Hannah to leave the Rubins alone, but now I wish I hadn't done anything."

"Why's that?"

"Millie got so depressed when Hannah took off, Bernard said it was as if their daughter had died again. They went into Sunny Day two months later."

"What happened when you confronted Hannah?"

"I expected tears and an apology, something! I mean, we had been *friends*. But she simply said, 'That's fine, I was leaving anyway.' "

"She said that?"

"She was completely heartless. I said that maybe we could work something out, write up a more formal agreement between her and the Rubins, because I knew Millie was going to be heartbroken without her. But Hannah didn't care. She didn't bat an eye. Said she'd be out by that night. Then I find out that she'd had a huge fight with her boyfriend over God knows what. I thought maybe he'd found out too."

"Her boyfriend, Kenneth Russo?"

"Yes. And then she was gone. And you know what happened to Kenny, right?"

"Yes." Megan's heart skipped. "That was a week after Hannah left, correct?"

"Yes. We don't have crime here. We have a security patrol and gates and until Kenny was killed hardly anyone even locked their doors, everyone was comfortable walking at night. But now? My residents are scared. At night they barricade themselves in, and few people come to my evening events. Friday-night movies and Saturday-night dancing? Attendance dropped in half. It's just started to grow again." She stopped talking. Megan was about to thank her for her time, when Paula said, "So did Karin have something to do with Kenny's murder?"

"We don't know— Karin?"

"Yes. I told you I found out her real name, right? Karin Standler. A physical therapist from New York."

Megan didn't know whether she said thank-you or just hung up the phone. Officer Dodge said something, but Megan didn't hear the question. Her face was clammy, her hands shaking, as she looked down at her Black-Berry screen to view the e-mail that had come in from the sketch artist in Texas.

Karin Standler had been Megan's partner.

The woman who had shot her in the back twelve years ago stared at her from the BlackBerry screen.

Karin Standler was a sociopath.

Megan had come to the conclusion slowly, disbelieving. She'd ignored the signs because they were partners, friends, sisters. For three years they'd worked closely together, and Megan had learned so much from the senior agent. Karin was smart, sharp as a tack, and believed wholeheartedly in the job. "I love this job," Karin said time and time again.

As it turned out, Megan realized, Karin loved it too much. She loved the badge, the power, the ability to scare people—criminals or not. True, she had clean cases, impeccable attention to detail, and her arrests had the highest rate of imprisonment through either confession or conviction.

Megan discounted Karin's moodiness—Megan's mother had been moody. Megan ignored Karin's running commentary on the failings of the justice system, or the leniency of the courts. A lot of cops had a problem with a system that let violent criminals out early or let them plead to a lesser offense. Karin may have had extreme views of crime and punishment, but they weren't any more extreme than the views of Megan's own father, who, after drinking a bit too much on occasion, would lament a failing country he risked his life for. That he'd died defending the rights Americans hold dear wasn't lost on Megan.

Karin slept around, but never had a steady boyfriend. She told Megan she was too independent and temperamental to live with someone. Megan felt like a prude around Karin.

But even with all of Karin's flamboyant acts, Megan saw the compassionate woman inside.

Or so she'd thought. After nearly three years, she'd realized it was an act. That Karin had been playing her all that time, and Megan had sucked it up because she wanted a big sister, a mentor, a friend.

It was two months before Karin shot her that Megan made the first turn toward suspecting that her partner was overzealous in her pursuit of criminals. They had been part of an annual drug raid in coordintion with the Washington, D.C., Police Department, DEA, and ATF. Megan and Karin were assigned to a periphery post and Karin was displeased with the position.

"They're putting us here because we're women," Karin complained.

Megan had been nervous—this was only her third year in the Bureau, and she'd never worked the annual roundup. Last year, two cops had been shot, one seriously, even with all the vests and protection they wore.

At the time, Megan thought she was being a coward and perhaps Karin was right. After all, they had a lot of experience working the drug cases with the DEA.

As soon as Operation Wild Wild West—named for the location they were hitting that year in west D.C.— began, Megan sensed they were in serious trouble. The cross streets they were assigned became the primary exit route of the criminals—mostly parolees who didn't want to be caught with drugs or weapons and be sent immediately back to jail.

Megan had called for backup and Karin had a fit, but they didn't have time to argue. Six gang members, notorious for trafficking drugs, ran down the alley toward a car parked half a block from Megan's location. Karin immediately began pursuit, and Megan couldn't let her partner go off without her, even though she felt it was too dangerous in this situation without having backup in place.

Five of them escaped in the car, leaving the slowest behind. The kid—Megan learned later he was sixteen and his older brother was one of the five who escaped—kept running.

Megan had to find cover as the car made a second, then third pass, trying to kill them and get the kid. Karin disappeared from view and Megan began to panic. She couldn't leave her partner. The car finally left, and Megan ran toward where she saw Karin turn into an alley.

She didn't see the shooting, but she heard it.

Megan had thought Karin was dead.

Instead, Karin was standing and the kid was dead, lying in a filthy alley in the worst part of Washington, D.C.

"Karin! Are you okay?"

Karin whirled around, her gun still out, and aimed at Megan, then she pulled it up and relaxed. "Just fine."

It had been a righteous kill. The kid had a gun out; Karin had no choice but to fire.

Megan didn't dispute that.

But in her mind, she couldn't forget the look on Karin's face when she turned around, gun drawn: excitement. Nor could Megan forget her calmness after the shooting. Megan questioned her own competence because she knew she wouldn't be so calm and collected if she'd killed a human being—and that bore out the two times she was forced to draw her gun and fire. Megan had been calm on scene, but she'd been a basket case for two days afterward and grateful for the forty-eight-hour administrative leave.

Megan had done a little research after that incident and learned that Karin had killed or shot more suspects in the line of duty than any other active agent. Every shooting had been investigated and ruled unavoidable. Yet . . . Megan knew Karin was a good liar. She had caught her fibbing about little things. It had never bothered Megan too much because it hadn't affected her. But suddenly Karin's rages against the system and criminals who got off with a slap on the wrist took on a far more ominous meaning.

Her mistake—Megan had realized when she thought she was about to die in an alley two blocks from the D.C. jail—was not sharing her concerns with someone. Maybe they could have given Karin a psych test or counseling. Maybe Megan was wrong. She had hoped she was. She'd hoped she was very, very wrong. After all, the people Karin killed were criminals. They were wanted fugitives or suspects in violent crimes. She had no compassion for anyone. Her strength in the FBI had been her relentless and dogged pursuit of criminals. She worked extra hours, took extra training, volunteered for dangerous undercover missions, and turned in clean and prosecutable cases. The U.S. attorneys had loved her. She'd taught Megan to cover all the bases, not giving the bad guys any wiggle room.

But Karin was a sociopath. Because of their friendship, Megan had ignored or excused Karin's actions for far too long. She couldn't avoid the truth after the kid in D.C. was killed. Megan might have done the exact same thing in the same situation facing a gun, but it wasn't the shooting itself that had disturbed her. It was the aftermath. The glee. The satisfaction on Karin's face.

The day Megan almost died, Karin had confronted her about an in-depth report Megan had on her desk about officer-related shootings. It wasn't an FBI article, but there were law enforcement statistics about drawing one's weapon, firing, injuries, and fatalities. Big-city cops were in daily and consistent danger, more than the average FBI agent, but individual cops fired their guns less than half what Karin did.

Not proof of anything directly related to Karin, but enough that Megan wanted to keep an eye on her.

Megan lied about the article, but she was a pitiful liar and Karin didn't say much the rest of the day. Megan was about to leave when Karin ran up to her, excited. "I have a location for Rentz! Let's get him!"

Stanley Rentz, twenty-five, was a college dropout wanted for molesting prepubescent girls while traveling the country as part of the stage crew for an alternative rock band. When local and federal agencies figured out who the rapist was, they put together a sting, but Rentz had slipped out before it went down. He'd been hiding out for weeks, and his mother worked as a consultant in Congress. The FBI had received information that Rentz's mother was helping him financially, so they had kept a close eye on her, her office, home, and commute route.

Megan followed Karin out. "Who's our backup?"

"Marty and Ted. They're meeting us at the station. My contact in the building said Rentz's mother was acting nervous all day. I put a tail on her, and she's waiting at a different Metro Stop, taking the blue line north instead of the orange south."

This was the break they needed. Megan was relieved that Karin wasn't privy to her investigation. She had been feeling guilty about it as it was, but knew she couldn't go to her boss about Karin without something solid. Something more than her gut. Karin had been preoccupied for weeks; maybe that was her way of handling the trauma of killing a suspect, Megan didn't know. Maybe all this would come to nothing, and Megan could forget she thought Karin was trigger-happy.

The first inkling that something was wrong was when Megan didn't see Marty and Ted anywhere at Metro Center. They'd worked with the two agents multiple times when apprehending a fugitive, both as the primary team and as backup. Even though the men were undercover and the station was crowded, Megan should have been able to pick them out.

"Where are they?" Megan had asked Karin.

Without answering the question, Karin pointed out Rentz's mother to Megan. The fifty-year-old accomplice was carrying her briefcase, her purse strapped over her shoulder, and a small black backpack. She glanced over her shoulder several times as she looked down the tunnel, nervously waiting for the approaching train.

"I told them to get on at the stop before this one," Karin said absently as the train pulled up.

That made sense, Megan thought as she followed Karin onto the train.

They split up—Megan in the front, Karin in the back—inside the car as Rentz's mother entered. She got off at Stadium-Armory, a transfer station. She didn't cross over to another line, but took the escalator up to the street level.

They followed. Though it was dusk, the gray drizzle that had dampened the streets all day had turned into a steady, cold November rain, making visibility poor.

Rentz's mother approached a small, driverless car parked illegally across the street, near the corner of C and Burke Streets. She opened the passenger door and dropped the backpack inside, then turned around and walked back toward the Metro.

Karin spoke into her walkie-talkie, "Follow the mother."

Megan turned to her. "What? Rentz is going to be here. We need them here."

"You're a wimp, Megan. I always suspected it, but now I know that you can't do this job. You follow her, I'll take Rentz down myself."

"No," Megan said. "He's desperate, and desperate criminals do stupid things." She didn't want Karin to get hurt. The irony of this thought at that moment stayed with Megan the rest of her life.

"There he is," Karin said three minutes later. Megan saw a figure that could have been Rentz walking with his head down toward the target vehicle. "We need to get him before he gets to the car."

"Let him get closer," Megan said. "He's too far—"

But Karin jumped. "Rentz! FBI! Stay right there. You're—"

Rentz ran. Of course he did, he was more than fifty feet from them. Easy to get away. He dodged traffic and ran through the grounds of D.C. General Hospital.

Karin went after him. Megan followed. Karin motioned for her to circle around. Megan saw the plan and agreed—if she could get to Rentz before Karin, she could talk him into surrendering. She was good at it, had gone through extensive training in hostage negotiations, which helped with talking to fugitives as well.

But the alleyway was dark, and although initially it had been a good idea, Megan realized that they were in a vulnerable situation. On this side of the hospital, lighting was poor, there were no public entrances, and Megan couldn't see or hear Karin or Rentz. Worse, Marty and Ted had no idea where to meet up with them. Megan radioed her location over the open channel, but all she got was static. What was wrong with her earpiece?

The pop of a gun was far closer than Megan thought. Cautiously, gun drawn, she rounded the corner and nearly tripped over a body.

Karin?

She bent down, and realized immediately it wasn't Karin but Rentz. He'd been shot in the stomach, blood poured from his mouth. "I-I-I didn't see. She-she shot me." He was shaking and Megan knew he was dying.

"Call an ambulance!" Megan screamed. She searched for a weapon and found none.

"Watch out!"

It was Karin's voice behind her. She started to turn,

then heard the loud pop of a gun followed immediately by an intense pain in her lower back and the smell of gunpowder. She fell to her knees.

Karin stood over her. There were shouts and voices Megan didn't recognize. She vaguely remembered as she lost consciousness that she was in the loading dock for a hospital.

She thought she heard someone say, "Traitor."

But maybe it had only been in her mind.

CHAPTER
THIRTY-ONE

When Karin Standler had met Ethan two years ago, he was barely surviving—a government-sanctioned drug addict. His shrinks had him on so many meds it was a wonder he could communicate.

Karin had been working at a gym that had special services and equipment for the disabled. She hated her job, but there were perks. She could work out whenever she wanted for free. So she maintained her body to perfection, stronger than she'd ever been in the FBI. The pay was decent, and she took private jobs when she could.

But she missed the badge, the power, the authority that went with being a cop. All because of Megan Elliott.

Twice after Megan's shooting incident, Karin had prepared to finish the job and kill her traitorous partner. The first time had been a week after the Office of Professional Responsibility forced her to resign. Karin had sat outside Megan's D.C. apartment, gun in hand, waiting.

Reason prevailed. If Karin shot the bitch in the back of the head, they'd look to her. Prison was not an option—Karin would rather be dead.

So she took a page from her mother's handbook.

"Be patient and plan ahead," Crystal Standler had sagely advised. *"The cliché 'Revenge is a dish best*

served cold' means if you wait long enough, you can kill
your enemies and no one will look at you."

Crystal Standler had known exactly what she was
doing. She'd killed four men that Karin knew about, including two husbands, and no one had ever suspected
the dainty Southern lady of anything illegal.

So Karin kept tabs on Megan. Nothing overt. After
her termination, she still had friends in the Bureau, guys
she could have drinks and sex with and they'd talk
about the job. She tried to pick men who were disgruntled because they were most likely *not* friendly with
Megan, the FBI's very own Rebecca of Sunnybrook
Farm.

Five years ago, Karin learned from her on-again, off-
again boyfriend that Megan was being promoted to supervisory special agent and relocating to Sacramento. It
was the sign she'd been waiting for. Time to act. Megan
would be three thousand miles away, and Karin could
kill her while plausibly being on the East Coast. All it
took was planning.

Karin took her vacation in Los Angeles that year.
From L.A., she rented a car and drove to Sacramento.
She had an unregistered gun, an alibi just in case, and
the cold rage necessary to put a bullet or six in Megan's
body.

She followed Megan home from FBI headquarters
that day, planning on walking straight up to her, making
sure Megan knew exactly why she had to die, and then
Karin would put a bullet in Agent Megan Elliot's head.
In her mind, Karin watched Megan's blood and brains
hit the wall. The shock on her face, the panic, the fear.
The end.

Karin had been so close to pulling the trigger.

But she wanted Megan to suffer. To pay for her treachery and deceit. At one point, they were supposed to have been practically sisters! Karin had shared everything— nearly everything—with Megan. Karin liked having a trainee who listened to her with rapt attention. Karin had wanted to train Megan the right way, and after, Megan would be to Karin what Karin was to her mother—her protégée, her pawn. Karin would train Megan to kill.

But because of Megan, Karin had been forced to kill her own mother. Because of Megan, Karin had been forced to resign from the FBI. Because of that fucking *bitch,* Karin was now a nobody.

Killing Megan wouldn't be entirely satisfying. Making her suffer, on the other hand, would nearly make up for everything Karin had lost.

So in the end, Karin left Sacramento without pulling the trigger. She drove back to Los Angeles, then flew back to Washington, D.C., quit her job, and found a similar position in New York City. She learned everything she could about Megan Elliott—all about her brother, Matt, and her half-sister, Margo. About her ex-husband, Mitch, and her friends and neighbors. She had a whole scrapbook on Megan, and she made plans. Karin considered killing everyone Megan cared about, one by one. Her ex-husband—word was that they were still friends. Then Dr. Hans Vigo, who had been their boss in the D.C. office. He had moved over to Quantico, but Karin could get to him. She could get to anyone.

After Hans, she'd move to her neighbor. Then a colleague. Her best friend from college, who Karin had met years ago. Then her half-sister. And then her brother.

Karin loved the research and the planning and she had been about to put her revenge plot in motion when fate intervened, introducing her to Barry Ethan Rosemont.

When she learned that he'd been tortured by acupuncture, Karin knew right then that she had to learn everything about torture. Because while killing Megan's friends and family would be satisfying, that would only hurt Megan temporarily. Maybe ruin her life. But physical pain and suffering? Where Karin could watch Megan's body fight uselessly? Where Karin could listen to her beg for mercy? Where Karin could hear Megan scream? Much more satisfying.

She would slowly, over days, maybe weeks, torture the life out of Megan. Her ex-partner would die slowly and in excruciating pain. Karin even considered kidnapping Megan's brother, now a high-and-mighty D.A., who Megan had always worshipped. How would Megan react to watching her brother being tortured to death?

But Karin wasn't a monster. She killed only those who deserved it. That was her pact with herself. It was the way she could justify that her actions were righteous.

She'd saved Ethan's pathetic ass time and time again. All she wanted in return was knowledge. She wanted to learn how to use those needles as effectively as Ethan. Unfortunately, pulling the information from Ethan's diseased brain had been harder than expected. Karin had to convince him that the only way he would ever be cured, the only way the nightmares would stop, would be to seek revenge on those who turned him over to the Taliban. It took time. Nearly two years.

But it was worth it.

The needles gave Karin power. She would keep

Megan in a constant state of pain. Make her beg to die. Just like Ethan had when he was held captive.

Karin wanted to see that bitch on her knees begging for mercy, begging Karin to shoot her in the head and put an end to the pain. She wanted Megan to see that Karin's way was the right way and that Megan had ruined everything.

I was given the knowledge of good and evil and I was punishing the wicked for the sake of the innocent. All those who got away. All those who would get away.

For the innocent. For the meek. For those who wouldn't or couldn't defend themselves, Karin was their savior, their avenger.

She'd fought and saved herself, hadn't she?

Because she couldn't save everyone. She hadn't been able to save her father from himself. If he hadn't made her mother angry, if he hadn't seen things he shouldn't have seen, Karin wouldn't have been forced to act. She'd thought Daddy was strong and loved her, but he was weak and pathetic. So ultimately, Judge Standler's death had been his own damn fault.

"Karin, you have to stop."

She looked at her daddy and frowned. He was very white and his hands were shaking as he drove the car through heavy traffic in the rain.

"Stop what, Daddy?"

"I know you killed Grandma's poodle."

"Why would you say that to me, Daddy?" Tears poured out of her eyes. How had he found out? She'd been so careful. She was always careful.

"Grandma doesn't know, but I found Daisy's collar in your desk drawer. Along with your diary."

"You read my diary?" The tears stopped flowing and anger took their place. So much anger she had no outlet, no way to stop it, molten lava coming up the center of a mountain. The top was going to blow . . .

"Not just Daisy, but those other pets. You can't do that, Karin. I-I love you, but I'm scared for you. I want you to see someone."

He'd read her diary. She'd written everything in her life in that book. About how Margaret Fletcher flirted with Tommy Dressler when Margaret knew that Karin liked Tommy. Margaret kissed Tommy after the softball game when Karin had pitched a no-hitter.

Karin had gone to school with Margaret since kindergarten. So she knew that Margaret had allergies. Lots of them. Like peanuts. She'd seen Margaret go into anaphylactic shock in the second grade when she accidentally took a bite of Dina Huntsberger's chunky peanut butter and banana sandwich. She didn't even swallow, but her face turned red and her neck swelled up and Mrs. Burgess had to stick her with a needle to get her to start breathing right.

Tommy wouldn't like Margaret if he saw her swell up like a balloon and pee on herself.

Karin ground a handful of peanuts into a powder so fine it looked like beige baby powder. The next day at school she walked by Margaret and sneezed in her face, blowing the fine dust of peanuts into the air. Margaret yelled at her, called her a bitch.

You didn't use those words in Catholic school. Especially not when Sister Pauline was walking by.

But before Sister Pauline could take her to the office, Margaret started choking. Her face turned red and her eyes rolled to the back of her head. Sister Pauline acted *fast, pulled an epinephrine kit from Margaret's back-pack, and stuck her with a needle.*

Karin watched in amazement as Margaret thrashed on the floor of the hall, wheezing. Sister Pauline told her to get the nurse and another epinephrine kit. Karin did, running as fast as she could. She didn't want anyone to blame her. And it gave her time to wash her hands, after getting the nurse.

Karin didn't know then that sometimes people went into comas because of peanut allergies. But that's what happened to Margaret. She was in a coma for three days and when she woke up she couldn't talk right. Sister Pauline explained that her brain had been without oxygen for too long and got damaged.

No, Daddy couldn't have read about Margaret and the peanuts, that was last year, in fifth grade. Karin had already hidden that diary.

"Are you listening to me, Karin?"

"I can't believe you read my diary."

"Karin, this is important! I love you, but I can't let you hurt animals. You have a lot of rage inside. You need to talk to someone who can help you find a healthy outlet for your anger."

But she hadn't been angry when she'd drowned Daisy in the pool. She'd just wanted to see what would happen. And the damn dog always barked at her. Her mother hated the noise. Her mother told her to take care of Daisy. "You know what to do, Karin," Crystal had said. And she had even watched when Karin did it. "What did you feel when you drowned that poor help-less animal?" Mom asked, as if mocking all those shrinks and busybodies out there.

Karin shrugged. "Not much."

The lava of anger inside her continued to rise as she realized that her father could get her into big trouble. Her mother had told her someday he would have to die. Karin didn't want to do it. She had loved her father. He bought her beautiful clothes and presents and took her to museums and wonderful places all over the world. Her mother didn't like to do anything fun.

"You hurt people!" Karin told her father.

"I've never hurt anyone."

"Yes you do. You judge them and send them to the electric chair. Zap!"

Her father shook his head, hands tight on the steering wheel. "They were very bad people. They killed innocent people, Karin. They were guilty of awful crimes."

"So it's okay to kill someone if they're really, really bad?"

"That's why we have a criminal justice system."

"Daisy was really, really bad. She bit me." It was a lie, but it made Karin feel better to say it.

"I'm so sorry, honey, but dropping Daisy in the pool was wrong. She's just a dog. She didn't know any better."

"I thought she could swim back. I didn't know she would die. I made up that stuff I wrote in my diary." She burst into tears. She did know Daisy Dog would die. She had made sure of it. She had held Daisy under water when the dog paddled close to the edge. When she had looked at her mother, her mother had smiled.

But Karin hadn't written that part down in her diary. She'd been learning, taking lessons from the master herself.

"It's okay, Karin. It's going to be okay. I'll make sure you're okay."

Daddy was acting strange. "I don't have to talk to any stupid doctor, do I?"

"It's for the best. I love you, I know what's best."

"Mommy knew."

"What did your mother know?"

"That I killed Daisy."

Her father jerked his head toward her, shock on his face. "Why would you say such a thing, Karin? Your mother would be heartbroken—"

She took that moment to scream at the top of her lungs. "DADDY! LOOK OUT!"

He startled, jerked the wheel, even though there was no obstacle in front of their car. She pretended his swerve shoved her across the seat, and she banged against the steering wheel. She didn't know if he saw her grab the wheel or not, she liked to think he did, and then, when it was too late, she realized that maybe turning the car into oncoming traffic wasn't the smartest idea she'd ever had . . .

She woke up the next day and her mother was at her bedside. Karin had a broken arm and a bandage around her head. She hurt all over and felt small bandages on her face and legs.

"Daddy!"

There was a policeman in the room as well.

Karin wondered if she was going to jail.

She began to cry. "Mommy? Mommy? What happened?"

"There was an accident, sweetheart." Her mother took her unbroken hand and said, "You're going to be okay. Thank God, you're going to be okay."

"Accident? Why is there a policeman here, Mommy?

Did I do something wrong? I don't remember being bad, Mommy. Why is the policeman here?"

"He's here to help."

"I'm not bad, Mommy."

"Of course you're not bad. Witnesses say that—"

The policeman cleared his throat. "If it would be okay with you, Mrs. Standler, I'd like Karin to answer in her own words." He smiled at her and Karin liked him. She could tell in his eyes that he felt sorry for her, which was good. If someone felt sorry for you, he didn't think you were bad. If someone felt sorry for you, he believed what you told him.

"Karin, your father picked you up last night from your friend Tanya's house."

She nodded, winced.

"Mommy, my head hurts." Her head really did hurt.

"I'll have the nurse bring some Tylenol in a minute."

The policeman said, "It was raining. Do you remember?"

"Yes. It was raining hard."

"Was your father upset about something?"

"Daddy doesn't cry."

"Maybe he wasn't crying. Maybe he was mad. Yelling. Or sad and not talking at all."

Karin blinked back tears and looked at her mother. "Mommy?"

"Tell the policeman. It's okay. I promise, it'll be okay no matter what happened."

"Daddy . . ." She sniffed and let the tears flow. She had loved her father, in her way. "He was sad. Mommy and Daddy were getting a divorce." She looked at her mother. She nodded, smiled in that way only Karin could see.

Karin kept going. "He wanted me to tell the judge that I wanted to live with him. But I didn't want to. I love my mom and my dad. I didn't want to choose. I started crying. Daddy said crying was for babies, and that made me cry more."

She stopped talking, glancing at her mom for clues. She knew she was talking too fast, so she took a break. Played with the sheet, rubbing the material between her fingers.

"Karin?" The policeman prompted.

"I don't want to say anything. I don't want you to arrest Daddy. He didn't mean to do anything wrong. He's not a bad man."

"Honey," her mother said, the tears coming from her eyes now. "Oh, sweetheart, I'm so, so sorry. Your father died."

Karin's lower lip trembled. She hadn't known for certain until her mother said it. "Why?" She cried, her mother hugged her. "Why, Mommy? Why did he do it?"

The policeman asked, "What did your father do?"

"H-he said that h-he would choose for me. Then we were driving in another lane and there were cars and horns and everything got really loud. Then nothing."

Karin would not let Megan Elliott—that *twit!*—get away with destroying her perfect life. She had been doing exactly what her righteous father did: sentencing bad people to die. She had continued his proud tradition of sitting in judgment. It's not like she killed people for the fun of it. She always had a good reason. Self-preservation or justice. She liked to think that she targeted the bad guys as a legacy to Daddy.

If there was *some* fun in murder it was the irony that

she provided a better system of justice than the court system her father lived for and believed in.

She'd learned an important lesson the day her father died. She could get away with murder.

Karin was no quitter. The last twelve years of her life had been spent planning how best to make Megan Elliott suffer. And now that she was so close, she was most certainly going to see this through.

She'd sent Price's dog tag to Megan to make her worry. In the back of her mind, she would wonder how long she'd been followed. How long she'd been watched. She'd start jumping at shadows, looking over her shoulder. She'd be following the investigations through the grapevine, never knowing what exactly was going on, not knowing who was next, and if it was going to be her.

Karin had planned on sending Bartleton's tag to her as well, until the pathetic Ethan killed two innocent people. That had been the last straw. He'd gone from borderline crazy to full-out lunatic. After Hackett, she was originally going to talk him into killing himself. That would have been no problem, considering she'd stopped him from blowing his brains out a half dozen times. But Karin couldn't be sure of him anymore, and when he used the wrong gun . . .

She broke out into a sweat. That had been her one mistake. She should have gotten rid of the gun she'd used to kill Kenny Russo, but she liked to have it with her for the memories. Her five-month affair with Kenny had been the most fun she'd had in a long time. She'd manipulated him beautifully, he fell in love with her, and she learned everything about his former Delta team. What she didn't know, she obtained through his computer and e-mails to his friends and colleagues, ostensibly from him.

Unfortunately, she had to kill him. She kind of liked him, but he would have known she'd stolen George Price's dog tag. Kenny looked at the tags all the time, teary-eyed and lamenting his past mistakes.

"I should have put my foot down and told General Hackett we couldn't have a reporter with us on the mission. But we're trained to obey orders, and Hackett wanted a P.R. piece like the Marines had."

Price's dog tag was Kenny's way of punishing himself. And Ethan insisted, besides. *"All of them or nothing."*

Now Ethan was gone, and Father Cardenas was safe. She didn't want his death on her conscience. She was already to blame for one man of God dying.

She squeezed her temples as she followed the patrol car.

Crystal killed Father Michael, not you.

You might as well have pulled the trigger yourself. You told him too much!

I just wanted Crystal out of my life.

She was smarter than you. She was always smarter than you.

Maybe. Until I gassed her in her sleep. She never saw it coming.

Because you're weak and pathetic and couldn't confront her yourself. Because she would have won. She always won. You cheated.

Maybe I cheated, but who's pushing up the daisies?

Karin didn't care how she got what she wanted, as long as she came out on top. And finally, victory was within her reach. Megan had won twelve years ago, but today? Today Megan would be the big loser. Fate had handed Karin the opportunity of a lifetime. If she hadn't been watching the police canvass the resort, if she hadn't been curious about what they were doing and how much they knew, she wouldn't have seen Megan Elliott get into the patrol car. She wouldn't have been in a position to follow.

It was a sign, an omen. A very, very good omen.

She continued watching, glanced at the clock on the dashboard. Any minute . . .

CHAPTER THIRTY-TWO

The patrol car sputtered and died.

Barbara Dodge barely managed to pull over. "I don't believe it! No gas. It was full when we left." Dodge radioed in that an officer needed nonemergency assistance.

Megan stared at Karin Standler's image on her Black-Berry.

"You're the sister I never had, Meg."

Why—*how*—had Karin gotten involved with Barry Rosemont? Megan didn't want to believe that Karin had been in any way involved with killing the soldiers, but there was no doubt in her mind that she was capable of such violence. Karin had shot Megan in the back and gotten away with it.

Her excuse had been stress. Her mother had committed suicide three weeks before and Karin hadn't told anyone. She had been embarrassed and angry and depressed. The shrinks all agreed that Karin was suffering from acute depression. OPR removed her from duty because of "reckless disregard for human life and proper procedures" but with extenuating circumstances. As long as she went to counseling for a year, she wouldn't be prosecuted for manslaughter and attempted manslaughter in shooting an unarmed suspect and her partner in the back.

"It was an accident," Karin sobbed at the hearing. "I saw the suspect going for Agent Elliott's gun. I thought I did. It happened so fast, and I reacted." She looked across the room at her still-recovering partner. "I am so sorry. Megan, I am so sorry. I love you like a sister, you know that."

But Megan had been immune to Karin's pleas and lies. It had taken three years, but in that time Megan learned that Karin was a pathological liar and a murderer.

OPR didn't believe her.

"Agent Elliott, you are justifiably enraged by what happened and this panel is taking this situation and your accusations seriously. But in light of Agent Standler's mother's suicide, we can't help but consider the extraneous circumstances that impaired Agent Standler's judgment."

Procedures and changes were made to prevent situations like this in the future. More counseling, more feel-good measures to make sure that the agents didn't have external pressures that could lead to "reckless disregard for human life."

It was all bullshit, Megan thought. Then and now. Karin was a sociopath, only now she was far more dangerous. Megan dialed Hans. She hoped that Jack had received the sketch from Texas as well and that Hans was already jumping on tracking down Karin Standler.

Officer Dodge said, "They're sending a patrol with a gas can. I feel like an idiot."

"It happens to the best of us," Megan said lightly. She was irritated only because she wanted to jump on Karin's trail.

"I'm going to stretch my legs. If you want to—"

"I'm fine here, thanks," Megan said. They were on a

narrow turnout on the Pacific Coast Highway. Five feet away from Megan's door was a cliff and a short guardrail. Megan wasn't scared of heights, but she'd just as soon stay in the car. She also didn't want to admit that she was nervous about Karin. Her ex-partner still scared her. Ironically, it was because of Karin's lies that Megan herself had learned to discern truth and fiction from suspects and witnesses, one of the reasons Megan had ended up being so good at her job.

Officer Dodge stepped out, stretched. Traffic had improved. "Once we get gas, forty minutes, tops," she told Megan before walking down the shoulder.

Hans picked up. "Meg, I was just trying to call you."

"It's Karin Standler."

"I know—you got the sketch from Father Cardenas, then."

"Yes, but I also found a witness in Orlando who says that Karin had been dating Ken Russo for months and left just prior to his murder. Russo had Price's tags, but the police didn't find them after the homicide."

"I screwed up, Meg. I didn't consider that the contact the killers made with you was personal. I assumed it was to taunt the police. I'm sorry."

"How could we have known about her? No one has heard from her in years. Last I knew, she was a physical therapist somewhere. Did you get my text message about Ken Russo?"

"Yes, and Rick Stockton is sending four agents to the community to interview everyone who saw her, starting with Paula Andrews. Good work, Meg."

"Don't pat me on the back. Karin's at large and we need to find her ASAP. I don't have to tell you she's extremely dangerous."

"Are you okay?" Hans asked.

"Yes. But I'll be better when she's behind bars."

"I've already sent out an APB and her picture is going out to law enforcement."

"You need to do a picture with shorter, blond hair. The witness said she dyed it."

Movement behind the car caught Megan's eye. She turned and the driver's door opened.

The woman wore black jeans and a black T-shirt. Her short streaky blond hair looked like she'd cut it herself. But her wild blue eyes and the smug hatred on the woman's face told Megan that nothing had changed. Karin Standler was still a sick, twisted sociopath.

She had a gun in her hand.

Megan dropped her BlackBerry and reached for her gun, but it happened too fast.

Karin pressed the trigger. Megan expected to die, but there was no gunshot, only a faint pop. Her left shoulder stung. Her head felt thick and her gun fell from her hand. She reached for something that protruded from her shoulder and the last thing she heard was Karin laughing while Hans shouted from far away, "Meg? Megan! *Megan!*"

Thirty minutes later Jack stared at the empty police car on the side of the Pacific Coast Highway. He pushed aside the quiet sobs of Officer Barbara Dodge who had been shot with a tranquilizer that had left her disoriented and ill. He ignored Hans Vigo and Detective Holden and a dozen cops walking around the area, looking for evidence—clues—as to where Karin Standler had taken Megan. He avoided looking at the plastic bag that held the tranq dart that had most likely been in Megan's body, or the bag with her phone and her gun.

He focused on being the soldier he was. Not the man still grieving for a friend who'd been cruelly murdered. Not the man worried about a hostage. Not the man falling in love with a woman who may not even be alive.

She's not dead. That bitch doesn't want to kill her easy.

Jack closed his eyes and took a deep breath to push away the image of Megan tied to a chair, screaming in pain as she was being tortured with a thousand needles.

Megan's strong. She'll survive. She has to survive until I find her.

"Vigo!" Jack shouted. They weren't doing anything. Not even planning their next move.

Hans approached. "We're doing everything we can to find her. We have roadblocks—"

"We were too late with the roadblocks. Standler had ten minutes before we even knew where the damn car was!"

"We have aerial sweeps, until it gets too dark."

Which was imminent.

"We have to find her fast." Jack didn't want Megan to suffer one needle of pain. He'd gladly take the torture to spare her.

"Dammit, Jack, I know that! Everyone at Quantico is working on this. We're looking into Karin's bank records, credit cards, property she may own, vehicles, everything."

"The woman likely has cash and fake I.D.," Jack said. "And a car that isn't registered to her."

"What do you want me to do? Give up?"

"Think like a killer."

"I knew Karin. I was her boss. I didn't recognize her for what she was."

"Beat yourself up about it later. I need Megan's phone."

"Why?"

"She has friends who don't always play by your rules."

"We're doing everything—"

"Give me her phone. What was that name again? J.T.?"

"Caruso."

"Right. Rogan-Caruso."

After Hans nodded his ascent, Jack ran over and snatched Megan's phone from the evidence bag. He quickly found J. T. Caruso's number and called it.

"Hi, Meg, I saw the news and—"

"This is Jack Kincaid. Is this J. T. Caruso?"

The voice turned from friendly to dead serious. "Yes. Where's Megan?"

"Rosemont's accomplice kidnapped her. Karin Standler. The feds are working it, but she's been missing an hour and no one knows where she is. Standler could have taken her anywhere, though most likely someplace driving distance from Santa Barbara."

"I'm on it. Keep this phone on you, I might need information." He hung up.

Jack felt marginally better calling in the cavalry. Rogan-Caruso was the top private security firm in the country. They would do everything they could to find her. Jack had to believe that.

"Jack—" Hans began.

"I'm calling Dillon," Jack interrupted. "He knows this stuff." Walking away from Hans and the others, he dialed his brother on his own cell, keeping Megan's free for a call back from Caruso.

"Jack?"

"Megan's gone. Kidnapped by Rosemont's accomplice."

"Megan knows the woman." Dillon stated it as a fact.

"Yes. It's her former partner. Karin Standler shot Megan during a fucked-up operation and was fired, but Megan said it was deliberate, not an accident. Get into her head, Dillon. I need to find Megan now."

Dillon said quietly, "I'm not psychic, Jack. I need information."

"I don't know anything!" Jack ran his hand over his head, staring at the ocean without seeing the setting sun. "Where would Karin Standler take Megan?"

Dillon began slowly. "We need to assume that Agent Elliott was the target all along. That however Karin became involved with Rosemont, her primary purpose was to abduct and torture Megan. Which means she's most likely still alive."

"I already know that. She's alive, and about to suffer horribly if I can't find her. If I know where she is, I can extract her. That's all I need, a location."

"Is the FBI running property records? Credit? Any—"

"Yes, all of it. Megan is one of theirs, they're doing everything they can." *Megan is mine.*

"Does Hans know this woman?"

"Yes. He was Standler's boss back then."

"Put him on the phone."

Jack motioned for Hans to come over. "It's Dillon." Jack put it on speaker. He wasn't about to miss any of it.

"What have you got?" Hans asked.

"Do you have any of Standler's aliases?"

"No, though we're pursuing a lead at a hotel near the resort where General Hackett was killed. During the canvass, officers found a witness who saw a woman in a red bathing suit and sarong enter through a side door with a card key. She looked disheveled and matched the description we had from the bartender. We now think she registered under the alias Erin Hunter and are pursuing that lead."

"What about Russo?" Jack said. "And the elderly people she conned?"

"Rubin," Hans said. "Hannah Rubin."

"What's this about a con?" Dillon asked. "I need to know how she's pulled all this off."

Hans explained how Karin passed herself off as the long-dead daughter of an elderly couple in order to get close to Ken Russo. "That's where she got Price's dog tags, and likely where she found the location of the other Delta team members. She was there for five months."

"Do you know anyone else she conned? Where are her parents? Siblings?"

"She's an only child. Her father was a Virginia Supreme Court judge killed in a car accident when she was twelve. Her mother committed suicide twelve years ago. Right before she almost killed Megan."

"Did anything else lead up to that attack on Megan?"

"Meg said she was quietly investigating Karin's actions in the field. She felt that she'd shot a suspect without provocation, then reviewed all Karin's reports and learned she had a high rate of shootings. Karin found out, according to Meg, and tried to kill her by setting up a sting for a fugitive and putting Meg in the line of fire."

"And she's not in prison?"

"There was no proof to Meg's accusation, and Karin was diagnosed with severe depression. Her mother had just killed herself. Three psychiatrists, one FBI and two independent, all came to the same conclusion."

"How long was Megan looking into Karin's record?"

"I don't understand."

"Longer than three weeks?"

Hans said, "It was longer than a month. Meg never came to me about it, though. Why didn't she say something?"

"And accuse her partner of being a vigilante killer?" Jack said. "She wanted proof. Cross her *t*'s and dot her *i*'s, especially something this serious."

Dillon said over the speaker, "I'd bet my life savings that Karin killed her mother. How did she die?"

"Carbon monoxide poisoning. There was a suicide note."

"Typed? On a computer?"

"Printed. But Crystal Standler's prints were on the keys, no one else's. Believe me, the FBI looked into the suicide after Karin's actions."

"I'll still bet my reputation that Karin killed her mother or forced her to kill herself."

"This doesn't help us find Megan!" Jack said. "They've been gone over an hour."

"Two things. Karin has taken Megan to a secluded place where she can be confident that not only will no one hear Megan, but they wouldn't know where to look. The property will likely belong to someone she knows, who is either dead and the land is in probate, or it was willed to her but she never changed the ownership. Possibly property that is owned by the elderly couple—the Rubins—if they own any, but it would have been purchased in their name when she was living with them and they might not even know about it."

"So we run property searches for the Rubins, Judge Standler, Crystal Standler—"

"Did Crystal remarry?"

"I believe so, but she was a widow when she died."

"Check that husband's name as well. And Ken Russo, plus any of the other victims, though I don't think she did that. She'll want to feel perfectly secure, and that means a place set up ahead of time that she doesn't think anyone will find."

"Why not break into a vacant house?" Jack asked.

"She wants a base camp. A place where she feels safe, in control, and away from prying eyes. She'll take Megan to the one place she thinks she can do anything to her and not be discovered."

"Dillon," Hans interjected, "there is no national property records search. We have to go state by state. It'll take days."

"She's close," Dillon said. "She's not going to want to drive for three days. I'd guess twelve hours, tops. Start in those states."

"California, Oregon, Nevada, Utah, Arizona, New Mexico, maybe Montana, Idaho, and Washington. That's still a lot of territory."

"Then we'd better get started," Jack said. "Are you sure we're not just chasing our tails? If this takes hours and doesn't lead anywhere . . ."

"I'm confident in my assessment, Jack."

Jack had a hard time trusting anyone, even his

brother. But Dillon had proven himself in the past; Jack had no choice but to trust him now.

"Thanks," he said quietly.

"She means something to you."

"Yes."

"You'll find her."

"God, I hope so."

"Where's your friend, Father Francis?"

"Hidalgo. Why?"

"There's something to that. I've been reading Rosemont's records in more depth. He was extremely obsessive-compulsive."

"Which means?"

"Father Francis should have died."

"We already figured they didn't have the time to kill both Scout and Padre, or were interrupted."

"No. Rosemont wouldn't have left unless it was complete, or it would bother him so deeply he would be compelled to return."

"And if he couldn't?"

"He may start acting erratic and unpredictable, like he's trying to scratch an itch he can't reach."

"Perhaps like killing two innocent civilians for no reason."

"Perhaps."

"Why is Padre important?"

"He saw Karin at the church. They talked. She knew he was a priest and that he was part of the Delta team. But she couldn't set him up. I think she had a Catholic upbringing. Team up with him; he may be able to talk her into letting Megan go. She has a healthy dose of respect for and fear of priests."

"Fear?"

"I probably said that wrong. I meant, she respects and admires priests, but has a fear of God. That if she hurts a priest, that's it."

"She's already going to Hell, Dillon."

"I'm not making a moral judgment; I'm getting into her head. She justifies her actions because she's not killing a man of God. Everyone else is guilty of something."

"So she's a religious nut job killing for God?"

"Absolutely not. She's not insane, and she knows exactly why she kills."

"Why?"

"Because she can get away with it."

CHAPTER
THIRTY-THREE

Icy water hit Megan across the face like a brick. She jumped and kicked, her thoughts jumbled. She was drowning. She coughed, breathed air through a raw throat, then received another slap of cold water.

Kicking again, Megan realized she was restrained. She shivered uncontrollably and opened her eyes, but even the dim lamp light made them ache.

"Come on, Meggie Eggie, time to wake up!"

Karin. The tranquilizer. She'd been talking to Hans and then . . . her ex-partner appeared.

"Karin." Megan's voice was low and raw from disuse. How long had she been unconscious? She squinted through dim, artificial light. Outside was complete darkness.

Megan had no idea where she was. She inhaled deeply, smelling the fresh, cold, pine scent of mountain air. What mountains? More pine than redwood. The room was large and open, like Jack's cabin in Hidalgo but larger and lived in.

She couldn't stop shivering and realized she had no clothes on. Only her bra and panties. She was tied to a table that had been tilted at a forty-five-degree angle.

"Karin," she repeated.

"Great, you figured it out. Took you long enough." The sarcasm rolled off her tongue.

"What do you want?"

"I want to hurt you."

Megan's head was still fuzzy. She started to ask another question, her training reminding her to keep the kidnapper talking, to buy time.

A prick like a bee sting pierced the back of her hand. She opened her mouth to protest, but screamed as pain shot up her left arm. Megan couldn't think. She could scarcely breathe. Her arm convulsed against the restraints.

Then the pain was gone, only a residual throb.

"I've learned a lot," Karin said. "I've learned that my mother was right. Revenge is best served cold. You didn't see me coming. If Ethan hadn't fucked up and used the wrong gun, I wouldn't have had to act so quickly. But it was fate. I never expected to find you down here. The FBI has gotten lenient over the years, letting you roam outside of your jurisdiction."

"You killed Ken Russo with the same gun you killed the Hoffmans, General Hackett, and Barry Rosemont."

Karin made a buzzing bee sound with her mouth and pierced Megan again, this time in her neck. Instantly, Megan's head felt like it was on fire. She moved it side to side trying to alleviate the pain.

Karin was laughing.

"I didn't kill those people. They weren't a problem. Ethan just lost it. He was insane, you know."

Megan took a deep breath, mentally pushed aside the residual pain as best she could. "But you're not, Karin. You know exactly what you're doing."

"If only I were a better shot, we wouldn't be having this conversation."

"Why didn't you kill me back there? Twelve years . . . you had twelve years to what? Seek revenge because I turned you in for being a fucking sociopath?"

Karin pricked her on her right hand this time. Megan bit her lip to keep from screaming. She tasted blood. Her eyesight wavered and a sob escaped.

"You can do better than that," Karin said, poking behind her ear.

Megan's body convulsed, she lost control. Tears streamed down her face and she cried out, a primal sound she'd never heard before. Her vision blurred as a tidal wave of pain crashed over her. Then everything turned gray.

"No, no, no," a distant voice chanted. "You can't pass out on me! We're going to have fun. Well, I'm going to have fun and you're going to suffer exquisite pain."

Megan's vision slowly returned. Karin stood before her, staring. "I could have killed you, but I've killed before. It's fleeting. When I met Ethan, I found someone who could teach me about suffering. He suffered. Those soldiers who were supposed to protect him? Why should they live happily ever after while poor Ethan was tied down and poked?" Karin stuck a needle between Megan's toes. "And prodded." Another needle between two more toes. Megan's chest heaved with sobs—she didn't want to let go. She didn't want to give Karin the pleasure of her pain. "And tortured for *months*."

A needle slid into the sensitive area next to her small toe and Megan screamed, turning her throat raw. Through tears, she looked at her foot and saw three needles protruding.

Through the haze of agony, Megan knew beyond a shadow of a doubt that Karin didn't give a shit about Rosemont's pain and suffering when he was held captive in Afghanistan.

"You don't care about anyone, not even Ethan." Megan swallowed, her breath labored.

"Ethan was a whiner. Do you know how many times I saved his pathetic life? The nutcase should have been committed."

"If it weren't for you, none of those men would have died. They didn't deserve it. They didn't deserve to be cut down and tortured like prisoners of war. You pushed Rosemont into murder."

"He thoroughly enjoyed it, though he never actually killed anyone before those people at the rest stop. Killing was my job. He would have stuck needles in those bastards until the end of time if I didn't cut him off. So far, only one of them died in the process."

"John Doe. Heart attack."

"Give the special agent a blue ribbon! Or should I say *supervisory* special agent?"

Karin stuck a series of ten needles on the underside of each of Megan's arms.

The pain came in waves that never completely receded. The throbbing increased and decreased in rhythm with Megan's heart. She thought of her family, the father she'd adored, the brother she would miss. Her younger half-sister she barely had the chance to know.

Jack.

Karin would tire of this. Eventually, she would kill Megan. Either "accidentally" like with John Doe or with a very deliberate bullet to her head. Megan had no idea where she was or how she got here. She didn't even know how much time had passed. Hans knew who to look for, but would he know where? She didn't even have her cell phone, did she? No, she remembered dropping it. Her BlackBerry had a built-in GPS. It didn't help if she didn't have it with her.

She looked around. It was dark outside—the high windows near the roofline were uncovered. Was it the same night she'd been taken? She didn't feel as if she'd been unconscious for days. She couldn't assume anything, though. She turned her head, saw a digital clock on a table against the wall: 1:34. That would be a.m. based on the dark. Officer Dodge ran out of gas around five in the afternoon. It had been at least eight hours she'd been in Karin's control.

Karin would tire of hurting her. She had always been impatient.

Jack, I wish we had more time together. I found something special with you, and now we can't see it through.

Could she be so upset to lose something she barely had?

"Oh, Meggie Eggie, are you sad?"

"You're going to kill me—just get it over with."

Karin jumped up and down with glee. "That didn't take long! You think it's almost over? You won't know when it's over until you feel cold steel against the back of your head."

Crossing the room, Karin took a .357 from a desk drawer. She waved it at Megan. "This is my favorite gun. I haven't used it on anyone yet. I was saving it special for you. But when you're dead and buried, no one will find you, so it won't matter! I'll go back and take care of some of the other traitors who made me talk to those asshole shrinks."

"You fooled every one of them. You're good, Karin. They believed every tear, every word."

Karin smiled brightly. "I am good. I'm even better now." She put the gun to Megan's temple and cocked the hammer. Megan willed herself to stop shaking, but she couldn't.

The loud click of the hammer hitting made Megan scream. Karin laughed uproariously, greatly enjoying Megan's terror.

She yanked the needles out of her captive's underarm and tossed them on a table.

"I must have forgot to load it. Silly me." She crossed the room to the desk and took out a box of ammunition. Put six bullets in the cylinder, snapped it closed. She pointed the gun at Megan and said, "Bang."

"Bitch." Megan bit her tongue, wishing she hadn't said anything.

Knowing that she'd gotten to her, Karin grinned as she put the gun down on the desk.

"I've waited twelve years to pay you back for investigating me. *Me!* Your partner. Your friend. You didn't even come to me first, didn't talk to me about it so I could explain."

"What would you have said if I told you I thought you killed that kid on purpose?"

"I would have said yes, then I would have blown your head off."

"I should have turned you in sooner."

"Shoulda-woulda-coulda. Don't live in the past, Meggie. That's why I have to do this. Once you're gone, I'll have nothing hanging over me. No debts to repay. You're the last thorn from my past." She picked up a pack of five needles.

Megan tried not to stare at the shiny stainless-steel weapons. "You conned two old people into letting you impersonate their daughter."

Karin's smile faltered. "I don't know what you're talking about."

"Of course you do. Bernard and Millie Rubin, *Hannah*."

Karin slid a needle under her thumbnail. Megan bit back a cry. She managed to control the pain through sheer will. Karin slid another needle under the other thumbnail and this time Megan screamed out, her neck straining, trying to control her reactions.

"You're not in charge here," growled Karin.

"Give it up, Karin. It's you and me. I know what you did." Why did Karin think she wouldn't have figured it out? "I'm not stupid. I found out about Kenneth Russo. Killed in a robbery. So I followed up. Talked to his neighbor. Talked to the community director. Learned all about Hannah Rubin."

Karin yanked out the needles. The pain slowly receded, now Megan throbbed all over. "I should have killed Paula. She was too much like you. Nosy bitch."

"You can kill me."

"I will."

"But you'll never be free. They'll find you."

"They have to know who they're looking for."

"They do. Francis Cardenas—*Father* Cardenas—remembered you so well, he was able to describe you to a sketch artist. I wasn't the only one who got a copy."

"You lie."

"It's not just killing me you'll have to pay for. It's killing American soldiers, a general, a family. You won't be able to hide. You can pretend to be anyone, manipulate another senile old woman, and they will still hunt you down and put you in prison."

"I. Don't. Believe. YOU!"

This needle came down and simply pricked Megan. It didn't hurt like the others. Karin stabbed again and again, drawing small amounts of blood. She threw the needles across the room and stomped off, kicking furniture and knocking chairs over. She left the room.

Megan tried to slow her racing heart, but she'd never been so terrified in her life. She didn't want to die like this, when she had so much to live for.

Karin wanted to hurt her, and she would. Megan would fight the pain, find some way to survive. She tugged at her restraints; too tight to escape, too strong to break free. She would take the assault and agony as long as she could, hoping—praying—that Jack and Hans found her before Karin put a bullet in her head.

Karin returned with a bucket. She poured more icy water over Megan and the federal agent almost passed out.

"Better," Karin said.

Megan couldn't talk. Her lips chattered.

"I can improvise. We never used ice water, but Ethan told me about it."

Karin pulled over a chair and sat in front of Megan. She stared at her on the table, grinning. But her eyes were as icy as the water she'd drenched Megan with.

"You stole everything I loved. My job and the respect I got from it. Was it so wrong to dispense a little frontier justice? I think not. They were *criminals,* Meggie. The bad guys. Or are you so worried about the damn rules and regulations that you'd rather have a guilty man walk free?"

"Y-yes," she said.

"Right, but—"

Megan interrupted her, teeth chattering. "Y-you didn't care who you k-killed, Karin. You j-just wanted to play God. You kill and hurt people b-b-because you like it. You feel good inside, don't you? You're nothing but a brutal, monstrous serial killer."

Megan couldn't bait her this time. Karin had calmed down. She smiled wider. Megan couldn't quite see what Karin was doing near her feet. But—

Megan screamed. She didn't even know where Karin had pricked her, but her entire left side felt like it burned from within.

"I learned some new tricks, Meggie, just for you."

Megan's screams were so loud her head hurt. Then there was nothing. No pain, no sound, no hope.

Jack paced back and forth in front of Scout's Cessna Caravan.

It had been ten hours since Megan was kidnapped. Three a.m. and no word from her, no word from Karin Standler. Karin didn't want to ransom Megan, she wanted to kill her.

Megan could already be dead. Suffering. Terrified. Jack closed his eyes and pictured a group of POWs he'd rescued ten years ago. The hollow eyes of men who had endured so much pain and suffering that they looked more dead than alive. Broken in every sense of the word. Hopeless.

"Don't do this to yourself," Padre said.

He'd flown out as soon as Jack hung up with him the

night before. Padre stood with his friend on the airfield, trying to help.

"What are the damn FBI doing?" Jack said. "Taking a coffee break?"

"Jack, they found the truck Rosemont was driving when they killed the Hoffmans. They're going over it with a fine-toothed comb, something will—"

"Have you called in favors? Is there anyone you know who can help with the search?"

"The FBI have the high-end toys in this case, Jack."

"And they don't know how to use them!"

A small plane landed on the lighted airstrip, and taxied over to the main area. Jack watched it, wishing he could take Megan away, right now. The two of them, no one else, on a beach, in a jungle, in the mountains. He didn't care where he was, as long as Megan was with him.

Be strong, Blondie. You're a survivor.

He was still watching the arriving plane when he heard a car squeal through the open gates of the small, private airstrip outside Santa Barbara. It slowed, headlights so bright Jack had to put up an arm. Out of instinct, he had his hand on his gun and stepped out of the direct light.

The doors opened and two tall men stepped out. Dressed in khakis and black T-shirts, they were armed.

"Kincaid?" the brown-haired man questioned.

Jack nodded. "Jack Kincaid."

The brown-haired man extended his hand. "Matt Elliott." He gestured toward the black-haired man. "And J. T. Caruso. Meg's my sister."

Jack nodded. "Elliott. Caruso."

"Where are we?" Matt asked.

Hans approached from where he'd been talking in the hangar. He obviously knew both men. "We're looking for property that Karin Standler owns or has possession of. We believe she took Meg to hold her captive, not kill her."

"Torture her, you mean," Matt said. "Then kill her."

"We have time."

Matt's jaw tightened. "J.T." was all he said.

J.T. took out his phone. He pressed one button and said, "Jayne, you're up. What have you found?"

"The program's still running, J.T., I'm going as fast as I can."

"I'll wait."

Out of the corner of Jack's eye he saw a familiar figure walking from the runway. Turning, he saw his brother Dillon. He couldn't have been more surprised.

Dillon approached the group and gave Jack a tight embrace and slap on the back. "I'm here to do whatever you need."

"You didn't have to come from Washington."

Dillon raised his eyebrow. "You're family. We don't turn our backs on family."

The emotions coursing through Jack were violent in their intensity. Family. Matt Elliott came for Megan, Dillon came for him. And Jack hadn't asked either.

Family mattered.

"I got it," Jayne said over the phone.

"Give it to me," J.T. said.

"Four possibles. A house outside St. George, Utah, owned by Kenneth Russo, Sr. It's vacant, on five acres and in probate. Has been for more than a year.

"A hundred-plus-acre ranch outside Amarillo, Texas,

owned by Barry Rosemont's brother-in-law, Bryce Tyson."

"Is it occupied?" Dillon asked.

"Yes, but Tyson has a record and the ranch has been in the red for years. He's facing foreclosure."

"Next?" Jack said, impatient.

"A cabin in Lake Tahoe owned by Bernard and Millicent Rubin."

"That's it," Hans said.

Matt asked, "Where in Lake Tahoe?"

"I'm looking on Google Earth right now. It's on about one acre fronting the lake. They've owned it for more than forty years and a rental company manages it."

Hans called in the information to his office for them to immediately contact the rental company.

"What's the fourth?" Jack asked.

"A cabin in Flagstaff, Arizona, owned by Crystal Gardner."

"Who's that?" J.T. asked. "That name wasn't on the list I gave you."

"I did some research. Gardner is the maiden name of Karin Standler's mother."

"That's it," Dillon said.

Jack opened the door of the Cessna. "I need an address. I'm taking off in two minutes, whoever wants to come."

Hans said, "We need to send in the local sheriff. It'll take at least an hour to fly there from here. By then, Meg could be dead!"

Jack's jaw tightened. "You don't need to tell me that, Vigo. I'm aware of the danger."

Dillon said, "Have the sheriff's men approach with caution. Do not expose themselves. If Standler thinks she's cornered, she'll kill Megan and run. She has an escape plan, probably multiple plans. They have to approach cautiously and devise a rescue plan. Ascertain where the hostage is and the layout."

Jayne said over the phone, "I'll get a layout and send it to you, J.T."

"Thanks, Jayne. Send me the coordinates and the closest level area to land a Cessna Caravan." He hung up. "Let's go."

Jack and the five men boarded the plane. Within minutes, Jack was airborne and pushing the capabilities of the Cessna, while Hans placed as many calls as he could to get Arizona law enforcement to locate the Flagstaff residence.

Dillon slid into the co-pilot seat. "We're going to find her. Alive."

Jack couldn't speak. He focused on the plane's controls. "Caruso," he said, "where are we heading?"

J.T. rattled off numbers and Jack made adjustments. As soon as they were level, he pushed the plane as fast as it could go.

"ETA?" Matt Elliott asked.

"Fifty-five minutes."

Hans said, "The county sheriff has been briefed and dispatched."

"They'd better not fuck it up," Jack said.

"They're aware of the seriousness. The city of Flagstaff has a SWAT team and they're sending it out as well. The cabin is off the major roads. They're about thirty minutes out."

"Good," Dillon said. "We don't want to spook her."

"What will she do?" Jack asked.

Dillon looked uncomfortable. He glanced from Jack to Megan's brother.

"I'm a big boy," Matt said. "I want to know exactly what's happening and what Karin Standler plans to do with my sister."

"It's only an educated guess," Dillon said cautiously, "but if Standler feels threatened, she'll kill Megan without hesitation."

J.T. pulled out a laptop and brought up a map. "I have the specs of the cabin and the terrain. We don't have a lot of time to plan this mission, and there is no room for error. Kincaid, I need you here. This is your specialty, right?"

Jack glanced at Dillon. "Can you handle the controls?"

Dillon nodded and took over flying the plane.

Jack crossed to the rear where J.T. had his laptop open. Jack forced himself to think of Megan as a hostage, not as the woman he was falling in love with. It was the only way he could focus on the mission, and not on his fear.

"We have one thing going for us: it'll still be dark when we land. But not for long. We'll have less than thirty minutes to get in position and execute the plan. There's no room for error," he repeated.

Dillon said, "We have one more thing going for us."

"Besides darkness?" Jack asked.

"We have Father Francis," answered Dillon.

"What does Padre have to do with this?"

"Karin Standler didn't kill him."

"I'll break open the champagne," Jack snapped.

"I did some research while flying out here, and I think

I know why she spared him. Remember when I said I thought she had a religious background?"

"So?"

"Karin Standler went to Catholic school for elementary and high school, and then was a registered parishioner at St. Thomas More during college. The pastor, Father Michael O'Malley, was murdered in a confessional when Karin was a senior."

"She killed him?" Jack said, glancing at Padre who had a poker face.

"No," Dillon said, then frowned. "Maybe she did, but I don't think so. The murder was thoroughly investigated and there were no suspects."

"Then why is this important?"

"Because he was a religious figure who was important to her, for whatever reason. I don't know when Karin Standler started killing, but Father O'Malley's murder may have been the trigger that sent her down this path. And Father Francis may be able to temporarily replace him."

Padre nodded. "I agree."

"What?" Jack said. "What are you talking about?"

"I'll talk to her."

"No. No. You're not risking your life, Padre. We go in like a traditional rescue mission. We've done this hundreds of times."

"This isn't a traditional rescue mission," Padre said. "The soldiers we face have orders and protocols and their goal is not to kill their hostages, but to barter with them."

"I agree," J.T. said.

Dillon added, "If Standler feels threatened, she'll kill

Megan even if it means her own death. We need a distraction."

"I'll do it," Padre said. He looked at Jack. "You know this is the only way."

Jack didn't want to risk Padre. He didn't trust Karin Standler. And Dillon couldn't give him good enough odds that Padre would come out uninjured. Or even alive.

"We'll assess the layout when we get there," Jack said. "If this is the only way, that's how we'll do it."

THIRTY-FOUR

Megan was jolted into consciousness by waves of pain radiating from her right foot. Her entire body spasmed, then she went limp like a rag doll. She had no energy. No strength. Both her feet throbbed as if they were buried in burning coals. It was all she could do to open her eyes.

"Much better!" Karin said. "I don't like it when you get tired. It's no fun. And if it's not fun for me, I'll just kill you."

Megan worked her mouth, but no sound came out. She was so tired. She tried to look at the clock, but the red numbers were a blur. She squinted and still couldn't see them. She thought it was still dark outside, but she didn't know if an hour had passed or a full day.

"You know, I thought you had potential. I thought you understood. But you're a people pleaser. Teacher's pet. Hans liked you better because you fawned over him, you told him how smart he was, it was sick. I thought you had a thing for him, then I realized that you had replaced your father. *No one* could replace my father. Certainly not Hans. I was really sad when he had to die."

Megan couldn't have heard that right. Hans? Dead? No. "Wh-at?" she squeezed out of her raw throat.

"He read my diary. Asshole."

She wasn't talking about Hans. She was talking about her father.

"He wanted to send me to a shrink. I couldn't—not then. I didn't have the shields up. My mother always told me never to write anything down. I had them hidden, but he found them. I hated it when she was right."

Karin had killed her father. It made sense, a very sick, logical sense. Yet—she'd been only twelve when he died. "H-how?" Megan asked.

"It was raining. I had the poor road conditions going for me. It was really stupid, but I was young. See this scar here?" She pulled down the collar of her T-shirt and pointed to a faded white scar—thin, about three inches long. "Piece of metal hit me in the neck. But I was young, I wasn't thinking, I thought because I had my seat belt on and he didn't . . . Well, it still worked and I was only in the hospital for a couple days. I think that was the first time my mom was actually proud of me. Maybe the only time." Her voice trailed off.

Megan's stomach rolled. She couldn't believe what she was hearing about Karin's sick family. Her mother knew that Karin was violent? That she'd killed her father? Condoned it?

"I've hated you for a long time, but never more than when you had me fired."

"You tried to kill me!"

"See, that's the thing. They didn't even believe you! But they *still* fired me. I had to play this emotionally strung out depressed nervous wreck just to prove I didn't shoot poor Meggie Elliott on purpose. I hate you for that. I hate you for being such a goody two-shoes, a premium saint. You know, there's nothing wrong with executions, with or without a righteous judge. And I had hope for you, but you started investigating *me*. Looking into *my* life. *My* family. No. *Not allowed!* You crossed the line, and I had to take care of it.

"But," she continued, "I do owe you one. A small one. I finally had the courage to take care of my mother. That fucking bitch was a thorn in my side for years, but when she—" Karin spun around and Megan couldn't see her face. "She went too far," Karin said, her voice low. "Just like Ethan."

"The police." Megan swallowed. "They thought it was suicide."

"Yeah, well, it wasn't too hard. A few pills to make her sleepy, a running car in a closed garage, a note on the computer . . . the only thing I regret is I couldn't do *this* to her."

Karin stuck in a needle and, although it hurt, it didn't hit a nerve.

Karin frowned at the needle and threw it across the room. Took a deep breath, calmed herself, squeezed her hands open and shut. Megan watched the process, wanted to keep Karin talking because that seemed to distract her so she couldn't concentrate. The reprieve gave Megan time to regather her strength and time for someone to find her.

"I don't understand." Megan tried to relax. She was so cold she couldn't feel her fingers or toes. "Why did you have to kill your mother because of *me*?"

"It's called planning. First, I wanted her dead. I had been trying to figure out a way to do it for years, but I didn't want to be caught. Nothing worked, or there was too great a risk to me. Then you started investigating me, and all of a sudden, the plan unfolded.

"See, you always need an out, a Plan B. A Plan C doesn't hurt, either. My Plan A was to put you in the line of fire and have a bad guy take you down. With my help but his gun. But if that didn't work I might go to prison. Sure, I thought you'd be dead, and prison is not ideal, but I was willing to risk it. Then I thought—wait, Plan B. If my mom commits suicide and I don't talk about it, start acting a bit different, but not strange enough to get myself committed, then if something went wrong and it was my gun that killed you, I could claim emotional distress. I might lose my job, but most likely I wouldn't. Maybe administrative leave and counseling, then I'd be back. But *you* testified against me. *You* had me fired."

There was a sick and twisted logic in her reasoning. Megan felt ill from more than the pain and cold.

Karin picked up another needle and held it in front of Megan's face. She tried not to show fear, but it was impossible. She'd never been this scared in her life.

The needle twirled in Karin's fingers. Megan couldn't stop staring at it, shaking, half-frozen, pained and panicked. The anticipation of pain was almost as emotionally devastating as the pain itself.

Karin pressed the needle gently against Megan's chest without puncturing the skin. Using it like a pen, she moved it down Megan's body.

Megan had *thought* Karin hadn't cut into her, but a long, thin red line oozed out of a hairline incision.

Down her stomach, her right calf. Megan shook uncontrollably. Karin brought the needle slowly down to the backside of her knee and then poked.

Megan screamed in a voice so hoarse she thought she might lose it forever.

But she wouldn't need her voice if she was dead.

Karin inserted a needle behind her other knee. Megan saw bright stars, then nothing at all.

J.T. and Jack met with the local SWAT commander, Lee Beck, around the bend from the cabin where Beck's team had confirmed that Megan Elliott was alive, but restrained.

"What condition is the hostage in?" Jack asked, his stomach twisted in knots.

"Alive, but not in good shape. We have a sniper in position, but there haven't been any clear shots. The target has at least one gun on a table about ten feet from where the hostage is restrained. She may have more, we don't have confirmation."

"We'll integrate into your team," Jack said, "but we have a plan. We can't leave Agent Elliott in there much longer."

"Agreed," Beck said. "She is unconscious right now."

Jack's head jerked up. "Why didn't you say so?"

"Because she's alive. And when she passes out, the suspect leaves her alone."

"Where's the suspect now?" J.T. asked.

It was all Jack could do not to make a fool move on the cabin right then and there. He itched to see for himself that Megan was alive and breathing. But rash action would get her killed.

Beck asked for a status report, listened to his earpiece, and told them, "The target is standing two feet to the right of the hostage, back to my man, bent over a table. He can't see what she is doing."

"Does he have a clear shot?" Jack asked.

"Negative," Beck responded. "The angle is bad. She needs to be directly at the window or at the front door to take the shot."

Jack didn't like the plan. They needed more time to infiltrate the cabin. Jack did not want to risk Padre's life, but he couldn't see another alternative. They needed to buy time to extract Megan, and because Megan was in no condition to assist, it would take more time to bring her to safety.

Dillon and Hans approached them. Hans said, "Two entrances, front and back. Beck's men have the cabin completely surrounded. But I think your plan will work."

"Did you see Megan?" Jack asked.

"No," Hans said. "We didn't want to get too close and tip our hand."

J.T. said, "Daybreak is in thirty minutes. We'll lose the cover of darkness. Ready, Kincaid?"

"Hell, yes. Let's get Megan out now."

Torturing Megan was less fun than Karin had thought it would be.

Three hours and the wimp had fallen unconscious three times. When Ethan did it, the other victims didn't lose consciousness more than once. Was she being too rough? Or was Megan just too weak and pathetic?

It also disturbed Karin that Megan knew about the Rubins. If she knew the truth, others could learn it. And Karin would become a fugitive. She didn't want to live in hiding with a fake identity and no future. She wanted to continue doing what she'd been doing for as long as she could remember. Serving justice.

Megan had said Karin just liked to kill. Had a taste for it, so to speak. Maybe that was true. What was wrong with liking your job?

But all these months—years, really—had culminated in tonight, and Karin now felt let down. Slowing killing Megan was supposed to be the highlight, yet when Karin thought about it, last night, when she shot Hackett and Ethan, *that* had provided a headier rush of power.

She was going to have to move on. Disappear for a while until she could confirm whether Megan told the truth.

It was Megan's fault, the bitch.

"Wake up, sugar," she said. She took a needle and pressed it into her skin. Nothing. She took another. Another. Another. Soon Megan had dozens of needles hitting all major nerve points, and nothing. Was she dead? No! That wasn't fair! How dare she die like this.

She took a needle and slid it behind her ear.

Megan woke with a scream.

"Good, you're not dead." *Yet.*

The bitch was dumping tears out of her eyes. Rolling them across her face. Her lips were blue. Maybe the ice water hadn't been such a good idea.

But *that* part had been fun.

The sound of an approaching vehicle raised Karin's hackles. She picked up the gun and walked to the front door.

It was a pickup truck. A lone driver. Lost? No. She was too far off the beaten path.

The man got out. Tall, Hispanic, serious. He wore a white collar under a black shirt.

Father Frank Cardenas.

*   *   *

The SWAT sniper was told to take the first clear shot, provided that the hostage was not in the target's line of fire.

Jack, J.T., and Matt went around the back of the cabin, low and to the ground. SWAT had provided outstanding intelligence, and the back door was exactly where it was supposed to be. J.T. silently picked the lock.

Matt slid into the cabin first, toward the kitchen where the circuit breaker was. J.T. and Jack waited for the count of thirty. It was evident that the two former Navy SEALs had worked together in the past; they shared the same silent understanding that Jack had with his soldiers. The familiarity and ease working with them gave Jack greater confidence. But Padre was at the greatest risk right now. He had these thirty seconds to stay alive.

"Father," Karin said. "How did you know where to find me? Why are you here?"

"You didn't come to confession, I was worried about you."

Something was wrong. She glanced behind her; Megan was exactly where Karin left her, frozen in pain.

She looked back to Father Francis.

"You're not alone." This wasn't supposed to happen. She'd been so damn careful!

"Neither are you. I know about Father Michael."

Karin's heart rose to her throat. No one knew about Father Michael. *No one.* How could he know?

He's a priest.

"I tried to stop her," Karin whispered.

Father Francis stepped toward her. "You tried to stop who?"

She frowned. He didn't know. If God was talking to him, he would know her mother killed Father Michael because Karin went to confess everything and beg for forgiveness. Karin confessed not because she felt bad for the people she hurt, but because she was in love with Father Michael. She wanted to share everything with him. If he forgave her, she'd try to stop for him. For his love.

She'd never loved anyone else.

She shook her head. "No. No, no, *NO!*"

She raised the gun. The lights went out at the same time she pressed the trigger.

Chaos.

Jack had no time to fear for Padre when he heard the gunshot. The lights went out as J.T. reached *one* in his countdown and they both flipped down their tactical night vision monoculars. Everything Jack saw was in crystal clear shades of green. J.T.'s equipment was state-of-the art and could ultimately save Megan's life.

Jack quickly moved through the back of the cabin and directly to the table where Megan was restrained. He turned the table to shield her body away from where Karin stood. The suspect was partly obscured by the door and a bookshelf. She stood there, staring outside.

You'd damn well better be okay, Frank.

Megan's entire body was violently shaking and he immediately thought she was going into shock. She was practically naked, her skin ice cold to the touch and soaking wet. The floor was slick with water as well. Several thin needles protruded from her bruised and bloody body. Jack had to force overwhelming emotions of rage and fear down deep; reacting would put Megan's life at greater risk. He silently motioned to J.T., who nodded his acknowledgment. While Jack cut off the wrist and ankle restraints, J.T. carefully removed the needles. They couldn't extract her until he was done, but they didn't want to risk permanent damage, or death.

Jack whispered in Megan's ear, "It's okay. It's Jack." He didn't think she heard him; she didn't seem to be aware of anything happening around her.

Matt Elliott was moving around the interior perimeter to get into position to take Karin down.

Ten seconds had passed since the lights went out.

Movement from Karin's side of the room accompanied the loud *slam* of the front door shutting. Jack stepped in front of Megan and pulled his weapon while J.T. finished removing the needles.

Karin stepped into the main room. She looked stunned, blinded by the dark. A .357 revolver was in her hand, the muzzle still facing out. Jack had a clear shot.

Megan cried out, then bit it back on a sob.

Jack saw the moment when Karin's night vision cleared. She saw their silhouettes and movement.

"She's mine!" Karin said and pressed the trigger.

Jack fired simultaneously, and heard the report of a rifle from his left—Elliott—and from above—the sniper— competing with his own rounds. His breath was knocked out of him as Karin's bullet hit him dead center in the middle of his chest, stopped by the Kevlar vest he wore. He stumbled back, shook it off, watched Karin's body jerk as each bullet fired hit her. The sniper's round took off half her head, her brains hitting the wall behind her. She crumbled to the floor.

J.T. shouted at Jack, "Are you hit?"

"I'm okay."

Jack turned back to Megan while Matt inspected Karin's body and kicked her gun away, then reported through the radio.

"Target dead. All clear."

A shout from the back of "Lights!" had the three soldiers removing their night vision eyes.

Megan's injuries looked far worse in normal light. She was dangerously cold, her lips blue, and her skin so pale she looked translucent. Smears of blood covered her body. Jack and J.T. inspected her for any serious external wounds. None of the cuts were still bleeding and they all appeared superficial. But there was nothing superficial about the pain Megan had suffered.

Jack pulled a thermal blanket from his pack and wrapped her in it, then picked her up and held her. "It's me, Megan. I'm right here. You're safe."

Matt approached, his face tight and grim. "How is she?"

"Alive."

That was all that mattered. They would overcome what happened tonight because Megan was alive, and they were together. He wasn't letting her go.

"The medics will be here in two minutes," Matt said. They'd been waiting a half-mile down the road.

Matt touched Megan's wet hair and cold skin. "What did Standler do to her?" he asked, his voice hard.

J.T. said, "Ice water. Needles. We need more blankets."

Both J.T. and Matt removed their thermal blankets

and Jack wrapped those around Megan as well. "Come on, Blondie, talk to me."

She didn't open her eyes. Her body was still shaking uncontrollably.

"She doesn't know we're here," J.T. said, his tone clipped with restrained worry. He glanced at Matt with concern.

"Jack." Megan's voice came out a faint, hoarse rasp.

"I got you." He held her tight against his chest.

She didn't say anything else, and Jack felt her entire body relax against him and grow heavy. She'd passed out again. He had to get her to a hospital. He didn't know what else Standler had done to her . . .

Padre.

Jack carried Megan out of the cabin, side-stepping Karin Standler's bloody body without a glance. The ambulance approached, the red twirling beams casting odd swaths of light against the breaking dawn. A generator roared to life and lights came on around the periphery.

Padre lay in the dirt fifteen yards from the front door. Dillon was there working on him. Jack ran over and squatted, still holding Megan tight against his chest.

"Dammit, Frank! You promised you wouldn't get shot."

"I'm okay."

"She missed the damn vest," Jack said.

Dillon was holding a field dressing hard against Padre's left upper arm, where the shoulder met the bicep. The dressing was already soaked red. Blood had spread under him, soaking into the earth. "He's lost a lot of blood," Dillon said.

"We have the same blood type. I'll give in the ambulance."

"He'll need it."

"I'm okay," Padre said again. "Megan?"

"Alive."

"Is she okay?" His voice was weak, his breathing labored. J.T. strode over to the medics to push them to move faster than they already were.

"She will be." Jack had to believe it, even as she lay unconscious in his arms.

"And Karin Standler?"

"Dead."

"The plan worked," Padre said, closing his eyes.

"Not well enough. Don't you dare die on me, Frank."

A half-smile crossed Padre's lips, but he didn't say anything. When the medics rushed up to them, he was unconscious, too.

CHAPTER
THIRTY-FIVE

Megan sat in the hospital room feeling like an old woman. Sore and so bruised she could hardly move, she was finally being released. Six days was five days too long to stay in a hospital.

The door opened and she thought it was Jack; instead, it was Hans.

She hadn't seen him since her first night in the hospital. Jack told her he'd flown back to Quantico the next morning. She'd been pretty much out of it.

"Megan."

"Hi."

"I heard you're being released."

"Finally." She tried smiling, but faltered. Hans wasn't the same man she'd begun this investigation with.

"You're looking better."

"Better is kind of relative." She'd lost too much weight, had had borderline hypothermia, and then a severe fever from infection. She didn't feel like her old self, but she had turned the corner. She was going home. Jack was flying her back to Sacramento today. He hadn't left her room except to check on Padre.

Hans sat next to her on the bed.

Several minutes passed before Hans said, "I owe you an apology."

"You don't. Hans, whatever it is . . . we're friends, right?"

He took her hand. "Always." He paused. "I used to be married."

Megan was surprised. She certainly hadn't known that, or even suspected it. "Why did you keep it a secret?"

Hans stared ahead at the white wall of her room. He didn't answer her question directly, but said, "Her name was Miriam. She was eight months pregnant with our daughter when she was killed in a robbery." His words were choked. On a sob he said, "Because I didn't . . . I didn't get her ice cream."

Everything came clear. Hans's reaction and preoccupation after learning about the pregnant Loretta Hoffman being gunned down. Seeing her body, remembering his wife.

Megan wrapped her arms around Hans. She murmured sounds, not words, in his ear, to soothe him, and her. She'd never known he'd suffered such a violent tragedy. But he still should have trusted her with the truth.

"You could have told me."

"I should have told you. I was having a hard time and I didn't realize it. I didn't see it right away."

"Why did you go to the morgue to see Loretta Hoffman? You didn't need to do that."

He took a deep breath and pulled away. His voice caught. "I had to. Miriam . . . she was alive for a few hours after the shooting. I told her the baby was okay. I named her Jennifer, just like Mimi wanted to. But the baby didn't live, never even took a breath, and neither did Mimi. She died there, after telling me to take care of our baby girl. I couldn't stay—I didn't want to see her dead. I didn't want her to be dead! We were only twenty-one. We had our whole lives ahead of us. After she died, I couldn't look at her, I couldn't say good-bye. Now . . . I wish I had. I wish I had seen her one last time."

Megan took his hand. "Maybe she wouldn't have wanted you to see her like that. Isn't it better to remember her as she was when she was alive?"

"Maybe you're right. But . . ." He kissed her hand, tears in his eyes. "I'm here for two days to work with Detective Holden to finish the reports."

"You can call me. I want to help."

"I probably will."

Jack stood in the doorway. "You're not supposed to go back to work for another week."

"I won't. Just a phone call or two."

"I'll be watching you, you know that."

She smiled. "I know that."

Hans shook Jack's hand. "Jack, take care."

"You too."

Hans left and Jack sat down. He gently pulled Megan into his lap and kissed her. "How are you?"

"Ready to get out of here."

He held her close to him. "Sweetheart, I'm so sorry I couldn't stop her from hurting you."

The pain in his voice made Megan's heart twist. "It's over. It's been over."

"Are you okay? Really?"

"I'm sore. I'm tired. I'm not going to forget, but I'm going to be okay. I have you."

He rubbed her back and whispered in her ear, "I love you, Megan."

She drew in her next breath sharply. She hadn't expected that sort of confession from Jack. She knew he loved her through his actions, but hearing it meant the world to her.

His hands held her face. "I know what I want. I don't play games. When you walked into my life nine days ago, I never wanted you to walk out. Now I'm not going to let you."

"I—"

"You love me, too, Megan. Say it."

She couldn't help but smile and shake her head. "You're sure of yourself, aren't you?"

He kissed her lightly, then harder, then his hands were in her hair and her body was flat against his.

She broke the kiss only to say, "Yeah, I love you, Jack. I don't know how it happened, but I love you."

"Good. Then we're getting married."

"I—Jack. We don't, I don't, we should—"

"I don't think I've ever heard you speechless."

"Maybe we should get to know each other better."

"Life's too short. And I know what's important." He stared at her, held her chin in his palm. "Life is important. Family is important. *You* are important to me. *You* are my family. I know what's in your heart, Megan. I know what's in your soul. All the other stuff—whether you leave the cap off the toothpaste or gargle in the middle of the night or sing opera on the weekends—it doesn't matter. What matters is who you are, and that I know. You're mine, I'm yours, and nothing is going to change that."

"I have a cat."

"You think a furry feline is going to scare me off?" He kissed her.

"Okay."

"Okay what?"

"I'll marry you."

He smiled, and her heart melted. "I didn't ask."

Three Weeks Later

Jack walked up the pathway that led to his parents' house. For twenty years, he'd been estranged from his father because they would never agree on what happened in Panama. But after losing Scout and nearly losing Megan and Padre, he couldn't leave his relationship with his father unresolved like this.

Megan took his hand and squeezed it. "This is the right thing. You won't regret it."

Jack wasn't so sure. He didn't know if his father would talk to him. Listen to him.

But he wanted Megan to be part of his family, and that meant his entire family. Somehow, with her by his side, in his life, he gained the courage to stand in front of his father and ask for forgiveness.

Not for his decisions, because Jack knew he'd done the right thing in Panama, even if his actions could have gotten him court-martialed.

But for not understanding his father's role, his need to enforce the rules, and his fear for Jack's life and career. Maybe if he hadn't been a rash nineteen-year-old, they could have resolved this earlier. Or maybe if Pat Kincaid hadn't been an overbearing colonel who couldn't see that not all orders had merit, and some were flat-out immoral.

Rosa, his mother, opened the door. "Jack!" She

hugged him tightly. She smelled of spice and tortillas and cookies.

She turned to his fiancée. "Megan, Megan! Welcome to our family. This is a beautiful weekend to get married." She hugged her. Megan was a bit overwhelmed by the enthusiastic welcome, but she was smiling.

"Thank you for letting us use your home, Mrs. Kincaid."

"Rosa! Or Mama. Or Mom. You can start with Rosa, I don't mind."

"Thank you, Rosa."

"Come in, come in!"

"Is Dad here?" Jack asked.

Rosa said, "In his office. He's waiting for you."

Jack hesitated a fraction of a moment.

Megan kissed him. "And so am I. Go. Do it now, Jack. Tomorrow we start the rest of our life together."

Maybe it was loving Megan, or simply understanding forgiveness and letting go of past regrets, or seeing his brother Dillon and Megan's brother, Matt, put family first, even when they weren't asked. But for the first time Jack thought he could have his whole family back. Including his father.

He caressed her face with the back of his hand, ran his thumb over her lips, then walked down the hall to make peace with his dad and to reclaim his family.

Read on for an excerpt from

FATAL SECRETS

the second book of the FBI Trilogy
by
ALLISON BRENNAN . . .

Published by Ballantine Books

"They'll fire you."

ICE Agent Sonia Knight gave her partner a sideways glance and rolled her eyes. "Not if we succeed."

Trace shook his head. "I want this bastard as much as you, but we're walking a real fine line here."

"We're close."

"We could both end up dead."

"Our witness has risked everything to give us this information. If Jones even gets a whiff that Vega is turning state's evidence, he—and his pregnant wife—are dead."

"Don't think it."

"You know it. He hasn't checked in for three days, which isn't like him."

"But Kendra Vega is fine. We've been checking on her constantly."

"For now. But Vega could be getting spooked. It's one thing to talk about getting out of the business, but doing it is another story. These people are ruthless and Vega knows it."

"And you pulled every string and called in every favor to get them into Witness Protection *when* he delivers the goods. You can't do squat for him unless he comes back with the intel."

True, but Sonia worried that Xavier Jones was untouchable. He'd been getting away with trafficking humans for years because his instincts were sharp and he trusted no one. That one of his top security men came to her three weeks ago to make a deal was a miracle. She wasn't going to blow it—she wanted Jones in prison and the Vegas safe. That's why not hearing from Greg Vega for the last three days disturbed her. Where was he? Why hadn't he checked in?

"I wish we had better information," Trace said, not for the first time.

They were hiding among the pine trees near Devils Lake, appropriately named considering the son of the devil, Xavier Jones, owned hundreds of acres in the area. She could see his house with field binoculars, and tonight, like the last two nights, it was dark.

"It will happen this week."

"This is our third night watching Jones's place. He's out of the state, like Vega reported last time he checked in. The kid could be wrong."

"He's not." They'd contacted the Transportation Security Administration but Xavier Jones hadn't used his passport. He usually traveled by private plane, both retaining a pilot and being a pilot himself. Tracking small crafts was much more difficult, making the last few days even more frustrating. He could be back in Northern California now for all they knew.

Sonia had spent her days talking with Andres Zamora just to get him to trust her. He told her everything he remembered about his family's abduction and his mother's murder. It all held together, and he had the scars to prove it.

"I should never have run."

"You did the right thing. Your brother told you to go."

"I should have stayed with them. Emilio is all I have."

"Don't give up on Maya."

"How could she survive what they do to her?"

Sonia didn't have an answer, because she didn't know if she could find his sister. Eight days was a long time in the vile underworld, and thirteen-year-old Maya had most likely been sold before she ever set foot in America. If she ended up in America. They'd been separated during the journey, and Andres had no idea where they'd been when she'd been taken away. He and Emilio ended up here, being smuggled in first by truck, then by boat.

"If you're worried about a reprimand, I'll tell them I lied to you like I lied to the rest of the team." She hadn't wanted to lie, but she felt like she had no choice. Her boss wouldn't have authorized this stakeout on the word of a ten-year-old illegal immigrant.

Trace slammed his fist on the ground. "I can't believe you said that."

"I'm sorry." She stared through the binoculars at the dark house. She didn't want to hurt Trace, but he hadn't been in the trenches long enough to know how brutal this business was. That the buying and selling of humans was even thought of as a *business* angered Sonia and kept her focused on the prize: slapping cuffs on Jones and getting him into an interrogation room.

"No you're not. You think you're protecting the team, but you're only hurting yourself. Don't be the martyr, Sonia. You're too damn good. I'm a big boy, and I could have told you to fuck off, or told Warner that Vega didn't give you this intel. I backed you up because

I trust your instincts. I just don't want you to be blinded because—"

Their earpieces came to life.

"Beta Two reporting three vehicles approaching from the west at approximately forty miles per hour, headed toward the residence."

Beta Two was stationed at the fork, and there were only two private homes off this road, one being a vacation home belonging to a Silicon Valley executive who came up here quarterly.

Adrenaline flushed her system and she was ready to rock and roll. *This* was what she lived for. It was 0100 with a near-full moon.

"ETA?"

"Ninety seconds to our post."

"Stand down. Do not engage—Beta Four, circle—"

She was cut off midsentence. "They're fibbies," Beta Two said.

"*What?*"

"Grill lights just went on. Red, white, and blue."

Sonia slammed her fist on the dashboard. She watched the road and seconds later red and blue lights flashed intermittently through the trees lining the private road off Lake Amador Drive. She heard someone— sounded like veteran Joe Nicholson—say, "She's gonna fuckin' blow like Mount Vesuvius."

"Wish I could see it," his partner replied.

"Wish I were on vacation."

They were talking about her, and they were right. She had had more problems with the fucking FBI than any other law enforcement agency. They'd blown her operation. How did they get wind of the stakeout? Why didn't they call and find out if anyone was investigating Jones?

They acted like they were the only federal law enforcement in the country. Jones was ICE territory, and Sonia was going to make damn sure the FBI knew it. Innocent children were going to die if they screwed this up.

She watched as three black Suburbans drove onto the wide, circular drive in front of Jones's towering home, lights flashing, screeching to a halt as if they were in some B-movie.

Federal heads were going to roll. Sonia would see to it. Personally.

She issued orders to her team, then turned to Trace. She was about to tell him to stay put, but shut her mouth. He was no longer a rookie, having been with her team for two years. "Ready?"

He nodded. "Don't be rash."

"This isn't the first time the fibbies have screwed up one of our ops."

"You don't have to tell me that, but still—more flies with honey, right?"

"I don't want to capture them, I want to swat them."

She and Trace ran low to the ground toward the residence. They were a good hundred yards or more off, but made to the rock-strewn edge of the drive through sparse foliage without being seen by the Feds. They halted behind a boulder where they could watch the SUVs stage their raid. Doors opened and at least eight fibbies oozed from the interior, black bulletproof vests with bold white letters proclaiming their authority: FBI.

Homeland security trumped the FBI every time, and she'd make sure the idiots who drove into her stakeout damn well knew it.

They were dressed in black tactical gear, and she pulled her hat from her pocket that identified her as ICE and clipped her badge to her belt. Trace did the same. She motioned to her partner and mouthed "On three," and then they emerged from the trees only feet from the nearest agent. If she had been one of the bad guys, she'd have an ideal head shot. Hell, with her weak hand she could have taken out three of them without breaking a sweat. Incompetent jerks. Did they know who they were up against in Xavier Jones?

She strode toward three agents surveying the layout. One black-vested agent tried to stop her, flashing his badge and saying, "Ma'am, we'll have to ask you to speak with—"

She pointed to her badge and glanced at his name sewn onto his vest. "Who's in charge, Ivers? Elliott? Richardson?"

"I—"

A black-haired agent approached. Sonia recognized Sam Callahan, the Sac FBI's SSA for white-collar crimes. Political bribery and money laundering. What was he doing here when Jones's crime was far more international—and deadly—in scope? "Callahan. Surprised to see you here."

"Right back at you, Sonia." He nodded at Trace. "Anderson."

She couldn't hold back her frustration. "You just destroyed nearly two years of work! Is covert not in your vocabulary? We're in the middle of a major investigation. Did you just not feel like contacting us?"

Callahan straightened and reddened. "We have a subpoena."

Subpoena? "For what? No one cleared it with me. This is my operation, we're dealing with immigration and human trafficking here, a bit out of your jurisdiction." She was just getting started. "Dammit, Jones probably has people watching this place. And I know he has security—" She gestured toward the security cameras her team had identified three days before. "You blew it, Callahan."

She started to kick the door of one of the SUVs, then pivoted before her boot made contact. She was pissed off, but she'd take out her frustration on the racquetball court later tonight.

What was she going to tell Andres? She pictured his troubled face and his warm brown eyes begging her to find his brother. Andres had been here, at the Jones house. He'd seen the gate, had known about the mermaid fountain—completely out of place in the Sierra Nevada foothills. This was where Andres had last seen his brother; this was where Sonia had to start looking.

She needed to talk to Vega, but she couldn't jeopardize him, not when they were this close. He'd missed two scheduled contacts, and she desperately wanted to pull him now, but her boss made it clear: no hard evidence, no witness protection. Toni Warner was playing hardball with Jones's key man because Vega was certainly no saint. Complete immunity and witness protection would only be worth it for ICE if they got something, or someone, big in return.

The passenger door that Sonia had nearly taken her anger out on opened. A man stepped out, clearly in command as evidenced from the quiet that descended among the FBI agents. Unlike the rest of the agents in black SWAT-gear with FBI-logo jackets, this man was dressed like a wealthy corporate attorney in a sharp charcoal-gray suit, crisp white shirt, and dark blue tie. He filled the suit beautifully, but looked like he'd be more at home wearing a black flak jacket and carrying an M16.

The suit shut the door and stared down at her with eyes so dark brown she couldn't see the pupils. Sonia unconsciously straightened. She realized he wasn't as tall or big as she thought—just over six feet and 180 pounds was her guess—but his commanding presence made him appear much larger. She noted that he wore a double shoulder holster; on one side, the standard-issue Glock, on the other a definite non-issue HK Mark 23, a .45 caliber pistol that was used in U.S. Special Operations Forces.

Who *was* this guy?